The Tantalus Case

Tom Oliver Publishing
PO Box 951
Stockton-on-Tees
TS19 1PP

First published by Tom Oliver Publishing 1/07/2010

ISBN: 978-0-9566063-0-3

Cover design by the Author
Photography by Ian McCann - Middlesbrough

Printed in the United Kingdom

Mixed Sources
Product group from well-managed forests, and other controlled sources
www.fsc.org Cert no. TT-COC-002641
© 1996 Forest Stewardship Council
FSC

PEFC
PEFC/16-33-415

PEFC Certified
This product is from sustainably managed forests and controlled sources
www.pefc.org

*This book is dedicated
to my wife Janette.*

*Her help and inspiration
made this book and the
Aitken and Allen series possible.*

Chapter 1

★ ★ ★ ★

~Ten seconds of Hell~

In suburban England it was a Saturday in June. The sun is already shining brightly. The dawn chorus was some five hours ago. The Andersons in their smart home in Shelley Walk were just settling down to breakfast as a family. This would be the last time that they would gather as a family. They are sat unsuspectingly around the kitchen table, James Anderson his wife Emily and their son Jason. They would soon be joined by the fourth member of the family, their twenty four year old daughter Amy.

She is decidedly looking worse the wear from the previous night.

Jason looked up as his sister approached.

'Good grief, look at yonder vision. Have you wet the bed? You're up and it hasn't gone ten o'clock yet… and it's Saturday.'

'Piss off you!' was his sister's response.

Her Mother chided her. 'Amy, don't use that kind of language here.'

'Well, he's a wanker.'

Her father lowered his paper and intervened.

'That is quite enough. If you can't be civil just keep quiet.'

Amy sat down opposite Jason and scowled at him. James goes back to reading his paper. Emily got up to get Amy something for breakfast.

'What would you like dear? Do you want toast, cereal, fruit or porridge?'

'Nothing, just juice will be fine.'

'Grammatically incorrect Sis, nothing means nothing.'

Amy glared at her younger brother.

'You need more than just juice,' said her mother. 'I can make you scrambled egg on toast.'

Emily was not accustomed to seeing her daughter for breakfast at the weekend and was slightly at a loss.

'Mum! I told you, just juice. That is all I want.'

'OK dear, no need to snap, I was only trying to give you a decent start to the day.'

'Juice will be a decent enough start to the day.'

Emily goes to the fridge to get some juice.

Amy glares at her brother and makes the action of wanker with her hand. Jason mouths 'slut' across the table. Hostilities are ceased as their mother returns with Amy's juice.

'There you are dear. What are you up early for?'

Jason laughs sarcastically and says, 'Early?'

Amy glares at her brother.

'Nothing really, I am just meeting some people to go into . . . .

She never finished her sentence because at that moment the kitchen door flies open and two people dressed from head to toe in black explode into the kitchen. Each has a handgun. The one that was in front shoots Amy through the head. This throws her body back over the chair and the second gunman immediately shoots her through the chest. They immediately turn on their heels and quickly walk out.

Emily Anderson just stood where she was. All she could do was scream hysterically.

Jason just sat there with his mouth wide open. He was frozen and found it impossible to move or to make a sound.

The first to move was his father, James. For a split second he too had been frozen. The sequence that had developed in less than ten seconds was like some nightmare. The problem was this was no nightmare. This was very real. What snapped him out of his frozen state was the sound of the car engine as it sped off. James shouted to phone an ambulance and ran to the door just in time to see the car slow to join the main road at the end of the cul-de-sac. The car was a grey BMW, the model before the latest one. He couldn't see the whole of the registration but there was an F and a 7 and he thought either a six or a G. He ran back into the house to get his car keys and gave chase but he knew it was a hopeless cause.

He never saw the BMW again and he turned round and headed home. James had served in the army and had seen active service in the Falklands. He knew his daughter was dead before she even hit the floor.

When he got into the kitchen Jason was trying to comfort his mother even although there were tears quietly running down his cheeks. His mother was sobbing uncontrollably.

His daughter lay where she had fallen. She lay in a huge pool of blood, which was slowly spreading across the tiles of the kitchen floor. She looked like a rag doll with a leg lying at a crazy angle trapped under the chair she had been sitting on. The glass that held her juice had shattered as it hit the floor and the orange juice was starting to mix with the spreading pool of blood.

'Did you phone the ambulance Jason?'

'They are on their way and I phoned the police.'

'Well done son. Take care of your mum please. Take her out of this room. You haven't moved anything have you?'

'No, I couldn't go near her. Amy's dead isn't she?'

'Yes Jason I'm afraid she is.'

It was like Emily Anderson had never heard the exchange between the two men.

'She's going to be all right isn't she?' she asked.

'No Love, our daughter is dead.'

'What do you mean dead? She can't be, once they get her to hospital they'll save her.'

'I am sorry Emily; there isn't a hospital anywhere that can save our lovely daughter. She is dead, murdered.'

Emily Anderson started sobbing again. Her hands were clenched in tight fists and her whole body shook. Before they could say anything else the sound of sirens and cars screeching to a halt at the door announced the arrival of the police with the ambulance hard on their heels. James went to the door and met the police coming up the path.

'This way please, Amy's in the kitchen.'

The first policeman spoke, 'I am PC Wright and this is PC Stephenson. What has happened? The 999 caller was almost hysterical. A shooting was mentioned.'

'That was my son Jason. He actually did well. Two guys burst in and shot my daughter right in front of us. I am positive she is dead.'

The two policemen followed James into the kitchen. PC

Stephenson bent down beside Amy's crumpled figure. He felt her neck for a pulse. He looked up to his partner and just shook his head.

'You haven't touched anything have you?' asked PC Wright.

'No, absolutely nothing.'

'Then I am going to have to call this in, CID this one.'

PC Wright turned to the paramedic who had now arrived in the kitchen.

'Can you double check for signs of life please.'

The paramedic did exactly the same as the second policeman, right down to lifting his head and shaking it.

He spoke to the policemen.

'Sorry, there is absolutely nothing we can do here. It's pointless us hanging around as it's going to be some time before you can move her.'

The Paramedic then looked at the family and almost apologetically he said,

'I'm so sorry; there is absolutely nothing we could have done even if we had been here the moment it happened.'

PC Wright said 'Mr Anderson, can you please take your family to another room. We have a crime scene here and must maintain its condition.'

'Yes….. Yes, we will be in the lounge. Come on Dear, we need to leave the police to do their job. Come on son let's get your Mum into a seat. I think I'll give her a brandy to help with the shock. I could do with one myself but I might have to drive.'

PC Wright said, 'The CID will be here shortly and the forensic team as well. If you feel you need a brandy Sir, have one. We'll do any driving you need.'

'Thanks, I do need one.'

Chapter 2

★ ★ ★ ★

~ Take One~

For the Andersons what followed was like some surreal dream. The events appeared to be happening in a rush but at the same time it was like they were happening in slow motion. They were sitting trying not to think about what had happened. For James he could only think about images of Amy as a child. She had been a little beauty. He could remember seeing her for the first time. She had been born whilst he was on active duty in the Falklands. Emily had sent photos but he couldn't wait to see her in the flesh. She was nineteen weeks old when he saw her for the first time. The photos did her no justice, she was simply gorgeous. She would grow up that way. Raven hair and the most beautiful blue eyes with long eyelashes. Twenty-four years old was all she was. He couldn't believe it. Her life snuffed out, just like you would snuff out a candle. All he could think about was his last words, a reprimand, not a serious one but a reprimand nevertheless.

Sitting at the other side of his mother with an arm around her shoulder Jason was thinking similar thoughts. The last thing he had mouthed at Amy was 'slut'. He wished that he hadn't.

Emily Anderson was simply numb. She couldn't think beyond the fact that her beautiful daughter was dead. She just couldn't stop crying.

The lounge door opened and a very smartly dressed man entered followed by an equally smartly dressed woman. The man introduced himself and his colleague.

'Sorry to intrude, I am DCI Jeremy Aitken and this is DC

Louise Allen. I recognize that the events are extremely traumatic for you but we need to get facts as quickly as possible as it can help. Can you please tell us exactly what happened and as far as is possible I mean exactly what happened. We are going to interview you separately as you may have a different take on events or one of you saw something that the others didn't. Would you care to go first Mr Anderson? Can you look after your Mum Jason . . . it is Jason isn't it?'

'Yes…I mean, …yes I am Jason and yes I'll look after my Mum.'

James Anderson thought that there was something very businesslike, almost unfeeling about DCI Aitken. Somehow there was also a feeling that if anyone could catch Amy's killers this was the guy. He didn't know why he thought this but he just did. The cool very beautiful blonde Detective Allen gave off that same feeling.

'Thanks Jason, right Mr Anderson can we go to another room?'

'We'll go to the conservatory. It will be quiet there. Do either of you want a tea or a coffee?'

The moment he said it James regretted it, so bloody British a cup of tea in a crisis. Anyway the kitchen was off limits.

'Thanks but no thanks; I think we need to get on with things.'

There it was again, that ruthless efficiency.

In the conservatory all three sat down in the comfy wicker furniture. The conservatory looked on to a small but beautifully tended garden. This was Emily's domain and she kept it well tended the whole year round.

Aitken said, 'Right Mr Anderson in your own time and own words.'

James Anderson took a deep breath and very slowly expelled it before he started to speak in a low but surprisingly steady voice.

'Well it had started differently. For starters we never see Amy at the weekend before midday as she is usually out at the weekend partying with her friends.

Jason made some smart comment. Amy told him to 'Piss off' and her mother got on to her. Amy then called him a wanker. At that point I rebuked her and told her that was enough. That reprimand was the last thing I said to my daughter. I went back to reading my paper. I'd had breakfast at that point and I like to read the paper on a Saturday and a Sunday after breakfast. Emily was wittering on that Amy should have a good breakfast but all she wanted was juice and my wife must have gone to fridge to get it. I was behind the paper; in fact I had just closed it to come in here for a bit of peace and quiet when they came in, burst in, the more accurate term. They came in fast, shot my daughter, turned and walked out. Probably less than ten seconds. We all sat transfixed. It was Emily starting to scream like a banshee that snapped me out of it. The sound of the car at our door starting up galvanized me into action. I ran to the door but these guys weren't hanging about. They were at the bottom of the cul-de-sac turning on to Park Avenue. The car was a metallic grey BMW three series; four doors the model before the latest one. I only got an F and a 7 there was also a G or a 6. I cannot be sure about the G or whether it was a 6. I ran back indoors to grab my keys but it was hopeless I never saw the car again. Oh, I forgot, I yelled at Jason to get an ambulance. I have no idea why. I knew my precious daughter was dead before she hit the floor. I was in the Falklands and saw casualties there. Both guns were heavy calibre, a .38 and a .45 mm. The sound in the kitchen was enormous. Just like two huge explosions. When I got back in Emily was in a terrible state and Jason was comforting her. Poor Amy just looked like some rag doll that a disenchanted child had cast aside. Ten minutes earlier she had been a vibrant living, breathing person. Now she just lay there, all life extinguished.'

At that James Anderson paused, the sheer enormity that his Amy would never again be a vibrant living person overwhelming him. The two detectives sat quiet while the internal cauldron bubbled and seethed inside James Anderson. The tears welled in the eyes but he quickly brushed them aside. The cauldron was threatening to boil over.

Aitken spoke in a very quiet calm voice. 'It's OK Mr Anderson, take your time, go on when you are ready.'

James Anderson then managed to put the lid back on the cauldron.

'I asked Jason if he had called the ambulance. He said he had, plus he had called you guys. I asked if anything had been touched or moved. Jason said he couldn't bring himself to go anywhere near Amy. He seemed to know she was dead. Emily thought that once the ambulance arrived they would save Amy. I told her that our precious daughter was dead but she couldn't seem to grasp that. Then your colleagues turned up and the rest you know.'

Aitken got up and walked to the window. He stood looking out the window for a full ten seconds then he spoke.

'Good Mr Anderson, now I want you to try and remember every detail about the two gunmen, every detail.'

'The trouble was it all happened so fast. I had just folded my paper and I was just about to stand up when the door burst open. The first guy was straight past me and over to beside Jason. He leaned across the table and shot Amy through the head. The impact of the bullet was so great, or Amy was trying to avoid it that she went over backwards. The second guy was so close behind that he shot her through the chest. I looked at her after and I am sure it was through the heart. She would have died instantly from either bullet. As the first guy went past me I started to stand up but the second guy pushed me hard back into the seat. I think I said 'What the hell do you think you are doing?' I tried to stand up as they left but the same guy that had pushed me into the seat pointed his gun at me and shook his head as if to say 'Don't even think about it.' None of the two spoke.

With that they were gone.'

DC Allen spoke. It was the first time James Anderson had heard her speak. She had the same calm voice as her boss.

'What were they wearing? Do you remember anything distinctive?'

'No, not really, they were all in black even down to the gloves. There wasn't a square millimetre of flesh to be seen. They were white though and both had black hair. The first guy in was about five feet eight maybe but solid, probably nudging twelve stone. The second guy was big probably six two and he was really fit. I would put him at twelve and a half stone. The top was close fitting and he was in great nick. The smaller guy had the palest blue eyes, really icy. The second guy had very dark brown eyes. The smaller guy was probably the older.'

Allen spoke again, 'How do you reckon that?'

'It's hard to say, probably the age in the eyes. I only had a split second of eye contact. I cannot remember anything else.'

Aitken spoke, again that calm interrogative manner.

'I am sure you can. It comes back slowly. You said you were a serving soldier so what can you tell us about the guns. Could you identify them in the future?'

'I couldn't identify the exact gun but I would recognize the type.'

'That's really what I meant.'

'The first guy had a .38 Smith & Wesson, short barrelled job. The tall guy carried a cannon. I mean in size of calibre. It was definitely one of those plastic Glocks. I think it was a Glock 30, the .45 ACP, the sub compact. When you dig the bullet out of the wall you will probably find it has octagonal rifling. That is a feature of that weapon. I was a weapons expert in the Falklands and I have retained some interest even if I actually hate guns. I just love the beauty of the engineering but their use is against everything I believe in. I never thought my knowledge would be pertinent in this manner.'

James Anderson went silent and just sat there shaking his head.

'That's OK Mr Anderson, you have done really well. There is a lot there. In the meantime can you now send your son through? I know you need to comfort your wife but do not talk about what you have said to us. Her own version of evidence is what we want. Try and go over what you have said to us and if you can think of anything else, however trivial, let us know.'

Chapter 3

★ ★ ★ ★

~Take Two~

James Anderson joined his family in the Lounge. He was glad to see that Emily had finally stopped crying. She just sat there staring at a spot in the carpet.

'Jason, the police want to speak to you now. Are you up to it?'

Jason looked at his father and shrugged his shoulders.

'I suppose so. I don't imagine I've got much choice.'

'You do Son; nobody is making you do this.'

'Dad, if it helps catches the people who murdered Amy I'll talk to anyone.'

'Thanks Son.'

Jason walked into the lounge. The man was standing at the French Doors looking into the garden; the woman was seated in one of the armchairs. As he entered the man turned round and spoke.

'Take a seat Jason. If you didn't catch our names as we came in, I am DCI Jeremy Aitken and this is DC Louise Allen. Your father has given an excellent account. We are very interested in your account. As we said to your Dad, in your own time and in your own words.'

Jason's account was almost as exact as his fathers except that he couldn't give the colour of the gunmen's eyes nor could he give information on the guns. One had a short barrel, the other longer.

'That I think is all I could remember. Oh there is one thing though, the smaller guy has psoriases.'

'Now that's very interesting,' said DC Allen. 'How do you

know that? I thought none of them had any flesh in view.'

'I am a fellow sufferer and I would know the smell of that cream to treat it anywhere. He definitely had that cream on his arms. He pushed me aside as he leaned over the table and I am absolutely positive about that cream. The tall guy was the younger.'

Aitken said, 'Your Dad said that. He said it was their eyes that told him but you didn't see their eyes. How did you come to your conclusion?'

'Footwear, the small guy's shoes were rubbish, definitely wrinkly class. The tall guy had some serious black Vans. He had huge feet about size twelve I would guess. I think that is all I remember.'

Allen spoke, 'You've done well Jason, brilliantly in fact. If there is anything else you remember let us know. Can you send your Mum in? Thanks. By the way how did you get on with your sister?'

'All right, as far as you can get on with a sister who was eight years older than you. Sad fact was the last thing I said to her wasn't very nice but she had been calling me names. We were pretty close when we were at school. She was big sister and she looked out for me. We drifted apart a bit when she went to University. She never had time for me then, too busy with her own mates. Always got me cool birthday presents though. As a sister I suppose she was OK. I'll send in Mum.'

Chapter 4

★ ★ ★ ★

~Take Three~

W hen Mrs Anderson entered, Aitken was back standing at the French Doors looking into the garden.

Just as when Jason entered he turned round. This time it was DC Allen who spoke.

'Come in Mrs Anderson, please sit down,' said DC Allen. She made the same introductions as Aitken had with Jason.

'If you are not up to this we can do it later. We shall be sending in counsellors to help you get through this awful time.'

'It's OK. I am not sure what I can add to what my husband and Jason has probably told you already.'

'Oh you would be surprised,' said DC Allen, 'anyway just take your time. Just remember that you might have seen something that might help apprehend these men. They were both men weren't they?'

'I'll try. They were definitely both men.'

'How do know that?' asked Aitken.

The line of questioning had slightly surprised Emily Anderson. The oddball nature of the question had a strange effect in making her think very clearly.

'Just the way they moved. No woman could move that way. Actually that makes me remember something about the smaller one. The one that came in first has the tiniest limp, almost imperceptible. Even though he was moving fast it was there. There is something wrong with his left hip. The last person I saw with that identical movement was my cousin Harriet who had Polio as a child. Strange thing was that she survived Polio to die in a stupid accident when she fell off a small stepladder. Hit her head on the corner of a coffee table.'

Emily Anderson's account pretty well matched that of her husband's and her son's. Both the CID officers were impressed with how calm she was. Apart from a constant clasping and unclasping of her fingers she was remarkably composed. That night the dam would burst further but the two Officers would not be there to witness it.

DC Allen encouraged her.

'You are doing well. Your accounts match extremely well considering the brevity and speed of the event. Is there anything else you can remember, anything at all, no matter how trivial.'

'I was just about to tell you and it isn't trivial. The second chap was coloured, not deep black but more coffee. The smaller guy doesn't have black hair. It is more likely to be ginger.'

'Now that is big,' said Aitken. 'That is not big, that is huge. What do you mean the tall guy was coloured? Both your husband and son said they were white with black hair. We would normally arrange for a photo fit expert to come and create an identikit likeness from your testimonies.'

'You are wasting your time as they were wearing prosthetic masks. They were extremely expensive ones and they had to be fitted by an expert.'

Aitken asked with obvious intrigue, 'What do you mean masks? Surely your husband and Jason would have noticed.'

'No not necessarily, I am a make up artist. I do a lot of make up for the major film studios and I use those types of masks a lot. It is not work that I recognize. Usually this type of work is almost like having the signature of the person who created it. Some one did it and it was definitely someone who was an expert. I can see them a mile off because I know what to look for. Most people would be fooled. The shorter guy had eyelashes that were definitely ginger. The taller one had the tiniest scrap of skin showing at the joint of his mask to his own eye. He was definitely coloured. He also wore Hugo Boss aftershave.'

'How do know that?' asked Allen.

'When Jason was about fifteen he fell in love for the first time, you know what I mean. Can't live without you, we'll be together forever. Never works out that way. Now that he is nearly seventeen Rebecca has come and gone as has Mel and Kate.

Forever isn't quite so long when you are fifteen. Anyway his father was quite pleased about Jason's interest in the opposite sex. He had shown not a great deal prior to the lovely Rebecca who arrived in his life complete with braces on her teeth. Jason also had braces at the time. Amy rather wickedly suggested that she magnetise Jason's braces and that would have guaranteed an attraction to the lovely Rebecca.'

A wan smile passed across Emily's face as she recounted Amy's plan for matchmaking. It vanished as quickly as a snowflake on a summer's day.

'I am sorry, I am digressing.'

'It's alright. I take it Jason's Dad gave him some Hugo Boss aftershave,' said Aitken.

'He did, didn't last long though as Jason was a bit generous with it. He stank of it, the place stank of it and that tall guy definitely stank of it, albeit a lot more subtle than Jason.

That is brilliant,' said Aitken. 'Just one last question Mrs Anderson, can you think of anyone that would wish to kill your daughter or anyone that hates you or your husband enough to kill your daughter purely as an example and to hurt you?'

'I have been turning that over in my mind. Was there something about our daughter we didn't know? Was it a case of mistaken identity? I have entertained all manner of notions I can tell you. Bottom line is I think I know my daughter. Whatever happened here today was criminal and I do not think my daughter was involved in anything criminal. She was opposed to drugs. I think she drank too much at times. She was just starting to suffer real hangovers and that was starting to see a change in her drinking habits. No, Amy was a pretty popular person. She got on well with most people. We have no enemies that I know off. I am not bosom buddies with the woman at No.2 at the bottom of the cul-de-sac but that is simply because she is a gossip and I have no time for that kind of thing. She thinks I am, as she put it to Mrs Williams at No. 8 'a snooty cow'.

DC Allen smiled and asked Emily, 'Can you gauge what Amy's mood was like when she came in for breakfast? Was she tense, worried? Can you remember?'

'I do not think it was too great. I think the previous night had been a little too much drink and unlike the past she was suffering. As I said she was starting to show signs that the hangovers were getting worse. I heard her complaining to one of her friends about it on the phone. She said she couldn't drink like the Uni days, suffered too much now. The youngsters all drink far too much these days. The only thing different this morning was the fact that she was up early. She was going to meet up with her mates and go into town I think. She never did say where she was going, as she never had the chance. Those murderers, how could they shoot someone like that? It was like, well, it was like you would slaughter an animal in an abattoir. In fact, that's probably a lot more humane than what they did to my little girl.'

Emily stiffened and the tears welled in her eyes but she fought them and composed herself.

'I don't think there is anything else I can add. What happens now to Amy?'

Aitken answered, 'Well, the forensic guys should be about finished. Can you please not use the kitchen tonight as they might need to come back tomorrow? We shall remove Amy and take her for a post mortem. This is a murder enquiry and as such we will not be able to release Amy until all that has been completed. The moment the coroner is finished we shall inform you immediately. I am so sorry if that sounds all very brutal but we need to prepare you for what is possibly a lengthy wait until you can put your daughter to rest.'

'OK then, whatever, can I go now?'

'Yes and thanks for your help,' said Allen. 'As we told your husband and your son if there is anything else you remember do not hesitate to contact us.'

'Oh my God there is one thing. I have no idea where my head is. The smaller guy has four rings on his left hand.'

'I thought they wore gloves,' said Allen.

'They did, but as he stuck the gun across the table the gloves were so tight that the shapes of the rings showed through the material. The ring on his wedding ring finger is probably a gold sovereign and the one on his index finger probably a half sovereign.

DCI Aitken immediately picked up on the significance of what she had said.

'Are you saying the small guy was left-handed? He had the gun in his left hand? Your husband or your son never mentioned that and it is pretty important.'

'Oh he used his left hand alright the murdering .. .words fails me. I do know what I would like to do to him.'

'I have one final question Mrs Anderson and we shall let you get back to your family. Amy went to University, what did she study?' asked Allen.

'Accountancy, she was always brilliant with figures. Amy was simply brilliant with computers. She had a fabulous career ahead of her. This was her second job. She was head hunted to join this company. They are a fairly young company but they were rising fast and Amy seemed to be doing well with them.'

Chapter 5

★ ★ ★ ★

~Looking at the Rushes~

Emily left the room and the two CID officers sat there in silence. It was Aitken who spoke first.

'What do you think? They were very corroborative in their accounts. This was also a paid for hit.'

'What if she was a mistaken identity and it was meant to be someone else?'

'No, it was too quick, too clean. Those two guys knew exactly what they were doing. My problem is what the hell has happened here? Amy Anderson was murdered and there had to be a reason behind it. She wasn't just murdered at random. This was as cold and clinical as it gets. She was a bloody accountant. No one hates accountants, they are too bloody boring to hate. Nobody murders accountants.'

'They do in the Mafia, Sir. By the way my Uncle's an accountant. Mind you, you are right, he is bloody boring. You had to admit, we got a lot from those three interviews. Good stuff from all three. Firstly there was the father's evidence regarding the car and the guns also the other bit about the eyes and the age of the assassins. Then there was that very acute observation by the son regarding the guy's psoriases. His different take on the age thing. Then Emily Anderson with her stuff about the masks. They must have been fantastic masks to fool the men. The left hand issue as well. I am surprised neither the father nor the son picked up on that.

'Yes, for what were ten of the most hellish seconds in their collective lives I have to admit to sheer amazement in the detail they supplied. To get one reliable witness is fantastic. To get three is a bloody miracle. I take it that you got in touch with traffic about the BMW?' asked Aitken.

'Beat guys had already phoned it in. I'll go and check.'

'There's not a lot else we can do here Allen. Let's get back and get things rolling.'

As they left they spoke to forensics.

'How you getting on?' enquired Aitken

'Alright Chief, almost finished, we are just about to bag the victim. Pretty bloody brutal, she stood no chance at that distance. That distance being about six inches for the bullet in the head. I think the bullet through the heart was a very large calibre and hollow. Good job for the family she landed lying on her back. The exit wound is not pretty. The problem is there is so little actual evidence. It is almost like these guys didn't exist. They were definitely pros. I haven't seen anything this clean in a long time. Have you guys got anything from the family or were they just too shocked?

'Actually they were quite fantastic and we are both amazed at what they managed to see in what must have been a nightmare and one that lasted no more than ten seconds. Your bullet through the heart was probably courtesy of a .45 Glock 30. We await your results. See you back at camp,' said Aitken.

In the Den the three members of the Anderson family were speaking about their evidence to the detectives.

James Anderson said that he thought Detective Aitken was very professional but a bit cold.

'I think he is very professional,' said Emily but I do not think he is as cold as you think. The woman is sharp as well. These two know exactly what they are doing. If anyone is going to bring the murderers to justice I feel they will be the ones to do it.'

'That's funny dear; I thought exactly the same thing about them. What did you make of them Jason?'

'I am not sure. I have never met a detective before. I suppose they were good at their jobs. They certainly made me think, so I suppose they must have been good at their jobs. Did you notice the way they both dressed? There were some very expensive threads hanging from the both of them. I thought the police weren't well paid but the two of them must be. Strangely enough I have been interested in a career in the police but the salary levels has been putting me off. Do you really believe they will catch Amy's killers?

'I do not see why not son,' said his father, 'I just do. There is something about the pair of them. They are a brilliant example of the Swan syndrome.'

'What do you mean Dad, the Swan syndrome?'

'Well you know how elegant and relaxed a swan looks on the water. Cool and sophisticated on the surface but below the surface the feet are going like crazy. Those are a couple of swans.'

Chapter 6

★ ★ ★ ★

~Trying to make Sense out of the Senseless~

Back at the station they gathered in the briefing room.
'Right,' said Aitken, 'let's settle down. Let's have a bit of hush.'

When things settled down he continued.

'At 9.37 this morning PCs Wright and Stephenson responded to a 999 from No.11 Shelley Walk. This is a cul-de-sac off Park Avenue in the Rollins Park area. What they found was a young woman who had been shot by two gunmen. The gunmen had taken great care to ensure that they were unidentifiable. They wore black from head to toe. The woman was shot once by each gunmen. The first was a shot in the forehead and the second probably passed through her heart. The PM will tell us a lot more. The young woman was an Amy Jane Anderson, twenty-four years old and the oldest of the two children of Emily and James Anderson the owners of No.11. James Anderson is a Falklands vet. He now has his own plumbing business and by the look of the house the Andersons look comfortably off. We estimate that from the moment that the two gunmen entered the kitchen where the Andersons were sitting round the breakfast until they left was about ten seconds.'

There was a collective intake of breath.

'Forensics says that it was one of the cleanest crime scenes they had ever seen. This was a professional job. I am positive about that. They had intelligence on what they were going to meet and more importantly where their target was going to be. Amy was never normally in the kitchen at breakfast on a Saturday morning. Most Saturday mornings she was super glued to her bed until at least midday on a recovery from the previous night. New job, new found wealth had seen Amy become quite the party animal. She was a bit hung over when she came down for breakfast. The gunmen knew exactly where she was going to be as they never went upstairs.'

The DCI then drew up where the Andersons were in relationship to each other and the room the moment the gunmen went in. He then detailed all the information gleaned from the family. The assembled audience were equally impressed.

'There you have it. I am sure you have questions. Yes Dave?'

'Have we picked up anything on the car? Is anything showing up on the cameras?'

'Not a jot. There are two cameras on Park Avenue, none of them bloody working.

Park Avenue is quite long but all the roads off it are dead ends. The next exit is onto Jodrell Road which is a T Junction. The next cameras are the ones on Jodrell Road. If they turned right or left onto Jodrell Road they had to go through one of those. Nothing is showing up for the time in question. It's like they disappeared into thin air. We have guys all over Park Avenue to see if they could have holed up right beside the crime scene. That little trick has been done before. We also have guys all over Shelley Walk and so far nothing helpful. What is it Laura?'

'Would the gunmen be able to see the girl if they had been watching the house?' she asked.

'No, not really and the curtains in Amy's room were still drawn. The house is one of the two at the end of the cul-de-sac so is set back. The kitchen is at the back and even from the garden you cannot see into it. What are you getting at?' asked Aitken.

'Just this Sir, if they were so informed in their knowledge of the target, what if their intelligence was via a bug already planted.'

A voice from the back of the room said, 'You've been watching too many cop shows on telly Laura.'

A ripple of laughter ran round the room.

'Hold on there,' said Aitken, 'maybe Laura has something. It would mean that if there was a bug or bugs someone had to put it there and probably recently. We need to sweep the place. Andy can you organize that, and Laura, if that sweep comes up with what you think I want you to go and interview the Andersons. We need to know who all have been in their house, tradesmen and meter readers, anyone that has been over their door in the past few months. I just have this gut feeling that you might be right Laura.'

'Boss, Park Avenue'

The speaker was Jimmy Austin.

'What is it Jimmy?' asked Aitken.

'I know Park Avenue pretty well, my Nan and Granddad used to live there and I went there a lot as a kid. There is a weird 'S' bend about half way down where there aren't any houses just an old gas depot. Used to be a big storage yard full of them yellow plastic pipes but there are just the two big tanks left now. The tanks are scheduled for demolition and I think they are planning to build houses on the site. If you wanted to lose a car in Park Avenue that's the only place you could and you would have to be mighty quick. They could have changed the lock so that they could get in and out and probably change vehicles.'

'Not bad Jimmy, the funny thing is that just before I started this briefing I was speaking with our Sarge co-ordinating things at Park Avenue. The only thing that anybody had seen unusual was a large van, like a furniture van, coming out of the gas depot. A passer by was walking his dog. It was blue so he just thought it was a gas wagon. There were three guys on board. One guy locked up the gate and they drove toward Jodrell Road. By now our witness has got onto the second half of Park Avenue which leads to Jodrell Road. The junction is still some quarter of a mile away. They turned left onto Jodrell Road. How did the witness remember that? The only reason was that the usual boy racer in his Citreon Saxo had gone screaming past our dog walker and tried to cut up the van just before it got to the lights. Boy racer suddenly realizes when he is alongside the van that he is not going to make it. He slams on the anchors and nearly has a head-on with a guy coming the opposite way. Citreon Saxo finally pulls his horns in, the van turns left and the Saxo goes right. Our dog walker walks home probably shaking his head. Anyway if those were our gunmen they have picked up a third member. If they did indeed go left there's a pair of cameras on Jodrell Road beside the infants school. They were put there for the idiots that drive like our boy racer. The van had to go past those cameras so we should get front and back. Jimmy, get onto the gas people and see if they had any reason why people would be in the yard this morning. You can also get onto Sergeant Peterson who is co-ordinating on the ground. Tell him to look and see if the lock on the yard gates is a new one and if it is, do not touch it. We will get the forensic boys over to see if they can get prints off it. The moment that's done we will get in and check the yard. The car might still be there, you never know. Go back and check with our dog walking friend. See if there is anything else he can remember. The Sarge has his name and address. Right, we all know what we have to do, let's get to it. We'll meet back here at 16.00 for an update. Right Louise, you and I need to do some investigating ourselves.'

With that the assembled cast got up and cleared the room.

'What had you in mind boss?' asked Allen.

'Can I turn that round Louise and ask you what would you do?'

'What would I do? Well I do not think this case is going to be straightforward and it isn't going to be easy to find these guys, not with what we have got so far. They planned this to the very last detail. No residues at the scene of the crime so I can guarantee the stakes here are going to be high. So I would start trying to find a motive for her killing and what Amy Anderson was involved in and with whom. We need to check out her parents as well. Who were her friends, acquaintances? We need to do the complete background check. We need to shake the tree to find what may drop down. Do you not think it was rather an odd killing?'

'I am intrigued Allen. Go on, what do you mean it was an odd killing?'

'Well simply there was no need for the second guy or even his having to shoot Amy. That was superfluous; it was like it was a demonstration of power. Neither gunman used a silencer. I think this was to get the message across. Don't screw with us if you know what's good for you. This was most definitely an execution.'

'I agree that struck me as odd too. You are right in that it could have been a warning. Anyway we better get back to her parents and see what they can give us by way of background. I am not looking forward to this, their emotions are going to be red raw and bleeding. I'll tell you there are times when this job really sucks. This is one of them.'

Chapter 7

★ ★ ★ ★

~An Unwelcome Hyena~

O n the way over they drove in silence, it was Aitken who broke the silence.

'What is usually at the root of most of the crimes we have?'

'Money,' said Allen.

'Yes, almost every bloody time. Who handles money apart from you women, banks and supermarkets?'

'That's probably sexist. We don't all force our men to hand over what they earn.'

'That is not what I meant at all. Women do actually handle far more money than men. Household bills, feeding, clothing, it is normally the women who take care of that.'

'Accountants,' interrupted Allen, 'and Amy Anderson is an accountant, well was an accountant. What if she had discovered something and was silenced.'

'It's possible. At this moment in time I am ruling nothing out. Oh Shit, No! The sodding hyenas are here. There's that sleazy bastard from the Mercury. I can't stand him or the bloody rag that he writes for. Don't let him come near me or I'll be the one facing a murder charge.'

They had just turned in to Shelley Walk and Louise could see up the road to the large number of reporters and camera crew outside No.11. She could see the bald pate of Don Sullivan of the Mercury and the great long ponytail of straggly locks of what was left of a follicle challenge that he patently had not won. The DCI absolutely detested him. As they drew up Sullivan stepped forward.

'DCI Aitken, when were you thinking of making it known that there had been a murder here?'

'As far as you are concerned, never is the answer.'

'Charming,' said Sullivan.

Aitken brushed passed Sullivan and dropped under the tapes. The two beat policemen were standing guard.

Aitken spoke to them. 'It's Allan and Graham isn't it?'

'Yes Guv,' replied Allan.

'When did this lot appear? What have you said to them?'

PC Allan responded, 'Less than an hour ago. That creep Sullivan was first.'

'Trust that bloody vampire. Go on.'

'They started to appear in dribs and drabs the last guy about ten minutes with that TV crew.'

'Don't even look at them,' said Allen. 'They even use lip readers.'

PC Graham spoke, 'They asked what had happened but we said we knew no more than they did as we had not been allowed in. We were simply here to ensure that no one entered the house. Seemingly it was the woman at Number Two who phoned the press and TV. I heard this from one reporter speaking to another. Most of them have been to see her and they have tried the neighbours but our lads restricted their activities. Nobody from the family has looked out.'

'Well done lads, you've played a blinder,' said Aitken. 'We will have to issue a statement but not just yet.'

Sullivan shouted at Aitken and Allen, 'Are you going to tell us what has happened or not? Bet it's the daughter. She's supposed to be a real looker, a babe seemingly. Bet there's sex involved.'

'Sullivan, only you could jump to that kind of conclusion and worse print it. Why don't you crawl into that sleaze pit that you came from? For the rest we shall be giving a conference in approximately ninety minutes from now.'

There was a clamour of questions from the assembled media corps but the DCI was adamant.

'Sorry, but we have work to do. Come on Louise, let's get on with it.'

One TV Reporter called out, 'DCI Aitken, are you here to make an arrest?'

Aitken turned and saw it was John Horden, a highly reputable reporter on TV.

'John, I can categorically tell you that we are not. Equally you can all leave this location as you are simply wasting your time. Your organizations will all be duly informed prior to our statement. We anticipate Railton Police Station ninety minutes from now. There is definitely nothing going to happen at this location. I suggest you all go back to the office and wait. You are going to see nothing here or hear nothing here.'

'Thanks DCI Aitken, we will await your announcement, me? I'm going back to camp.'

'Thanks John, we will see you at Railton.'

'How come he gets a civil answer and I get rubbished,' asked Sullivan.

'You shouldn't need to ask,' said Aitken.

Chapter 8

★ ★ ★ ★

~*A Bug's Life*~

Inside the door they met the two guys who had been doing the sweep for bugs.

'Well Laura was spot on. Each room has a listening device. Much more important is the type they are, absolute bloody state of the art ones and totally undetectable. Not available to the great unwashed. We don't even get these. MI5 do. I know about them but I have never seen one, not until now.'

'You'll be back at the station before me. Pass on the information to Laura please. Thanks Lads,' said Aitken.

The two detectives found the Andersons in the lounge where they had left them.

'Can we come in please?' asked Aitken. 'There are a few more questions we need to ask you. Can you handle that?'

'If it'll help catch those murdering bastards, come in. In fact if you want and it helps, you can take up residency. Do you want us separately again?' asked James Anderson.

The two CID officers could feel the anger in his voice. At their first interview he had been strangely calm and efficient. Now he was obviously feeling angry.

'No,' said Allen, 'this is fine as a group. You will probably be able to help each other with the answers.'

Emily Anderson spoke, 'I would offer you a drink. Lord knows, I would love a cup of tea, but the kitchen, it's off limits anyway.'

'Sorry,' said Allen, 'we sort of forgot in the heat of the moment you need sustenance. Look, the kitchen can be used, the forensics say that there is nothing else they can get here. Best get food in. I'll go and make us all tea if that's OK?'

'I'll come and help,' said James Anderson. 'I know how they all take their tea and coffee.'

Five minutes later the two were back with tea, coffee and biscuits. There was juice for Jason who never touched tea or coffee. Emily was first to take a drink.

'That tastes fantastic. I'm sorry; I was so ready for that. What did you want to know?'

'We believe that this was a contract killing. We have just learned from our techs here that the entire house was bugged. Someone placed them here. A Laura Baynes shall be here shortly to go over all the people that have been over your doorstep in the past few months. The bugs detected exactly where Amy was in the house. The gunmen knew exactly where Amy was located. We sealed Amy's room earlier but we shall need to go over it with a fine toothcomb. We are sorry but it is going to be hard on you.'

'What do you mean a contract killing?' asked Emily.

'I mean these were probably hired assassins. They will have done similar assassins previously.'

Emily gasped, 'Good God! That is horrible!'

James spoke, 'One thing puzzled me. Why did both men shoot my daughter? Surely one guy was enough.'

It was Allen who gave the answer. 'We have already spoken about this and we think…. well it's only a hypothesis at the moment, we think it was to make an example, to send a warning.'

Aitken picked up the thread, 'Somewhere, somehow your daughter crossed someone big time. She was either involved in something herself or learned something about someone. Given her background we favour the latter. An involvement with or a knowledge of something would prove fatal to Amy. What we are here to do is to try and get from you a background into Amy, her friends, her lifestyle, everything that will open up the windows on your daughter's life. Something that happened out there caused someone to take a cold-hearted decision to end you daughter's life. It is not enough to catch the murderers we must apprehend those who probably paid them. We are not going to rest until that has been done. We are pretty confident that these guys will have been paid.'

At that moment Aitken's phone rang.

'Sorry, I am going to have to take this.'

He got up and went to the hall.

'Yes Dave. What have you got for me?'

Back in the ops room Dave reported the latest situation to Aitken.

'Some important stuff Guv, looks like Jimmy got it spot on. We finally got onto the Gas company. Well it isn't a Gas thingy anymore, it's a redevelopment site but you know what I mean. Not easy finding people at the weekend. They say they have in fact sold the site to a developer. There was nothing that would be happening in the yard in connection to them. They gave us the name of the developer. They in turn say that they had nothing happening. The Sarge went back to the Gas depot and looked at the lock. It is new. The developers say they got the keys from the gas company and as far as they knew the old lock should have been in place. Again we got lucky and got the guy just as he was going out. The guy from the developers distinctly remembers the lock because he was at the site when the Gas Company handed over the keys and the Gas guy had said that the chain and the lock were big enough to keep out most tea-leafs. Someone changed it. When we got in we found a loading ramp, a big one where they must have loaded the gas vans from. We think they loaded the Beamer onto the wagon there. There's tyre marks and stuff on the loading bay. They would have needed some kind of ramp because of the height of the wagon and apart from marks to that effect, we found no actual ramps. Forensics did over the lock and chain before we removed them.'

'Good, we must be able to find the van though. The guy walking his dog said it was clearly marked with the Gas Company's name and logo.'

'It might not be now. The Sarge went back to interview our dog walker, a Mr Edwards. The old boy used to own a small sign writing business. When the Sarge tried to see if he could get more info on the wagon or anything else about the three in it he was told the only things he could remember which was that the signage was magnetic.'

'What do you mean magnetic?' asked Aitken.

'Seemingly you can get signs that are magnetic and they stick to the metal of the wagons or vans etc. He thought nothing about it at the time, as it is a common enough practice with hired vehicles. Because the vehicle was a curtain-sider, that's a vehicle where the trailer is covered in curtains instead of being solid, because of that the signage was only on the tractor unit.

'I know what a curtain-sider is but the signs I didn't know that, you learn something every day. So if they can be stuck on instantly they can also come off instantly. I see what you mean.'

'The old boy says the wagon was a Scania. He knew that because he used to own a Saab. Bored the ears of the Sarge about it being the same company and how wonderful a car it was. His last piece of info was a cracker though. The guy who closed and locked the gate was not very tall and walked with the tiniest bit of a limp. The reason he noticed was that his wife suffers from arthritis. Although it is in its early stages she walks just like him. He said to himself at the time that you are going to suffer lad, in later life.'

'Good stuff Dave. Well it looks like we have our two gunmen but now joined by a third party, probably the guy actually driving the wagon. We can call off our search for the car and concentrate on the wagon. Tell the Sarge he's done well and thank Jimmy. We are going to be here for a while yet. Let's hope we find that damned wagon.'

'Now Sir, that's the problem. We picked it up on the cameras at the school on Jodrell and we even have a registration which turned out to be from a vehicle that has been written off. Even stranger, the wagon did not go through the camera at the Oscar Road junction. The problem is that there is nearly a mile between those two cameras and loads of exits off Jodrell. They could have turned off at a number of exits. We have cars scouring the area.'

At that point Aitken could hear Dave's mobile ring.

'Guv, can you hang on a sec this is from one of the cars in the area.'

Dave spoke to the caller on his mobile.

'Sorry about that Guv. That was one of the cars saying they had just been flagged down in Acacia Avenue by an old boy, a Mr Hendricks of the local neighbourhood watch. They got an earful for not being around earlier. 'Never there when you are needed,' you know the type.'

'All too well Dave, all too well,' said Aitken.

'Well he reported that a large blue truck had come thundering through earlier, this was an area where no trucks are allowed. In the past, trucks had used the route to avoid the huge jams at the end of Oscar Road. The route normally meant they were heading west. The timing is exactly ten minutes after our dog walker reported them at the gas Depot. Our lads asked Hendricks if he could tell them whose truck it was. He said that was the strange thing, it had no markers but fortunately the outraged conscience of the people took the registration. It was our guys definitely, signage removed.'

'These guys are going to a helluva lot of effort to make them untraceable. Someone is spending dough and large amounts of it to make sure of that. Further, this was very much premeditated. There is absolutely no mistake, the girl was the target. You think they are heading west, anything on the cameras?'

'Guv, more bad news, we have come up with absolutely nothing. They do not show up on anything. The route they were taking would have seen them able to access the motorway in about three and a bit miles from Acacia Avenue. Our cars are now concentrating on that area but it is mainly residential.'

'Tell the lads to look for anywhere that a wagon of that size could hole up. The extent that they are going to cover their tracks is amazing. Most people would just burn a car; they must have some plan for this vehicle, a compactor or something. I do not think they are going to turn up locally. Check every damned camera we have in the area. I am positive they are going somewhere and with a purpose. Thanks Dave, if you get anything else let me know.'

'OK Guv, talk to you later.'

The DCI returned to join the family and Louise in the lounge. Louise looked enquiringly at him.

'Progress Sir?'

'Yes, I'll discuss it later.'

There was that crisp business like efficiency of Aitken thought James Anderson. He had discovered something but it wasn't the right moment to make any announcements. James thought he might as well ask.

'Have you found them?' enquired James Anderson.

'No, not yet, but we are getting information on their movements. It's just a matter of time. How are we getting on here?' asked Aitken.

'OK,' said Allen, 'there is just such a lot to cover. Amy has only been back home for fifteen months. She was in Manchester doing her Accountancy degree for the four years prior to that and did about a year's work with a company in Manchester. That company was an accountancy company who specialised in insolvencies. She came home when she got her position with ADI. They are a comparatively new company, within the last five years, who have come on in leaps and bounds, hedge funds, all manner of things. Full of rising young executives. If you are over forty you are from an extinct species.

'Gee, thanks,' said Aitken

Allen continued. 'She was making good money for basically still a trainee. That explains her increased activity on the partying front but seemingly that was only ever Friday and Saturdays. The rest of the time she turned up for work as sharp as she could possibly be. They all follow a carefully mapped out career development path. Work hard, party hard, but the party hard must never interfere with the work hard or you were out. Amy was destined for great things. She was brilliant at figures, but not only was she brilliant at figures she was also brilliant with computers. The guys that swept her bedroom said there is the most fantastic and incredible set up in there.

'Tell me about it,' said Jason. 'A couple of months back my laptop crashed and I had to do stuff for school the following day. Amy wasn't around so I thought I would use her computer. I had only turned it on when she came back in. She went mental. When she finally calmed down she told me I must never, never touch her computer again. I told her I wouldn't, as it was a waste of time anyway. I couldn't fire it up, it had that many passwords.'

'I think,' said Aitken, 'we need to have a serious look at Amy's computer. She might have something on there of interest. Did she have a boyfriend, a closest friend or friends? Was there anyone from her work that she hung out with?'

'I've already asked that Sir. There hasn't been a boyfriend since Manchester days. A few dates since she returned but nothing serious, she has been concentrating on her career. As for friends there is a Melissa Harcross who lives on the Pendleton estate. They became friends at University in fresher week when they found out that they lived half a mile from each other and they have been good friends ever since. Melissa is a lawyer.

Aitken said, 'We'll need to talk to her. Does she know yet?'

'Unfortunately yes,' said James. 'The reason Amy was up early today was that she and Melissa were meeting up to go into town shopping for a wedding outfits. Melissa is getting married in five months time and Amy was to be the chief bridesmaid. When Amy no showed she called Amy's mobile which was still in the kitchen. Your forensic team took it through and I spoke with Melissa and told her that Amy had been murdered. I wasn't thinking. I didn't know what to say. She just screamed and burst into tears. I couldn't get any sense out of her. I phoned her parents to say what had happened. Her father had just got back home after running Melissa to the station. So he went back to find her. They called about half an hour later and Melissa was in a terrible state. I should have just said Amy was ill and couldn't make it. I wasn't thinking, I just wasn't thinking, poor lass.'

'Look there is nothing to reproach yourself for. She would have had to find out anyway. Better that you tell her than her seeing it on the TV,' said Allen.

'I suppose so. I didn't just blurt out Amy had been murdered I tried to break it gently. Trouble is it's not something you can break gently.

Chapter 9

★ ★ ★ ★

~I never saw you as the caring type~

Going back in the car to the station Aitken brought Allen up to speed with the wagon scenario and how it had vanished into thin air.

'They can't have just vanished, it's impossible to hide a truck that size,' said Allen.

'That's true and I am sure they will resurface, the question is where? As I said they have taken the car to ensure absolutely nothing remains for any kind of forensic testing. I had to feel sorry for the father in there. He had earlier seen his daughter murdered, in fact it goes beyond what I deem a murder, this was an execution. He had seen all that and yet he was concerned that he had upset her best friend Melissa. How decent a bloke is that?'

'Yes,' agreed Allen. 'I think we can safely rule out any involvement by the family. We'll check it out but I am positive this was and is, just a nightmare for them. They are probably all hoping to wake up and find it was just the most awful dream and Amy is fine.'

'Not going to happen though, that is why I will not rest until I nail their arses to the wall.'

'You and everyone else involved in this case Sir. I think I know what you mean about it being an execution.'

'My feeling is that big money is involved here. No expense spared so far. I hope Laura throws up something with the Andersons. Poor sods are getting hit with questions from all sides. We need to tell the counsellors to get involved after Laura is finished. Tell them to offer their services again this evening but unless they specifically request a visit not to actually go back in until tomorrow. None of them will sleep. The only time that three will sleep is when total exhaustion sets in. The best thing for them is to leave them for the rest of the day, they need each other and that should be private.'

'Christ Guv, I never saw you as the caring type.'

'Thanks a bunch Louise, you know as well as I do that you have to insulate yourself against what we see at times. That doesn't mean it doesn't get to you in the wee small hours when everything is quiet.'

'Sorry Boss, I know exactly what you mean and we haven't had something as callous as this for ....in fact, I cannot remember anything this cold blooded. As you say it was an execution.'

Aitken switched straight back to his professional mode.

'Back to business, any ideas yourself? Who, what, why? Are you getting anything at all?'

'If I was a gambling man and I'm not.'

'You're not even a man never mind a gambler.'

'My God you've noticed. I thought by your language at times you thought I was a bloke.'

'Do not tell me that you do not swear, I am not buying into that.'

'Me swear?'

She left a pause then said.

'Of course I never would.'

The way she had phrased it tickled Aitken and he burst out laughing. That amused Louise as well and she started laughing. There had been nothing funny said but it was the very first bit of light relief in what had been a very tough day.

It was Allen who switched back to serious mode.

'You asked about my thoughts. I said if I was a gambling person I would be having a few pounds on the company she works for or something from her Manchester days. For me, her current company deals in huge amounts of money. I smell money at the root of things here. If it was Manchester it would likely be drugs. I do not think it will be Manchester. The girl has made no attempt to cover her tracks. No, I think this company needs investigating and I don't know why but I just feel Amy's computer is going to tell us something. Maybe she is not the blameless character we think. What if she was blackmailing someone and got in out of her depth.'

'You do right to keep an open mind; she might be a total fraud. Strange thing I have this gut feeling that Amy really is a victim. I hope you are right about the computer. Yeah, blackmail is a possibility. My instinct is the same as yours, this high flying financial company; we need to find out everything about them.'

By the time they got back to the station people were starting to go home. The Super had been on TV with a press release about the murder. He had simply given a very basic outline and described the men exactly as they appeared at the shooting. The Super, Frank Purbright had called DCI Aitken before he had made his TV release. They had decided just to run with the tale of looking for two gunmen exactly as they had appeared to the Andersons. They went with the grey BMW and what they thought was letters in its registration. DCI Aitken thought it was best that they did not let the gunmen know that they had been rumbled with regard to the wagon and the fact there was now three people involved. Maybe, just maybe they would make a slip up if they thought they were safe and the police was on the wrong scent. Purbright was back at the station from the television studios and called Aitken and Allen into his office.

Chapter 10

★ ★ ★ ★

~Frank Purbright~

'Right, take a seat and update me,' was Purbright's opener for ten.

Purbright was a policeman of the old fashioned school. He was as straight as the day was long. He had come up through the ranks, he backed his men and his men loved him for it. It was like he was one of them. He should have been further up the tree but he had what one Commissioner described as an unambitious mouth. Frank Purbright told it like it was. He didn't give one whit about whose feathers he ruffled.

If you got a rollicking from Frank Purbright you usually deserved it. The men and women who worked for him would have gone through a brick wall for Frank as they knew he would be first to go through the wall with them. He was a tall man, six feet four and although only a couple of years from retirement he was still an impressive man. He was almost solely responsible for cleaning up organized crime in his Manor when he was a DCI. He had been shot at an armed robbery they had been called out to. Fortunately it was the robber's last bullet that he had fired into big Frank. Before he could reload the badly injured Frank had bounced the guy off the wall, breaking his nose and cheekbone. He disarmed him and cuffed him before passing out. It had been touch and go and he nearly died. The Force stuck him inside after that. He was far from happy. Being a desk jockey wasn't his scene. The powers that be finally relented and let him loose again amongst the criminal fraternity. It would be a political scandal that would be his undoing. He tried to nail a master crook that was hooked up to an MP. They were busy legitimising illegal immigrants, a nice little side earner which, when they were finally nailed, was estimated to have put just over two million in the MP's bank account. Frank knew they were at it but he just could not tie up all the loose ends. The crook and his MP sponsor knew that Frank was onto to them. The crook most certainly knew Frank's reputation and had his sponsor remove Frank from the equation. The MP claimed harassment for his constituent, a most law-abiding individual. Frank Purbright's actions were besmirching his constituent's good name, harming his business. Frank wanted to harm his business all right.

Frank was duly promoted to Detective Superintendent and moved out to Railton where he remains to this day. Railton was the most affluent neighbourhood Frank had ever worked. The force knew exactly where they were putting him. There was no damage he could do in Railton. There was crime alright but usually perpetrated by a band of wandering players from other Manors. The previous murder in the patch was eleven years ago.

What our MP had underestimated was Frank's tenacity. Frank's partner at the time had been a DS Chris Jenkins. Frank helped Chris to crack the case and in the end our MP got ten years, as did his partner in crime. Frank raised a large Scotch that night.

The move to Railton didn't suit Frank and for about a year he railed against it. His long-suffering wife Barbara caught most of this incessant complaining about how bloody peaceful Railton was. Salvation would come about in a rather peculiar manner. Frank's salvation came from massive housing estates, seven to be exact, in an area known as Tranter's Hill.

They had originally been in another Manor but parliamentary boundaries had been re-defined and this now fell within the Railton area. The Government of the day had no chance with Railton as a constituency but include these seven housing estates and they would certainly get the seat.

These were large sprawling estates built in the sixties. There were numerous high-rise buildings and some sixty eight thousand people lived there. The place was referred to as Beirut by the honest burgers of Railton. This was a reference to the war torn Beirut and not the one that had been the jewel in the eastern end of the Mediterranean. The reason it was called Beirut was that quite a few houses had bullet holes in their walls. Drive past shootings were commonplace.

With the very large area now under Railton as the main office Frank was promoted to Detective Chief Superintendent and he now was back at doing what he did best.

Frank Purbright was delighted the day it was announced that Beirut was now within his jurisdiction. The guys on those estates didn't play at crime. They really were criminals. Frank was ecstatic. He couldn't wait to start getting them locked up. Frank was very definitely old school. He wasn't all that interested in criminal backgrounds such as broken homes and all these bleeding liberals and their excuses. As far as Frank was concerned there was right and there was wrong. You knew from an early age which was which. If you can't do the time don't do the crime was Frank's attitude. The lads at the Tranter's Hill nick were also ecstatic to get Beirut off their hands. That ecstasy would be short lived as a number of them were transferred to Railton, as they would need additional resources to cope.

Frank was glad he had just over a couple of years to go. He would have never fitted in with the modern force. Most were career orientated. Promotion was a must. No one was content to be just a constable anymore. In his young day guys could be twenty, thirty years a constable, sometimes their whole working life but they were the backbone of the force. Now it was all psychometric tests, Myers Briggs assessments, annual assessments, career development, targets, deliverables and so forth. As far as Frank Purbright was concerned it was a right load of claptrap. You had to watch what you said or you were up for bullying and harassment. When he thought back to when he was a young copper on the beat, some of the ear bashings he had got from one Sergeant James Alexander Dunbar, a Scot whom he often wished would bugger off back north of the border from whence he had come. Then he realised that underneath the rough exterior of Dunbar there was a man who was extremely loyal to his troops. He remembered well being torn out a strip by the station Super, a particularly nasty character. A cock up by someone else landed at Frank's door and the Super had given him no chance to explain things. Frank was getting hell from him in a corridor when in walked Sergeant Dunbar. That day had been a monsoon and Dunbar was drenched through. The moment he saw what was going on he was straight in. 'Sir, what is going on here, I hope you are not tearing a strip off my man. That's my job. Now if you just go back to your office I'll get to the bottom of things and report back. Thank you Sir.'

The Super looked totally chastised and left mumbling, 'OK Dunbar, I shall await your report.'

He remembered Dunbar saying, 'Right laddie, follow me and let's get this sorted.'

Frank had been given the chance to explain the situation and the still soaking wet Sergeant went to see the Super.

Later that day the Super had met Frank in the corridor once again. 'Purbright, I believe I owe you an apology.' That was it, the Super kept walking.

Constable Harcross, a colleague with twenty-two years experience told Frank, 'I bet Dunbar made the Boss apologise. You don't bloody argue with Sergeant James Dunbar, well not if you know what's good for you. As a Station Sergeant he'll back you to the hilt.'

Frank never forgot it and tried to do the same with his men and women.

As he sat down he briefly looked at DC Louise Allen. She was the encapsulation of the new breed of police officer, smart, sharp and university educated. There was only one direction that her career would take and that direction was up. She was trained in all sorts of different things that he had never even heard of when he was a Police Cadet.

Psychology, body language, interrogation techniques, victim counselling, the list was endless. He liked her though, she was ambitious but she wasn't a back stabber. If she screwed up she put her hands up to and didn't try to shift the blame. She had dropped a couple of clangers early on but she was a quick learner and was making sure that there wouldn't be repeats. She worked well with Aitken. They had been partners for nearly a year. Another woman had been his partner for about three months but she couldn't hack it. She asked to be reassigned to another partner as she thought Aitken the coldest, most unfeeling bastard she had ever met. Purbright had seconded Allen from Deanend or Deadend nick as it was known locally. He knew that he had made the correct decision in getting her transferred. Purbright liked to handpick his team and had been very successful at doing so.

Purbright liked Aitken. There was a more than a little bit of himself in Aitken. Unlike Frank he was able to embrace modern methods. He had been transferred over from Beirut at Purbright's request. Prior to that, he worked south of the river in Alderlea, an area that was probably even tougher than Beirut. It was because of an incident there that he had been moved to Beirut. He had a partner who was kidnapped then taken into an abandoned warehouse and executed by firing squad as a message to Aitken to back off or he would be next. Aitken nailed them all but from that day onward he really was a cold unfeeling fish. At long last Purbright had found a partner that got on with Aitken and it looked like he was happy with Allen. Purbright settled into his big high backed chair. The gunshot wound had left him with a pain in his back. It was worse on rainy days. He always sat side on to his desk when he was conducting these interviews and side on to anybody else at the other side of the desk. He stretched out his long legs and crossed them at the ankles. The two officers knew what came next. Frank would put the tips of his sausage like fingers together along with the tips of his thumbs. He then pursed his lips and put the tips of his forefingers against them. He then stared at a spot on the office wall.

'Right what have you got for me?' was his question.

The two officers briefed him and he kept touching index fingers against his pursed lips. Occasionally he would move his fingers from his lips to say 'carry on' but that was it. When they had finished he sat staring at the wall for another full two minutes. Louise was going to say something but Aitken put his hand on her arm and put his fingers to his mouth to signal her to stay quiet.

'OK, definitely a contract killing. I think it's worthwhile to check out the victim's background and in particularly her company. The wagon cannot disappear. I agree that these guys were heading somewhere. I am positive they wanted to hit the motorway, east or west I have no idea. I'll leave you to it. Come in early and we will have a meet before your daily briefing. This has been a tough day for all of us. Large Scotch country for me tonight, helps me think. Got the habit from a station Sergeant I used to work with, Sergeant James Dunbar, long gone now but a bloody great cop.

Chapter 11

★ ★ ★ ★

~Beware of Greeks bearing gift~

The two worked well into the evening.

'That's it for me, I'm knackered,' said Aitken. I can think of better ways to spend the weekend. I thought we might have dragged up something else. Mind you we have a lot on the ADI finance company. Laura was right on the bugs. We now know that they gained access through supposedly free wall cavity wall insulation and loft insulation. That was only ten days ago but I can guarantee everything about these guys was a con. They certainly did the work according to Laura. I've read her report; she's just e-mailed it in. Have a look, as I'm pretty sure Laura is spot on. These are the guys that bugged the place.

Laura had comprehensively reported that two guys in suits had turned up at Emily Anderson's door. She answered the doorbell. She was normally at work but shooting had been delayed on the set.

'Oh, what are you selling? There is nothing we want and we are not religious so you are wasting your time.'

'Mrs Anderson we are not selling nothing.'

Mrs Anderson felt like saying that was grammatically incorrect but decided to keep quiet.

'No, in fact we are actually giving you something for nothing. We are from Railton Borough Council and we have received funds from Central Government which we have to spend in ecological causes. You know the thing, Green this, green that. That said it is a pretty good deal. Insulation for zero cost, can't be bad, so let's not worry about the whys and the wherefores. We have only got a few million but it is better than nothing. We decided on how many houses we could do. We then limited the service to people who had lived here at least a year. We then balloted or to be more accurate had the computer come up with who was going to be eligible.'

Emily again resisted the urge to say 'whom' but stayed silent.

'You were the lucky one in this street. We are doing either cavity wall or loft insulation. We cannot afford to do both.'

'Our walls were done a few years ago and I am sure the loft is insulated.'

The second suit spoke. 'Probably is but most is only 100mm between the rafters. New regulation is 250mm. I would be amazed if you have that. Have you a loft ladder; it will only take a moment to check. Oh, sorry, we had better get formal so that we can come in. Here's my ID.'

With that he briefly flashed a card that looked like it was a Railton Borough card with his photo and Environmental Services on it.

Emily said, 'I suppose you had better come in.'

The first suit took down the loft ladder and poked his head into the loft.

Emily said 'There's a light switch to your right just behind your shoulder.'

'Oh yes I see it. That's better. Yep, just as my colleague thought it is the old 100mm. You will qualify for an upgrade no problem. I'll tell you, put this in and you will notice a big difference on the old fuel bills. You will need to sign an acceptance so that we can get the insulating company to do the job. We only use the best of contractors. Anyway I shall shut up and if you are in agreement we can get things moving.'

The second suit spoke. 'The company that covers this area is from Henby and they are called Insulpak. Make sure you check their credentials. You just cannot have anyone wandering across the threshold.'

That night the Andersons received a call from Insulpak. Emily answered the call.

The man from Insulpak said. 'Mrs Anderson, the council has arranged for free loft insulation at No.11. We have a cancellation on Monday morning because the house we were supposed to do, the woman has had to go into hospital. Is Monday 10:30am OK for you otherwise it will be five weeks time.'

'Well I go down to old Mrs Winterbottom to take her some meals to help her through the week. I always leave about quarter to eleven. How long does it take to complete the process?'

The Insulpak man said, 'Just a little over the hour.'

'Well, I suppose I could let them in. I'll be back before they are finished. Yes go on. They might as well do it, the quicker they do it the quicker we see the savings you mentioned.'

That Monday the Insulpak van arrived and two guys got out and introduced themselves.

Emily asked them, 'You do know I am going out shortly?'

The first operative said, 'Sorry we didn't. How long are you going out for? Strictly speaking we are not supposed to work on the site without you being present. I hope you are not going to be far away.'

Emily told them, 'Only half an hour. Your company said you would be here for at least an hour. I'll be back before you are finished.'

The second operative spoke, 'as long as you are because we work to a very tight schedule. We have to do six houses today and you need to sign off the work here. No signature, no pay.'

Down at Mrs Winterbottom's Emily was telling the old lady what she was getting done. Mrs Winterbottom thought she was mad to leave two total strangers in the house.

'This was arranged by the Borough Council I would have thought they would be reputable companies.'

Mrs Winterbottom said, 'I wouldn't care if it had been arranged by the Archbishop of Canterbury himself I still wouldn't be leaving two strangers alone in my house. Look at Mrs Beckett at No.52. She let two guys in. Twenty-eight stitches and three weeks later she got out of hospital. You just cannot be careful enough these days. I think you ought to get your coat and get back home without delay. Have a good look round the house. Make sure nothing is missing.'

Emily hurried home. Mrs Winterbottom's warning had caused her concern. She was glad to see that the van was still in the drive. As she turned the key in the lock one of the men was coming out of the master bathroom which opened on to the upstairs landing.

'Oh good Mrs Anderson you are back. We are just about finished. I'm sorry, but I had to use your bathroom, call of nature.

Don't worry, the wife has me very well house trained.

Emily spoke, 'Do you want a cuppa or anything?'

'Thanks but no. We have a twenty-minute break after the third job, flask and a sandwich. Appreciate the offer. I had better crack on.'

He picked up a roll of insulation and headed up the ladder. Emily looked around her but everything was exactly as she left it. She quietly toured the bottom floor but everything was in place. She didn't want to appear as though she was checking every room in case they worked out she was checking up. The two men came down stairs fifteen minutes later

'Right Mrs Anderson can you have a look around at the top of the stairs and go into the rooms upstairs to make sure we haven't left you with a hole in the ceilings?

Emily was delighted to do so and to her relief everything was undisturbed. She went back downstairs.

A very relieved Emily said, 'everything's fine, the landing's spotless. That's great.'

'Fine, then we need you to sign that we have been. It might be free to you but it is not free to the council. Sign there, date and the time. Thanks.'

Emily signed and two minutes later the van was gone. That night James Anderson had a look in to the loft. When he came downstairs he looked quite pleased.

They made a good job of that. I've been meaning to do that for ages. Tell you what, it'll make a difference this winter.'

'It's good they were only here for just over an hour, it is worth about £500 they were saying.'

Chapter 12

★ ★ ★ ★

~Dinner's probably in the Dog. ~

Yes the timing is perfect,' said Allen. 'I notice that Laura thinks that the choice of time meant that they had been keeping the Andersons under observation. Looks like Amy had discovered something or was part of something and she was ready to blow the whistle. Yes, I think it is time to go home, I am knackered and we have an early start with the Super. He wants us in early. Christ another takeaway. I am going to look like a Chicken Chow Mien shortly. Mum and Dad gave me a case of Daniel Barraud Pouilly-Fuisse for my birthday last month. After such a crap day I think this is a good enough reason to open one, Dad keeps asking if I have tried it yet.

'I didn't know it was your birthday. You might have said.'

'Over thirty a woman doesn't.'

'I thought you were only twenty eight.'

'I wish, said Allen. 'No that was the big three O'

'Daniel Barraud, that's a bit special. Your parents cannot be short of a bob or two. If that particular tipple is chilled just right, it becomes divine.

'Well, well Detective Chief Inspector Aitken I didn't take you for a wine buff. That's twice you have surprised me today. Dad isn't loaded but he trades in wine. Knows his stuff back to front. If you are into wine he might be able to get you some at really good prices. Anyway this baby is in the chiller and set for being perfect. I think I shall have some fish with it. To hell with the takeaway, I'll do a warm sea bass salad; the express way of course, is there any other after a hard day at the office? What about you?'

'Rosemary will probably have wasted her time, yet again, making dinner. Dinner's probably in the dog. That dog gets more of my meals than I do. Only damned dog in the street that lives on a Mediterranean diet. No wonder the bugger's fat and I'm thin. Bet he has great cholesterol though. I might just take you up on that wine offer, there's a Sarafin Givery Chambertin, . ..forget it, maybe another day, or if I ever make Super I might be able to afford it. Let's get out of here. I get worried when you become on first name terms with the office cleaners.'

The following morning, Sunday, they both arrived within minutes of each other. Louise arrived in a new black Toyota MR2. Aitken who was walking from his car waited until she caught up.

'When did you get that? I thought you had a beetle?'

'I still have it but that was my birthday present from Jonathon.'

Aitken thought if the parents aren't loaded the boyfriend sure as hell is. All he knew about the boyfriend was he was some big shot in the city.

'The problem is I love my Beetle. Beautiful as the MR2 is, I am not sure I prefer it to my Beetle, there is more room in the Beetle. Jonathon would be crushed if he knew that.'

'Grease my palm with silver and I'll not tell. Anyway, how was the Daniel Barraud?'

'It wasn't. I had a Chicken Chow Mien and a diet coke.'

'I know exactly what you mean. That damned dog had Kidneys Turbigo and I had Welsh Rarebit. Bloody wonderful! Let's go and see what the Super has to say. God, I hope we make some progress today.'

'By the way I spoke to Jonathan and asked him if he knew anything about ADI. He was very, very, curious as to why I wanted to know about them. You know he works for KES, Kaye, Emmett and Smythe; well ADI has come up so fast that Jonathan's company thought it might be worthwhile buying out ADI before they became too expensive so they did some background research. According to Jonathon there is something very rotten in the state of Denmark. They have funds all over the world but with connections back to some very dubious people in places such as, Colombia, Afghanistan, and Myanmar. KES decided to do some more digging and brought in specialist help using the Emmett connections, probably old retired CIA guys were hired to find out a bit more. The resultant report would mean that KES would not touch ADI with a ten foot tarry pole.'

'Good stuff Allen; I knew it had to be money. Our Miss Anderson probably found out far more than was good for her. What we need to know is what was it that would get her killed. I am sure her computer will kick up something. I wonder how that is going.'

'Sir, I can tell you now. Very slowly is how it is going. I spoke to the tech guys last night and they are inundated, at least a week, ten days before they can start on it.'

' Did you tell them it was a murder case?'

'Yes I did but they pointed out it wasn't the only murder case they were working on. The Sallini case was taking up a lot of their time. They also pointed out in very terse terms that it was Saturday evening.'

'Oh, like that was a priority. It's our Saturday too. Crime doesn't do nine to five. I need to lean on someone, call in a favour Christ! Frankie Sallini. Who the hell is interested in finding whoever popped that little weasel? The guy did us all a huge favour by giving that little scumbag lead poisoning courtesy of an UZI. Seemingly he had up to thirty-three bullets in him. His scrap value would be substantial. When these guys 'sauf of the river' do it, they make sure they do it properly. He was about a stone heavier when they took him to the morgue; there was so much lead in him. Christ, the Super will have a bloody fit.'

Chapter 13

★ ★ ★ ★

~Crime doesn't take a weekend off. ~

When they got inside the Super was in his office. He stood beside his desk, his shirt brilliant white and starched. Trousers with a crease so sharp you could have cut yourself on it. The shoes gleamed so brightly Louise could have put on her make up with them.

There were no apologies about their Sunday being screwed up. Purbright was straight to business. He had obviously given things a lot of thought since last night.

'Good morning, take a seat. I've been thinking. My question is, are we looking for the right colour of wagon?'

Aitken responded. 'We have two sightings by members of the public and both cameras at the school in Jodrell Road. That wagon was blue all right.'

'Yes but was it actually blue. The tractor might have been but what if that was also a disguise. The signage was removable, maybe so was the paint job. There are these new plastic coats that can be applied and they simply peel off. That was a curtain-sider so maybe a fresh set of reversible curtains in a different colour. I think we should take a very close look at the trailer section; maybe it wasn't blue, maybe it was only the tractor that was blue. These guys wouldn't want to take too much time to change its appearance. Odds on, it was only the tractor that was painted. I think we need to look for a Scania with a curtain sided trailer but the last thing it will be is blue, probably re-plated as well. Check that area again north of Acacia Avenue. There has to be an area, a warehouse or somewhere you can work on a truck without someone seeing you. There is that old abandoned filling station and garage on Deal Street. That's only a short deviation on the route to the motorway. That has to be a possibility. Problem is, it is mainly residential. They could have crossed under the motorway into Beirut. There are too many cameras for that. They would have been picked up somewhere. I suggest that we go back to the motorway cameras, service stations, check the whole bloody lot. I would have thought that they were hitting the motorway no more than an hour after leaving the gas depot. Right, let's get on with it and keep me posted. We need these guys to make an error. I am sure they will, especially if they think they are away and free. They surely wouldn't go far as there is always the chance of a roadside VOSA spot check. They couldn't take the risk of being stopped.'

'Yeah, but I think it very likely they could have legal papers from there on. No expense has been spared here so fake documentation would be used. Right Sir, unless you have anything else we shall get on with it,' said Aitken.

'No, I think that is it. Keep me posted.'

'Oh yes, there is one thing Sir,' said Aitken, 'Tech cannot start on the murdered girl's computer for at least a week. The Frankie Sallini case is the hold up. They also informed us it was the weekend. Can you help?'

Purbright was out of his chair and on his feet in a flash.

'You're damned right I can. The weekend, the bloody weekend. Crime doesn't take the weekend off. They'll all be in shortly and on it first thing when they come in. Frankie Sallini, I ask you. As far as I am concerned whoever took him out did a lot of people a favour. There should be fewer addicts with that scumbag out of the way. Yes, we want to catch his killer, we cannot have people taking the law into their own hands, but I can assure you I shall thank Sallini's killer before he is locked up.'

Back in the office they covered all the latest developments with the team. Some of the team were muttering about the hard time they were getting from their loved ones but by and large they were all there to do a job.

'Well team,' said Aitken, 'firstly a few thanks are in order for contributions that brought things forward, Jimmy, Laura, good work, needless to say that goes for you all. Excellent police work all round. We have just come from the Super's office. Interestingly enough, he thinks we are looking for the wrong colour of wagon.

He reckons the colour was probably a plastic type spray on and could be peeled off. Yes, what is it Lloyd?

'Sir, I got an earful from a woman on Deal Street. We were door to door on whether anyone had seen the blue wagon. She said she hadn't seen a blue but a dirty grey big thing came roaring out of that old disused garage on Deal Street and nearly ran her over. At the time she was pushing her fifteen-month-old son in the pushchair.'

'Odds on our guys, the Super even suggested that old filling station and garage on Deal. It's in the middle of a quiet section with no houses opposite. They could have wheeled it in to the garage at the back of the filling station and peeled it back to its base colour. Right, let's get this show on the road. Check the garage on Deal Street and then back to the motorway cameras and filling stations, grey Scania this time round. OK, give me good news next time we meet. Laura, we need a word.'

Allen liked that about Aitken, it was never me, me, with him. We need a word, it was inclusive and she liked him for it.

The team dispersed to their various tasks.

'Right Laura, Louise here has used her other half Jonathon to give us some background into ADI. Not good news as there is something that his company discovered as to make ADI a bit shady. So Laura, I think we need to check out this ADI. Jonathan may know more than he can release, so we might call upon his company to see what they dug up.

'Sir I wouldn't want Jonathan to be involved. What he told me was in strictest confidence,' said a slightly concerned Allen.

'Don't worry Louise, he'll not be mentioned. We'll just say that as you are in the same line of business do you have any opinions. Make it clear they are only one of several companies that we are running a check with. Right Laura, can you see what you can dig up on ADI, I have a feeling that they are at the root of the troubles here. Find out if they are politically connected. Do they have a political 'sponsor?' I am sorry to load all this on you but with you DS breaking his leg last week coupled with the fact you are the best researcher we have it should keep you busy. Are you happy with that Laura?'

'Yes Sir, no problems I will get on to it right away. Might be a bit difficult though, seeing it is Sunday. I can run a lot of background checks so hopefully I should manage to come up with something substantive.'

Aitken thought as Laura walked away that she probably would come up with something substantive. She was a very good detective. Purbright had purloined her from another Manor about a year ago. She had been rather quiet when she first arrived but again Purbright had got his facts right. She was showing herself to be very sharp and she was gaining in confidence.

Aitken was keen to see some progress. He disliked working weekends so it was only ever good for him if it was worthwhile and produced results.

I wonder if they are going to start work with the computer. Why do I wonder? I'm damned sure that the Super has got it underway.

Chapter 14

~*Melissa Harcross*~

'Let us first pay a visit to the friend from University days, Melissa Harcross. Who knows, Amy might have confided in her, especially if they were as close as Amy's parents think. Right Allen let's go. You can drive.'

Twenty-five minutes later they were standing knocking on the door of Melissa Harcross's house. A man, about fifty-five years old, answered the door.

'Mr Harcross?' enquired Aitken.

'We have been expecting you. You had better come in. Melissa is here, in a bit of a state. It's all been a terrible shock. They were as thick as thieves the pair of them. They were just two young women, setting out on life's path. Amy, what can I say, Fiona and I, sorry, Fiona, that's the wife, well, we just can't take it in. I am sorry, I'm rambling on. We have had to get the doctor in to Melissa. She is still a bit woozy from the sedatives she was given yesterday. She's in here with her mother.'

The two police officers followed Keith Harcross into the living room. The room wasn't very large but comfortably furnished. The first impression was that it looked like a home. Family photographs were scattered around. A photo in a large silver frame showed Melissa in her graduation robes hung on the wall lit by a small down light. Next to it, another photo hung, this was of a young lad of around ten years old in his school uniform. The photo was black and white and was obviously taken a number of years ago.

Sitting on the sofa were two women, the older woman plainly

Fiona Harcross, the younger her daughter Melissa. Both shared red hair and when they looked up both shared the same green eyes. The younger woman was an exact facsimile of the older one, just about twenty-five years apart. Although not classically beautiful both women were quite striking. DCI Aitken blinked momentarily, a movement picked up by Keith Harcross.

'Like as two peas aren't they? Glad to say Melissa took her looks from her mother and not me. Melissa, these two police officers need to ask you a couple of questions. Are you up to it?'

'It's OK Dad, I'm not sure there is anything I can tell you but please sit down and ask away.'

Her mother spoke. 'Dad and I shall leave you to it. Can I get you a coffee or a tea?' she asked the two Officers.

'Thanks,' said Aitken, 'coffee would be fine for me, just black, no milk, and no sugar.'

'Yes that would be lovely. Coffee as well, milk, no sugar. Thanks,' said Allen.

'What about you dear, Juice? Her and Amy, neither would drink tea or coffee. Me, I am not lovable, sorry Freudian slip but probably correct, I am not liveable with, was what I actually meant to say, without my morning cuppa.'

'No Mum, I am fine at the moment thanks.'

When her parents had left Aitken started interrogating Melissa.

'Melissa, thanks for agreeing to answer our questions in such difficult circumstances. I'm DCI Aitken and this is my colleague DC Allen. In your own time I just want you to tell me a bit about your friendship with Amy.'

'Well, we met by chance at Fresher's Week in Manchester. Discovered we came from three quarters of a mile apart and we have been great friends since. The one and only thing we disagree on is football, I introduced Amy to football at Manchester, my own team, our local mob here, was in town to play United and I convinced Amy to come along. She got hooked. Her Mum and Dad even bought her a season ticket. A United fan she is, or was.'

At that Melissa stopped and both officers heard the sharp intake of breath. The young woman's body stiffened and her head dropped. A tear formed in her left eye and slowly rolled down her cheek before dropping off her chin onto her lap. She brought her head up and composed, she carried on.

'It is just so hard to believe I shall never see her again. That's my brother in that photo there. He was killed outside our door in a hit and run. He was ten at the time and I was seven. I just could not believe at the time I would never see Harry again. I loved my big brother and my feelings of loss at the time were unimaginable. I have never really got over Harry and now that terrible visitor, grief, is back residing within me. The car and driver were never found.'

'That's awful about your brother. Was that why you became a lawyer?' asked Allen.

'Possibly, you imagine as a child you will eventually catch the guilty party and that they will spend the rest of their days behind bars. Yes it is possible that's what was embryonic in my becoming a lawyer but not any more. We both had four happy years at Manchester and rather strangely we both eventually came back home to work locally. I am with Reyrolle, Simpkins and Heighway.'

'Oh yes, know them well,' said Aitken. They have been around a long time. Reyrolle, Simpkins and Highway Robbers as they are known locally. Actually they are my Dad's lawyers. My Dad being Aitken Publishing.

Melissa smiled the briefest but most dazzling smile. Her face actually lit up when she smiled. DCI Aitken thought, you are quite an attractive young lady.

'Yes, the one and the same. I have met your Dad then. He is ever such a charming man. Amy had got her appointment with ADI and I had done well in my company. So we suddenly found ourselves with a bit of money in our pockets so we started to party a bit at the weekend. We just had plain old fun, nothing else, and nothing that ever interfered with our jobs. Sometimes a little too much to drink but nothing that ever made us forget what had happened the previous evening.

Amy enjoyed a drink but drink didn't enjoy Amy. She had started suffering from hangovers so she kept a rein on the booze. We never touched drugs. That's a real mug's game. We had left them well alone at Uni and we certainly were not going to start now that we were in good jobs.

'Did you talk much about your work?' asked Allen.

'Not really, the nature of my work means it cannot be discussed anyway. The only thing of that nature that ever came up was about men. At Highway Robbers they really should wear masks, there isn't one piece of decent talent but Amy's place on the other hand is dripping with young rising executives. Recently we had a few good laughs about two guys at our respective workplaces.

For me it was Mr Nerd or to be more accurate Mr . . ., sorry let us just leave him anonymous. Mr Nerd is simply besotted with me but this sadly for Mr Nerd will always be an unrequited love from afar. For Amy it was even funnier. All those young men around and Amy is gorgeous so you would have thought she would have been pestered from every department but it was a wrinkly who hit on her. The guy was close to fifty.

Louise Allen smiled inwardly, she could almost feel Aitken cringe, he was still a few years yet to the big Hawaii, the state of being 50, but it was the next big decade for him.

'Yes, we had a few good laughs about the pathetic efforts they both were making.'

Allen asked, 'Neither of you had a regular boyfriend then?'

'The odd date yes, but nothing since Uni days.'

'What about boyfriends at Uni?' continued Allen?

'I went around with a guy for about eighteen months. Amy was going out with a Canadian at around the same time. He was a year ahead and when he finished his degree he returned to Canada. The communication between them lasted for around six weeks after he went back. I imagine he is still in Canada. With my boyfriend I found that I wasn't in the first team as I had thought. I was in fact on the substitute's bench and even that was at a push. The rat already had a first eleven and I mean a first eleven. Amy and I were both going into our final year so we decided to concentrate on our studies and boys would be in the future.

'Yep, there are a few rats around, I know that only too well,' said Allen.

Aitken could almost feel the bond that the two women made and he thought, that's good Louise has made a connection.

'We are not all rats you know,' said Aitken in defence of men.

The two women just looked at him then looked at each other and their expression was enough to convince Aitken that an awful lot were rats in their eyes. At that moment Melissa's mother entered the room. She carried the most enormous tray of food, a large cafetiere of coffee and plates of scones, toasted teacakes and various biscuits.

'I have warmed the milk. I always think it is better than cold milk. The teacakes are toasted and already buttered so I hope you are OK with butter. There's a selection of jams, as I didn't know your preferences. Are you sure that you don't want a drink dear?'

'No Mum, I'm fine.'

'Right then I leave you all to it.'

With that Mrs Harcross left the room. The two police officers looked at the tray sagging under the weight of food. They had both been in early and were now starting to feel a little peckish. That tray was bursting with treats. Melissa caught their mood.

'Bad news but I am afraid you are expected to shift most of what you see before you. Mum believes in feeding the five thousand even if only two or three turn up. Five loaves and two fishes, that's a snack. Everything on those plates, coffee and milk apart is produced from Mum's kitchen. She is a brilliant homemaker, too brilliant at times. Dad cannot cope with all the food she serves up.'

'He doesn't look overweight to me,' said Aitken'

Oh, he isn't, you just haven't seen his garbage disposal unit that is our poor Labrador have you? Poor beast really needs to go on a diet.'

'Yeah I have one of them at home, that dog has more of my dinners than I do,' said Aitken.

Chapter 15

★ ★ ★ ★

~*Pull pin, count to three, throw grenade*~

The two police officers got stuck into Mrs Harcross's goodies and the stuff was absolutely delicious. Aitken thought he could have scoffed the lot and just phoned in for a stretcher to take him away. DC Allen surprised him by tucking away a substantial amount of what was on offer. The coffee was simply beautiful. Aitken could feel the food have a restorative effect on him. Melissa had stopped speaking, giving the two police officers a moment to tuck in. She was quite pleased to see that they were doing so with gusto and that her mother would be quite pleased. Her next utterance would stop the two police officers assault on the food.

When she did speak it was a hand grenade that she threw into the conversation.

'I am pretty positive that ADI are behind Amy's murder. I think they simply shut her up.'

Coming out of the blue in a moment when Aitken and Allen were slightly distracted by Mrs Harcross's epicurean delights it had the effect of snapping both officers back to the job in hand.

'What did you just say?' said Aitken.

'Sorry, but it is what I believe. I cannot prove it but I just know they had something to do with it. Just over two months ago we were having a meal at that new Thai restaurant on Grenville Road and Amy suddenly became very serious. She said that she had uncovered a very serious situation at her work. As she had never mentioned her work in a work context I knew instinctively that it was something serious. I asked her if it was anything that I could help with. She said no, this was way too big and it would be a lot better if I didn't know. I said thanks a bunch, you have just put me on a horse and not given me a ride. She said sorry but it was best that way and to just forget what she had said. I pressed her to allow me to share a problem but she was adamant. She was convinced that it was better for me that I didn't know. As quickly as she had opened up she closed up.'

Melissa stopped for a moment. She was obviously with her lawyer's background carefully considering what she said next. She continued.

'The matter didn't rest there. The next thing that happened convinced me that something was up with Amy at ADI. I was at work and had just gone to have a bite to eat at a local restaurant I frequent. I had just sat down when a chap asked if the seat opposite me was taken. The place was busy and there were few seats so I said go ahead, help yourself. He sat down and started eating his sandwich. He then said… Miss Harcross, I believe you are a friend of Amy Anderson; in fact I believe that you are her best friend. What I would like to know is, does she ever discuss her work with you. I immediately heard alarm bells. I replied no, she never does but that is absolutely no business of yours whoever you are. He replied that in fact it really was his business. His name was George Kennedy and that he was with the HR department at ADI. 'Miss Anderson is still a comparatively recent employee and as she deals with some huge accounts it was important that she maintained a silence about what she did for a living.' He said that this type of routine check up was frequent during an employee's first three years with the company. They could lose major accounts through employees being loose with their tongues. I said that Amy never spoke about her work probably because I never spoke about mine, as I was a lawyer. The only thing that I knew about Amy's work was that she seemed to be enjoying it. I light-heartedly threw in that she mentioned there was some seriously good looking talent but she didn't believe in dating anyone from the office. That is good news he said. We are keen that she enjoys her work. You do appreciate that we would prefer if our confidential check up remained that, confidential. Some people are likely to get bent out of shape if they knew we were checking up on them. I knew that this was more than just a check up. They really were fishing to see if Amy had passed on anything to me. I took particular notice about the guy. He was about five feet eleven, dark brown hair and dark brown eyes. I would estimate his age at forty. A few things about him were distinctive. He had a tiny star tattooed on his thumb and it was recent. He also had a scar on his left eyebrow, long healed up but visible nonetheless. Add the fact that his nose had been broken at some time. Again it was almost imperceptible; it was like he had been a boxer when he was young. His hands were that of a boxer except they were immaculately manicured. His clothes were very expensive. If he was from the HR department he was extremely wealthy. He had a Duomètre.'

You have lost me,' said Aitken.

'It's the latest watch from Jaeger-le-Coultre in pink gold, costs over £20,000. That is serious money for a watch. Mind you it is a serious watch, stunningly beautiful.'

'How did you know it was this watch?' asked Allen.

'Well it was my dad's birthday a couple of weeks back and I was planning to get him a watch. He has always fancied a decent watch but he thought it was frivolous to spend a few hundred on himself for a watch. Amy jokingly said I should give him the Duomètre. A guy had rolled in at her work with one. Listening to the boy's talk about it she said it had a quarter-second display. I have no idea why anyone would want a quarter-second display, must be a bloke thing but this guy's watch had that display and I am positive it was that specific model. I am afraid Dad got something nearer a thousand but he was over the moon with it.

'What accent did this guy have?' asked Allen

'Almost Estuary English but there was a well masked controlling dialect underneath and that dialect was Mancunian. I know after four years oop north. The one convincing fact that this guy wasn't who he said he was, on his right hand little finger he wore a very expensive signet ring engraved WY. I naturally told Amy about the meeting. She was obviously worried, even scared I thought. Seemingly they did have a George Kennedy at her office. He had nothing to do with HR. He was a spotty faced seventeen year old who worked in the mailroom. WY was in fact the guy with the watch. His name is Walker Young. He is something heavy in security in the company.'

At that moment the Aitken's phone rang, it was the office.

'Excuse me for a moment,' said Aitken. 'I need to take this.'

Chapter 16

★ ★ ★ ★

~Caught on Camera~

He took the phone call in the kitchen; it was Dave from the office.

'Yes Dave have you got news for me?'

'Quite a bit Guv, First we have traced the grey Scania and we have good likenesses of all three and they match the description from the Andersons and our dog walker. They went sixty-five miles west and got off toward a small village called Swaffendale. We have the wagon on cameras in the town. The registration they are using is from a wagon that was a total wreck. The next village along from Swaffendale is Oxenbridge but we didn't pick them up there. They didn't go through there.'

'So where did they go?' asked Aitken.

'Well, that's where we got a big break. A local farmer has a farm adjoining what was an old quarry. The quarry is now filled with water about five hundred feet deep. Our farmer was in a field close to the quarry when he heard a big crash coming from the quarry. There is a lot of fly tippers who use the quarry but the crash was too big for something like a bike or a car being dumped. By the time he climbed up to the quarry edge he was just in time to see a grey BMW disappearing under the surface. As it was a fairly new car he was concerned someone had been in it. Then he noticed at the other rim of the quarry opposite there were three guys walking away. They were going back down the slope from the rim; he only momentary saw them from the waist up as they disappeared from view. Two were about the same height and the third was shorter.

Obviously they were fly tippers and he thought no more about. He spoke to his wife at breakfast this morning about what had happened and she thought that he should report it just in case somebody actually was in the car. So he went into Swaffendale this morning and did exactly that.'

'They probably opened the windows of the wagon so it would sink fast but must have forgot the windows on the BMW, that is probably why it took longer to sink. That is a mistake by them. They will make more.'

'Actually they have. We worked out that if they had dumped the truck they must have had to get transport again. Well, we studied the footage from Swaffendale and Oxenbridge cameras. Twenty minutes after the farmer reported seeing our three lads, a Smart Four by Four was pictured driving through Swaffendale heading back to the motorway. The driver was a white male in his thirties, probably six feet. The passenger was also at least six feet and his colour and I quote Mrs Anderson was 'coffee'. These Smart cars are a bit nifty and have a fabulous glass top. Through our top we could clearly see the third passenger in the back. He was much smaller and guess what colour his hair was?'

'Ginger?'

'In a word, helluva observation from Mrs Anderson. When we nail these bastards she will have played a huge part in catching her daughter's killers. They took the Smart car with them on the wagon.'

'I take it we have some leads on who they are and the car.'

'Working on it Guv. Nothing yet from records and the car registration belongs to a car registered to a Mr Devon of Highgate. Gave him more than a bit of a shock when we turned up on his doorstep. His car was in the drive so we are positive the registration is a clone even though the car is the right colour. Two weeks ago a Smart car matching this one was stolen from a car park in Alderlea. Anyway we followed our friends and they travelled twenty-six miles east to the Ravenswood service station. There all three went into the shopping area. The driver bought cigarettes and the other two took a brief comfort break. When they came out of the toilets the two walked up to a fourth man who was playing one of the slot machines. There was a brief conversation then all three walked out to a large 500SL Merc and drove back onto the motorway heading easterly.'

'Did it look like they the two knew the fourth man?'

'Hard to say, Laura says from their body language they did. I couldn't see it myself but it was a very quick meeting. They both sat in the back of the Merc and we have nothing on camera about any exchanges between them. The driver of the Smart car stayed and had a meal in the café. He left in the Smart car on his own and drove back onto the motorway. He got off at junction 2 but we lost him after that. We next pick him at Flatford station where he caught a train and we finally have him on camera at Sidebolt station in the Alderlea area.'

'Looks like Alderlea is his home patch so we need to concentrate on the criminal fraternity from that area. We also need to look around the Flatford area. I can almost bet that you find a scrap yard with a compactor and I bet there is a nicely cubed Smart car in the stock of compacted vehicles.'

'I'm about to come to that Sir.'

'Sorry,' said Aitken. 'What about the other three?'

'Well they also got off at Junction 2 and the passengers were dropped off at Flatford station. There they also caught a train to Sidebolt. The Merc is registered to a Philip S Ridgeon of 4 Demeter Way, North Easterby. No form at all. Moved there just over a year ago. On Laura's suggestion we checked out where our man might have dropped off the Smart car and only a mile from the motorway is a car crushing plant. We haven't got to it yet but two are on their way to see if, as you said, we can find a Smart car which has been made much smaller.'

'That is really good work Dave, maybe we are making progress. Anything else?'

'Yes, the super was right. We went to the old disused garage on Deal Street and we found tyre marks and the tiniest fragments of a blue plastic style coating.'

'That Dave, is another piece of the jigsaw in place. We have a couple of corners and some of the straight edges, it's a start. I shall be finished here shortly and I think I shall visit Mr Ridgeon. If he is innocent he is not going to be expecting us. If he has something to do with this then he still will not be expecting us. He is likely to react after we leave. Keep away from him at the moment. Louise and I shall visit him shortly. Is that it?'

'That is it at the moment, Sir. Do you want to know of any other developments? Oh, I almost forgot the Tech guys, who are very pissed off bunnies to say the least, say that Amy's computer is a minefield. The password is twelve letters long and the problem is our guys think that if we get it wrong there is going to be a lot of files lost and maybe most of the stuff. Can you phone her parents and see if they know the password.'

'Yes, but I shall be back at the station in about half an hour. There is something I need to get before I go to see Mr Ridgeon.'

Aitken phoned the Andersons but drew a total blank from all three as to what her password was. Aitken then walked back into where Louise and Melissa were still talking. Louise looked up enquiringly. Aitken just nodded.

'How are you getting on here?'

'I do not think there is much more Melissa can tell us but she is positive she would recognize the man who sat down beside her in the restaurant. Melissa asked Amy to go to the police but she said there was no need to do that and I was never to mention anything about this ever again. She was definitely scared. Are we making progress?'

'Yes, Tech have all turned up in their Sunday best. Some have had to miss Church. They have started on the computer but it has a twelve-letter password and they think that if they get it wrong there are minefields that will wipe out whatever is on it.'

'Twelve letters, I wasn't sure computer protocol allowed for that many letters.

'Don't ask me, I haven't a clue.' said Aitken.

Melissa spoke. 'Computer protocol on Amy's computer could be totally non-standard. She was a genius with a computer, an absolute genius. Twelve letters you say. I cannot guarantee it but I think you will find the password isn't a single word but three. I believe her password might be thereddevils, you know, Man U. It's all rather coincidental that it is twelve letters.

'Melissa I hope you are right. We think Amy's computer holds things that may help us. Do us a favour and keep things we have discussed private and please do not speak to the media,' said Aitken.

'Amazingly they have already been here. Dad said that I was under sedation and wouldn't be able to talk to anyone until tomorrow. They said they would return tomorrow. Dad told them they would be wasting their time'.

'We will leave you in peace now Melissa. If there is anything else you can think about ring DC Allen. Her number is on her card. Big thanks by the way, you have given us another piece of the jigsaw. We'll see ourselves out and please, thank your Mum for the spread it was great.'

'Yes Melissa, Thanks. If you think of anything ring me,' said Allen.

On the way back to the station Aitken brought Allen up to date. By the time they had returned Allen was up to speed.

'Can you wait in the car I shall only be a couple of minutes,' said Aitken

'Sorry Sir got to pee, all that coffee gone right through me.'

'Too much information Allen, noticed you tucked the toasted teacakes away. Where do you put it all?'

'Boy that is rich coming from you. You had your snout well into the trough.'

'Alright I admit it, boy, can that woman bake. I just had this mental image that we were going to be joined by the most obese Labrador you have ever seen.'

Allen laughed,' I really got to go Sir, you are not helping the situation.'

Chapter 17

★ ★ ★ ★

~You sound like a Music Hall Act~

Forty-five minutes later they were sitting outside the gates that led to Demeter Way. There were only six houses in Demeter Way and the whole road was blocked by two enormous gates. They got out and approached the gates. At that moment a car pulled out from the second house on the right. A young blonde woman in her early thirties was at the wheel of a convertible Bentley. The gates glided open and a security guard stood up from a small hut just behind the large pillar of the gate and touched his cap. The young woman smiled sweetly at him and drove out. The two police officers stepped inside the closing gates.

The Guard snapped at them, 'What do you think you are doing? This is private property; you cannot come in here without an appointment. Do you have an appointment?'

'No,' said Aitken.

'Then I must ask you to leave immediately.'

'We are here to see Mr Ridgeon at No.4,' said Allen

The Guard was starting to get a little testy. 'You said you had no appointment so I must ask you again to leave.'

'Oh I think he will see us without an appointment. I am, as you can see by my warrant card, DCI Aitken and my colleague here is DC Allen. Show the nice man your warrant card DC Allen.'

The guard looked momentarily perplexed then he went into his guardsman's hut and made a phone call.

He came back, 'Mr Ridgeon shall see you now. His house is the one at the end on the left.'

As the two walked toward it Aitken observed that they didn't need much instruction to find number four when there were only six bloody houses. The 500SL Merc was sitting in the driveway. The registration matched that from the motorway cameras. As they walked up the driveway to the door it was opened by a man in his late forties. He was casually dressed in very expensive clothes with no socks inside a pair of clog styled shoes. The hair was immaculate although it had started to recede at the temples.

'Good morning I'm Philip Ridgeon. Sorry I should say Good afternoon, it's past midday. Our guard dog Butcher tells me that you are police officers. What can I do for you? It surely can't be time yet for my contribution to the police charities. I thought that was still a couple of months off.'

'No it isn't that at all. I'm DCI Aitken and this is DC Allen. We are here on official police business.'

'Then you had better come in. Aitken and Allen you sound more like a Music Hall act.'

I'll Music Hall act you, you smarmy Bastard, thought Aitken. My gut feeling is that you have something to do with all of this.

They followed him through a large hall with a huge atrium that went up the two floors of the house. They went through double doors into a large room. The room was beautifully decorated and furnished. Through a window at one end they could see into a huge garden which had a large swimming pool in it. Whatever Philip Ridgeon did for a living he got extremely well paid for it. He sat down in a winged armchair and gestured to the officers to sit down.

'Right then, how can I help you?'

'Simple. Yesterday evening you dropped two people off at Flatford Railway station. Are these acquaintances of yours? Do you know who they are?' asked Aitken.

'Do I know who they are. No I certainly do not.'

'Then can you explain how they come to be in your car?'

Louise picked up on the rather terse statements from Aitken that something had got up his nose, probably the Music Hall comment. She was right.

'Certainly, I had been to Bristol on business for the day.'

'Yesterday was Saturday, do you usually work all day on a Saturday?'

'Look around you, do you think that you pay for this working nine to five. No, I am a Management Consultant and frequently

my work is at the weekends so that none of the staff are even aware
I have been to their company. I save corporations large amounts of
money by telling them what actions to take. Quite often that action
is to get rid of people so weekends and evenings are often the only
times when boards will see you.'

'Who were you seeing in Bristol?' asked Allen.

The question momentarily threw Ridgeon or maybe it was the
fact that Allen had spoken as she had not said a word prior to that.
Whatever it was it seemed to knock him out of his stride.

'Oh a company called,' he hesitated then said, 'Cyrus
Investments, surely that doesn't matter. I thought it was the two
people I had dropped off that is of interest to you.'

'So it is. How did they come to be in your car?'

'Simple really, they approached me at one of the filling stations
on the way home. I had not meant to be so late so I went in for last
minute flowers for my wife. My dinner was likely to be in Barnaby
our Old English Sheepdog so I thought I would pour oil on
troubled waters with some flowers. Didn't work though. Still
sulking this morning. Taken herself off to see her sister. My ears
are probably burning right now. The two men said they were trade
plate drivers and if was I going east could I give them a lift. They
had trade plates on them so I thought they were kosher. As I get off
at Junction 2 they asked to be dropped off at the nearest station and
that was Flatford. They thanked me and got out. They were both
quite coarse types. Language was quite appalling. What have they
done that interests you?'

'Collectively they haven't done anything. We just want to talk
to one of them. We have no interest in the coloured guy.'

'So what has the smaller one done?'

'At this moment we'd rather not say. We just need to talk to
him.'

'Was he dangerous, my goodness, I could have been robbed or
had my car stolen.'

'No, he isn't dangerous. If you must know, it's identity fraud.
We think your guy is the same guy that we have on camera in
Alderlea, in the big Tesco there using a stolen credit card.'

'Oh is that all!'

'What do you mean, is that all. It's a very serious crime identity
fraud,' remonstrated Aitken.

'Sorry I didn't mean to be flippant.'

'Did either man use the other's name?' asked Allen.

'Do you know, I don't think they actually did. As I said they were typical of their class, quite coarse and vulgar. I was more than a little glad to get them out of my car. My wife gave me a bit of an earful for picking them up in the first place.'

'Where exactly did you pick them up?' asked Aitken.

'Either Torcross or Ravenswood or it could have been the one after that. To be honest I wasn't paying too much attention.'

'I wonder what they were doing out that far, up to no good likely.'

'Guilty until proven innocent, surely that's a bit back to front Detective Chief Inspector. As I said they claimed to be drivers so they could have been an awful lot further out. I didn't actually ask them where they had come from. In fact I hardly spoke to them.'

'You're right; this may not even be our guy. If you cannot think of anything else we'll be off. Sorry to call on a Sunday.'

'I did wonder about that. I would have thought it was only something serious that brought you guys out on a Sunday.'

'I would normally say yes. Truth is we are down on meeting our targets and we have a Super who had given us all a kick up the … well, I'm sure you know where we all have been kicked. Normally I wouldn't even be touching this low level case and certainly not on a Sunday but we are trying to get better stats. The problem is the picture from the hole in the wall at Tesco's is so poor. There was a torrential downpour at the time. This guy will probably get off anyway.'

'I take it your heart is not in this today.'

'You could say that but we have to persevere. Do you mind if I use your bathroom before I leave, early start and too much coffee,' said Aitken.

'Not at all, you have a choice. There are nine bathrooms and another three additional loos.'

'Nine bathrooms, that is amazing,' said Allen. 'Mind you it is an amazing house and the gardens look outstanding. I was just sneaking a peek through the window there.'

'Why do I not give you a whistle-stop tour while your colleague takes his break?'

He turned to Aitken and gave him instruction.

'Through that door to your right and at the far end of the hall.'

'Thanks.'

Aitken was waiting for Allen when she returned.

'You ought to see these gardens, they are simply beautiful. My dad would kill for any of the themed gardens. The Japanese one is particularly exquisite. My Mum would die for the herb garden. Thank you, Mr Ridgeon, for introducing a very bright spot into an otherwise dull day.'

'Right Allen, we need to get back to our dull day. Thanks again Mr Ridgeon for your time. If there is anything at all you recall you have my card.'

Chapter 18

★ ★ ★ ★

~An illegal Bug's life~

Back in the car they drove around the corner and stopped. Aitken pulled a small device from his pocket about the size of a Dictaphone. Ten seconds later the device was given off a ringing sound. The next thing that was heard was someone, a man, answering the phone.

'Oh my, you little beauty. Even better than I could have hoped for. He's using the speakerphone.'

On the small device in his hand they could hear Ridgeon making his call. Roberts is that you. I thought I sodding told you never to ring me at this number unless it was a dire sodding emergency.

'Kind of is. I have had two plods round here looking for the weasel. Seems he has tea-leafed somebody's credit card and used it illegally at a hole in the wall. They picked our friend up off a station camera at Flatford. They came here to ask if I knew them. I said I had picked them at a motorway service station, trade plate drivers. I said they had asked to be dropped off at the nearest station to where I came off the motorway. I sure as hell wasn't going to say I had just paid them a hundred big ones for a termination.'

'Are you on that sodding speakerphone thing? What if your wife overhears? Don't even say things like that on the phone.'

'She wouldn't need to be here, not with your language. She's at her sister's and will not be back until this evening. I was going to play golf.'

'What the hell were plods doing out on a Sunday? That gives me some concern.'

'Don't worry, I covered that off. Their station has not been performing and they have received a good arse kicking. The DCI was a right self-important prick. This type of case was below him. He usually only went after big time crooks. Pompous bastard. The DC was a woman and I'll tell I could have given her one, she was seriously fit.'

'Check out if the little weasel has actually done the crime. If he has we'll get an Eastern European contractor and get shot of the three of them. Make it look like a gangland hit. I still have a niggling bad feel about this. A guy we use for a contract the day before and they pick him up on the station camera at Flatford. Their other image is in Alderlea. Mind you that is his home patch so he might have been a naughty boy. Still it's a big coincidence, almost too big. Are you sure that plod was as dumb as you think?'

'Oh he was thick alright, thick as they come. Just remember that they had no interest in my second passenger.'

'Yeah but our pompous plod might not be a pompous plod at all but a very smart one instead.'

'No this plod wasn't too bright; you could see he was overwhelmed by the house. An old-fashioned retainer, touch the forelock, knows his place in society, although he thinks that he is important. The DC was the one with the brains. She would have happily stripped off and swam in my pool. I wished to hell she had done. She was bored both with the job and the idiot she works with. I shall check out our friend's activities. There was one amazing thing about our plod, his suit was bloody fantastic. Could even have been Saville Row, it was that sharp. Come to think of it so were all of his clothes.'

'You really are thick. Do you honestly think some plod dressed like that is your average plod? I will guarantee your plod was very interested in the weasel but sod all to do with fraud. You have had smoke blown up your arse. I think you just got teamed. You can go ahead if you want to check the weasel out but I have made up my mind already. I am bringing in a contractor. You can make the payments again but do not get caught on camera anywhere or you'll be the next contract.'

'Do what you have to, I'll check him out. I know you are wasting your time. I'll wait to hear your instructions.'

There was a click, the voice on the other end hung up. They

could then hear another number being dialled. Again Ridgeon was using the speakerphone. A voice answered, 'who's this?'

'It's the Paymaster General, who do you think it is? I think you have been a naughty boy. I dropped you off last night at Flatford. Two plods have just left me. They were looking for you. They say that you are guilty of identity fraud. You are on camera at your local Tesco purloining funds with someone else's credit card. Your photo from the station matches the one from the Tesco hole in the wall.'

'Not bloody me they haven't. What the hell would I do going to a supermarket? I live on my own. Tesco's a mile away from me. I have a minimart only fifty yards away. Tesco's full of food I would need to cook. Bollocks to that. I have two Indians, Two Chinese takeaways, a Polish restaurant plus a Fish and chip shop within two hundred yards of my front door. You tell me, what the hell do I need Tesco for?'

'OK, I get the message, so it really is mistaken identity. For your sake Dobra you better be telling the truth or the Lord High Executioner shall live up to his name. He is pretty pissed off with the plods looking for you. Low profile it, same goes for spending your cash. Low profile that too. You have been warned.'

'Fine, I get the point. If that's all, I am going down the off licence to get some beer in for the match this afternoon. I take it I can do that?'

'Yeah fine, Low profile.'

Click, the phone went dead.

'You just bugged his house. That is absolutely illegal. What happens when they are found?' demanded Allen.

'We shall cross that bridge when we come to it. I shall momentarily hang my head in an act of contrition. Nothing we have heard or more accurately recorded, is admissible in court. I need to know a lot more after that little visit. We need to get the numbers of the callers, Ridgeon, or is that Roberts. Who is the Lord High Executioner? Who is Dobra? We have our hit team, of that I am certain but we need to stick this on them. It is one thing knowing who done it, it is quite another thing proving it.'

'I think we need to find these characters and find them quickly or they are going to be dead.'

'Yes Allen, I thought about that. There is a temptation to leave them out there as bait and nail the top dog and the rest of them.'

'That is a very high risk strategy.'

'I would need Frank Purbright to agree to that. OK let's get back to base and see what else has bubbled to the surface. Let's try to get a few gathered together for a briefing.'

Chapter 19

★ ★ ★ ★

~You got that right Son~

Back in the briefing room the team assembled in dribs and drabs. Laura had made an excellent job of bringing the wallboards up to date.

'Right settle down. We have a lot to discuss. Good work here Laura. We are going to make some additions to your wall. DC Allen and I have just visited Melissa Harcross, Amy Anderson's best friend and we also paid a visit to Mr Ridgeon the owner of the Mercedes 500SL. It appears that Mr Ridgeon may also be known as Roberts. He was also the paymaster for the two men who killed Amy. They received £100,000 for their work. The murder of an innocent young woman.'

'How did you come by this?' asked Jimmy.

'Ah, Jimmy that's the rub. I know this as fact but now proving it is a totally different matter.'

'Another Aitken special. OK we'll leave at that. Sorry Guv, didn't mean to interrupt.'

'What the hell, here it is.'

With that Aitken played his illegally obtained tape. They all listened intently. It was Laura who spoke first.

'I thought you said Ridgeon was British. He's not.'

'Records on him have him holding a British Passport.'

'OK, he could be British but he has undertones of being a Skippy. He has lived in Darwin at some point.'

'If that is the case you are truly amazing. I honestly thought he was British. How the hell did you pick up that,' said Aitken.

'Had a boyfriend from there once, he worked with Darwin Development. He was a lot broader than our Mr Ridgeon but it is all in the vowels.'

'No wonder you didn't pick it up Sir; you probably haven't bedded any Australian men. Truly amazing what you can pick up between the sheets,' said Keith.

Laura just smiled her sweet smile.

'Thanks Laura, just ignore Keith,' said Aitken. 'Melissa Harcross is convinced ADI is responsible for the death of Amy. She thinks that Amy discovered something about ADI but it was so huge that Amy was having difficulty coping with it. Melissa also gave us what she is convinced is Amy's password. The computer is, well I think it is, the key factor in our enquiries. Amy was an absolute wizard with computers so it stands to reason she would use it in such circumstances. The computer could almost be a confidante if there wasn't a human being that she was willing to share her secret with.'

At that moment the door opened and in walked DC Chris Atkins.

'Sorry Guv, bloody shunt held me up. Not me, some idiot hit a bus. You can imagine the panic in today's environment. What the hell has Johnny Clyde got to do with this investigation?'

'Who is Johnny Clyde?' came from a few mouths including Aitken's.

'Him up there, the coloured guy. He is Jonathon Clyde Robertson, son of mixed parentage and a real nasty piece of work. He hated his father, a Geordie from Newcastle. His father used to knock the living daylights out of his mother, a woman of Trinidadian descent. He hated his father and everything that he stood for. That is why he dropped the Robertson from his name, that and probably the fact that Johnny Clyde was a far cooler name for a young man about town. Rumour has it that when he was fourteen he returned home to find his father fuelled by that dark brown stuff. You know the nuclear shit they drink up there in Newcastle. Well he was beating the living daylights out of Jonathon's mother. The young Johnny tried to intervene. The father then turned his attentions to young Johnny. Problem was the father had not really noticed that young Johnny, though only fourteen, now stood six feet tall and was built like a brick outhouse. He beat his father to death. Of course it was never proven, his mother was not going to testify against her son who adored her, that and the fact that they never found the body. Mrs Robertson's story was that her husband had finally abandoned her and hopefully he would never come back. Good riddance as far as she was concerned. Clyde then kept on with a life of crime, going up through the gears. The thing was, he was very clever. Nothing could be pinned on him. We know of one instance where a head of a gang was giving Johnny a hard time over his name. This guy was one serious heavyweight dude. He was saying that you walk around calling yourself Johnny Clyde, cool and all that shit. He then made the whole café laugh by saying your real name is Jonathon Robertson. Not much bloody cool about Jonathon Robertson. Johnny turned and left the restaurant and the gang chief said 'That's right, is Mummy's boy going home to Mrs Robertson. Maybe like 'The Graduate' you have a thing for Mrs Robertson. Two minutes later Johnny walked through the café door with a baseball bat. He broke the guy's legs and arms and no less than eight of his ribs. Punctured a lung, the sod was lucky to survive. Nobody who was present in the café that night would give evidence against Johnny. It was two years later before we actually pinned him down, armed robbery and GBH. He got eight years. He should be safely ensconced in Parkhurst, Isle of Wight.

You are not going to tell me he is a suspect.'

'Well, that was certainly descriptive enough Chris, to the point of being brilliant. To answer your question he is more than a suspect he was definitely one of the shooters. If you know our friend there, do you know the other guy? Does Dobra ring any bells?'

'Jimmy 'Dobra' Perkins or The Weasel, I have never actually met him. He was a sidekick of Clyde. Clyde was like a protector to Jimmy. All I know about him is that he has red hair.'

'The Dobra nickname, where did that come from?' asked Aitken.'

'No idea Guv, probably something from his childhood.'

'Right, we actually now know who our killers are and who paid them for the hit. We do not know who sanctioned it. Roberts or Ridgeon refers to him as the Lord High Executioner. Now this guy has decided to take all three out. We need to find out who the third guy is, the driver that is. Odds on is that he is also a resident of Alderlea.'

'That's south of the river and not our patch Guv. We cannot go poking about there without alerting Colin Naismith. You should know that better than anyone. Him and the Super have previous. Purbright is of the opinion that Naismith is bigger than any of the crooks on his patch. Lot of bad blood there. We go poking around and Naismith would use it against our man.'

'Who said anything about poking about there?' asked Aitken. 'Well, certainly not official like. I didn't think we were banned from having a drink at places like The Three Crowns and The Midshipman. We could have a meal at The Fat Lobster. Good places to go for some food and wine. You do have to be prepared to rub shoulders with some of the criminal classes who have a tendency to frequent those establishments I have just mentioned. It's a small price to pay for good food and some excellent ale to wash it down with.'

'You'll get us all shot some day Guv.'

Sergeant Bill Armstrong spoke. 'If the main guy is going to knock off the three who murdered the girl why cannot we offer them a protective deal in return for evidence?'

'Bill, do you want to nip next door and run that one past the Super. As far as these three guys and Frank Purbright is concerned, we erect three crosses, we hand him a hammer and a bunch of big nails. He'll nail these bastards to the cross personally. I am not going to be the one to try putting that plea bargain to the Super. He'd be nailing my arse to the cross. It would be me he would crucify.'

Outside in the corridor and out of sight of the people in the room Purbright smiled and turned to walk back to his office. He could just be heard to mutter to himself, 'you got that right son. I would have nailed your arse to the cross if you had proposed that deal.'

He sat down in his chair stretched his long legs, crossed them at the ankles and stared at his spot on the wall. He nodded his head. Aitken was making progress. Maybe not all too politically correct, but he was making progress. Aitken knew how to catch crooks.

Chapter 20

★ ★ ★ ★

~Just like school, the comedians sit at the back~

In the briefing room Aitken continued.

'No, we have to take the whole damned lot down. Money is at the root of this and ADI are up to their necks in it'.

At that point Louise Allen came into the room.

'Sir, a few things to report. Firstly, Melissa was correct. That was the password. Unfortunately that is only the beginning. Amy's computer is so well protected that it is proving very difficult for the Tech guys to navigate their way through the minefield. They talk about her in glowing terms. Hopefully they will have something for us shortly. Secondly, we have traces done on the two phone calls that Ridgeon made. The first was to a mobile. Nothing unusual about that except it was answered in Rangoon. The owner is one John Collins or more exactly Christopher John Anthony Collins, Chief Executive Officer Operations for ADI.

I have bounced Ridgeon off Interpol, as he seems to have been a recent immigrant to the UK although he claims to be British. He isn't British, he is in fact an Australian or I think he is. A Philip Bruce Roberts is wanted by Interpol for running huge amounts of drugs into Australia. He came from, yes, you've guessed it, Darwin. I think a round of applause to Laura. Most of his drugs originally came from Myanmar or Afghanistan, but for the last two years of his activities he had added Colombia to his suppliers. The Interpol guys and the Australian authorities were just about to gather up Roberts and his cronies but they reckon someone on high tipped him off. I couldn't poke about too much without getting Interpol actually involved and that would put a spoke in our wheel. Interpol and the DEA probably have bigger fish to fry. Anyway as far as Roberts is concerned, the height and age match but the face probably has had plastic surgery. He is very fit.'

A voice from the back said, 'he seemed to think the same about you.'

Laughter ran round the room.

Another voice at the back. 'We also now know that Ridgeon has poor eyesight.'

More laughter.

'It's strange,' said Louise, 'it's just like school, all the comedians sit at the back.' 'Carrying on, Jonathon Clyde Robertson is no longer in Parkhurst. He was released over three months ago on a technicality. The arresting officer made a pig's ear of things. Robertson's lawyers appealed and won. He's out on the street, as we now know to Amy Anderson's cost. Lastly, CRO have made a match with the third man, the wagon driver. He is a David Earl Jones, originally from Cardiff, a petty criminal and usually the driver for jobs. Has form, three years for being the driver at a convenience store robbery. A frustrated Grand Prix driver, grew a bit too big and heavy for that. He resides only two streets away from our ginger haired friend. He probably doesn't go to Tesco either.'

This brought a laugh from the audience.

'Right,' said Aitken, 'we have all the murder gang plus our Australian Ridgeon a.k.a. Roberts, who is very fit. So what do we do with that info? Do we go out there and drag them in? If we do not get a confession we need to release them. I think it is going to be difficult to prove the case. We would need to recover the wagon and the BMW from 500 possibly 600 feet of water. That is going to be costly and time consuming. I am sure that the water immersion will not help forensics. That said, I am positive that the masks they wore went down with the wagon. I think we can nail them. We have enough CCTV from various cameras to make their movements very accurate. Our problem is that we must be able to make it stick when we take them in. If we have to release them, all it does is speed up their execution. Or is that a bad thing? Should we in fact let them go? We could tell our friend Roberts that we did indeed pick up his hitchhiker and that he might be guilty of something really serious. That would shake the tree.'

Constable Peter Adams spoke. 'I thought we were supposed to prevent crime not initiate it.'

'Semantics Peter, semantics, nothing more. Whilst we are prepared to initiate the intent to commit a crime there is no intention to let that crime happen. It is the intent we require.'

'Sorry Sir, I just thought that you were willing to let the three be murdered.'

'Peter, the trouble is they deserve to be eliminated and it would save the country a small fortune. We are talking probably twenty-five or even thirty years for these lowlifes. That's nearly a million quid each that we, the taxpayer, are going to be stuck with. The trouble is and attractive as it is, we are the Police. We cannot allow actual murders to take place. We need to set the trap but spring it before the bait gets eaten. We have no idea how many more are going to be involved. Hopefully they can pay for their stay at Her Majesty's Hiltons themselves. Hopefully we can nail enough of their funds to ensure that their stay is paid for by their ill-gotten gains. I am in favour of holding off their arrest at the moment; obviously I need to clear this upstairs. Whatever happens, no matter how difficult it is to prove, I know we can nail Amy's killers.'

Out in the corridor Purbright was once again eavesdropping. He couldn't help but smile at Aitken's explanation. It was brilliant, but Purbright also knew that Aitken would not cry any tears if all three were wiped out.

'The problem is that her real killers are the ones who sanctioned the hit. Look, it's Sunday and we have made good progress. Let's go home. I'll go and see the Super and see if he agrees that we lay off momentarily.'

Again a voice from the back spoke. 'Are you going to get roast beef and two veg today or is it going to be roasted arse and two veg. Hell if I was married to a cordon bleu cook like you I wouldn't miss the amount of meals you do. I would also kick that greedy bugger of a dog into touch. My Alison is so crap at cooking that I feel like going home and kicking her arse for being such a poor cook. What does the lovely Rosemary have waiting for you? Coq au Vin? Beef Wellington? Go on make me pig sick.'

The DCI looked at his watch.

'Malcolm you are spot on, I do need to get home. One of my favourite meals awaits, Alfelia.

Malcolm said, 'I am none the wiser and I think I shall stay ignorant. Saves me killing my useless other half.'

Jimmy, who was Malcolm's partner spoke.

'I would love to hear what Alison's saying about you. I can just guess. She'll be looking at her watch and thinking that Mr Snout in the Trough is on his way home and whatever I make is not going to be good enough and certainly not large enough. I don't know why I bother. Too good for you Malkie, that woman is an angel.'

Malcolm's riposte had them all on the floor.

'If she's a bloody angel I wish she would take her place in heaven!'

'If she did you would sure as hell miss her.' said Jimmy.

'Yeah, I suppose I would. She's not a bad old stick, but I wish to hell she could cook.'

There was a good feeling in the room with the bit of banter going on. They knew they had made good progress but there was still some way to go.

'Right, if we have no other contributors I suggest we get home to our loved ones and that includes Alison Terry, beloved wife of one Malcolm Terry who, to avoid culinary disappointment, is going to take the said Alison Terry out for a well deserved meal. I am going to see the Super then I am going to make sure I beat that stupid dog to my dinner.'

Aitken and Allen went to see the Super. They knocked on his door.

'Come in, don't sit down. Good couple of days all round. Don't arrest those guys yet. We'll speak in the morning. Go home, Goodnight.'

'Good night Sir.'

'Yes, Good night Sir.'

In the car park Aitken and Allen said goodnight.

'Is the Daniel Barraud getting opened tonight?'

'I am going to do what I intended to do last night. Are you going to have a glass yourself?'

'Yes I shall open a bottle of Gicondas. We, the impecunious, cannot afford to drink Chateauneuf du Pape so we have to settle for its much poorer but worthy cousin.'

'There's nothing wrong with a Gicondas. Impecunious, that's a laugh. I thought you lived in Westbury Avenue. How much is that pad worth? Bit like our friend Ridgeon or Roberts and his street.'

'It's nothing like Roberts street, there are a lot more properties for a start and the street has neither gates nor security systems, anyway, the house was left to me by my father. I didn't buy it.'

'Was that Rosemary picking you up in a top end sports Merc the other week when your car was in the garage for its MOT. This Ford Focus you run is a total con. Inverted snobbery.'

'Hey, I happen to run the Focus because it is a cracking car. It has nothing at all to do with reverse snobbery. Rosemary's car has nothing to do with me. Royalties from the cookery books she writes bought that car, not me. OK I admit I might not be impecunious but I am not far off it.'

'Yeah, I believe you. Good night Guv. See you in the morning.'

'Eight o'clock we meet with Purbright.'

'How do you know that? He never even mentioned a time.'

'That's why I am a DCI and you are still a DC. Night.'

Chapter 21

★ ★ ★ ★

~The smile of a Fox in the Chicken Coop~

Jeremy Paul Martin Aitken did live in a mansion. One he inherited from his father long before his father died so as to evade death duties when his father would eventually pass away. His father was a publisher and brilliant at spotting writing talent. It was how Jeremy met his wife Rosemary. His father had just started to publish her cookbooks. Jeremy was twenty-nine when they met, she was three years younger. Their common ground was the English language. She the budding cook writing her cookbooks, he the police officer who had started his career a little later than normal because he had been to Oxford and had a Double First Class Honours in English Literature and History, then went in to the family publishing business. This had been wonderful for his father. For years he had wanted Jeremy to follow in the business but he was not going to pressurise him. Jeremy had always loved books and the English language so it was no real surprise that he opted to read English Literature at Oxford. The Aitken family had suffered tragedies. The distaff side of the family suffered from breast cancer. Jeremy's mother had died of it when Jeremy was only eleven, his older sister Ophelia would be claimed by the same terrible disease at only thirty-one. Ophelia was four years older than Jeremy and as a family they had been very close. When Ophelia died it was the second great tragedy in Jeremy's life after his mother's death. At the time of Ophelia's death he was going out with a girl that he had being seeing for about eighteen months. Things were progressing to the stage where she was just waiting for the proposal of marriage but she was to be disappointed as it never came. Jeremy had decided never to get close to another person. He thought the world of his father but he decided he needed to get away and he took off. Worked his way around the world following the harvesting of crops. Fifteen months later he returned and joined the police. He had decided that he didn't want to be office bound and the police offered a worthwhile calling. He started at the bottom because he did not apply for the position declaring his degree from Oxford. The Police did their stuff and checked him thoroughly but did not discuss with him his degree. They left that as something personal or he would have otherwise mentioned it.

He knew his father did not approve of his career choice but he would never articulate that disproval. Promotions followed and he rose up through the ranks then joining the CID. He was destined for the top, as he was one of the best at clearing up crimes.

His father had been a bit older than Jeremy's mother. He was devastated with the loss of his beautiful wife and threw his energies into the business. The company grew and grew and Aitken Senior was amassing a huge fortune. This he transferred to the young Jeremy to avoid death duties.

The publishing company would be the vehicle through which Jeremy would meet his wife. He had called round to see his father at his house. His father answered the door asking him in and saying that he was just winding up a meeting with a new writer. He frequently held interviews at home. He told Jeremy that he would be a few minutes. Then he stopped and thought for a few moments and suggested that Jeremy was good at judging characters in his profession and could he come in and cast his eye over this writer. Jeremy followed his father to the drawing room. On a rather large Chesterfield sofa sat a woman with her back to the men. A shaft of winter sunshine shining through the window struck the raven hair which tumbled off her shoulders. The sunshine picked out auburn highlights which were completely natural. The plush carpeting hid the sound of the men's footfalls and Mr Aitken was almost at her before she looked up.

'Rosemary I should like to introduce you to my son Jeremy. He is a detective. Jeremy this is Rosemary Smith; she is going to make herself and me a fortune.'

The woman would stand up and extend her hand and in doing

so she looked Jeremy straight in the face. Jeremy's breath was taken away. Rosemary Smith was not only beautiful she had the most amazing pure violet eyes. They were simply arresting, appropriate considering Jeremy's profession. He knew that there was all kind of contact lens that you could use but he was convinced he was looking at the real deal.

'Nice to meet you, I do not think that I have ever met a real detective.'

'That is good because it means that you have been a very law abiding member of society.'

'Well I have met the odd policeman. My one and only vice is my car. The thing is it's slightly sporty and slightly feisty. Brian, that's his name, you know Life of Brian, silly I know. Well he does have a tendency to nip on and has landed me in trouble on a couple of occasions, not my fault really.'

'My goodness, what have we here, a criminal with no sense of remorse. Doesn't even acknowledge her guilt, even blames another party. I think I need to keep an eye on you.'

Standing to one side Mr Aitken smiled, the smile of a fox that had just found a hole in the fence around the chicken coop. He thought to himself I am positive that you are going to keep an eye on this one son. I am in fact positive you will keep both eyes firmly on Rosemary Smith.

He had recognised that magic moment. The one he had had all those years ago when he had met Fiona, his own lady. A special magic, one that had never disappeared until that terrible disease cruelly took her from him.

Rosemary Smith flashed the most dazzling smile, perfect white teeth in a gorgeous full mouth. That smile could disarm any man.

'Actually I think that this introduction is your father being rather devious. He has travelled with me and knows of my teeny weeny habit of occasionally going over the speed limit. I think he is trying to get me to slow down. What better way than to introduce me to a law enforcement officer.'

'I am only looking after my investments,' said Mr Aitken.

Aitken Senior was definitely being devious. He saw the expression on his son's face the moment Rosemary's and Jeremy's eyes had met. He smiled inwardly. He was looking after his investments all right but they weren't necessarily monetary ones.

Chapter 22

★ ★ ★ ★

Stuck in Heavy Traffic

Two weeks later he would phone Jeremy. 'Where are you? Are you at home?'

'Actually I have just got in, what can I do for you, Dad?'

'A huge favour son, I was due to have dinner with Rosemary Smith to discuss her book launch. I am in heavy traffic, not even moving. There is no way that I am going to be on time and I cannot raise her on her phone. She's due to be at the Athenaeum for seven thirty for drinks. Sorry to drop this on you. I should only be about forty-five minutes if I ever get moving. Can you help me out?'

'I suppose so but what I am going to talk about. I can cook but not like she can, if that is all she writes about.'

'Good grief Man, what do you mean? You do not know what you will talk about? Cabbages and Kings Man, there should be some payback from studying English at Oxford. You two are about the same age, whatever it is that people of your generation talk about, that's what you talk about. If you cannot make it, just say.'

'Steady on Dad, I didn't say I wouldn't do it. I'll be there. Just try and get there as soon as you can.'

'Thanks, I'll be there when I arrive.'

Aitken Senior smiled to himself. No, you didn't say you wouldn't do it. There was never any chance of you saying that. He looked out the Bentley's window at the mass of traffic passing by. He was sitting in his car, in a lay-by, not moving. He was doing The Times crossword. He had only described his situation; it was

Jeremy's interpretation of the message that made him assume that his father was struck in a traffic jam. The reason Aitken Senior was not going to be on time was that he had no intention of being on time especially when Jeremy was going to be there at seven thirty. An hour later might be a timely entrance. Jeremy was seated at a table in the bar of the Athenaeum when Rosemary arrived. She looked around the room and he waved. She looked slightly surprised to see him.

'I am sorry but my father. .'

'Is Mr Aitken all right?'

There was a definite air of concern in her enquiry.

'No, he's fine. I was just going to say that he is in traffic and will be late. I shall have to do in the meantime. Can I get you a drink while we wait Dad's arrival?'

'Good news is that I am not driving. I know you are a policeman and I am not just saying it, I never ever drink and drive. I think I shall have a . . . what is that you are drinking?'

'It's a Kir Royale, they use quite the most superb champagne here. My one weakness, wine. I do not have the car either so it's an opportunity to enjoy the odd luxury.'

A waiter brought their drinks and asked if they wanted to look at the menus. They did and he brought them immediately. Jeremy explained that his father would be coming as soon as he could.

'Have you dined here before?'

'Many, many times, this is my Dad's favourite watering hole. When I finally fled the nest he found the house a fairly lonely place and he become a frequent visitor. He'll sit, normally in that corner over there, with a Large Bombay Sapphire and Tonic and his beloved Times crossword. He loves the place and the staff love him. He gets spoiled rotten in here. He gets service that nobody else gets.'

An hour passed before Jeremy's father came in. He was delighted to see the two in animated conversation.

'Sorry about that Rosemary, awful traffic out there. Anyway I am here now.

Oh, thank you Martin. Yes please, the usual.'

A member of the staff was standing by waiting to take Mr Aitken's hat and coat.

'Have you ordered yet?'

'No Dad, we were holding off until you came.'

'I am slightly peckish. I take it you are staying to dine Jeremy.

There is not going to be too much shop talk. I hope you have brought your appetite Rosemary as the food here is quite divine.'

'Oh I think I will manage something. Do you have any recommendations?'

'Trouble is that it is all good here. Is there any kind of food you do not like?'

'Not really, I am certainly not a vegetarian. But you knew that anyway from my books.'

'Good girl, people of my age are predominantly carnivores and I think we were meant to be.'

'Rosemary beware, you are dangerously close to seeing my father get up on his soapbox. There are many things he has views on.'

'At least I am not a bigot or a racist. I simply like old-fashioned values, good manners and respect for my fellow man.'

'He reads too many books my Dad. Believes in Utopia, Shangri La, and Samuel Butler's Erewhon.'

'Don't you believe him Rosemary, he has the same standards. Just tries to give the impression he's a hard-bitten cop made bitter by the dregs of society. All an act, don't be fooled, it's just a front. To answer your question as a starter the Gravadlax, the saddle of Roe deer is now in season and that is mouth wateringly delicious. If you opt for that we shall have a gamey type wine. My son has a slight weakness for wines and I think we can safely leave the choice in his capable hands.'

The food and wine was, as Mr Aitken had said, divine. The evening passed all too quickly. Jeremy was more than amazed to find out that this beautiful creature was not married nor was there anyone waiting at home. She was equally amazed that he was in similar circumstances. Over Armagnac for the men, and a coffee for Rosemary, Mr Aitken lobbed in his grenade.

'I cannot but thank you Rosemary for spending the evening with us. Mind you we had plenty to celebrate. You two should do it again and then you can talk about what young people talk about when there isn't an old duffer around.'

'Dad,' protested Jeremy, 'Rosemary might not want to. Do not put her in a difficult position.'

'Are you going to tell me that wasn't a very pleasant evening, extremely convivial. I know I pressed you into service but it was far from a hardship. Entertaining beautiful and elegant company is always a pleasure.'

'You two stop please, yes, I would be quite happy to do it again were you to ask Jeremy.'

'There you are young Aitken, resolution, thank you Rosemary. Go ahead man ask the lady out.'

'Dad, please!'

This would be the start of many pleasant evenings they would spend together. Jeremy's intent to avoid ever becoming close to another woman went out the window. Those violet eyes were mesmeric. Eighteen months later they were married to the delight of Mr Aitken Senior. They honeymooned in Mauritius. A year later Amelie arrived and just over a year later she would be joined by a baby brother Charlie. Mr Aitken Senior was in heaven.

Chapter 23

★ ★ ★ ★

~Sometimes Thanks is an inadequate word~

T he next few years for the Aitken family were fabulous. Jeremy's career was going from strength to strength. Charlie doted on his grandfather. It was nearly impossible to find the one without the other.

Rosemary's career had gone into overdrive and she would become internationally famous.

Then one evening, when Amelie was nearly five, and just about to go to school the grandfather called a family conference.

'Pour us a glass please Jeremy, my usual. I have a small announcement to make.'

Jeremy thought he was going to announce his retirement. He would be proved right but his father had a few cards up his sleeve.

When he had got his drink he started.

'As you know I am seventy next month. I have decided to call it a day. I have had a General Manager more or less running the business for the past three years. Chris, he is a bloodhound. He has an uncanny knack of sniffing out a winner. I am sure he is gay but you would never know it. I think he has a partner. I thought of selling up but that would mean someone else coming in, a stranger whom my staff wouldn't know and I couldn't guarantee their jobs so we are to carry on as usual. The company brings in far more money than I need. At my age I have more money than I can possibly spend, without guilt, in what time I have left. I am also moving.'

'You're moving Dad. You cannot. I mean, this is the family home. You wouldn't be happy anywhere else.'

'You see, that is exactly where you are wrong. I would be extremely happy if I knew this was a family home. This place is far too big for me. There are rooms, rooms that my cleaner is the only person who has gone into in several years. The gardens are beautiful thanks to Ken but they are very large. I have bought a bungalow on Park Drive near the golf course. Lovely walled garden, very private. The house is light and airy and has enough bedrooms should any grandchildren require to sleep over.'

At that moment all the three adults could suddenly hear was a lot of giggling and laughter from Amelie and Charlie who were playing in the next room.

'That is the very thing I am trying to get across. This house needs to ring again to the sound of children's laughter. The tree house in the old oak needs to be used again. Some other boy needs to break a pane of glass in the greenhouse window with his football and dread having to tell his father'.

Rosemary smiled, she knew Mr Aitken was obviously reminiscing. Mr Aitken carried on.

'No I think this old house is ready to meet a new family, a big Christmas tree with loads of presents under it, Christmas morning, a roaring fire in the hearth, shrieks of excitement from young children. I am not using this house to its potential and that is why I have put the deeds in your name. Both of you will raise your family here and if you are happy as Fiona and I were I shall be delighted for you.'

'Dad this is all too much. You cannot possibly give us your home.'

'Who says I cannot. I already have. The deeds are already in your name and lodged with our Solicitors.'

'I don't know what to say Dad. It is all too much'.

Rosemary was in total agreement with Jeremy. She also recognised that Mr Aitken would not change his mind. They were faced with a *fait accompli*.

'Yes,' said Rosemary, 'I agree with Jeremy, sometimes, a thank you, is rather an inadequate word; this is one of those times. Dad, I am totally speechless. If you are sure this is what you want then our way to thank you is to cherish this house as a home, just as you and Fiona cherished it.'

Rosemary got up and hugged her father-in-law. He could feel the damp from the tears running down her face but he knew the reason. How he wished that Fiona and Ophelia had known this lovely woman. They would have loved her.

'That would indeed be a wonderful thank you. This is a great place for Amelie and Charlie. The gardens will be fantastic for them and their friends. Hopefully I have some time left to see them and yourselves completely at home here. I will not live in your pocket. I just want to babysit from time to time.

'You had better want to babysit. Those two so look forward to Granddad's tales at bedtime,' said Rosemary.

Aitken Senior laughed, 'Just as I look forward to telling them.'

'I must admit I look forward to what you spoke about, a big Christmas tree and my two children holding their Grandfather's hand as they try to convince him it was OK to open just one present from the pile under the tree. I would love to see you trying to wriggle out of that.'

'You have a vicious streak in you son. That job has hardened you. How you would put an old man in such a position is cruel.'

That is how Jeremy Aitken came by his house and at forty-six he and Rosemary had lived there for just over eight years. Amelie had just become a teenager and had inherited her mother's looks and her violet eyes. Young Charlie was a clone of his father. There was absolutely no need for a DNA to establish who his dad was. He looked exactly like photos of Jeremy at the same age. Jeremy's father was starting to fail. He had reluctantly given up his beloved golf on the advice of his doctor.

His company was still doing extremely well under the stewardship of Chris. Chris was now the Managing Director. Christopher was gay, a fact that Mt Aitken had confirmed one evening when he visited the Athenaeum with the Times under his arm. They had just taken his hat, coat and scarf and he had a brief look round the room and there was Chris sitting with what turned out to be his partner, a man of the same age called Geoffrey. Mr Aitken walked over and said 'Hello'. Chris was obviously slightly embarrassed as he regarded Mr Aitken as being of the old school. Chris stood up and shook Mr Aitken by the hand.

'Mr Aitken, I should like to introduce you to Geoffrey. Geoffrey is my ...Chris hesitated momentarily.

'Your partner. Nice to meet you Geoffrey. Glad to see that

Chris has someone to go home to considering all the hours he works. Are you just dining or are you celebrating something tonight?'

Chris said, 'Actually we are. It's the fifth anniversary of our civil union. So this place is a bit special. Expensive, but worth it. Are you dining Sir?'

'Not tonight I have just come in to do my crossword; I shall simply have some Tapas at my table. I hope you two have a wonderful meal. Try and get him to reduce his hours Geoffrey, I have been telling him for ages.'

'I shall Mr Aitken. Nice to meet you, I have heard so much about you.'

'Good I hope.'

'Very good, believe me.'

'I think I detect a Bombay Sapphire sending seductive vibes from that table in the corner and I shall go and see what clues my devious compiler has set me today. You two have a wonderful evening.'

As Chris and Geoffrey were called to their table they found a bottle of vintage champagne there already chilled to absolute perfection. The waiter explained that it was from Mr Aitken to wish them happy anniversary. When they came to pay their bill they were informed that it had already been settled by Mr Aitken. They went to the bar to thank him but the corner table was now occupied by a couple.

Chapter 24

★ ★ ★ ★

~Who told you I was head of the House?~

Aitken rolled his Focus up to the large wrought iron gates at the entrance to the drive. He pressed the remote control and the gates swung open. He thought thank goodness that Louise Allen didn't see those, she would have had a real dig. The motion sensor closed the gates behind him. Another button on his remote opened one of the garage doors and a light came on in the garage. He drove in and parked, grabbed his briefcase and went through the door in the garage into the house. Rosemary would either be in her den where she wrote or in the kitchen where she experimented. Charlie had gone to his grandfather's who was teaching him the intricacies of chess. Rather too well as he recently beat Jeremy. Amelie was at a Gymkhana and it would be another hour before she would be home. From the garage a short passageway took Jeremy to the main entrance to the house. The architect / designer of the original house had actually lived in it for about fifteen years. Jeremy's father was its second owner. An outstanding feature of the house was the entrance and the hall. A huge double staircase rose inside an atrium that was the whole height of the house including a beamed cathedral ceiling. He was really glad Allen couldn't see this as it was much grander than the one in Ridgeon's house. Heating the hall in the winter should have cost about as much as heating a three-bedroom semi. Fortunately our architect had been ahead of his time and there was all manner of heat conservation measures in place. He popped his head into

Rosemary's den, it was empty. She had to be in the kitchen. She was.

'Oh, you're home early. I wasn't expecting you.'

Aitken walked over and hugged her and then started a mock interrogation.

'Why, is there someone else here that I should know about. Is Ken the gardener up in the bedroom.'

'Thanks a bunch, Ken the gardener is seventy-one years old. Do you think that is the extent of my pulling power? Rather strangely, seeing you mention it, I do need to talk to you about Ken. I think that these gardens are too much for him. I've noticed lately that he is slowing down. I spoke with Mrs Ken and she says he is definitely failing. Problem is those gardens out there are his pride and joy. I think we need a younger man.'

'There you go again I knew you wanted a younger man.'

'Be serious Jeremy, I meant that Ken needs help, a younger man to help with the heavy work. It's Sunday and Ken is down in the greenhouse working. I suggest that you go and see him. Mrs Allardyce's son Ian is doing a lot of gardening jobs and according to her is looking for some other clients. He's really keen to learn the trade. He studied geography at University and apart from teaching the topic, which he doesn't want to do, he really cannot find the right job. He started with gardening odd jobs and now he is hooked on it.'

'Why the hell did he read geography then?'

'For exactly the same reason as someone I know studied English Literature and History at Oxford, even got a Double First and became a Policemen.'

'Touché, you've got it all worked so why do you not go and speak to Ken?'

'Why should I? You are the head of the house, so it falls within your remit.'

'Who told you I was head of the house? Not a single soul that knows us both. As far as being head of this house it can only be a figurehead thing, it carries no authority. The authority sits very close to me but definitely not with me.'

'Jeremy, just go and speak to Ken.'

'Fine, question is, can we afford an extra body. I only have my DCI's salary.

'Well that was something else I have to tell you. Chris phoned me Friday to tell me that they are giving me a huge advance on three more books and another serialisation on TV. If I commit it will be a lot of hard work. Two years work basically. I have to give a response by Tuesday. I enjoy the work so I am taking the offer. So finances are not an issue. Besides years ago your father transferred huge amounts of cash to you and what have you done with it? Zilch, zippo, de nada. You sit on it like a Scrooge. Other than an expensive taste in clothes what have you spent?'

'That's not true. As long as my Dad is alive I am not going to be seen splashing his cash. He worked damned hard to earn it.'

'Let me assure you that your Dad is concerned that you haven't spent on anything at all. He hopes you would buy a decent car like a Bentley.'

'Yeah, I can just see me parking that down at the station. I'm happy with my Focus.

'That could be perceived as inverted snobbery.'

'My God that is the second time I have been accused of that in a day.'

'Who else accused you of that?'

'Louise. That's who. I am not a snob, either conventionally or inversely.'

'She's a sharp one that Louise.'

'I know she is, but she is wrong.'

'How can she be, she is a woman.'

'That is totally sexist, I am going to speak to Ken, at least he is a man and logical.'

'Thanks Dear, I thought you might.'

Jeremy walked down the gardens to the greenhouse realising that he had been tactically mugged. Rosemary always came across as the most likeable person, she was liked by both men and women. She was extremely feminine and gentle but there was a razor sharp intellect behind those amazing violet eyes. An only child, that her parents absolutely adored, she could have grown up spoilt but it was quite the opposite, she was extremely well adjusted. Jeremy went into the green house. Ken was busy pricking out plants.

'Hello Mr Aitken, bit of a cold wind out there, it's a lazy wind, can't be as bothered to go around you, goes right through you instead.'

Jeremy had always been Jeremy to Ken as a child. When he returned to take over the house he became Mr Aitken. He tried to get Ken to call him Jeremy but he persisted with Mr Aitken. For Jeremy it felt like something had changed in their relationship. He could remember many happy hours spent in Ken's company on their knees bedding in plants. He had learned a lot about plants as a youngster and because it was learned at an early age it had stuck.

He remembered complaining to Rosemary about Ken calling him Mr Aitken. He felt that something had gone from their relationship. Rosemary's answer nailed it exactly. What had gone was his youth. She pointed out that the last time he had lived there he was a young eighteen year old about to go to Oxford. His father was Mr Aitken and at the time he was Jeremy. He was now the Mr Aitken of the house and Jeremy had become Charlie.

'How is it going Ken?'

'Just starting to get some plants hardened up for the beds. Was there anything that you was as wanting me for?'

Jeremy loved the almost archaic phrasing that Ken used.

'Yes, it's about your age.'

'I've been waiting a while now for that as to come up. I've been enjoying a bit of a longer run than I was expecting. When are you a wanting me to finish?'

'Good grief, no one said anything about you going, not unless you want to. Once you hear me out I hope you will stay for some time yet. No what I meant was that you are seventy one and an encyclopaedic amount of gardening knowledge resides in that head of yours. I am concerned that you should now be passing on that legacy. My wife's been speaking to Mrs Allardyce about her son Ian. He's keen on gardening, bit of a self-starter, self-educated as far as gardening is concerned. I just thought you might take the time to pass on some of that huge reservoir of knowledge. The timing is perfect, you are going to be mighty busy shortly. A bit like an apprenticeship. That would mean for young Ian a bit of hard graft. I am sure as a youngster you would have gone through that.'

'Now that is indeed true sir, the senior gardeners didn't too much heavy tilling I can assure you of that. I know the lad anyway. He came into the Grey Mare's Tail the other night and asked if I knew of anyone who would be as wanting some jobs done in the garden. There's always someone as is but I couldn't for the love of me bring anyone to mind seeing it was at the moment. I told him to use the local free sheet, somebody might take the bait. We had a pint of Bert Findlay's finest. I liked the lad.'

'Well then I think it is time to see if young Allardyce wants to be a gardener or not. If you are in agreement I shall get him to come for a proper interview with you. We'll pay him a decent rate; you'll have to guide us there. I just think it would be criminal not to pass on that knowledge.'

'Yes and we all know what you do to criminals Mr Aitken, you lock them up. I don't as sure be as wanting that, so I think you had better tell the lad as to come and see me. My goodness, are you be looking at the time there. I think I had better be finishing for the day or she who must be obeyed will be busy setting up a right ear bashing.'

'Right then that's settled and I shall see you anon. Thanks Ken.'

As Ken walked away Jeremy could have sworn that there was jauntiness to his step.

Jeremy walked up the garden rather pleased with how he had handled that.

That night as Ken tucked into his roast beef and Yorkshire puddings he told his beloved Kate the events of the day.

'Had Mr Aitken down today. He wants me to take as like an apprentice. Wants me to pass on what's in my head to that son of Harry and Betty Allardyce.'

'Then it'll be a pretty short apprenticeship for the lad. That shouldn't take long for there's not a lot in there and I'm not sure you should be passing what's in your mind to any young innocent lad.'

'Away with you woman, Mr Aitken was talking about my gardening knowledge nothing else.'

'Ay and you be sure that is exactly the knowledge that you do pass on, we wouldn't want the child corrupted.'

'Child, he's not a child. He's a twenty two year old young man. As far as corrupting is concerned it's more likely that he could corrupt me. Mind you when I think back to what we did when I was at twenty two.'

'Ken Winstanley that is quite enough at the dinner table.'

Kate Winstanley however could not suppress a smile.

'Aye lass, it's maybe not a bad idea. I'm not of a spring chicken anymore. It's hard work some days. There's those three acres in that garden. You know the architect had himself planned to build another two houses on that plot but decided to take the space for himself in the end. You do know that?'

'Yes Ken I do, you've told me often enough. More roast potatoes?'

'Please, if there's another one in the pot.'

'I wouldn't be offering you another one if it didn't exist, now would I?'

'I suppose not dear.'

Kate Winstanley smiled again to herself; she knew that Rosemary's Aitken's hand had guided this deal through. She had known that Ken had been struggling for some time and when Rosemary phoned expressing her concern she knew that it would be quickly resolved to the happiness of all concerned. Ken still had his beloved gardens, the extra money was great and he would be doing far less of the actual hard graft needed for such a large garden. Ken had been devastated when Mr Aitken Senior broke the news that he was moving to a smaller property to be immediately overjoyed with the news that young Jeremy and his family was taking over and that the status quo in gardening terms would stand. Young Charlie had the same inquisitive nature as his father. For Ken it was déjà vu. Charlie was like having Jeremy kneeling beside him except that over three decades had slipped through with the sands of time.

Chapter 25

★ ★ ★ ★

~That's too much information~

Jeremy was extremely pleased that things had gone well with Ken. He knew Rosemary would be looking for a positive outcome and that had been achieved.

'Ah, you're back. Charlie's home, straight on to his computer again.'

'I think he spends too much time on that computer,' said Jeremy.

'I think they all do but he is doing brilliant at school. He has actually said that he wants to go to Oxford like his dad.'

'He's never mentioned anything to me.'

'He's not going to tell you is he?'

'Why not, I am his father.'

'God, for a top-notch detective, you do miss some of the most obvious clues. Your children, well, they are at that awkward age. Amelie is coming up fourteen, no longer a little girl but not a woman either. She thinks she is ugly. Your son is on the way to being a young buck. He wants to flex his muscles. Show that he will be a big buck someday.'

'Amelie thinks she's ugly. You have got be joking, she's absolutely beautiful. I have told her often enough.'

'Yes, you are her father and you would say that. You would be the last person to tell her she is ugly. She expects you to say she is beautiful. She needs some young lad to tell her that.'

'She's a bit young for that.'

'Oh, you think so. Totally wrong answer. Your daughter is, as you say, very beautiful but she's been having periods for well over a couple of years, she has pubic hair and she wears a bra.'

'Good God Rosemary, that's too much information.'

'Maybe so, but they are not problems that you have had to deal with. All I am illustrating to you is she is growing up. Like most men it has not been a problem for you as you have not been exposed to it. I shall predict that we are going to need those gates at the end of the drive to keep the young lads at bay. You are about to enter a very tough period as a father, when you suddenly realise that you are no longer the most important male in her life. Now take your son, what have you told him about sex. Have you spoken to Charlie about the opposite sex, masturbation, condoms, whatever?'

'For God's sake Rosemary, he is only twelve. They get all that kind of stuff at school. His mates will probably tell him anyway.'

'I cannot believe that someone of your intelligence could say that. What expert advice is he going to receive from boys of his own age? Were you masturbating at his age? Probably. Did you know at that age when a woman was at her most fertile in a month? When the most dangerous time to have sex was? Need I go on?'

'Good grief Rosemary, I can't remember.'

Jeremy went slightly red and he could feel his face flushing.

'I bet you can, selective amnesia is more like it. What makes it worse is that the amnesia might not be selective. Your son is thirteen not twelve.'

'Oh my God, so he is. How did I get that wrong?'

'Because Jeremy, you are seldom here that's how. What I am simply trying to get across is that your children are just starting to cast aside childish things. Your son is quite definite in what he wants to do. He wants to take over Granddad's business. He has had this in his noodle for some time.'

'Never, ever, said anything to me about that.'

'I think this has been accidentally germinated by your father. He told Charlie a few years back that he had hoped that you would take over the business but of course, after trying it, you decided against it. Charlie informed his granddad not to worry; he would take it over once he was grown up. Granddad said that would be great, more to keep Charlie happy than anything, but much to his Granddad's surprise he has persisted with his plan and is getting more and more inquisitive about the business. He had been pestering your Dad to let him visit the company more and more to see what all they do. He has been a couple of times and dogged round after Chris. His interest really is genuine and your father is actually very impressed with both his budding business acumen and his ability to pick things up. Chris is delighted to assist. So the family business may yet stay in family hands.'

'Seems to be a lot going on in this family I know nothing about.'

'Not really. Charlie thinks because it didn't suit you that you might tell him not to get involved.'

'You know that is not the case. What Charlie does in his career should be something he wants to do and if he wants to take over the family business then brilliant and good luck to him. He should spend some of his holiday there, paid of course and made to work. I wouldn't be so keen on him following in my career.'

'I thought you loved what you do.'

'I do but it is a dangerous task and getting more so in today's society.'

'I think Charlie would be delighted to do that, especially if he knew that you suggested it.'

At that moment Charlie came into the kitchen.

'What would I be delighted with that Dad was suggesting?'

'Your Dad thought it was time you were earning your keep. So he is suggesting that you start working during your holidays.'

'I do work, I help Ken heaps in the garden.'

'We know you do. I am just teasing. What your Dad was actually suggesting was that you should start working at your Granddad's business. You will get paid as well, according to your Dad. Your Dad thinks you would find it interesting and whatever you do in the future, the business grounding would help. You are old enough to start getting interested in these kinds of things. Obviously we need to speak to Granddad and he would have to clear it with Chris.'

Charlie was by now grinning from ear to ear and clearly excited at the prospect.

'There's no way Granddad will say no and Chris won't mind.'

Rosemary had her back to Jeremy so Jeremy couldn't see her wink at Charlie.

'We do not know,' said his Mum. 'Chris might not want a thirteen year old under his feet. So let us speak to Granddad first. He's coming here tomorrow night. We'll ask him then, OK?'

'We could phone him now.'

'I think we can wait; you have five weeks to go before your holidays.

'OK, when's dinner going to be ready? I'm starving.'

'You are always starving. Once Amelie gets home we can dine.'

'Why is it I am always waiting for meals through no fault of my own? It's either Dad or Amelie who are late. I am never late for meals.'

'You can say that again, you are usually first to the table. Oh, there's your sister now, your prayers have been answered. Hello dear, how did your gymkhana go?'

'Hi Mum, Bruv, I thought you were working Dad? Got a silver and a bronze, Arabella just got pipped for a bronze so I felt a bit sorry for her. She seemed OK about it coming home in the car. I would have had a First except that I put Brandy in the wrong place between four and five. The fence was awkward, that half stride out, we all had the same problem. Kimberley won and she had problems with that jump as well. Brandy's still a novice like me but you can feel him getting more and more confident. He's a big animal and I am only starting to get to grips with him, big change from Tinker. Why are you home early Dad?'

'Finished for the day that's why. Should I not be here, am I cramping your style?'

'No dad, I am pleased to see you. We can all sit down and have dinner. What kind of case are you working?'

'Murder I am afraid, but you know the rules there is nothing I can discuss.'

'I take it it's that Amy girl that was murdered. She was really beautiful and vivacious . Arabella says her brother Eddie is quite devastated.'

'Why is he devastated and how do you know she was vivacious.'

'He worked with Amy. Eddie is an IT wizard at ADI. He tried to date her a couple of times but she didn't want to go out with a colleague. He was dead keen on her, who wouldn't be. I don't think Amy was keen to get into a heavy relationship. She was lovely when I met her at Arabella's.'

'Well dear daughter you are full of surprises.'

'Yeah and I think one of them might be I stink. I am going for a shower. Give me half an hour Mum.'

'I am starving and she is going to be another half hour. Mum!

Can I least have a biscuit.'

'No you cannot, you'll spoil your appetite.'

'You are joking Mum. A biscuit is only going to whet my appetite.'

'OK then but just the one and not a chocolate one.'

Chapter 26

★ ★ ★ ★

~Casting aside childish things~

Dinner was fabulous and very relaxing for Jeremy. A serious case like this was very intense and demanded immense concentration. There were moments when you had to switch off or you would go insane. There were the odd moments when Jeremy would question whether he had chosen the right profession. He wasn't sure if he would rise to the very top. He refused to play the political game that the youngsters were so adept at. He knew that Frank Purbright had given him very good reports but he equally knew that Purbright would finish his career well below the level that he deserved to be. He knew Frank saw bits of himself in Jeremy. Then when they nailed some scumbag down, especially the child molesters and the rapists or some young thugs beating up the elderly and the infirm to rob them, when you nailed them the job was all worthwhile. There were some really bad people out there and his work was to scoop them up when they did wrong and deposit them safely behind bars where they could no longer be a menace to society. Jeremy wasn't too concerned about them reappearing back in society. As far as he was concerned those types would, in the main, re-offend and behind bars was the best place for them. The bleeding liberals, as he viewed them, only made his job more difficult. Rosemary said that he made Judge Jeffries appear a moderate. There were times when you collared some particularly obnoxious criminal, someone who had beat up an old woman, you felt like getting in and closing the cell door and seeing how he would fare against a man. There were times when you felt like beating them to a pulp but that of course would be a grave mistake as you would then be no better than the criminal.

Charlie was clearly excited at the prospect of actually working in Granddad's company. He couldn't wait to speak to his Granddad about it and his mother and father finally relented allowing him to phone after dinner.

Everyone was in good form and it was one of the best family dinners for ages. They were all relaxing after dinner with the exception of Charlie who was patiently waiting for a decent interval to elapse so that he could leave the table and phone his Granddad.

Amelie then made an announcement that took them all by surprise.

'Dad, you know how you asked me a couple of months ago what I wanted to do in life. Well I have decided. I want to enter the world of Artificial Intelligence. I will need to go to Oxbridge and possibly MIT.'

'That's quite a lofty ambition, you mean robotics, that kind of thing.'

'That kind of area yes, but not necessarily robotics. The Japanese are strong in this area so I have started learning Japanese as a language. Robotics is going to be rather exciting in the future. I think we are about three decades away from artificial intelligence outstripping man. We will be able to create artificial brains capable of incorporating human feelings.'

'I find that all a bit scary,' said her mother. 'I imagine them taking over. You've never mentioned an interest in this before. What's brought this on? Can you handle the extra requirement study of another language?'

'Dad asked what I wanted to do and I have given it a lot of thought and it is in an area that the subjects I need for University are the subjects that I excel in at school. I love languages and Mandarin is next. As far as time goes I intend to back off on the show jumping.'

'I thought you were more interested in getting into show jumping.'

'That was when I was young, I was eleven.'

Both her parents stifled a smile.

'I soon realised that I might be better than average at show jumping but that was all. No, I still want to ride but more recreational than anything. When you watch Alexandra Huxley then you realize what a God given talent really is. If she doesn't make it to the Olympics some day I'll eat my riding hat. You can cook it Mum. By the way I do not believe in God but you know what I meant.'

'Well Miss Aitken we are learning a lot about you today. Have you got any further revelations of interest.'

'Quite a number dear father but I think we should keep them back for another day. I am not sure if your old heart could take them.'

'You keep that up young lady and you will not even reach my age. Off you two go. I want to speak to your Mum.'

The two left the table thanking their Mother for the dinner. Charlie was picking up speed as he left the room, his mother telling him to walk not run.

Chapter 27

★ ★ ★ ★

~Amelie's Godparents~

'What was it you were saying about casting aside childish things? Well that was quite a bombshell from our daughter. As you said, she is becoming a young woman and one with very definite ideas. I wonder where she gets that from?'

'You're not looking at me I hope. I wouldn't say boo to a goose.'

'You might not say boo to it but I bet you could still cook it, just as my goose was well and truly cooked over Ken. Ken was getting an assistant whether I wanted it or not. I got mugged there. A smiling assassin.'

'Mugged? A smiling assassin? You are spending too much time at that police station. Not everything is a crime.'

'You know exactly what I meant. Anyway what do you think about Amelie's chosen profession. Believe me we might as well accept it that some ten years from now we will have a hugely qualified daughter who will work in the field of Artificial Intelligence.'

'Yes and an atheist at that. Have we failed her in that department? Maybe we should have gone to Church more.'

'Neither you or I are deeply religious so what would have been the point of us attending church every Sunday. I do not think that we would influence our daughter in that direction. Dinner with our daughter was extremely revealing. If we failed in our religious instruction so have David and Jennifer, they are Amelie's Godparents and must be found wanting in their duties. I shall bring this to Mr Collins attention next time we meet. I'll be dead serious and enjoy watching him squirm,' said Jeremy.

'I think after a lapse of thirteen years in the religious guidance of his godchild the accused Mr David Collins is unlikely to have his feathers ruffled by you declaring his goddaughter an atheist. I think the same goes for Jennifer. She's more liable to instruct your daughter in the use of a rampant rabbit.'

'Rosemary, don't even joke about that. What the hell made you say something like that?'

'Because, rubbish detective, it is very likely to be true. Jennifer gets more attention from that damned rabbit than she gets from David. They even sleep in separate bedrooms now. He's being having it off with his secretary for a couple of years now.'

'What do you mean having it off with his secretary? Do you mean Mrs Wills? You are joking she's ten years older than David and put politely rather well upholstered.'

'You mean she is in her fifties and fat. Life doesn't stop when you reach your fifties and it obviously hasn't for Mrs Wills. She's obviously capable of taking more down than just shorthand.'

'That's a bit rude from you and anyway nobody does much shorthand these days.'

'Well I am not very pleased with David. He's really hurt Jennifer and she is my friend. If you ever do that to me you will find my new recipe book will include a recipe for pan-fried seared testicles, yours. As I say repeatedly I thought you were supposed to be some super detective, are you telling me you knew nothing about this?'

'No I did not. I cannot believe it, Mrs Wills of all people, she looks more like his mother. Jennifer is a beautiful woman and a nice one to boot. She has made sacrifices for David. What the hell is he thinking about? He was my best man. Has he lost the plot? I know he can be a selfish bastard but Jennifer doesn't deserve that. She accepted that he didn't want any family getting in the way of his career even though she wanted family herself. She would have been a good mother; you know what she is like with our two. The absolute Bastard, what the hell is he thinking about? Well stuff him! I don't need a friend like that. She should kick him into touch.'

Rosemary could tell that this had definitely come as news to Jeremy and not news that made him happy.

'That's what I told her but she still loves the lying cheating rat.

I told her she has a good job and could survive without getting a penny from David but I also recommended that she get every penny she could, the house, the car, the pension the whole bloody lot.'

'Wow I can see this recipe for seared testicles has quite a long list of ingredients, the house, the car, the pension, the money. For someone who would not say boo to goose I do not think I would like to seriously upset you. I definitely do not think it would be good for the health if I got caught playing away from home.'

'Never mind getting caught just don't even think about any kind of playing away from home. The gorgeous Miss Allen is decidedly off limits.'

'Rosemary, I'll agree she is a good looking young woman but she has a steady boyfriend. One who gives her expensive sport cars for her birthday so it must be serious? I see her more as a cop than a woman and a damned good cop too. She will probably tell you if you met her that she gets treated like a bloke. She is going to the top that one so an affair with a married man would ruin the image. Even if I was to try it on, it is likely to get me kicked testicles as opposed to seared ones. As I have no wish for damage in that department I more than happy to be a very faithful husband.'

'Good and don't you forget it. Are you going to say something to David?'

'No, why should I? I would not have known a thing about the affair until you told me. I am not poking my nose into their problems. That kind of thing is like walking through a minefield with a big stick and hitting the ground. It is only a matter of time before you hit a mine. No Rosemary, that is fraught with danger. The only thing is that it has changed the friendship. He might ask if he notices things are a lot colder on the friendship front. Then if he asks I shall give him a frank chapter and verse.'

'Jennifer kind of hoped that you would have a word with him, you do not need to say it was me that told you so that it doesn't look like Jennifer was involved. Just say that you had heard rumours, you know the usual thing, there is always someone ready to spread the gossip around, especially if the person involved is known to you.'

'Rosemary, David holds down a job where character is everything. His company principals are very old fashioned. If he has been horizontal jogging with Mrs Wills he has been very discreet about it. Had the principals, Mr Palmer or Mr Hewitson got the slightest sniff his arse would not have touched the ground until he hit the sidewalk. Actually he would not have touched the sidewalk it would have been the street he landed in. Maybe all Jennifer needs to do is threaten to go and talk to the partners about the situation to see if they can separate the pair for the sake of her marriage. David is so image conscious he is not going to downgrade to Mrs Wills for the works dance. No this is nothing more than sex, I know he has been taking Viagra lately. Now I know why. If Jennifer doesn't want to tell the two Partners she could tell Mr Wills. He is an absolute giant of a man. He is in his fifties and built like a pro wrestler. I visited David one day at five o'clock and Mr Wills was there to pick up Mrs Wills. He came through the door and he had to bend down. The other obvious thing was that Mr Wills doted on his Mrs Wills and I think that would also be a jealous type of doting. David might just find his balls not seared or kicked but missing completely if the Silverback ever found out that David had been exchanging bodily fluids with his mate. Do not forget David is a serious coward. Jennifer is an even a bigger sheep. Were she to change over to take the dominant role David would buckle down rather quickly. Your small warning of pan-fried seared testicles carried a very big health warning because you well and truly meant it. She needs to do something similar to David. David has used Jennifer as a doormat. She needs to wipe her feet on him. She will not lose him even if she scares the crap out of him. She needs to tell him like it is, very cold, very deliberate. He can either toe the line or be humiliated at work and then half killed by Mr Wills.'

'Quite a speech Mr Aitken, but good, I'll give you that. I think it might just work. I need to get to her as soon as possible. You've made me feel much better. I love you for that.'

Chapter 28

★ ★ ★ ★

~That was definitely a full broadside~

The following morning was cool and cloudy. Jeremy was up early. Rosemary moaned something about it couldn't possibly be time to get up yet.

'No it isn't you have an hour yet before you need to get up.'

'Oh, Good.' She rolled over and snuggled down.

In the shower the water was invigorating. Jeremy just stood there and let all the pressure jets hit his body. Then he finished with the waterfall feature that the shower had. Rosemary would use that with cold only. Aitken came to the conclusion he was too damn soft for that. He let Rosemary talk him into doing it with cold once. That was freezing, really freezing. She said it closed your pores. Closed them, froze them over more like.

Dried and dressed he went downstairs to the kitchen. Sat at the table reading a book was Amelie. She had an orange juice in front of her. She looked up as her father came in.

'Morning Pater, you are up and about early. Going in early?'

'Well not that early, we have an eight o'clock meet with Purbright. So I am a bit early even for that. What gets you out at this time of the day?'

'Something that came up in our Science lesson last Friday. More specifically, Darwin's Theory of Evolution. I gave Mrs Arnison a bit of a fit. I sort of put her in a bit of a state and I think she may revisit the theme today and I am making sure I have my facts at my fingertips. Hopefully the nature of the discussion might have been enough for her to bury the topic. She is really very religious and always goes on about how you can be both a scientist and religious too. I have no problem with her views just please do not ram them down my throat. Problem is you have for the sake of politics to say nothing. She was on about how at the time, Darwin's theories had originally challenged conventional religion and it was much later that the obvious compatibility between creation and evolution were accepted. I found it impossible to concede that there was an obvious compatibility. As far as I am concerned that is not the case. I just keep quiet about my own theories. Totally screws up the status quo. Saint Gregory's does not approve of anyone upsetting the status quo. You sent me to a school where the patron Saint is not noted for flexibility in learning and religious standards. His legacy seems to have been in the hands of some excellent stewardship over the centuries. Mrs Arnison is just another disciple.'

Jeremy thought about Rosemary's comment of casting aside childish things. This was no child sat speaking to him. This was a young woman, articulate, witty and with political nous. She wasn't a rebel; she was obviously far too bright for that. She might change things but Jeremy was sure that she would do it in an extremely skilful manner.

'So what did you say that holed her ship under the water, a full broadside or a single cannonball.'

'You are wicked Father, I almost feel that you are hoping I say a full broadside. Sadly I must disappoint you, a single cannonball but one definitely below the waterline. The old girl listed and nearly sunk before she made the port of blustering. She had been in full flow about how the fittest and strongest survive. I merely pointed out that this was not the case with Homo sapiens. Her voice rose a couple of pitches.

'And Howww do you reach this conclusion in opposition to Darwin's scientific papers Miss Aitken.'

She becomes frightfully affected when something displeases her. I then said that in the case of Man it was not necessarily the strongest that bred and that there were anomalies there. The case was disproved by the fact that women could only breed for a limited period up until the menopause. I could see her cringe even at the use of the word. Undeterred I continued on by saying that men could carry on breeding right up until they were in there seventies. Were we to compare men to animal bulls then as old bulls it was very obvious that in a physical confrontation to access breeding rights to the fertile females the old Bulls would get soundly beaten by the stronger and younger bulls. In other words we have moved on from Darwin as far as the fittest and strongest survive, well certainly in the case of mankind.'

'I think you need to redefine your definition of a cannonball that was definitely a full broadside. I take it you brought down the sails.'

Amelie smiled. 'I suppose you could say that. She was actually saved by the bell. So we had to go to the next period. Things had not been helped by a lot of sniggering when I started about breeding and bulls and all that.'

'Mind you, she would have to admit it was an excellent point you made. I always felt it odd that any male in his seventies would even consider fathering children. The likelihood of not seeing your children grow up is for me irresponsible. I know your Granddad was older when my sister and I came along but he saw us both to adulthood. You're a young woman now and Charlie is a teenager. So he is seeing the next generation grow up. I want something for breakfast. Do you want some cereal with fruit and toast?'

'Yes, if you can be bothered.'

They sat there and chatted for another half hour. This young woman he was talking to certainly wasn't the child he had known a brief few months ago. There had been a metamorphosis, the child was now a husk and a beautiful, articulate, smart young woman had stepped out from it.

Just as Aitken got up to leave Rosemary came in. Rosemary was not a morning person.

'You going to work, if you are, get your son out of bed before you go. He's welded to that damn bed. I do not understand it. He is hopeless at getting out of bed in the mornings.'

Jeremy looked at Amelie and they both smiled. The comment was a bit rich coming from Rosemary.

Chapter 29

★ ★ ★ ★

~Catching Tuna~

Jeremy could not get over his conversation with Amelie at breakfast. When he walked into the office Louise Allen was sitting in Purbright's office. She looked up as Aitken entered and said 'Good Morning, the Super's not far away. He told me to sit down.'

'I'll be two ticks. I am just going to my own office.'

Five minutes later he was back. Purbright almost followed Aitken into the room.

Good Morning, hopefully we are going to have a good week. Hopefully better than you look Aitken. You OK man? Something on your mind?

'Oh, I'm fine Sir, I was up early this morning and went to the kitchen to get my breakfast. There I met a very witty and beautiful woman. A woman I have never met before. I just feel very old.'

Purbright looked at Allen and they both smiled.

'Oh, you met the young woman that is your daughter. Aye, that indeed makes any man feel old. I remember when it happened to me. Our lass and I were going to take our daughter Melissa out for her fifteenth birthday when my Barbara took ill, a twenty-four hour bug. Well Barbara insisted that we go, all she wanted to do was to go to bed and die. Well I went to dinner with a child and left with a young woman I had never met before. Just like you Aitken, I felt bloody ancient in the Taxi on the way home. I am sure your father suffered the same Allen.'

'Probably Sir.'

'Right then Detective Chief Inspector we need to get your mind back on happier things such as catching vile murderers for starters. What is happening in the grey matter as far as our case is concerned. Looks like you have the guys that murdered young Amy Anderson. Are you sure you can make it stick? Are you even sure you want to arrest them at this moment? What is it that you are planning?'

'Many years ago when I was a kid I watched a programme about Tuna fishing off South America. These guys would go out in small boats and catch the Tuna with rod and line. The shoals swam in such a manner that they would start fishing with each man having an individual rod and line. The further they steamed into the shoal of Tuna the larger the Tuna became. The fishermen then changed over to two rods that were joined to a common line. It was all the fishermen could do to get the big Tuna on board. The only thing that I found slightly baffling was when the fishermen knew to change over to working in pairs. Still they had a strategy that worked. My problem is I feel we may catch the small Tuna and not be able to catch the larger Tuna.'

'OK then Aitken, how do you propose to catch the larger Tuna?' asked Purbright.

I am going to catch one of the smaller Tuna. Then I shall do a catch and release. I would expect the small Tuna to run straight to its fellow small Tuna and tell them that there are fishermen out there capable of catching them all. Hopefully he might even try to warn the large Tuna about the fishermen. They will not thank the little Tuna. More likely they will eat the little Tuna so that it didn't bring the fishermen to their part of the Ocean.'

'Interesting and which little fishie had you in mind to catch. I will right down on this piece of paper which little fishie I would catch and release. Give me a second Aitken.'

Purbright wrote a name on the small notepaper. He made sure that it could not be seen by either officer. He passed a small notepad to Allen. 'You have a go at this.'

'Right Aitken, Allen and I have our notepapers; put us out of our misery.'

'Jimmy 'Dobra' Perkins or The Weasel,' said Aitken.

Purbright held up his card as did Allen. Both were carrying the same message.

'Right,' said Purbright. 'Lets round 'The Weasel' up. I'll leave you two to do what you have to and interview him. Next topic, the big fish. How are we doing with the victim's computer? Are we making progress? Do we have any names we can work on?'

'No,' said Allen, 'they are struggling to get forward. They are really trying to tiptoe through what is a minefield of passwords and protection. Melissa Harcross gave us an entry point but even with that it is not coming up trumps. Our guys think they know where they want to go and what group of files they want to open up but they are well protected.'

'I might be able to help you there,' said Aitken. 'This new young woman of mine has a friend whose brother seemingly works at ADI and knew our victim Amy. He has the, sorry had, the hots for Amy but she wasn't looking for anything serious and especially not an office romance. The more interesting thing about Eddie is that he is a computer wizard. Who knows he might know something about Amy's computer.'

'Hopefully you are right Aitken. See the guy and try and get his co-operation. Anything else since yesterday?'

'Yes,' said Allen. 'I spoke with my Jonathon last night and he is looking at trying to get you the confidential report on ADI that his company commissioned. One thing he does remember at the discussions was that under many layers of shell companies a Wendell Fanshawe would appear to be a majority owner in ADI. The problem was that nobody could find out if Wendell Fanshawe existed. In fact they couldn't find out if it was indeed a person or was it an entity, another ghost company.'

'He sounds like one of these old Music Hall acts,' said Purbright. 'Wendell Fanshawe and his amazing doves.'

'Funny you should say that,' said Allen. I have been thinking about this case. It is all a bit theatrical. This whole episode is like something that would happen in a film like the sheer amount of steps and actions that were taken to ensure that these guys vanish. That and the disguises used by those who carried out the execution, way over the top. Bear in mind there was only short term planning so either a team did it or someone with a flair for the theatrical. This was way over covering their tracks. You get the feeling that they were almost laughing at us. You can almost hear them saying to themselves, 'they will never figure this one out.'

Purbright just sat looking at his spot on the wall. He never said a thing for fully two minutes.

'Do you know Detective that is one very interesting theory. In fact it is more than just interesting. Let us just assume for one moment that Wendell Fanshawe is a person then let our mind go further and consider that Wendell has connections with the performing arts. Has any film recently used the technique we have just witnessed in doing a hit, possibly reality imitating art? The problem is that if Jonathon's company do not know who or what Wendell Fanshawe is, and if we assume that he is a person we have no way of knowing his nationality. The obvious two favourites are American or British. There has to be Wendell Fanshawes in the world.'

'There are Sir, but surprising very few, they did pop up in some strange places,' said Allen. 'KES checked them all out. Rather strangely the very name has thrown up a bunch of eccentrics who bear the name. Only a couple were regular guys and they were in Australia. The ones in Britain, Canada and the USA were definitely different. Sadly the other fact was, that if you were called Wendell Fanshawe you were doomed to a life of the eccentric but in reality all very ordinary.'

'I find that hard to believe, being called Wendell Fanshawe would already have marked you out from the herd,' said Aitken. 'Your theory Allen is a bit 'far out there' but I can see where you are coming from. Do we have any film buffs aboard?'

'Just Doris Spedding, our voice in Dispatch and she is really an aficionado. She has been to the movies more times than I have had hot dinners,' said Purbright. 'She has visited all the major studios. In fact she has an amazing list of contacts in the industry. She has somehow even wangled a ticket to the Oscars, a couple of years back when our Kelly K won. I tell you I was impressed with that. Bounce the idea off her and if it has been used she will know.'

'She cannot have seen every film surely Sir, that's impossible,' said Aitken.

'She might not have seen every film but I bet she has seen the vast majority. She is close to sixty and she was widowed when she was only twenty-nine. Her husband was killed in a road accident. She took to going to the movies in her grief and simply became addicted. Damned good at her job though.'

That was Purbright both detectives thought. That last statement. She is damned good at her job. That was what counted.

'Right you two I can't sit here all day and chew the fat about films. I need to get the troops out there nailing our criminal classes. We'll talk later.'

'Right,' said Aitken 'lets go round up our weasel. Can you fix meeting up Doris for lunch in the canteen.'

'Not at The Isadora then? Doris doesn't rate The Isadora then?' said Allen winding Aitken up.

He didn't take the bait. 'We can take her to The Isadora if she helps us to crack this case.'

Chapter 30

★ ★ ★ ★

~*Jimmy 'Dobra' Perkins*~

An hour later they were at the door to Jimmy Perkins flat. They hammered on the door as there wasn't a doorbell.

'A voice from the other side said 'Hold your hair on. Do you know how bloody early it is? I have your sodding rent.'

They heard all the locks being taken off and the door opened. A very dishevelled Jimmy Perkins stood there in his boxers, a tee shirt and socks. The moment he saw who was standing there he tried to close the door. Too late Aitken was in.

'You cannot come in here. You're the filth. You are that bastard Aitken. The only reason I came here to live was you had bloody well moved on. You have no right to come in here without a search warrant.'

'We don't need to search the place we are simply taking you down the station for a small chat. You will be no more than a couple of hours.'

'In your dreams Aitken. You have nothing you can pin on me. So piss off.'

'I can have you come voluntarily or I arrest you. The choice is yours.'

'If you think you can stitch me up for that credit card job at Tesco, you are wasting your time. I never go near Tesco.'

'I have no idea what the hell you are talking about Perkins. We just want to speak to you. Your damn life may be in danger but if you do not want to know then that is down to you. We have come across some very interesting facts and they definitely endanger your life. You might be the target for a hit man.'

They two detectives saw Perkins visibly stiffen.

'Who the hell would want to take me out? You are bluffing.'

'Plenty, but at the moment it is an organisation. Get dressed and come to the station with us and we shall brief you. I have no idea why we are bothering but it might just save your worthless neck.'

Fifteen minutes later Jimmy was in the back of Aitken's car as they went back to Railton. He definitely needed a good shower.

'This isn't the way to the Alderlea nick,' said Perkins.

'We don't work there. I haven't come back here. You are having an away day. You are going to Railton,' said Aitken.

Perkins sat and said nothing but he was very obviously concerned about what was going down.

In the station they apologised but said it was necessary that he turn out his pockets from a security point of view. They could not be too careful these days. Perkins wasn't too happy to comply but under threat of arrest and having to hand over stuff anyway he reluctantly agreed.

A roll of twenties brought the comment from Aitken, 'you trying to dodge the taxman again Jimmy? You can hang on to that, I cannot see you mugging us with a bunch of twenties. Pick up the rest on the way out. I would give you your cigarettes but Health and Safety now dictates that this is a No Smoking Zone. Sorry!'

They sat him down in the interview room, got him a coffee and left him to stew for twenty minutes. They watched his body language through the two ways mirror. He sat for fully ten minutes with his head slumped on his chest and literally twiddled his thumbs but in a highly nervous manner. Then he jumped up and started walking round the room very quickly. The faster he went the more pronounced his limp became. He sat back down and put his head back over the back of the seat and stared at the ceiling. A few minutes later he jumped up again and started going around the room getter faster and faster.

He sat down again and this time he clasped his hands between his open legs and bent over until they were nearly touching the ground.

'Good,' said Aitken. 'Our bird is cooked. Even rotisseried himself. Let's go talk.'

They walked in on Perkins.

Chapter 31

★ ★ ★ ★

~Put one in that snake for me~

' **S** orry Jimmy to keep you waiting but the Super wanted to see us. Anyway can we get down to business? I am sure that you are more than a little interested in who is keen to terminate you. I shall read you a rather lengthy but detailed report. The reason it is so detailed and why that's important will become very clear to you. Please do not interrupt or say anything until I have finished the report. You will have plenty of opportunity to speak after I have finished.'

With that Aitken sat the dossier that he was carrying down, opened it and took out several pages of a document. He then started to read the document.

'Last Saturday morning the seventh of March you James Perkins and Jonathon Clyde Robertson drew up in a Series three grey coloured BMW to 11 Shelley Way in the Rollins Area. The time was nine twenty six. You entered that property with yourself in the lead. You were both wearing prosthetic masks and dressed in head to toe in black. Actually you were wearing the shoes that you have on now, Johnny Clyde wore Vans. You carried a .38 calibre Smith & Wesson and Robertson a .45 Glock. At nine twenty seven you shot one Amy Anderson through the forehead and Robertson shot her once, through the heart.'

Perkins visibly stiffened and opened his mouth to speak but Allen put her hand on his arm and put her finger to her mouth to signal him to stay quiet.

Aitken continued and read chapter and verse from the pages in front of him. He also showed Perkins all the photographs of him and his cohorts in vehicles.

Aitken closed the file and put it away.

'As I said Philip Ridgeon paid you one hundred thousand for this hit. You will not be able to spend it as they intend to take you out. Ridgeon has received instruction from his boss to pay Eastern European hit men who are going to take all three of you out. I can actually prove that to you. I know I have a lot of information at hand but unfortunately no team names yet or when this will happen. I can safely predict you have less than a week to live.'

'If you know all what you have just told me, why the hell are you not arresting me? At least inside I shall be safe.'

'I have no intention of arresting you, far easier that they take the three of you out. You are walking out of this station in the next five minutes.'

'I confess to the murder of Amy whatever her name was.'

'Anderson, Amy Anderson. You must have bloody known that when you took the contract.'

'Whatever her name was I did it. Things happened exactly as you described it. I will sign anything. You have to accept my confession.'

'Sorry Jimmy we shall review this case over the next ten days and if we think you have a case to answer we shall take you in for formal questioning. One way or another Jimmy you are going down. Twenty years or six feet, take your pick. My money is on the six feet down to be precise. Forget going to any other cop shop or the media. Go to the media and your death sentence will be instant. Screw with these guys and you might find that your death is far more horrible than you could ever imagine. Do not forget these guys will also use radioactive terminations.'

'Christ Aitken, you are one ruthless Bastard. Every thing they say about you is true and more. You cannot put me back out there, it would be murder.'

'You call Aitken a ruthless Bastard,' said Allen. 'That's rich coming from someone who a few days ago executed an innocent young woman. Now that they want to execute you and they shall believe you me, you are squealing like a stuck pig. I think we tell Mr Ridgeon that we are holding you. Boy will that speed things up. Especially if we announce that we are holding you in connection with Amy Anderson's murder. We shall intimate that we may have to let you go as we are still not able to tie all the loose ends together. We would even give him a time when you have to be released. I am sure he would send you a car to save you having to take a taxi home, not that you would be going home. That would only apply if you were religious. I didn't have heaven in mind, not for you anyway. Somehow you do not strike me as the religious type. What do you think Sir?'

'Do you know Detective Allen I think I have to agree with you. I am not sure that Jimmy is a practising Christian even if he keeps saying Christ.'

'You are both bastards, You are as bad as each other. You are no better than me. You know by releasing me I am dead meat. I have rights, you must protect me.'

'Protect you, our collective asses. You are a murdering scumbag. A body full of lead is exactly what you deserve,' said Aitken. 'Me, I cannot wait to see it happen.'

'I need to phone my lawyer,' said Perkins.

'What for? You are not under arrest. What do you need a lawyer for?' asked Allen.

'Listen bitch, I have rights. I need a lawyer.'

'No rights here Jimmy, just the same rights as you extended to Amy Anderson. You call a lawyer, raise your profile and all you do is speed up your demise. Right Detective Allen I think that we should take Mr Perkins back home. See if you can find a car.'

'I am not leaving this bloody station. There has to be someone in authority here. There has to be.'

'If it will make you any happier I shall speak to my boss. He is Chief Superintendent Purbright. Problem is that I think he will agree with us. Stay there for a moment Detective Allen.'

Aitken popped out and two minutes later he was back. Here's all your stuff back. Ring your lawyer at your peril. Right detective let's go and see the Super. Actually is he in? I haven't seen him since we came back in. Do not go away Perkins.'

'Oh bloody funny, sodding comedian, that's what you are.'

Standing the other side of the mirror Purbright smiled. Aitken and Allen were bastards all right, but only if you were a crook. Ten seconds later the pair joined Purbright in watching Perkins. As they had hoped he was on his phone right away.

'Hi Johnny, Dobra here.'

'What do you want?'

'Bad news mate we have been rumbled and I mean rumbled. That hotshot bastard detective Aitken picked me up this morning, him and his sidekick, the blonde bit. She's a cold bitch that one.'

'You didn't spill your guts did you?'

'No need for any confessions. They had everything even photos.'

'Jesus man, were we set up?'

'Oh we have been set up all right by the bunch that paid us for the hit. They are going to take the three of us out. They must have fed the police because there was no way the police had that detailed info without an insider tip off.'

'So I take it you are locked up then.'

'No they bloody refuse to charge me. They simply want to let me out so these hit men can take me out. Those two are worse than most crooks.'

'You are winding me up. You have to be.'

'I am not winding you up. I even tried confessing and they would have nothing of it. You need to give yourself up because the Old Bill is not coming to arrest you. I can assure you of that. I need to tell Dave Jones.'

'There's a problem. Dave has gone to Tenerife already. Left this morning. He booked an apartment in Las Americas. I bet he spends like it is going out of fashion. Are you really sure they weren't blowing smoke up your arse. If they had all that info they would have charged you.'

'You come in here if you like and they will take great delight in telling you the details. I mean they even mentioned your damn Vans.'

'We have obviously been taken for suckers Dobra. Sounds like we are between a rock and a hard place. Where exactly are you at the moment.'

'At Railton nick. The two have gone to see their Super. Hopefully he will afford us the security of being locked up. What are you going to do?'

'How the hell do I know? Sounds like we are dead men out here. I might try and get to that Ridgeon and take that snake out. Trouble is my shooter is at the bottom of that quarry. I think I know where I can pick up a nine mill Beretta. Three hundred notes but it will be worth it to ventilate that treacherous sod. What say you?'

'Do it Johnny. Put one in that snake for me. Balls and two in the guts job, don't make it easy for him.'

'Dobra, do you think they will already be watching us, not The

Bill, I mean the hit men.'

'The Old Bill aren't going to and I do not think Ridgeon's boss has organised things yet.'

'If the Old Bill are not watching us they will be unable to stop me topping Ridgeon. He is out today and tomorrow and I know where. If I get to him first he is a goner. If you are right I am down for the Anderson girl anyway. If that snake thinks he is going to wipe us out I'll wipe him out first. Right now I have a job to do. I am going to get that Beretta and hopefully get to Ridgeon. If you get thrown onto the street let me know. I think I know a safe house where we can lie low. Speak to you later.'

Behind the mirror Aitken said to Purbright.

'The only way we can stop Robertson taking out Ridgeon is to warn Ridgeon. If we warn him he will know that they have rumbled him. I would rather try and pick up Robertson. Ridgeon still has uses. Let us hope that we can keep Ridgeon alive.'

'I agree,' said Purbright, 'but it is no big deal if Ridgeon is eliminated. When thieves fall out and all that. Yes let's try and protect him by getting to Robertson.'

'I take it you are going in to see Perkins and instruct us to charge him. Keep him here in custody and all that, once we have a total written confession,' said Allen.

'In one, let's get it done.'

The three walked back in on Perkins. He was still pacing the room.

Right Jimmy,' said Aitken, 'this is our Super. He is willing to accept your confession but it comes with strings. You must sign a confession implicating both Jonathon Robertson and David Jones. You must also identify any of the ADI paymasters who paid for the hit. That should not be too difficult as it is the same lot that are aiming to get rid of you. If this is not to your liking then as I said you are out on the street. Once this confession is signed you shall be held in custody in a high security facility and in solitary until we can bring the organisers to court. This is for your own security. If you are in agreement to these terms we shall send uniformed to pick up Robertson and Jones.'

'I agree to the conditions but you will not be able to pick up Jones, he has gone to Tenerife this morning, rented a flat in Las Americas. I have no idea when he is back.'

'Right we shall go and pick up Johnny Clyde, said Purbright. I shall get in touch with the Spanish authorities. I shall get that underway. Even guilty, Mr Perkins, you do have rights. You two process Mr Perkins but I want to see you in my office first.'

Perkins smiled. He reckoned Purbright was going to shred their collective arses.

The three went back to the other room and watched him through the two-way mirror. He was straight on the phone again.

'Johnny, good news. The Super came in and overturned the two sods. The Super said I had rights, you're damn right I do. The Super has just dragged the pair off to his office. I got the impression he wasn't two happy with the way the so-called hotshots handled me.

How are you getting on as they are coming to pick you up and the Super guy is going to get the Spanish authorities to pick up Dave? Make sure you let that shit Ridgeon know that we know what was going to happen to us. Get to it boy.'

'OK Dobra, best outcome. We were in the shit anyway. I will be back at my flat by ten tonight.'

In the adjacent room Aitken said, 'Thanks Robertson, that save us a lot of wasted time. Trouble is we need to pick you before you get to Ridgeon.'

I think we'll struggle to pick him up,' said Allen. He is going somewhere specific.'

'I agree with you,' said Purbright. Go and do everything we need with Perkins. Absolutely by the book. We do not need some slippery legal eagle finding a chink. I shall prepare a press release for midday news.'

'I thought you were going to alert the Spanish authorities Sir?' said Allen.

'All in good time. I think his paymasters need to know how he is spending his money.

The pair walked back in to process Perkins.

Aitken took a small tube from his pocket and threw it at Perkins who caught it with his left hand.

'Seeing you are staying with us Perkins, you'll need that. That is for your psoriases.'

'How the hell do you know I have psoriases?'

'We know everything about you Perkins, everything,' said Aitken.

Perkins just shook his head, almost in disbelief

Chapter 32

★ ★ ★ ★

~You have a message from the Geeks~

An hour later with Perkins safely locked up they were all standing around the television.

Purbright came on and made a statement.

'This morning we arrested a thirty eight year old man in relationship to the murder of Amy Anderson last Saturday morning. We have a confession and subsequently we have charged this man. We are looking to apprehend a further two persons in connection with this crime. One is unfortunately out of the country at Las Americas in Tenerife. Spanish Authorities are helping us with regard to this matter.'

A journalist said, 'that is a very quick result Chief Superintendent. What contributed to such a speedy resolution?'

'I am more than delighted to say that the biggest contributory to solving this crime was Amy's own family. Her father, mother and brother gave an account of what happened in that most hellish ten seconds that was crucial. The level of observation and detail by all three was unlike anything I have ever experienced in my working career. Our team, led by Detective Chief Inspector Aitken, would be the first to admit that what the Anderson family contributed means that we can stand here and announce that we have a person, who murdered their daughter, in custody. Nothing we can say or do can help the Andersons at this moment in time but this will have made them feel good because they made it happen.'

In the station there was a huge round of applause.

Another journalist asked if they knew why Amy was killed. Was it a hit? Was the guy in custody simply an assassin?

'We are sure that it was a hit. At present we do not know why or who commissioned the hit. The man we arrested has not been co-operative in this area. His co-operation has been limited to a signed confession.'

'When do you hope to have anyone else in custody?'

'Probably before this day is out.'

'Can you release any identification on these people?'

'No I am sorry, at this moment we cannot release any names. We shall only do that when we have all three in custody.'

At that moment Aitken's mobile rang. The caller was Philip Ridgeon.

'Chief Inspector, I am just watching your boss on television. Now I know why you were interested in my car passengers. Were there murderers in my car? God, it makes me shudder. Was the other guy the one that went to Tenerife?'

'Mr Ridgeon, I shouldn't tell you this but seeing you had the pair in the car. Yes they were murderers. We have the little guy in custody. I hope that cures you of ever picking up hitchhikers in the future. The one that went to Tenerife wasn't in your car, he was simply their driver.'

'I didn't know they had a driver. You still have no idea who was behind all this?'

'No, our friend has clammed up in this area. Someone or something is scaring him witless. He's happy to confess to the killing but that is it. I do not think that even plea bargaining will work, the guy is just so scared.'

'Maybe your victim was involved in something shady. She could have crossed someone.'

'We thought of that, anyway was there anything I can do for you,' asked Aitken.

'No, it was just the news. Makes you shudder a bit when you think of having two cold-blooded murderers in your car. The wife will go ballistic. Anyway I need to go. I am at a course today and tomorrow.'

'Good grief, from the size of your house there wasn't much that you could learn.'

Let me assure you there is, International Law is one. Not a favourite topic and one that I struggle on. I will have paid out a damned fortune on this course and I will still be rubbish at it. I detest law, I am sorry detective, no offence meant.'

What did you study at University then?

I didn't, I went straight to work from school. I went into an architect's office.'

'That explains your ability in creating a fantastic house.'

'No, I am no Architect. I landed more by luck than good measure in Business Development and I made those Architect guys a fortune. Perth was just starting to grow back then.'

'Perth in Scotland, when was it on a boom like that?'

No,' Ridgeon laughed. Perth, Western Australia. My father was in Oil & Gas. I just happened to be there when I left school. Like all kids I took off and went to Darwin. Anyway look I am boring you and I got to go. I am sorry to have called you. The Press release somehow rattled me. They were probably armed at the time.'

'Actually they probably weren't. We think they had disposed of the weapons by then. I need to get going too Mr Ridgeon. Try and relax and forget about it. Where is your course as I hope you are not driving and picking up hitchhikers?'

'It's in Cambridge and I am going by train. 'Thanks for the concern Detective Aitken and goodbye.'

'Goodbye Mr Ridgeon, Goodbye.'

Allen who was ear wigging said. 'I can guess who that was. I take it he was trying to get the status on all three.'

'In one.'

'You didn't think to warn him about the danger he was in.'

'No Louise, we still have his phone being monitored and he's definitely making calls or getting calls on this topic.'

'Right we know he is on a two day course studying International Law in Cambridge. There cannot be too many of these going on. He was at school during some period in Perth, Western Australia and actually started working there. He was in Business Development in a firm of Architects in Perth. Odds on, he met Collins in Australia. Perhaps Collins met Roberts or whatever his name is when he was in Perth or when Ridgeon went walkabout in the Northern Territories.'

'I'll attend to finding out where Ridgeon is. Give me ten minutes.'

'Allen, you do that in ten minutes and I shall be a very happy bunny.'

At that point a uniformed policewoman approached Aitken.

'Sir, you have a message from the geeks. They want to speak to you.'

'Are they on the phone Jenny?'

'No Sir, they want you to go and see them.'

'Allen pass that to Ira, I need you to come with me.'

'Where are you going Sir?

'Geek Headquarters if Jenny Silverwood is to be believed. They want to see us.'

Chapter 33

★ ★ ★ ★

~The Tantalus Project~

On the way over Aitken said, 'do you know Allen we are no closer to rounding up the people behind the killing or the motive for the killing?'

'No Sir, what does the famous Aitken gut feeling say about this case. Another thing you haven't even given it a name yet. So answers please on a postcard.'

'I think we are in for a long haul. We wrapped up those responsible for Amy's murder very quickly. That will be a huge relief to the Anderson family. Thing is they are nobody's fools. Once they have got over the feeling of euphoria that Amy's murderers are locked they will start to ask why and who is indeed behind it. We have partially satisfied their need for justice but it is not sated. I think this is huge, so huge it may be taken out of our hands. If it is drugs, money laundering, SOCA will take over. Our chance is greater if this is British based. Do you know, the funny thing is I think your connection to the cinema or whatever has some merit? Wendell Fanshawe for me exists. I am sure he is a person. I cannot explain why. Oh shit. We were supposed to have lunch with our film critic. Totally slipped my mind.'

'She couldn't make lunch as her cover is ill. What she proposed was a drink in the pub at five o'clock. I covered off the topic with her and she is to give it thought before we meet up.'

'When were you going to tell me?'

'Five o'clock just before we met Doris.'

When they got to the IT headquarters they had to sit in reception until they could be collected.

They had only been there two minutes when a tall good-looking man approached them.

He extended a handed and said, 'Aitken and Allen isn't it? I am Malcolm Underwood and I am chief researcher here. Helluva problem you have given us. Please follow me. Right before we pop in here can you, in turn, please look into that device there.'

'Retinal recognition, what difference does that make as we will not be on any register.'

'Wrong Jeremy, can I call you Jeremy. Status and titles do not mean much here. Just look at that with your right eye.'

Three seconds later the machine flashed 'Positive Match'.

Allen went next and within another three seconds a 'Positive Match' came up.

'Looks like you have been breaching our civil liberties,' said Aitken.

Malcolm Underwood just shrugged his shoulders.

'Don't worry about it Malcolm,' said Allen. 'For my Boss to take umbrage about civil liberties being abused would be a bit of a double standard from someone who has bugged two mobiles and a landline illegally in the last two days.'

'Firstly I am not in the slightest worried if I am not a hundred per cent politically correct. What if Jeremy did obtain results that wasn't too politically correct. Good luck.'

Allen knew that Aitken was going to like Malcolm.

'They followed Underwood down a long corridor. He walked extremely fast.'

'You on bloody roller skates there Malcolm?' said Allen.

'Sorry, just habit. I started as a corridor messenger with UXL Computers. They played fast music in the corridors and the lifts to encourage you to walk fast. My super duper degree meant sod all at UXL. You started as a corridor messenger. Anyway we are here now.'

He swiped a card down the card reader and opened the door. Inside two people sat surrounded by computer screens.

'This is Jo Jo, she is Korean. We have truncated her name as we are unable to actually pronounce it. This far too good-looking son of a bitch is Chas Devine. Jo, Chas meet the famous Jeremy Aitken and his sidekick Louise Allen. How are you getting on?'

'Progress is slow Sir, but we are making progress. We have

crossed a number of minefields without setting off a mine. Amy was a genius as far as computers is concerned. We are slightly miffed it wasn't her degree subject. She was a bloody accountant yet she is red hot as a computer operator. If she was as good at accountancy as she was at computers she was some kiddie. The thinking is in the way she has stuff organised. This started life as a very good computer but it is now a fantastic computer. The problem is we have bits missing. Two memory sticks are not here and we know they exist. She has two very important files on sticks. One she calls the Tantalus file and one she calls two plus two equals five. Our guys found nothing in her room. She has a wide number of memory sticks but there is nothing on them to do with work. The most of them are of Computer systems,' said Chas.

'Your victim definitely discovered something and unless we can find these sticks we shall be struggling. She calls it the Tantalus Project because like Tantalus she cannot reach what is right in front of her. He was the guy that was punished by not being able to reach what was in front of him,' said Malcolm.

'Ask DCI Aitken here, he will probably give you chapter and verse.'

'I was right wasn't I?' said Malcolm.

'You were, there are a few different tales about Tantalus but the common one is he stole Ambrosia from the Gods thereby making himself immortal. He was punished by the Gods by being banished to Hades. There he was placed in a pool of water and a tree of lush fruits hung above his head. Every time he reached for a fruit the branches would move and take the fruits out of reach. Exactly the same thing with the water he stood in. Every time Tantalus wanted to drink the water it would recede out of his reach. Obviously her choice must have been influenced by circumstance. What have you got for us Malcolm?'

'Not a great deal but let us look at what is more a personal diary than anything else. They are not hugely detailed but they cover events for the eleven months of this computer's life. She was going to upgrade shortly. God knows how she was going to do that because most things on board are state of the art. There are gizmos here that we can only dream about. What I find slightly weird and something that pisses off Jo Jo and me is that she appears almost self-taught. She didn't even do computer studies at University. Frankly it hacks us both off that someone who is right up there without even doing a proper computer degree. I am sure we will both get over it. Less than five months after this beauty was commissioned the first diary entry that refers to something other than the computer. All the entries prior to this refer to her progress with the computer itself.'

'So what rang the alarm bells?' asked Allen.

Simple Louise, at first we thought that she had developed a bug or that a virus had popped up from somewhere. Look at this Monday, August 24th, 'There is something rotten in the state of Denmark.' This wasn't about the computer. No this is the start of a series of entries which relate to her work. We fast forward to the Friday the thirteenth of November. She enters 'There is decidedly something rotten in the state of Denmark. Typical Friday the thirteenth luck, I am gutted. I thought this was going to be the perfect job.' There is the first confirmation that she is definitely referring to the job. Look down the list and you will see an increase in entries as the year goes on. Trouble is they are in some shorthand and I cannot crack it. I think it refers to figure of money, that bit I am pretty sure about. Oddly she strays from conventional accountancy nomenclature or what I think an accountant would use and goes for a more mathematical notation such as 837.24×10^3. Here I think it simply an amount of cash, 837,240 pounds possibly, although US Dollars are a possibility. If this is money there are some very big sums being moved around. Each cash entry has To CR or To RM. Now is that a place or a person? Could it be Costa Rica or Charles Roberts? These initials are repeated. I have obtained the entire Personnel File for ADI. This is it here. Ask no questions how it was obtained. What we have done is place every person they employ for example with the initials CR and we have another expanded list here. By putting in their job titles we feel that we might be able narrow the search. Let me show you with this entry Tues 3rd November. Thirty-eight Million plus to RM. OK let's look at the RM's in the company. Ruth Morrison, works in the mailroom. Yes possibly she might mail money somewhere but I do not think so. No let us consider a Ross Morgan. Morgan is the Business Development Director for Asia. He only started at the beginning of October. Sure enough no RM entries back before the first of October but it is common after November all the way through to the week before last. My candidate for CR is Craig Reed who is the Business Development Director for Latin America. Look at Thurs 22nd of October, 2.6618 times ten to the power nine. We have moved into the billions class. I shall move this sheet of paper. You might get a surprise on the initials to whom this small sum was sent.'

'WF,' suggested Aitken before Malcolm could reveal the Initials.

My God, you are no fun at all,' said Malcolm.

'You are dead right about that Malcolm. I hate it when he does that,' said Allen.

'My sympathies Louise, everyone likes a little, no one likes a smart !

'Right Hot Shot Detective is WF a place or a person?'

'WF is obviously Wendell Fanshawe, a person,' said Aitken.

'There is no Wendell Fanshawe, he is not on my personnel list.'

'This is good stuff, in fact great stuff Malcolm. First class detective work never mind the computer part. There is a guy who knew Amy and he is a serious IT guy with this company. His name is Eddie Saunders. His sister Arabella is a friend of my daughter's. Rather spookily my daughter has met Amy Anderson. The problem is that if Eddie is a computer whizz kid he might know what they are up to already. He may even be involved.'

'I am not sure he would know unless he was actually poking about. That might be dangerous in that company. His job according to this is that he fixes and maintains the computer systems in ADI,' said Malcolm.

'A few weeks back Amy had considered telling this Eddie guy but ADI had got to Melissa and basically roughed her up.'

'Is that her pal, the Melissa that helped us get into this computer. Jeremy, this is going to have to be your shout. He might help us but on the other hand he might alert ADI.'

Chapter 34

★ ★ ★

~The Green Knight~

'What are the notations beside WF,' asked Louise. 'They are equivalent of Braille dots for two plus two equals five. The details of this transaction are probably on that $2 + 2 = 5$ stick.'

'That was some deduction to make, I mean the Braille.'

'Not me Jeremy, Jo Jo came up with that. In fact most of this work is Jo Jo's'

Jo Jo smiled sweetly. Apart from shaking their hands, Jo Jo had not uttered a word. It came as a huge surprise when she did speak.

'We badly need these sticks. I think the Tantalus stick will be the descriptive narrative and $2+2=5$ the actual money because it doesn't add up in accountancy terms. I think ADI is a huge money laundering operation and possibly a partner in drug activities. I think we are looking at a scale never seen. I do not think she would give the sticks to her friends. She was too scared to endanger them. No they are somewhere safe, the problem being it is too safe. I want to get into another file which I feel is pertinent. The file is named Sir Gawain and the Green Knight.'

'Good Grief, what is that all about,' asked Louise.

Your guess is as good as mine Louise but I think it has something to do with this case,' said Jo Jo.

'Sir, can you shed a light. I know who Gawain was; he was the perfect Knight of Arthurian legend. What has the Green Knight got to do with it?'

'No idea Louise,' said Aitken. The Green Knight story came later. It is a tale from the 14th Century. Sir Gawain met this mysterious knight who was totally green. Green Armour, green skin, green hair and beard. The Green Knight challenged any knight that he would allow them one blow with an axe providing that a year from this day he would be allowed one blow with an axe against his challenger. Sir Gawain accepts. One blow and he chops off the Green Knight's head. To Sir Gawain's surprise the Green Knight picks up his head pops it on and bows. The Green Knight departs saying 'One year from now we have an appointment.'

'I have no idea how this pertains. I will just go with your gut feeling Jo Jo. This file is not on a stick, it's on the hard drive, yes?'

'Yes Jeremy, it's there but again password protected and I am sure it has a self-destruct.

This has fourteen letters; it's just a hit or a miss. If she is sticking with her Man U theme it could be a player's name, can't be the Manager's, too many letters. Not the pitch's name or bits of it, for example the Stretford End. I think I get three chances.'

'Anything else?' asked Allen.

I think that these eight International Business Development guys are insiders and part of the whole corrupt affair. I have had one of our guys run their names and I think in all cases the names on the personnel list that Mal sourced are aliases. Ryan is accessing some files we are not supposed to. Don't worry; we are not hacking into the CIA or anything like that. He just happens to know some unbelievably well connected people. Ryan's dad was basically a spy, a real life James Bond,' said Jo Jo.

'Hang on a moment Jo Jo, I have Melissa Harcross's mobile. I don't think she will be at work today. I will give her a call to see if she can cast any light on what a fourteen letter Man U connection could be,' said Allen.

With that she called Melissa.

'Hi Melissa, Louise Allen here, can you speak at the moment?'

The answer was in the affirmative. Allen put her phone on the speaker system.

Right we are with the experts working on Amy's computer. Once again we are stymied by a password. Fourteen letters and probably Man United related. Any bright ideas? I know you are not a Man U fan but you know your football.'

'You are right about that. Fourteen letters you say. Could be a player, part of the ground. There was a pause, Melissa was obviously running options.

I think I might have it. Try *squeaky bum time*. That's fourteen and one of Amy's favourite expressions.'

By the time Melissa had finished speaking there was a triumphant yell from Jo Jo. 'We are in. She is brilliant. Want a job here Melissa?'

'I take it you could hear that Melissa. That really was brilliant. What you have given us so far is tightening the noose on the people behind the scenes who orchestrated Amy's death.'

'If that is the case Louise, that's what I would call brilliant,' said Melissa.

'Sorry to bother you again but hopefully we have made another step forward. Thanks Melissa, speak to soon.'

'Goodbye Louise, goodbye.'

'What the hell is 'squeaky bum time?' asked Allen.

'You are not into football are you?' said Malcolm.

'Cannot stand it,' said Allen.

'Right if you are wanting to see what the expression means look it up in the OED,' said Malcolm.

'You have to be winding me up? That is in the Oxford English Dictionary?'

'Absolutely,' said Malcolm. 'Anyway Jo Jo what have we opened up.'

'Well it is only a brief report. This concerns a George Royston. It seems that Mr Royston was possibly a founder member of ADI. Briefly WF gave him the shaft some eleven months ago. Thursday the 30th April to be precise. What's interesting is George Royston's response dated the 1st of May. That is contained in a copy of a memo to WF. WF is definitely a person and possibly another founder of ADI.'

A copy of the memo was in the file, it read.

'Dear Wendell,

You cannot stop acting as is so typical of your profession. You give me the shaft and you keep the mine. You see yourself as Sir Gawain the ideal knight. You are sadly disillusioned. All you can do is what you are good at and that is act, unlike Sir Gawain you have no moral fibre.

You may have beheaded me but beware Wendell, for I am the Green Knight. Seeing you love the world of Drama, let me tell you that exactly like the Green Knight, one year to the day, I shall return. On that day I shall behead you. We have an appointment, Saturday 1ˢᵗ May.

The Green Knight.'

'Seemingly, according to this,' said Jo Jo, 'Amy tried to trace George Royston but to no avail. She says that it's almost impossible that this company could have been formed by two shades, two phantoms. Interestingly she thinks that Wendell is in the theatrical profession. She lists a whole host of sources that she has searched and drawn a blank.'

'Thanks Jo Jo,' said Aitken. I can see why Amy thought this was a significant relationship. The memo would have been very private so somehow she managed to get a copy. Could she have accessed Wendell Fanshawe's computer, hacked in to it and signed her death warrant.'

'It's a possibility,' said Malcolm, 'but Jo Jo has not come across any files that suggest this is the case.'

'Right,' said Aitken, 'you are doing great and we shall get out of your hair. Keep us posted. We had better get back to Railton Allen. Thanks Malcolm, thanks Jo Jo. Oh before I go Collins and Ridgeon, what are their job titles?

Malcolm checked and said, 'Collins is CEO Operations; Ridgeon is Operations Manager for Europe. There are seven other area Ops Managers all reporting back to Collins.'

'Interesting,' said Aitken, 'that actually ties up the loose ends.'

At that moment Aitken's phone rang. He listened patiently.

'Good, thanks for that,' and he rang off.

Good news Allen, they have picked up Dobra's pal Johnny Clyde and he is now in custody. That keeps Ridgeon safe for the moment.'

Chapter 35

★ ★ ★ ★

Their Holy Grail is Money

On the way back to Railton the two discussed what had transpired with Malcolm and Jo Jo.

'That is it Allen. This is the Tantalus Case. I am going to go with that.'

'Good Sir, I was beginning to wonder if we were working on some untitled work.'

'Well, we need to let Jenny Silverwood know that Geek Central isn't actually inhabited by Geeks,' said Aitken.

'True, I think she might find Malcolm Underwood quite easy on the eye. They are probably about the same age.'

'What do you mean, Jenny Silverwood? I would have thought that one Louise Allen might have found Malcolm quite attractive as well. He is probably at the most three years older than you.'

'I am not on the market but Jenny is, two years now since she got divorced. There is no one on the horizon. Mr Underwood wears no ring so possibly he is unattached.'

'From a seriously top detective that is a rather huge assumption, Malcolm could have a partner, man or woman. He could be married but not wear a ring. There are, any number of reasons that he might not to be in a relationship or, any number of reasons that he is. What did you make of Jo Jo? If Jenny Silverwood came sniffing around Malcolm, Jo Jo might just send her packing. Those two are lovers, so do not start any matchmaking on behalf of Jenny.'

'How the hell do you know that?'

'Why are you asking me? You are the one that has studied all this body language stuff.

I would have thought it would have been obvious to you. Anyway what did you think of what has popped out of Amy's computer?'

'Very interesting her comment about a company formed by two shades, two phantoms. I wondered about her choice of words there, shade, phantom or the half dead. Mythical allegory or are Wendell and George Royston half dead already?' said Allen.

'Yes, I must admit I wondered about that. Amy Anderson obviously has or had a huge intellect. Her references are far from run of the mill. Your theatrical or film theory is looking good. What say you that Wendell Fanshawe is indeed the name of someone famous? Perhaps this is all some epic film scenario to him.'

'Possibly Sir, but somewhere there has to be a record if that is what he started out as. Maybe there is no such person, instead is it just someone acting as Wendell Fanshawe, George Royston's reference to acting. Do you want an even more far out theory Sir? Wendell Fanshawe and George Royston are one and the same person. They are a split personality, hence a situation that might explain those internal memos where you have one personality firing the other. You then have the other personality reacting and threatening revenge.'

'Now that Allen, is indeed very far out but strangely it could be right. Keep those ideas coming. There are eight of the international Business Development Directors. I would think they are all involved. I would think that somewhere there has to be accountant's involved. The bean counters are always involved and somewhere there are likely to be legal eagles. If you include Collins there are eight Ops guys. My guess is that Wendell Fanshawe probably doesn't see himself as Sir Gawain but more likely King Arthur and he has probably about twenty knights around the round table. The problem is their Holy Grail is money.'

' I wish to hell I knew if Wendell Fanshawe actually exists,' said Allen. 'The problem is he could also be a smokescreen. These guys could have invented him for convenience.'

'You are good at thinking outside the box Allen but I honestly do think Fanshawe exists. Your theory of a split personality is highly possible. That interests me greatly. We are supposed to be meeting Doris but he we had better go and brief Purbright first. I have great concerns when he isn't giving us a hard time.'

'I know exactly what you mean Sir. Last week John Simpson was complaining of exactly the same thing and then Purbright fell on him from a great height.'

'Yes, exactly what I fear.'

With that Aitken's phone rang.

Aitken smiled at Allen and she smiled back. Purbright was chasing information. The status quo was established. Aitken put Purbright on speaker.

'Are you two on a jolly or what? Do we have positive results?' growled Purbright.

Aitken briefed Purbright.

'I think Allen's thing that Royston and Fanshawe is one and the same person has merit. Do not ask me why I think that at this stage. Fanshawe knows that when he meets the Green Knight one year later that the Green Knight will aim exactly three blows and only the last one slightly nicks his neck. Fanshawe knows he is safe so I think it is all some figment of his imagination. Fanshawe is probably very, very clever but as mad as they come. We do need to track down our Wendell Fanshawe. Hopefully Doris can help you. I share your feeling he is originally from or may still be in the theatrical profession. I love a riddle like this. I take it Doris is in for a culinary treat?'

'If that means are we going somewhere posh such as The Isadora if that is what you are trying to find out, no, we are going to the, where are we going Allen?'

'The Pumpernickel, Sir,' said Allen.

'Well done Allen, glad to see someone has a responsible attitude to expenses. Poor Aitken, please be welcome in the world of the artisans, the ordinary people. I take it Allen you were responsible for this choice of location.'

'She was,' growled Aitken. He knew that would appeal to Purbright.

'Bye,' said Purbright. They could both hear him chuckling as he rang off.

Chapter 36

★ ★ ★ ★

~Doris Spedding~

When they got to The Pumpernickel Doris was already there.
'Ah Sir, that's great timing. I have just this minute walked in
the door. I was worried, as I had been delayed. It looks like it has
all worked out perfect.'

'What do you want to drink Doris?' asked Aitken.

'I will have a Port and Lemon please.'

Aitken smiled to himself, a Port and Lemonade was such a
perfect choice by Doris.

You Allen, what's your poison going to be?'

'I have Jonathon picking me up later, so I can have a drink. I
will have a Maraschino and soda.'

'This is not The Isadora, I would lower your sights, a white
wine maybe.'

'If you cannot get what I asked for then I shall have a white
wine.'

Five minutes later Aitken joined the two women at the table.
He served Doris her Port and Lemon and Allen her Maraschino
and Soda.

Allen said nothing, she just smiled and said thank you.

'You on the Gin there Sir?' said Allen.

'Yes, Dad is coming by to pick me up. I shall just leave the car
in the garage and get a lift from Rosemary in the morning. She is
flying to Edinburgh early doors.'

Aitken looked at Doris closely. He had seen her often enough
but she was like just part of the background. He knew her voice

better than he knew her as a person. He had heard her voice so often on the police radios. He knew she was popular with the rest of her colleagues. Her once black hair now had two white flashes a bit like Cruella de Ville in One Hundred and one Dalmatians. There was nothing however cruel about Doris. She was a very cheery soul. Aitken thought that Doris might have been quite a looker in her youth. She still had a very neat figure and the most beautifully manicure hands. A few small liver spots betrayed her age.

'Right, Cheers,' she said. 'That little problem you left me with. Was a murder committed in such a manner and did the people escape using the removable paint stuff that they used on the truck. Did someone ever put it into a film? I made a few phone calls before I met you. I am sorry but I even called a couple of friends in well, California to be truthful. I am so glad to say that I didn't waste the police's cash.'

'You found Wendell Fanshawe?' asked Allen.'

'Sadly No, but I did come across your murder scene. I have a good friend in Harrison Ford.'

'The Harrison Ford?' asked an amazed Allen.

'And I wish, no, my Harrison Ford shares only one thing in common with the other Mr Ford, they both work in the film industry. There the similarity ends. My Harrison is everything thing the screen legend isn't. He is short, overweight and bald. I have had dinner with Harrison Ford but very sadly the wrong one. That said my Harrison is a very nice man. He filters through potential films and scripts. He is extremely good at finding and choosing winners. When I gave him the description of the scene he said he had read it before as the opening gambit to a film script he had received. He thought it was a quite clever opening and he read on. Sadly that opening gambit was the only decent thing in the whole script.'

'Please tell me it was Wendell Fanshawe that sent it.'

'Harrison couldn't remember as it was about six years ago. He said the name sounds right but he couldn't be sure. What he could remember was the film's stupid title as he called it, the 'Last Train to Clarksville.'

'Exactly as the Monkees Hit,' said Aitken.

'Way before my time Sir.'

'Last Train to Clarksville was an anti Vietnam War song and was recorded by the Monkees. A good bit before my time never mind yours Allen.'

'Well there is the rub as the film script was anti war. That Harrison can remember. The sender was staying at the Hollywood Hotel all week and he expected Harrison to call and discuss the script.'

'Now that is useful. If we could only find out when that week was we could confirm whether it was Wendell Fanshawe or not.'

'Well you might just be in luck there. Harrison kept a file on every script that ever came through his door. He will search his archives and hopefully tie down during the week.' 'Maybe the hotel has Fanshawe as a regular. Perhaps we need to check there,' said Aitken.

Chapter 37

★ ★ ★ ★

~A very pleasant Dinner~

'A re we eating?' said Allen. 'I am starving.'
'Allen is always starving, it is a condition with her. I think she has something wrong with her,' said Aitken.

'The only thing wrong with me is who I have to put up with as a partner. He believes in the starvation diet Doris.'

'Eating is fine by me I shall phone my Dad and tell him not to collect me yet.'

Aitken returned two minutes later.

'He wasn't answering his phone so I left a message saying where I was and that we were eating. Have either of you eaten here before?'

Both women said 'Yes' in unison.

'My boss here might not think a lot of the fare served here.'

'I supposed that is understandable Louise when you are married to one of the finest cooks in the land. Actually though the food in here isn't all that bad.'

Aitken looked up as a very well dressed older man approached them. He stood up.

'Dad what are you doing here?'

'Hopefully, if you have completed your business, doing the same as you, eating.'

Louise also went to stand up and Mr Aitken, said 'Please do not get up on my behalf unless you are going somewhere. I am James Aitken, Jeremy's father and you must be the lovely Louise Allen. It is so nice to meet you. After all you are the one looking after my son. I take my hat off to anyone capable of such a Herculean task.'

Louise smiled. She thought, you could charm the birds out of the trees. She knew he was getting toward eighty but he was still a very handsome man.

Dad, this is a colleague of ours, Doris Spedding. Doris this is my Dad, James Aitken.

'Very pleased to meet you Mr Aitken.'

'Please call me James, are you OK with Doris? What is the food like here?'

'Yes I'm fine with Doris and the food is not bad. They make a homemade steak and ale pie that is excellent. They also do a superb bangers and mash that is really very good. The chef here makes his own sausages.'

'Thanks a lot Doris, I was mouth watering with the thought of the Steak and Ale pie, now those sausages seem divine. Do not tell me any more. I am already on the horns of a dilemma.'

He did it so smoothly that Doris almost giggled. Oh you are a charmer alright thought Louise.

'I could be really wicked and tell you about the Sea Bass fillets, the ultimate Lorelei,' said Doris.

'Stop, stop, I implore you, I am already dashed on the rocks,' said Mr Aitken Snr. in a mock anguished voice.

Doris was almost purring.

'So you two are colleagues of Jeremy here. I know what Louise does, so what do you do Doris?'

'Nothing nearly as grand as these two, James, I am just a dispatcher, on the radio simply sending people to crime scenes, road accidents, that kind of thing.'

'Well I would have thought that was pretty important. Do you not agree Louise?'

'I most certainly do and Doris is brilliant at it.'

'See what I mean Doris; you are far more than just a dispatcher as you called it. You are part of the team, an important part. Just remember that a well run company is a bit like an old fashioned Swiss watch, one that has big wheels, little wheels, springs, diamonds and jewels. What is obvious is that the watch does not keep accurate time unless all the wheels, cogs springs, jewels are all doing their job. So it really doesn't matter whether you are a big cog or a smaller one you are all equally important. If Louise is correct and I believe she is an exceptional detective, you may be one of the diamonds and by the way Doris, it is the sausage and mash.'

'You will not regret it James. As far as the sausages go try either the sun-dried tomato variety or if he has them on The Lincolnshire Red Spot ones.'

'Red Spot it is then, what are you two going for.'

'I am going for the Steak and Ale as I am famished,' said Louise.

'I think it is the catch of the day for me Dad, the Red Snapper. I am sorry but you are going to miss out on what is a surprising good wine list.'

'That is a pity but I will just have a non-alcoholic beer. Cannot drink and drive especially when your son is a policeman.'

'How can you drink that stuff Dad, it is ghastly?'

'You're not drinking it and I am fine with it.'

Chapter 38

★ ★ ★ ★

~You just have to be joking~

James Aitken's next question rather put Doris on the spot.
'How were you helping this two out Doris?'

Doris looked at Aitken almost pleadingly.

'Doris is a film buff and we were picking her brains to see if she could remember a scene in a film as we think it was either a copycat killing or the guy who thought up the idea finally used it,' said Aitken.

'And did you recall anything Doris?'

'No I didn't, but a friend of mine in Hollywood did. We are just trying to see if it is the Wendell Fanshawe, oh, I'm sorry Sir. I didn't mean to say that.'

'Wendell Fanshawe, my goodness that's a blast from the past,' said James Aitken.

'You know Wendell Fanshawe Dad? You just have to be joking,' said Aitken.

'Well I know of a Wendell Fanshawe and I do not suppose there are too many of them around. Trouble is it is nearly forty five years ago, possibly more.'

'Care to elaborate Father?'

'Actually come to think of it, it was nineteen sixty-six, the year

England won the World Cup. My company was doing well, after all the UK was booming. This Wendell Fanshawe sent me a book to publish. He said it was a world-beater just like England, that's how I remember it was '66. The book was going to be made into a film and as an actor he was convinced that it was a winner.'

'So he was an actor then?'

'I am not sure if he was good one. I only met him the once. He certainly was good looking. He was four years younger than me. I remember him saying he was thirty-two. I also remember asking him if he had done any TV work. He said he had been on the early editions of Z cars. I cannot recollect ever seeing him in anything.'

'That is interesting Dad, if we were to obtain tapes of Z Cars do you think you could recognise him? You said you met him in '66. When did Z Cars start?'

'Nineteen sixty-two,' said Doris.

'Good grief Doris I didn't think you would have even been around back then,' said James Aitken.

'Oh I am afraid so James. I was twelve in nineteen sixty two.'

'Well I never,' said James. Louise just smiled.

'So if he was in the early editions there cannot be that many to cover,' said Aitken.

'Problem Jeremy,' said Doris, 'you will be very lucky if any recordings still exist. I would doubt if you find anything in the archives. A lot of those early programmes no longer exist.'

'That's right Doris; a lot of the early classic programmes have been lost. Rather sad really,' said James.

'Dad, anything is worth a punt at the moment. He didn't say what his name as an actor was.'

'I cannot remember, maybe that was his stage name. Doris, have you got any ideas?'

'No James, as I told these two, it certainly isn't ringing any bells.'

'My brief association with Wendell Fanshawe came to a very abrupt end when I rejected his book for publishing. He became rather abusive and explained to me how big an idiot I was. The strange thing is that his book was all about computers and computer fraud. Strangely it was so far ahead of its time. The BBC might not have stuff in their archives but I probably have. I would have the devil of a job finding the stuff but I know where it is in general terms.'

'Ah here is our food,' said Louise. 'It is just as well that I am hungry because that is quite a plateful to get through.'

The food was excellent and the conversation went to other topics such as Doris's love of films.

'Fiona and I went to films quite a bit when we were young, before the family came along. The cinema was quite the place to go back then. I haven't been to the cinema for years. Last time I went I took my grandson Charlie and he was eight at the time. He's a teenager now. Funny thing is, what killed it for me was the smell of popcorn. The smell is just too invasive for me.'

'Some Cinema chains are considering banning it,' said Doris. 'I personally never buy the stuff, so I am easy but I know what you mean about the smell being invasive. How is your sausage?'

Helluva question thought Louise and smiled to herself.

'Absolutely fantastic. This really is quite superb bangers and mash.'

'Harald and I did most of our courting by going to the cinema, that and Top Ranking.'

'Top Ranking?' said Louise.

'Before your time Dear,' said Doris. Top Rank Organisation, they had a number of the best ballrooms where you could go dancing. Mind you they had the cinemas as well. Harald and I had some great times Top Ranking.'

'Does he still go to the Cinema with you?' asked James.

'I wish James. No sadly, I lost Harald to MS nearly thirty years ago. We had met at University, well more exactly through University. He was at Oxford and a neurologist; I was reading Politics and economics at Bristol. We met on University Challenge, incidentally another nineteen sixty-two programme launch. It was a few years later though that we were on, nineteen seventy to be precise. I was still an undergrad but Harald was doing postgraduate research. He was Norwegian, from the very far north of that country. It was a superb night as we absolutely stuffed Oxford. They were rubbish. No offence Sir, but they were. Harald was their only star and thanks to him they made it a bit of a contest. It was after the show we got talking. Anyway to cut a long story short, two years later we were married and another year later the first of my three children arrived. Timmy, who was followed by Chloe and then Helge. Then one April morning Harald woke up with pins and needles in his arm. He thought he had been sleeping the wrong way. Problem was it didn't go away. The diagnosis was MS and sadly severe and aggressive. Exactly twelve months later the sun in my life was extinguished. I was left coming up thirty with three young children. Fortunately Harald had provided well for us and between Insurances and Death in Service settlements we were well off, well off in the financial sense. Once the family had fled the nest I was at a loose end. I did a wide variety of secretarial work but didn't enjoy it. Problem was I wasn't qualified at anything in particular. I had never ever used my qualifications and now that would come back and bite me in the rear. So here I am working in the local cop shop. I actually enjoy it.'

'Sadly Doris, as you put it, the Sun in my life was also extinguished. I was widowed almost thirty-five years ago. Trouble was I suffered a double whammy; I lost my precious daughter Ophelia to the same damned killer, breast cancer. With the death of my wife and daughter my religion would also die with them. I am sorry but I just couldn't see what God's greater purpose was in taking my wife and daughter from me. If I am wrong and there is a God he had better have a bloody good explanation.'

Louise Allen could detect the bitterness in James Aitken's voice. She hadn't even been aware that Aitken had a sister. She had once asked him if he had any siblings and he had simply said no.

'Your husband must have had a very aggressive strain for him to go so quickly you can catch MS and although it gets progressively worse you often can have years.'

'That's true James; I remember in 1971 the Times ran an advert with a nude for the first time. I was only twenty-one at the time, I was close to graduating and I was home from Bristol studying. Dad was having breakfast when the paper arrived. Next thing was he nearly swallowed his cup of tea. Mum thought it was disgusting, Dad nodded in agreement and muttered something like 'Yes Dear' but he didn't actually condemn it. Me I was dead envious about how the girl looked. She was a total stunner.'

'Gosh I remember that,' said James Aitken. 'The Neves girl, 'The Body' as she was known. Yes that's right, it was a Fisons advert if I remember correctly. Your Dad would have known it was coming. There was a forewarning and the paper was completely sold out. I know where you are going Doris. She developed MS early on. She did live quite some time and sadly I think it was something else that killed her in the end poor girl. She really was very beautiful.'

'Did you complete the crossword that day Dad or were you

somewhat distracted. My Dad is a Times crossword nut.'

'So was my Harald. My goodness is that the time? It really does fly when you are enjoying yourself. I need to get home and let my dog out. Poor animal is probably cross legged by now.'

'I take it we can drop you off,' said Jeremy Aitken.

'No, it's OK, I live nearby in Pencaitland Avenue,' said Doris.

'Then it will only take a couple of minutes.'

When they had dropped off Doris, Aitken said to his father, 'You know, you never really know anyone. Doris surprised me. University Challenge, degree in Politics and Economics.'

'Why should that come as a surprise, she is obviously an intelligent woman with a good head on her shoulders. I liked her.'

Chapter 39

★ ★ ★

~The Invisible Man~

The following morning both Aitken and Allen were in early. Over the first coffee of the day they discussed progress to date and the dinner from the previous evening.

'Your Dad is lovely, he's a charmer,' said Allen.

'Oh he's that all right, he is also extremely good at getting his own way, so I would remember that.'

'I assume that Charlie is equally a charmer.'

'What makes you say that?'

'Because it is obvious the charm gene has skipped a generation.'

'I will smack you.'

'I rest my case.'

'Anyway if this is the same Wendell Fanshawe involved in this case he is now a man in his seventies.'

'There isn't an age limit for megalomania. History has proven that.'

'That's very true Allen.'

'We need a break here. Why are there no records on this guy? I find that totally baffling,' said Aitken.

'Yes, it's like he has been deleted in computer terms.'

'Do you know that is exactly what might have happened. I wonder if this guy has been smart enough to expunge his own records.'

'That would almost be impossible Sir, The number of places he would have to access.'

'Remember what Dad said his book was about, computers.

What if Wendell Fanshawe was a bit ahead of his time and before his theatrical career he was a pioneer in computers.'

'It's possible, bit of a long shot though,' said Allen.

'Yes but he would have had a lot less places to hack into and delete his records.'

'Yes Sir, but there would have been a whole lot of manual records and stuff on, what was it called, you know the newspaper system, microfiche that's what I am trying to say. How would he have made those changes?'

'What if and this is out there, what if he was involved in the computerisation of Government departments. Say he had access to the Inland Revenue etc. as they were switching over or upgrading. Just imagine someone removing himself from the IR records, no tax. That could have been the start and then it became an obsession. Wendell Fanshawe becomes the invisible man. Royston is born to replace him and even he is a figment of the imagination.'

'Well, that has to be a possibility and could fit Sir. Another possibility is that the theatre may have obsessed him. He could have financed his ambitions by a bit of early computer fraud. I wonder if any Government department suffered a loss in the sixties or early seventies. Do you know any Mandarins that could help? I would suspect either the Inland Revenue or Social Services, Pensions, that kind of thing.'

'As a matter of fact I do, probably a bit out there, but worth investigation. Anything else Allen?'

'Yes, shouldn't we be having doughnuts with this coffee?'

'All too American for me Allen, you need to stop watching these imported shows. The day I order doughnuts with my coffee is the day I pack in.'

'Couldn't agree more,' growled Purbright. 'Update needed.'

Purbright walked in and sat down in the spare seat in Aitken's office. He listened patiently during the briefing.'

'Well looks like you are fleshing out some facts on Fanshawe but I think finding him is going to be a huge task. This really is the Invisible Man. He is tantalisingly close but tantalisingly out of reach. Now I know why you call this the Tantalus Case. Most of our stuff is nothing more than supposition. Stick with it as most of your hunches are starting to come good. I bet Doris surprised you. Keep me posted.'

Purbright was gone.

'The Chief's right about one thing; Doris sure as hell surprised me. Things are never as they seem,' said Aitken.

'You posed the question yesterday, what if Fanshawe is someone famous. I actually do not think he will be famous. Great tabloid headlines but I do not think it to be the case. I think he finally got hooked on his Invisible Man scenario, so much so in fact that Fanshawe is possibly a recluse. That way he is even more difficult to trace. He possibly had a tilt at fame and failed. Every now and then he tries a tilt at a windmill, like six years ago a film script, every time he fails he becomes more reclusive.'

'Allen, I must admit you have a very weird mind but I like it. You always seem to come up with another piece in the jigsaw. I wouldn't be at all surprised if that little hypothesis stands up as fact.'

Chapter 40

★ ★ ★ ★

~His breakfast didn't agree with him~

At that moment John Durris came in.

'Morning John, what is it?'

'A news flash Sir, there is a report coming in on television that a British tourist couple has fallen from an eight-floor apartment in Las Americas in Tenerife. Guess who the man is identified as?'

'I could hazard a guess at David Jones. I would guess he was pushed,' said Aitken.

'That would win you a coconut Sir. They were found at four am this morning local time by some drunken revellers. Both were very much naked and very much dead. No foul play is suspected. Drink is thought to be the cause of what is seen as a tragic accident.'

'Sure, they were probably force fed the stuff before they were dropped over the balcony. I would assume the girl was just unlucky to be in the wrong place at the wrong time,' said Aitken.

'You have to admit it Sir, these guys are efficient,' said Allen. 'We probably need to increase security on the two we have in custody. In custody or not I would not be surprised if they take a pop at those two.'

'They are in isolation at the moment. I think they need to be informed of Mr Jones's demise. Might make them sing even more.'

'That's it for now Sir,' said John. 'If we get more news we shall let you have it.'

'Thanks John, we might need to pop you out there to liase with the Spanish Authorities as we suspect foul play.'

'OK Sir, let me know what you are planning.'

When Durris had left the room Aitken looked at Allen.

'You were right about one thing; these guys are efficient all right. That is seriously quick. That is serious money talking. We mention it on TV and instantly the guy is eliminated.'

There was a knock on the door and Durris almost burst in. 'Sorry to interrupt Sir but we have some more bad news. Johnny Clyde is dead.'

'What the hell do you mean he is dead? How in the name of hell could that have happened? He is in sodding solitary. We only arrested him yesterday.'

'Seems he has been poisoned Sir, his breakfast didn't agree with him.'

'That is bloody impossible inside a high security prison.'

'Appears not Sir.' Durris was a bit uneasy as he thought Aitken was about to explode.

'Please tell me Perkins is all right.'

'He is Sir. All this stress had got to him and he had a severe dose of the shits, sorry Ma'am,' he said to Allen. 'Anyway to cut a long story short he didn't touch a thing at breakfast. They took the plate away and stuck some of the porridge in the prison cat's bowl. The cat convulsed and died instantly.'

'This is all we bloody need, prisoners being murdered in high security units. The Press will have a field day with this,' said Allen.

'I take it a full investigation is underway. Does the Super know this yet?' asked Aitken.

'No Sir he is in a budget meeting with the administration guys,' said Durris.

'Christ, he is going to be in a foul mood anyway. This will really put the cherry on top of the cake.'

'Right John, you had better brief him when he comes out of the meeting,'

The panic stricken look on Durris's face told Aitken that was the last task Durris wanted to do that day.

'No, tell you what John, I'll tell him, in fact I shall send him a text and dig him out of the meeting. You get round to that bloody Prison and see what the hell happened. Make their life hell if you have to.'

'Thanks Sir, I am on my way.'

'Didn't fancy telling Purbright, did he?' said Allen.

'Cannot blame him really. He will go ballistic.

Aitken dug him out and Purbright did go ballistic.

'I bet that little waste of space Perkins will now clam up. We need him to stay alive. Without his evidence we are up the proverbial creek without the paddle. How, in God's name, can we have a prisoner poisoned in a high security facility?'

At that moment Laura popped her head in.

'Sorry to interrupt Sir, but the Media has got a hold of the Johnny Clyde story. They want us to comment as we announced these were the men in custody. The tenor of the conversations is that we might be responsible for their deaths.'

'Thanks Laura,' said Purbright, 'truth is we probably are. They were supposedly in protective custody. So they haven't got the facts that it is a poisoning we are dealing with. Probably a canary in the Prison who owns a forbidden mobile is singing but one that doesn't know the full facts. Christ this day just gets better. I have these clowns from Admin all over me like a rash. Your bloody expenses Aitken are why we are in the shit. The sodding Isadora is off sodding limits from now on.'

Allen smiled to herself, she wondered if the sodding Isadora had the same Michelin three stars as The Isadora had. She thought it was likely.

'Why the hell you cannot lunch at the Three Tuns like the rest of us mortals is beyond me. Don't give me that shit that because you happen to be married to one of the best cooks on the planet you must have a special diet of gourmet food. Shepherd's Pie down the Three Tuns is alright if you know you are going home to the meals that Rosemary prepares.'

'Thanks to the hours that I have to work here it's the damn dog that gets most of my meals,' said Aitken fully knowing the response that would elicit.

'Are you complaining about the hours? You are probably only a few years from being a Super then you will know what long hours are.'

Purbright was pacing round Aitken's office like a caged animal'

'Have we someone over there yet,' demanded Purbright.

'John Durris is on his way now,' said Aitken. 'I was thinking of sending him to Tenerife to try and get the Spanish Authorities to look into Jones's death. I was going to run it past you first Sir.'

Don't bother Aitken. If these bean counters are to be believed we need to start recycling toilet roll. We cannot afford to put anyone anywhere. I am looking into getting a tandem for the pair of you. The Spanish Authorities only need briefing into the fact that we suspect foul play. They will do their job no problem. I have to get back to this sodding meeting. No more bad news today from any of you or I shall shoot the messenger. Right now I am ready to dine on Administrators and you are on bloody sandwiches Aitken.'

Chapter 41

★ ★ ★ ★

~I am fed up with chasing shadows~

'God help those poor guys from Admin,' said Allen. Looks like you have to trim your wick on your expenses candle. I noticed last night came to a fair bit.'

Yes, I agree Allen, but it was value for money. I most certainly will not be putting Dad's share through on expenses.'

Laura before you go I want some legwork done. That young Anthony Johnson seems switched on. Can you have him go to Salisbury House and check the records for 1935 and 1936? Birth Certificates are numbered sequentially. Even when they ruin one they keep a record. What I want is to see if we can find a missing number in the sequence. If Fanshawe is British, which I suspect he is, there will be a missing record number if he has doctored the files as we suspect. It's a long shot but worth a try. Also see what Fanshawes were around the generation before. Assume the mother was in her twenties so she would have been born in the early part of the twentieth century. If he doctored the records he odds on eliminated his parents as well. I think an exercise in genealogy is called for. Can you organise that please Laura?'

'Yes Sir, right away. By the way Sir overheard Doris in the canteen this morning saying that she had met your father and it was easy to see where you got your good looks from. We are all clubbing together to send Doris to the local opticians.'

'Brilliant Laura,' said Allen.

'Out Laura or I will smack you too,' threatened Aitken.

'I have to put up with this level of threats all the time Laura,' said Allen.

'Let's see what we can unearth,' said Laura. She strode purposefully out of the office her blonde bob gleaming in the office lights.

'I really like her,' said Allen.

'You would, the way she treats me,' said Aitken.

'Actually nothing to do with it Sir but now that you mention it is most certainly another plus, a quite endearing quality. Laura is damned good at her job. She is a real professional.'

'Came up through the ranks did Laura, started in uniform, like myself. She was another Purbright 'acquisition' and he never gets that wrong. Her career has some way to go yet and I think she will go far. Right Allen, we are floundering here.'

'Back on your fish again, Sir. Floundering, flounders, you'll be in amongst Tuna next and not small ones, big ones.'

'You might be taking the mick Allen but you are spot on. I think it is time to go and catch some very large Tuna.'

'Thought you might.'

Aitken was quite impressed. Oh Allen was taking the mick alright about his fishing story but she was still spot on in her assessment of what was going to happen next.

'How would you propose that we catch some large Tuna Allen?'

'How do you catch any fish? Either with a rod or line or by using a net. A rod and line needs bait that the fish is going to take. We have only one small sprat that we can stick on a hook, Perkins. Problem is we must hang on to that sprat; it will be needed to land larger fish. To catch with a net we need to know where we can trawl. Problems all round I would say. They could snap up Perkins and simply leave the hook bare. In netting there is a whole ocean out there that they can hide in. I am open to suggestions Sir.'

'I agree with you Allen, much as I would like to hang Perkins out as bait he has become too precious to risk. No we need to go trawling. Let's get stuck into these so-called Business Development Directors. I am convinced they are part of the round table and every one of them a crook. There are eight of them and we know what parts of the ocean they swim in. Time to do some old fashioned legwork. I envisage a situation where we arrest all eight simultaneously. Let's look across at the accountants and the corporate legal eagles plus the Ops guys. Collins is definitely a

Knight, Ridgeon is nothing more than a Squire to Collins, a loyal retainer.'

'You are confusing me with your mixed metaphors Sir. First we have fish, now we are in Arthurian legend.'

'Right sorry, forget the fish. Let's use Arthurian legend as it is what Fanshawe alluded to with Gawain and the Green Knight. A knight is going to be someone from the inner sanctum and possibly has a direct line to Fanshawe. We need to flush out our information on them and identify whoever else might sit at the Round Table.

Aitken got up and went to the flip chart system in his office. He drew a rough circle and stuck WF at the top. Right, if we take this list that Malcolm Underwood gave us we have the following. Aitken filled in the eight Business Development Directors then round that he put the Operations people to match up.'

'There is no Ops Director for Asia,' said Allen There is Collins but he is CEO Operations. He must be doubling up. He took the phone call from Ridgeon in Rangoon.'

'Right, what other guys have we that we add to this list, two Corporate lawyers, one Company Accountant and one Company Secretary. First pass, some may be innocent, others may have to be added. How many do we have?'

Twenty exactly, plus Fanshawe,' said Allen.

'Well that's the basis for a Round Table.'

'Right Sir, then who is Sir Lancelot. My money is on Collins.'

'Not bad Allen. But there surely isn't a Guinevere or is there?'

'I wouldn't like to guess about that Sir. Let's try and nail these down. How are we going to do it? Share it around the team. We are going to have to be discreet as I reckon if this lot are definitely guilty and dealing drugs and laundering money they are going to be in the crosshairs of a few agencies including our own SOCA. This kind of activity is usually being monitored by someone somewhere.'

'That is a difficult one Allen. I would sort out who is getting what and brief them as best as you can on how not to raise their heads above the parapet. I am sure that the moment Amy got shot there were agencies looking in. We are probably under observation at this moment. Purbright is probably power brokering to try and get a run at this himself. He's no glory hunter or self-promoter and the SOCA guys recognise that. They are so pushed in terms of workload that they will probably be happy to get the groundwork done. I have a little project to attend to so I can leave you to allocate resources and get this going. Do only the Operations and Business Development guys first. I shall see to the Lawyers, the Accountant and the Company Secretary myself. Let's try and give all these mythical creatures some substance. I am fed up with chasing shadows. I shall see you in three hours time back here. Oh can you try and see if Royston is really a figment of the imagination. Has he risen from Wendell Fanshawe to become the split personality?'

At that Aitken's phone went and Allen left his office to start her tasks. It was Aitken's father.

'Hi Dad, have you got news for me on Fanshawe?' Aitken asked his father.

'Hi Dad, have you got news for me on Fanshawe, not how are you? Last night was great. No, straight to the jugular. Well you will be relieved to know that I have dug through our archives, I am covered in dust so I am sticking you with the cleaning bill, but it has been worthwhile I have an address for Wendell Fanshawe near Regent's Park.'

'That is brilliant Dad, just brilliant. I wonder if it was bona fide address at the time.'

'I think it was as I returned his manuscript to it and it was a recorded delivery. Any returned manuscript I returned by recorded delivery. Sometimes back then it was the only copy a writer would have. He must have received it as it never came back and he never phoned or wrote to say he had not received it.'

'That is just great dad; I know it is ages ago but it is worth a visit. I did enjoy last night. So did Doris according to jungle drums this morning. She thought you rather handsome it seems.'

'Well that's rather nice; I must admit I enjoyed her company. I liked your Louise Allen as well, she is razor sharp. I think she would have quite a wicked sense of humour. Anyway hope this helps. I take it Charlie is still coming to see me at the weekend about working in the business.'

'Wild horses couldn't drag him from that meeting.'

'Tell him ten o'clock at the Office. Chris will be there as he pops in most Saturdays.'

'Thanks Dad, I shall pass it on. Talk to you soon. Bye.'

'Bye, Son.

Chapter 42

★ ★ ★ ★

~A Working Girl~

Three hours later Aitken was back in the office meeting with
Allen.

'Are we making any progress?'

'Yes we are Sir, seven so far are not as they seem. They all have
shady pasts and that seven have all used other aliases. As far as I can
determine in the short timeframe we have been working, two have
been inside for fraud. The biggest breakthrough came from
Anthony who has had his nose in the records. A numbered birth
certificate is missing for the twelfth of December Nineteen thirty-
five. The Registrars are very baffled as no explanation exists. They
are equally baffled as to why we were even searching for such an
event and close to seventy-five years ago. He is now trying to see if
this is repeated for what would be Fanshawe's parents. How about
you? Have you made any progress?'

'I have Allen, but progress courtesy of my Dad. He went into
his archives and he actually has an address for Wendell Fanshawe
near Regent's Park and that is where we are going.'

'Did your meeting go well?'

'Yes,'

Allen didn't ask any more. When Aitken didn't want to discuss
something he just clammed up. Doris answered the question as to
what he had been doing. Allen went to the ladies before she went
out and in there was Doris.

'Oh Louise it's you, smashing evening last night. Mr Aitken
Senior is very handsome isn't he, very distinguished. You can see

where young Jeremy gets his looks. I was going to come and see DCI Aitken but it is a bad day for him. Two years ago to the day his partner was executed. I'm sorry I shouldn't really say that as you are the incumbent and God knows I wouldn't want anything to happen to you Louise.'

'It's OK Doris. Aitken took some time out and has just returned. I have a good idea where he may have gone.'

'A graveside near Virginia Water, that's probably where Louise.'

'I couldn't have been that exact Doris but thanks for the nod.'

'Jeremy Aitken changed a lot that day. Last night was the most relaxed I have seen him since that terrible day. I am sure you have contributed largely to that situation. You are good for him Louise, he trusts you.'

'And I him, Doris. Look I have to run, Mr Aitken Senior has given us an old address for Wendell Fanshawe and we are going for a nose around. You never know what can be found under some stones.'

When they got to the address it was a terraced street full of flats.

'This is it, number fifty-five. Flat eleven. That suggests Wendell lived in the top floors. Number eleven was on the fourth floor. A lift had been fitted, albeit a tiny one as it probably had to be shoehorned in to the space available. They knocked on the door of number eleven. A very elegant lady answered it. She was probably Egyptian.

'Aitken apologised for disturbing her and said they were trying to trace someone who had lived there over forty years ago, a Mr Fanshawe.'

I am sorry I cannot help. I have been here over twenty-three years I and cannot remember anyone ever mentioning that name. I took over from a Colin Dyer. Now he had been there for twelve years. That would take you back thirty-five years. Sadly Mr Dyer passed on some ten years ago. Goodness I am not thinking. Next floor up, number fifteen, old Daisy Sims, she has been here forever. She must be in her nineties but her mind is as clear as crystal. She moved in back in nineteen sixty-two, the year I was born. If a Mr Fanshawe stayed here she would know.'

Aitken thanked the lady and they walked up the stairs to number fourteen. They rang the bell and there was a delay until a voice said 'who is that?'

'We are the Police Mrs Sims.'

'If you were the Police you would sodding well know it was Miss Sims and not Mrs Sims. You can piss off or I shall call the real police.'

I am sorry Miss Sims, that was very presumptive of me. I am Detective Chief Inspector Aitken and my colleague is Detective Constable Louise Allen.

'Always the sodding same, a man in the sodding good job. Put your warrant cards to the camera. A person cannot be too careful these days. I don't open my door to just any bugger. Looks like you really are cops.'

'Actually we do not need to come in we simply have a question to ask you about a resident of number eleven in nineteen sixty-six.

'Sixty-six, you are going back a bit aren't you. We won the World Cup that year. Stuck it right up the Gerrys once again. Sodding wonderful, one of the best days of my life. We were round the corner at the Three Cornered Hat. We were pissed as newts by throwing out time. Ten o'clock back then. Number eleven you say in sixty-six. Oh it was that great poofter Fanshawe. A good looking bugger though. Thought he was some Shakespearian actor. RSC, the Royal Shakespeare Company, more like a right silly …sorry I won't say what I was going to say with a young lady there.'

Allen smiled, absolutely nothing politically correct about Daisy Sims, xenophobic, homophobic and probably racially prejudiced.

'I suppose you had better come in.'

There were a number of locks being unlocked and they were expecting to see a little old lady open the door. They were in for a major shock. Daisy Sims was no little old lady. She stood about six feet two and that was in her slippers. She had a huge shock of pure white hair. She extended her hand. 'Daisy Sims, pleased to meet you.' The handshake was strong and firm. Allen was amazed at the strength in the handshake.

'Can I offer you some tea or coffee,' she asked.

'Yes Please, if you can be bothered,' said Aitken.

'I wouldn't be bloody offering you tea and coffee if I couldn't be bothered. Park your arses down; the kettle is never too far off the boil. It's all I sodding do these days, drink bloody tea by the gallon and watch a load of shit on that sodding thing in the corner. Getting old is the pits but the alternative isn't too brilliant either.'

'What did you do when you were working?' asked Louise.

'I was a working girl.'

'Doing what?' asked Louise.

'Christ lassie, you must have had a sheltered upbringing. Tell her Aitken while I make the tea.'

Aitken explained to Louise that a working girl was a euphemism for a prostitute.

'God,' said Allen, 'I feel really stupid.'

Daisy returned with a laden tray.

'Up to speed now are you? Some very important people have had their brains shagged out through that door there, some of your lot, top brass, a couple of Bishops, the second one on referral from the first. Even a cabinet Minister has had happy days with my Fonz through that door. Fonz was my name for what I had downstairs. Happy days alright and I had a ball. I am ninety-six now but I have had a good life. Anyway tuck in, you look like you need a good feed Louise.'

'That was a mistake Miss Sims, she will eat you out of house and home,' said Aitken.

Just call me Daisy, Jeremy. Mind you when I was her age I could eat like a horse. I too was slim back then, mind you though I had bigger tits and a bigger arse than you Louise, which for my chosen profession was an advantage.'

Allen smiled to herself. She wondered what Aitken was making of this old woman.

'The other big problem of living this long is that I have buried both my boys, Richard, that's him on the left passed on two years ago and my Gerald last August. Bit sad really. Their fathers were both long gone. There is just me and my younger sister Adelaide. Don't even ask how she came to be called Adelaide. I think our father had visited it once. Bit of a hazy area. In fact it was a bit of a hazy area when father registered her birth. The haze was an alcoholic one. Anyway she's ninety-four and a right tight arsed cow. Still, she is my sister. She never ever approved of what I did. Anyway I digress. You are interested in Wendell 'the Poofter' Fanshawe. Jesus, was he an affected bugger. I used to love winding him up. Did three appearances in Z cars and I think that was the extent of his acting C.V. I am not sure he was a complete poof. Truth be told I think he swung both ways. As I said he was a good-looking sod. I would have been about twenty years older than him, in my early fifties but as they say many a good tune played on an old fiddle. Twenty years younger or not I would have sat on his face.'

God, thought Allen, I bet Aitken is cringing inside. He is sitting there with a fixed grin on his face.

'Fanshawe stayed for less than a year. Left in the November of sixty-six. Strange thing is that seven years later in June, I remember it well because my Mum passed on that year in the June, a couple of guys from the Inland Revenue, an older guy Leslie and his young sidekick a Mr Hayman. I was on the back foot when they called, Mum had died the week previously. Being a working girl the IR wasn't one of our favourite establishments. I realised quickly that they didn't have a clue about my activities. They were interested in a George Royston, who had given his address as number eleven some eight years previously. The guy they described was Wendell Fanshawe. I didn't straighten their ideas as far as Fanshawe was concerned. There were bits of his anatomy I would liked to have straightened out. Mind you I was retired, a pensioner by then. I would however considered coming out of retirement for one more time with Mr Christopher Hayman. He's probably married to some frumpy ugly bugger. You married to an ugly bugger Aitken because it wouldn't surprise me.'

'Actually quite the opposite Daisy. Our Detective Chief Inspector here is married to the celebrity cook Rosemary Aitken. This tea is beautiful. A tippy tea isn't it?'

'Well done Louise as least your sheltered upbringing has not been wasted. I made a fortune screwing and the upside is that it affords you the finer things in life. I still take two good holidays a year, Saint Lucia and Singapore last year. I love Singapore because I am so bloody tall they look at me like I am some goddess. I deliberately wear high heels. First time I went there I thought they regarded me as some sort of freak then I came to realise it was sodding respect they were paying me. They are so polite anyway. I just love the place. Yes, it buys me the finer things in life. I have a couple of gold plated Rampant Rabbits.'

Aitken sat there straight-faced.

'Christ you are a tight arse Aitken. That was a joke the Rampant Rabbits. Married to that delectable lady and working with this stunner you should be the happiest sod on the sodding planet. Lighten up man. This isn't a dress rehearsal; you are a long time dead. Anyway that is all I know about Wendell Fanshawe. I know it isn't much but it was a bloody long time ago.'

'Daisy, let me assure you that what you have given us was

absolutely amazing. To recall that kind of information from forty odd years ago is just fantastic. I cannot thank you enough,' said Aitken

'Well a gold plated…'

Aitken smiled a broad grin.

'That's an awful lot better Jeremy. Problem is I can remember every detail of what happened forty years ago. I get up to go to the cupboard and I cannot remember what the hell it was I got up to get forty seconds before.'

They said their goodbyes and headed the car back to Railton.

Chapter 43

★ ★ ★ ★

~*We can catch a person*~

'Well that was definitely different Sir,' said Allen.
'You can say that again. Daisy Sims is literally larger than
life. What a character. You couldn't help but like her. We did
extremely well out of that visit. So did you Allen, hoovered up
some poor old lady's cakes. That was probably her month's
supply.'

'In your dreams Aitken, did you clock the stuff that was lying
around. The little nick knacks were extremely expensive ones.
That painting on the wall was an original. That painting alone was
worth probably three to four hundred… thousand that is. Daisy
Sims must have done some amount of horizontal jogging to fund
her expensive tastes.'

'I just hope that Christopher Hayman is still alive. He might be
an interesting chat. I wonder why they were coming after Royston.
God do you see the time? Another day bites the dust.'

The phone rang, it was Laura. Aitken put her on speaker.

'Anthony has had a good day. He found the missing entry for
nineteen thirty-five. In nineteen thirty-three there are two entries
three months apart missing. Twenty-eight years earlier in nineteen
seven another entry is missing. In nineteen hundred another one
and in nineteen thirty-six another entry is missing. He decided that
he would come forward and sure enough in nineteen forty another
record is missing. Anthony thinks that nineteen hundred is the
birth of the father of Wendell. The mother was likely born
nineteen seven, odds on her death was in nineteen forty. The

nineteen thirty-three entry he reckons was a short-lived sibling. Nineteen thirty six is Wendell's father's death.'

'That is a helluva piece of deduction if it is to prove correct.'

'Give Anthony his due he went back even further and in eighteen seventy one up pops an Albert Fanshawe living in Rotherhithe in the East End. Genealogical research and Anthony came up with a Francis Fanshawe born in nineteen hundred. Albert had no more issue as his wife died giving birth to Francis. Anthony now jumped over to the records from the Great War. Francis Fanshawe served in the Great War and he was badly injured on the ninth April nineteen seventeen at the Battle of Vimy Ridge. His wife was Elspeth Fanshawe and she resided in Rotherhithe. Anthony then went and researched the records for the blitz and in particular the East End. In October nineteen forty a local Hall in Rotherhithe took a direct hit. On the stage at the time was a well-known singer in the East End, Elspeth Fanshawe. She was killed instantly. Her son Wendell was placed in the care of a local woman. The report mentioned that poor Wendell was now an orphan as he had lost his father in nineteen thirty six as a result of injuries he sustained in the Great War.'

'Laura that is nothing short of amazing.'

'I must admit Sir pretty impressive. Anthony has done well. Wendell Fanshawe is British and he comes from the East End. George Royston came from Highgate.'

'Laura, you have our undivided attention.'

'Fanshawe borrowed his new identity from someone that died about five months before he was born. George Royston was stillborn and his poor mother died in childbirth. Both are buried in Highgate cemetery. Fanshawe borrowed Royston's identity. He expunged the records as far as death certificates were concerned. Here he made his first mistake. He didn't allow for an anorak, one that compiled complete records of all the cemeteries in London going back as far as cemeteries have kept records. Trawl through this and you kick up George Royston.'

'Laura that is truly fantastic work, we needed some breaks. That is a serious piece of research and well worth it. We actually have been to where he lived in nineteen sixty six.'

'At least he is a person Sir. We can catch a person. We cannot catch a shadow.'

'That is ever so true Laura. Catch him we shall. What have the television reports been like?'

'Do not go there Sir. The Super is like a bear with a sore, well lets call a spade a spade, he is like a bear with a sore arse. The Governor at the nick where Perkins and Clyde are incarcerated is as slippery as an eel. Nothing is his fault. He is pointing the finger at everyone but himself. Trouble is John Durris is giving the Governor one hellish time. The Governor even tried to get Purbright to remove him because he was so hostile. Purbright said he would remove John but he would himself take John's place. The Governor declined that offer. The Super was dead chuffed with John's performance.'

'I bet he bloody declined Purbright coming in John's place. There are few people in authority who do not know about Purbright. I look forward to the news tonight. Laura, you guys have done amazing work, get home and we shall all meet up in the morning and take it from there.'

'Goodnight Sir,' and Laura rang off.

'Well Sir you too must be well chuffed with John Durris. I never thought he would say boo to a goose.'

'I think that only extends as far as Purbright. Do not worry about Durris, he is another Purbright hand picked job.'

'Will Rosemary be back home before you Sir?'

'No I think it will be about nine o'clock before she gets in. Are you doing anything tonight?'

'No I am on my own tonight. Jonathon is in France until Friday night. I might give my pal Amanda a call and see if she going to the gym.'

'Then you go to the pub I assume.'

'Yes, our training regime does include the odd hostelry.'

'Thought it might.'

Chapter 44

★ ★ ★ ★

~A Skill's Set~

That night at home Aitken heated up all the food that Rosemary had left. He went into the hall and shouted 'Amelie, Charlie, dinner is ready.'

Amelie came in and sat down in a couple of minutes. Charlie followed about five minutes later.

'Not like you to be last at the trough Charlie.'

'Mum's not cooking, you are.'

'Ah well that's where you are wrong. Mum actually did the cooking. I only had to heat it up. Even I can manage that.'

'Are you sure Dad?' said Charlie.

'Keep that up son and I shall forget to give you the message about your interview Saturday morning.'

'What do you mean interview? I thought I was just going there to arrange when I was starting at what I was doing during the holidays and how much I was being paid.'

'That is more than a little bit presumptive. Chris is giving you a formal interview. He will examine your skills set and see if it is worthwhile taking you on board.'

'What are you talking about, skills set?'

'Exactly as I say, you cannot undertake any task without having a skills set that allows you to perform the task.'

'Ah Bruv, you are just about to be rumbled. Chris is going to need a magnifying glass to find a skills set in Charlie Aitken. What you know about publishing you could probably write on your thumbnail.'

'I do so.'

'Well let's hope that your author's grammar is better than yours, otherwise you are in trouble.'

'Amelie, please stop winding your brother up.'

'And you haven't been winding him up, have you?' said Amelie.

'I thought I was actually going to acquire a skills set through training. I thought that was what was behind this work experience,' said Charlie.

'That is exactly what it is you are going to be doing. Ten o'clock Saturday morning with Granddad and Chris.

Later they were sitting watching television when Rosemary walked in.

'Hi gang, I'm home.'

'Good day Honey?' asked Aitken.

'Actually it was, I love Edinburgh and it was a nice sunny day. Cool when you are out of the sun. Planes were on time and we had a successful meeting. I had a most fantastic lunch in a restaurant just beside the Castle.'

'High praise indeed coming from you.'

'Hey, I am not that difficult to cook for. I am a good cook but there are many better out there.'

'Well I have yet to come across them.'

'You would say that Jeremy, you are biased. However this lunch was seriously top drawer. Have these two done their homework?'

'Yes Mum,' chorused the two children.'

'How was your day? Rosemary asked.

'A bit like the Curate's egg I am afraid. Bad, really bad in parts at the start but good at the end of the day.'

'That's better than the other way around,' said Amelie.

'We interviewed the most amazing woman this afternoon. Ninety-six and as sharp as a lance. She tried to tell us she was getting forgetful. She was a working girl in her earlier life.'

'What did she work at?' asked Charlie.

'She was a prostitute Bruv,' said Amelie.

'Do not worry Charlie, Allen asked exactly the same question when she said she was a working girl. How do you know that anyway Amelie?'

'I read, I watch TV. Pretty ghastly thing to do though.'

'Well I think she did it through choice and she must have been very good at her profession as she had some seriously expensive stuff in her apartment. She had a painting on the wall that Allen reckons is at least worth three hundred thousand.'

Half an hour later Rosemary said 'right you two it's late, off to bed the pair of you.'

'Good night' said Amelie. As she kissed her Mum she whispered in her ear. 'I enjoyed sitting there talking as a family, especially about grown up things.'

'So did I' said her Mum.

Charlie said, 'What if I fail the interview Saturday morning? What if I do not have enough of a skills set? What happens then?'

'Son,' said Jeremy, 'I do not think you will be failing the interview. I wouldn't worry about that.'

'What's this Jeremy? Charlie is going for a meeting about working at his Granddad's on Saturday. When did it become an interview?'

'Dad said it was an interview and I needed a skills set to get the job. I could possibly not get the job.'

'Good grief Darling, of course you'll get to work at your Granddad's. That is not even in question.'

'Well Dad said I needed a skills set and Amelie said I had no chance as I have no skills whatsoever. I am worried now that I might not be taken on.'

'Look you, get to bed. I'll sort your father out now.'

As Charlie hugged his Dad goodnight he whispered in his ear. 'That's for winding me up earlier on. See, I do have some skills.'

You little bugger thought Jeremy, you have dropped me in it with your Mum. He had to smile though.

As Charlie left, Rosemary said what are you smiling about? I do not think that making Charlie think it was an interview was very funny.'

'I'll tell you what I am smiling about. Our son has got skills alright and he has just used them on me.'

He told Rosemary how he had just been mugged. She laughed. 'Well you got your just desserts there. They are growing up.'

She told Jeremy what Amelie had whispered in her ear.

'Yes they are definitely growing up. At least it's good that they are happy to sit and talk with us. Problem is that it is going to be a tough world out there for these youngsters. I might have been joking with Charlie about a skills set but it will be necessary for them all in the future. Anyway they have gone to bed, come over here and sit beside me.'

'Yes Master, your obedient servant shall do your bidding.'

'Don't you start winding me up. One son doing it is enough.'

'Oh Diddums is in need of some TLC then,' said Rosemary as she snuggled up to Aitken.

'Oh you don't need to go the whole hog with TLC, I'll settle for just the TL.'

'Oh I'm sure you would,' Rosemary laughed that throaty laugh that Jeremy loved.

Chapter 45

★ ★ ★

~A Knight unseated~

Aitken's mobile rang at four forty five am. It was Railton, the Sergeant on the night desk.

Sorry to disturb you but there has been an incident that you might want to get involved in. Uniformed were called to an incident, the address of which is one Philip Ridgeon. They have just called back in to say they need the CID as it is a murder. The owner of the property has been murdered.

'Thanks I do want to be involved. Problem is it is not on my patch. Phone Purbright and brief him. He'll get clearance for me to attend. Phone Allen and tell her to meet me there. No, instead tell her to get ready and I shall pick her up in thirty.'

Thirty minutes later Aitken was at Allen's door. He was about to ring the door when she opened it with a coffee in one hand.'

'Sorry about this. We need to cover this. I think a knight has just been unseated.'

'No problem Sir, can you pull my door shut?'

'Why can't you?'

'My hands are full.' She just picked up a bunch of toast and armed with her coffee she walked past Aitken.

'I suppose you now expect me to open the door and let you into my car so that you spread a heap of crumbs all over my car.'

'I would think under the circumstances it is the gentlemanly thing to do. Especially after awakening a lady from her beauty sleep.'

'Lord knows you need it.'

'I was going to offer to share my toast but I think it will be my coffee you get. Over your head that is if you keep coming up with comments like that. I am well aware I may not be at my buffed and polished best at this time of the morning. I do not need reminding.'

'You look ravishing Allen, simply ravishing.'

'And you are so close to this coffee all over you. By the way I thought Ridgeon was simply a Squire.'

'I think I may have underestimated his position. He sat at the Round Table.'

When they got to Ridgeon's house there was a number of police cars there. When they got to the Police lines they asked the uniformed officer who was in charge. 'Roy Moss,' said the uniformed, 'he is inside.'

'Thank God,' muttered Aitken. 'Roy is one if the good guys.'

When they got inside the murder scene was in the bedroom. There wasn't just one murder. Ridgeon had been murdered, as had his wife.

They met Roy Moss on the landing.

Hello Jeremy, Hi Louise. My super said you were coming.

Hello Roy, apart from this, how are things going?'

'Actually, not bad at all Jeremy. When we got that bunch of scumbags that was the Desmond gang locked up we have had a little bit of a breather. Now this and I believe you have some interest in this guy here.'

'Yes we do. He was the paymaster for that Amy Anderson execution.'

'Hellish business, that poor lass. Then you have the Clyde guy knocked off in prison. That tells me you are dealing with some real heavy dudes. This was very much a pro job. They used two guys, a single shot through the head in each case. Silencers were used.

The departed are in here, not a very pretty sight. Nothing has been moved.

When they walked in Ridgeon and his wife were lying naked on top of their bed. Their pillows were soaked in blood.

'Fit bugger isn't he? or was! Well hung as well. She has false boobs and loads of liposuction. He has had an appendectomy sometime. That mark in his shoulder is another bullet entry hole from an earlier fracas. Have you checked this guy out because there is something strange about their records? His documents all say he is forty-one. He is fit but probably nearer fifty. She is supposed to be thirty-eight. She is more plastic than my bloody car. She will never see forty-eight again never mind thirty-eight. I would say she is older than him. She has spent some serious money to look like that. What tells me it was professional is that you will notice there are no powder marks on the victims and they have even policed their bullets. They dug the bullets out of the headboard, both bullets. Our forensic guys do not have high hopes of any DNA.

'Well I know who organised the hit but I have no chance of proving it. This guy was simply eliminated by his own boss for making a cock up in Amy Anderson's execution. His boss is John Collins and he is ADI's CEO for Operations. Our last known location for Collins was Rangoon. We think Collins is also an alias of an Australian drug dealer. You know as much as me Roy and even if you chase it down you will be unable to prove it.'

'Thanks for letting me know Jeremy. Saves a lot of bloody time just even knowing that. I take it this guy Collins was behind the lassie's death.'

'I think he gave the orders but we think someone above him gave him the nod. We think there is a Mr Big. Problem is, he is like a will of the wisp.'

'I think Jeremy, this guy probably got what he deserved so we can leave our Supers to work out the protocol of how we deal with this. I shall keep you posted with forensic and PM reports.'

'If they used silencers, how come the alarm was raised?' asked Allen.

'Simple, they got greedy. There is a wall safe in the downstairs study. They thought they would pilfer it. Damned thing is alarmed and much louder than the main alarm. Unable to kill the alarm they had to scarper. Complaining neighbour called about the racket and here we all are. We had as big a problem as them killing the damned alarm.'

'I sure as hell would like to see what is in that safe.'

'When we get it open we shall let you know.

'Thanks Roy,'

'Notice anything on our friend Ridgeon. He has a tiny tattoo on his left shoulder. It is a Tree of Life on a quartered shield. There are two quarters in light blue and two in purple. The Tree of Life is on the top right hand corner.'

'Why is that significant Louise?'

'I am not sure, I think it is possibly heraldic and might be a badge of office. Short of turning him over I will be very surprised if he has any more tattoos. That is a discreet tattoo, not one he wants to show off.'

'Interesting theory Allen, you think this lot are all going to have shields with a tattoo of the Tree of Life.'

'Possibly, but they might not all be the same colour. I am sure this is a heraldic use. The problem is I know zilch on heraldry.'

'You are not alone there Allen,' said Aitken. 'I think and I hasten to add think, that Azure or blue is loyalty and purple is Sovereignty. Does that mean loyal to the sovereign. I really do not know but the Tree of Life in Arthurian terms or Christian terms would be the interpretation that the Tree of Life was, as in the Garden of Eden, able to bestow eternal life. That said there are masses of interpretations of the Tree of Life in lots of different cultures.'

'You two talk in a different language,' said Roy. 'Obviously it works. There is no way I could ever have made any of that significance from a tattoo. If that is all you both want we'll bag and tag them for Post Mortem. I take it we will send their computers to Mal and Jo Jo. Hopefully they will get everything done by the end of the month. They are going to be out of circulation for three weeks. They are getting married in Mauritius. If she goes off to have family she is going to be a massive miss. She's the brains in that department and that is saying something as Mal is quite brilliant.'

'That's good Roy. Fancy a bit of breakfast somewhere. There's nothing more we can do here, we cannot bring them back to life. We know who ordered the hit. We do not know who carried it out but I can put money on it being Eastern European. You can check all flights for people who came in from the Eastern Bloc and who are flying back out now. Problem is they probably both came in as second men on HGVs but you can bet they do not have HGV licences. They will likely be going out on the Chunnel. You can always arrest them on a technicality, problems with their passport, documentation, whatever.'

'I think I shall give that a whirl Jeremy. Jack can you come here a moment.'

Roy briefed his man.

Chapter 46

★ ★ ★ ★

~I think that was air brakes~

'Right,' said Roy Moss, 'about this breakfast. I am sure Louise is up for food. I would be very surprised if she wasn't.

'Ah Allen your fame spreads before you, not so much a gourmet Roy, more a gourmand our Louise.'

'I really am going to smack you if you mention me and food in the same sentence again. You Roy Moss are in the crosshairs as well.'

'Oops Roy I think we had better tread carefully. Our Detective is maybe not a morning person.'

'There's absolutely nothing wrong with me in the morning, nothing that getting you two off my case wouldn't cure. Right Aitken, after that you are paying.'

'You do have to hanker for the good old days Roy. Yes, you really have to hanker for those days Roy. Those bygone times, times when the junior officers had to show some respect. Quite a bit of touching of the forelock, we knew our place back then.'

'You have it one Jeremy, sadly I must confess, your recollections are all too true.'

'What a complete pair of bullshit artists. I certainly cannot see you touching the forelock Aitken and I do not think you would either Roy Moss.'

Both Aitken and Moss laughed and Roy said, 'You might well be right at that Louise, you just might be right at that. Right we need to find a trough? This little piggy is starving.'

They had a very good breakfast in a Transport café that Roy

knew. Just as they were paying their bill Aitken's phone rang. Purbright was on the line. Aitken put it on the speaker.

'In the lack of an update, can I take it you lot are feeding your faces in some greasy spoon. You were supposed to get free information from Roy Moss not pay for it. I take it he is probably there.'

The laughter in the background told Purbright he was right.

'Get me off that stupid speaker thing and Moss you pay for your own bloody breakfast irrespective of however much assistance you have given us.'

'I can't Sir; Jeremy has already paid for us all. All my guys are here, Sorry that was sexist, all my guys and gals are here. We all appreciate the generosity of Railton. You will be the first to receive the forensics and the PM reports.'

'If you have stood that rabble from Coldwater breakfast, let me tell you that I will not be passing that particular expense, in fact, your arse will be in the shredder. And talking about arses you two get your collective ones in here as fast as you can. I take it I am off that bloody loudspeaker because Roy's a good guy and so is his Super but his top brass is a complete and utter waste of space. He is about the most pompous git going. He is the ultimate complete arsehole. He must not get wind of our co-operation.'

Roy Moss started to laugh and attempted to choke the laugh with his hands. What came out was a high-pitched squeak.

'What was that noise?' demanded Purbright.

Aitken switched off the speaker. I'm not sure Sir; we really are at a transport greasy spoon. I think maybe air brakes but not certain. Moss by now had the giggles and he had started Louise Allen as well. They had to go outside and when Aitken caught up with them they both had tears running down their cheeks.

'Sorry,' said Roy. 'We just lost it there. The air brakes, that was brilliant. Look I had better get back to my camp, I will keep you posted. I have been well warned not to let Pendleton know about our arrangement. My Super has the same opinion as Purbright has about Pendleton.'

Chapter 47

★ ★ ★ ★

~A meeting of the Round Table~

Back at Railton the two sat down in Purbright's office.
'What the hell possessed you to pay for breakfast for that bunch of vultures?'

'I didn't Sir, that was only Roy Moss winding you up. I only paid for Allen's breakfast that is all. Roy paid for his own breakfast.'

'So he was winding me up, that's OK Mr Moss, that's OK.'

Allen thought, Roy you are in the shit. Purbright is about to get even.

'Right you two brief me. Give me some good news before I go and meet the media vultures. This Prison poisoning business isn't going to disappear in a hurry. Fortunately the G8 meeting takes place tomorrow so I am hoping that slides us off the front page. That creep, the Ponytail Express from the Mercury was there yesterday. The sod asks the most difficult questions. I have to hand it to him on that score. Problem is I simply cannot stand the guy. These sodding bean counters are still here. They want us to have a greater efficiency, a higher collar rate and all of that with a five point seven percentage reduction in our budget. We topped the performance lists overall in the last three years. We catch more bloody thieves than any other Manor and they want us to cut costs. They are on a different bloody planet.'

'I have yet to find someone yet that likes Don Sullivan. He is married and has two children in their teens, so I suppose someone loves him,' said Aitken.

Aitken and Allen brought Purbright up to speed.

'Good work by young Johnson. A bit of initiative there,' purred Purbright.

'Spoke to Anthony last night to see if he had rooted anything else out. He attributed the success to guidance by Laura. He might be over egging the pudding as I think he has a thing for the lovely Laura. Likes the older woman obviously.'

'What do you mean older woman, Laura and I are exactly the same age,' said Allen.

'Then you can understand exactly what I meant about the older woman.'

'I shall talk to you later Sir.'

Purbright looking at his customary spot on the wall had a little smile just puckering the edges of his mouth.

'I believe Durris has made a breakthrough as well,' said Aitken.

'Yes he has. He has kept them all up all night at the prison. Seems our Governor had revolutionary ideas for cutting costs. He outsourced the food supply for the prison. The contractor seemingly put in new guys on Monday. They arrived with paperwork covering their contract with the outsourcer. The contractor cannot contact these people nor knows anything about them. The four regulars have also disappeared and that is a concern. We have obviously got good CCTV on them but after the masks that they used at Amy's murder they could be doing the same. According to the trusties only one was a Londoner. One was possibly American or Canadian. You can have a look at them on CCTV but I doubt if it will help. Anyway I have news for you. ADI are holding an extraordinary meeting of the Board and their Operations guys. I would suspect that events of the past two weeks have stirred things up. I would surmise that the death of Ridgeon will be a method of focusing the minds of the rest.'

'Where is this meeting taking place Sir?' asked Allen

'Ah, there is the rub Detective, it is in Singapore, in one of the luxury hotels there.'

'That's a bit of a pity Sir. I should like to have been a fly on the wall at that meeting.'

'That is exactly what I want you to be. The budget is shot for this year so we might as well be hung for a sheep as a lamb. That was one of Dunbar's saying. He once told me that there is a town in the North of Scotland, which I have forgotten the name of; where they were due to hang a sheep stealer called MacPherson. They got wind of the fact that a pardon looked like coming through so during the night they put the Town Hall clock forward an hour. The guy was due to hang at midday. They duly hung MacPherson and his pardon arrived long before the actual hour of twelve had been reached. He had heaps of these stories. Banff, no MacDuff, I remember it now, that was the place. How true it was I know not but it was a great story. I want you to get on a plane to Singapore to get everything you can on this meeting. I suggest you equip yourself well before you go. We obtained a few little gadgets, which were left behind at Andersons, and we need to see how good they might be. I have managed to actually come by some identical devices from a friend of mine. They will be waiting for you at your hotel.'

'When is this meeting Sir.'

'Friday at the Ascot Park Hotel in Singapore start 09.00 hrs sharp. Dress Lounge suits and ties. I know you have been up early but I want you to get out there later today.'

'Going east is more difficult on the body clock than going west,' said Aitken.

'Nearly eleven hours Sir so you can sleep on the plane. It will be morning when you arrive,' said Allen.

'That is when you both arrive. You are not sitting here twiddling your thumbs Detective Allen. You are going with him. Somebody needs to rein in his spending. Aitken, a five star hotel and an expenses account, no I need a governor in engine terms to slow things or a governess in behaviour terms to make him behave himself. You are on Singapore Airlines today. I hope we get a solid lead on Wendell Fanshawe.'

'We will just have a quick look at the prison CCTV stuff before we go Sir,' said Aitken.

'Feel free, you never know, you might just know someone.'

As they walked down the corridor from Purbright's office Aitken said, 'Seems the Round Table is going to meet and we are going to eavesdrop.'

'I would have thought that might not be as straightforward as it sounds.'

'No Allen, I don't suppose it will be. At least we have the opportunity to give it a try.'

Chapter 48

★ ★ ★ ★

~Another Knight~

They sat down to watch the CCTV from the prison. A camera was actually placed in the kitchens. The four contractor personnel appeared and they changed from their street clothes to the chef's clothes for serving the prisoners' breakfast. They could see the faces of the four of them no problem. They could see them obviously talking as they changed.

'Stop,' shouted Allen.

'What have you seen?

'Go back to that last guy getting into his chef's whites or whatever they call them.

That's far enough, now watch the guy. Here he is stripping off his shirt. See anything of interest Sir?'

'My God Allen, what a spot. The shield with the Tree of Life and I would swear it is exactly as the late Philip Ridgeon's one. Dave, can you run that back and when you catch a glimpse and that is all it is, try and freeze on the tattoo.'

'No probs Sir. There you are.'

'Can you zoom in Dave?'

'Yes, anything you like.'

'Dead ringer Allen. The club has a badge and I am sure it has Heraldic undertones.

This is a Ridgeon equivalent and odds on an operations guy. Malcolm's HR employee list for ADI did not have photographs. I am pretty positive they have no masks. This guy is identifiable. This is a big mistake by them.'

'At that moment Purbright poked his head around the corner. a message from Roy Moss. They took your advice and they are holding two lorry drivers and their so-called banksmen at Dover. The funny thing is the banksmen did not come in on the wagons. They flew in from Tbilisi and arrived in the UK twenty four hours before the Lorries came in.'

'What's a banksman?' asked Allen.

'Basically a lorry driver's assistant who helps when reversing and things like that,' said Purbright. I told Roy to strip them of their clothes and check for powder residue. I would almost guarantee one or both will have powder residue. We may even get lead particles if they haven't used one of these new green bullets. We have once again used the terrorist card. I told Roy to tell them we will hand them over to the American agencies and they could then expect a small flight to somewhere and a far more intensive interrogation. I reckon that will have the lorry drivers at least wetting themselves.'

'What is a green bullet?' asked Allen.

'Oh, they are getting rid of lead in bullets these days. Lead is bad for you. There is now a new range of bullets that are non-lead. Still kill you but you do not get lead poisoning,' said Aitken. Anyway Sir we have a little break here as well. Our guys have made a serious mistake. Eagle eyes Allen here spotted something of extreme interest. You got that print out ready Dave. Thanks. Take a look at this tattoo Sir, exactly the same as the one on the late Philip Ridgeon. Allen's Arthurian style Round Table is gathering momentum. This is probably another Knight.'

'Yes she might just be right. Big thing is this bugger is identifiable. We know that he is more than likely an ADI employee. Dave, get me as many pictures as you can of this guy from these tapes and I shall see if we can give him a name. You two watch your time. I don't want to spend money on fares that haven't been used.'

Chapter 49

★ ★ ★ ★

~A Fellow Traveller~

Two hours later Aitken and Allen were sitting in the departure lounge of Singapore Airlines.

'Glad to sit down, that was a rush. Have you been to Singapore before Allen?'

'No Thailand is the nearest I have come. Have you been before Sir?'

Yes but it was along time ago. A stopover on the way to Australia and that was only because of some technical problem with the plane. We were a bunch of students at the time. Qantas offered some fantastic deal to go walkabout. Six of us went down, five came back eight weeks later.'

'That sounds like tragedy struck.'

'No Allen, it wasn't anything like that. Neil Banks loved the place so much he stayed. He actually finished his degree in Sydney. As far as I know he is still there to this day. The annual Christmas card dried up a few years back. By then he had married a local girl and they had two young boys. He studied bio-chemistry at Oxford and I think the last time he sent a Christmas card he had gone back to University but this time as a lecturer.'

'Looks like we are on our way Sir, that's our flight being flashed up. My Jonathon swears by Singapore Airlines. He says that you get the finest of service.'

'Probably something to do with these beautiful stewardesses they have.'

'Down boy, you are a happily married man.'

'I know that, but you have to admit to the accuracy of the observation.'

'I'll give you that and it probably does influence Jonathon's thinking. They are all so damned graceful in those dresses. They don't seem to walk; they look like they are gliding across the ground.

'Not like you, you big horse.'

Talking of horses, keep up that kind of talk and you will be a gelding.'

'Ouch, shall we catch a plane. Glide on, I shall follow.'

Allen said nothing, she just glared at Aitken.

Aitken kind of wished he hadn't said big horse to Allen. His humour had backfired slightly as it was actually furthest from the truth. Allen was quite tall and she had lovely posture. She was very graceful when she moved. She might have been joking about the gelding bit but there was a bit of edge to it as well. Better just watch my step he thought.

They had just got on to the plane and they were just about to go up into Business Class when a stewardess came out of First Class and Aitken had a brief glance in. In the brief opening of the curtain to First Class he got a shock to see a tall man he recognised about to hand his jacket to a stewardess. He recognised him all right as he had seen him only a few hours earlier on CCTV. He was one of the four 'Chefs' on the prison video. Prison Chefs must be very well paid to be able to fly First Class to Singapore. Even Rosemary who was a celebrity Chef would think twice about that kind of money. She was just too practical.

'Aitken asked the Stewardess, 'Is it OK if I make an urgent mobile phone call? I am a Police Officer.' He showed her his Warrant Card.

'No problem,' she replied, 'we are still on the ground and not moving anyway.'

Aitken immediately phoned Purbright.

'You are never going to guess who is in First Class as a fellow traveller on this flight.'

'Probably your prison Chef. If he is a 'Knight' he is probably heading for this meeting.'

Purbright's response momentarily knocked the wind out of Aitken's sails. He recovered quickly.

'Shall I arrest him Sir or are you going to let him travel on?'

'He's not travelling anywhere. I have him on CCTV and I have him still in the UK. You sit down; have a nice glass of Champagne. Enjoy that because it doesn't show up on expenses. No I shall get my tail down there and arrest him myself. I'll need to get this flight held.'

'Good luck Sir, it is due to take off in twenty-three minutes. Keep me posted.'

'You are dead sure it is him?'

'Positive, Sir.'

'Good, then he's mine.'

Aitken sat down beside Allen who had the window seat.

'What happened to you? I was beginning to wonder if I was going to be on my own.'

Aitken relayed what had happened. He said that Purbright was going to hold back the flight and come and personally arrest this guy.

'This I got to see.'

'Fifteen minutes later the plane was reversing back from the gantry.

'Looks like Purbright didn't managed to get us stopped Sir.'

'I must admit I am surprised. That guy can pull in more favours than anyone I know.'

The plane was taxiing across the apron when it suddenly slowed down and came to a halt.

'The Captain came on and announced, 'Captain Lee here. I am sorry to announce that we shall have a short delay to our departure to Singapore. We have a small technical issue that has to be resolved. I would expect to be getting clearance in about thirty minutes. Fortunately there is a strong upper jet stream so we would expect to make up the time and we should be touching down in Singapore on schedule.'

Allen from her seat could see a set of steps being towed to the plane.

'Looks like something is happening, he might just have managed it.'

Ten minutes later Allen said' Oh my God, look out the window. It's the Super, Laura and Mike heading to the steps. How the hell has he got here this quick?'

'He could only have got here by helicopter, no other way.'

Five minutes later they saw Purbright, Laura and Mike take

their 'Knight' away to a now waiting Police vehicle.

Captain Lee came on and apologised for the short delay. 'We now have the all clear and we shall shortly be underway to Singapore. Our flight time is an estimated twelve hours and twelve minutes. We shall be cruising at an altitude of thirty nine thousand feet or eleven thousand eight hundred and eighty eight metres.'

A stewardess came and passed a note to Aitken.

'Mr Aitken this for you.'

'Thank you.'

The note was from Purbright.

Good spot, this is our man alright. That should cause a ripple or two in the Singapore meet. This guy is a George Vitra and according to your list, Operations Director for Russia. As far as we can ascertain he is actually an Afghan national of mixed descent. Will keep you posted on developments. Purbright.

'Tell you what Allen I don't fancy being in Vitra's shoes for the next few hours.'

'No I don't suppose it will be a picnic. The thing is I think these so called 'Knights' will be as tough as they come. They will probably all come from the wrong side of the tracks and they shall be career criminals, soldier mercenaries, guys of that nature. The common denominator is that they are all going to be tough as old boots.'

Chapter 50

★ ★ ★ ★

~A No Show~

The flight was as good as it get for a long haul flight and they arrived in Singapore exactly on schedule as Captain Lee had predicted. He wasn't just good at predictions but he was rather good at flying as well. The landing was cushion soft.

Allen said, 'It is amazing how they put something this big on the ground like that. You hardly felt it touch the ground. How you feeling Sir?'

'Alright, how about you?' asked Aitken.

'Surprisingly quite good,' said Allen.

As they walked through the airport to the passport check area, Aitken's phone was starting to pick up messages from Purbright.

'It's from Purbright, our man was George Vitra.'

'Oh the Operations Director for Russia,' said Allen.

'The same, seemingly he is an Afghan national and according to Purbright he is proving a tough nut to crack. He is finding it hard to slide out from under the fact that Purbright holds some excellent CCTV footage on him. Purbright knows that it is only a matter of time a high-powered lawyer appears to try and get bail for Vitra. Purbright is obviously fighting that bail.'

Through Customs and walking to their baggage collection Allen was completely impressed with how beautiful Changi Airport was. There were orchids everywhere.

'This has got to be one of the most beautiful airports in the world.'

'Yes, I must admit it is none too shabby.'

As they collected their baggage and cleared customs they went out to where a limousine driver was waiting for them with Aitken and Allen on a card. Five metres to their man's left another guy, in a chauffeur's uniform stood with a card saying Vitra.

'Well the situation is still not known this end,' said Aitken.

'Looks that way, that said, it should now become apparent something is up,' said Allen.

'I would have thought that one of his buddies would have been here to meet and greet.'

'Perhaps as a Knight you are expected to look after yourself,' said Allen.

'Could be, maybe he has a squire somewhere that does for him. Just not here it seems.'

'As a knight he could also have a horse just like someone else.'

'Ouch, I suppose I deserved that,' said Aitken. 'Even you must know it was an attempt at humour. You do not need me to tell you how graceful you are in reality. You are a swan and I am sure you know it. Anyway you are probably rubbish at accepting a compliment so I am going to shut up.'

'I think you had better. Do you think that chauffeur is an ADI employee or is he just an executive hire.'

The sudden change of topic told Aitken the matter was closed. He was very relieved.

'They do not have an office here. I would think he is just the same as our guy. Drugs and Singapore do not mix so it is a slightly odd choice of meeting place for what is a bunch of people involved in drug trafficking. Possibly appeals to Fanshawe's sense of humour. Hold a meeting about drug peddling in a place completely opposed to it. I think we will hang about just to see what he does. Tell our guy to hold on. I shall see how long this guy hangs about.'

Two minutes later Allen came over with their driver. The two drivers exchanged words in their own language.

Allen explained, 'I just told our driver here that we know of Mr Vitra and that he didn't make the flight. I said we were policemen and that Vitra was a drug dealer. Our man here is Jithu, a family man and one who detests drugs. This other driver here is his brother Zafran. If you want he shall call in and announce that Mr Vitra didn't make the flight so you can listen in on the radio.'

'I would be interested in listening to that provided Zafran is comfortable with that.'

'No problem Mr Jeremy,' said Zafran. I shall call Mr Collins's PA that Mr Vitra is not on the plane and let us see what happens.'

'What I would like to get across to Collins is that Mr Vitra was arrested and removed from the plane in London before it took off.'

'I have no problem with that either Mr Jeremy.'

He dialled a number that he had. A woman's voice answered, 'Nadine Kraft.'

'Hello Miss Kraft. Can you transfer me to Mr Collins please? There has been a problem with picking up Mr Vitra.'

'Why do you want to talk to Mr Collins about Mr Vitra? I am Mr Collins's Personal Assistant and you can discuss anything about Mr Vitra with me.'

'No, I do not think so, this is a man thing and I feel I should only speak with my employer who in this case is Mr Collins.'

'I was the one that hired you. Do not forget it.'

'I never could but there are things that only men can sometimes discuss. I have no wish to give offence.'

'Please just hold a moment.' said an icy Miss Kraft.

Half a minute passed and a man's voice came on the phone.

'John Collins here, what the hell is the problem here that you cannot resolve with Nadine?'

'It is about Mr Vitra.'

'For Christ sake man spit it out. Are you all backward here?'

My cousin Chok was on the flight from London. The flight was delayed at take off because the police came on and took a man out of first class in handcuffs. Mr Vitra is a no show so if he was travelling first class I am afraid he may be in custody in the UK. Why I wanted to talk to you man to man was that I still expect to be paid the full rate even though Mr Vitra did not turn up and is a no show.'

'You dug me out for that. I meant what I said about you sodding lot being backward.'

'I agree Sir there are quite a number of backward people here in Singapore. Fortunately for us Singaporeans they are mainly visitors.'

With that barb Zafran hung up.

'Brilliant Zafran, just brilliant Zafran. Took that pompous sod down a peg or two and got the message across. I loved that.'

'Zafran was all smiles. 'You liked that Mr Jeremy. I do not

think Mr Collins is a very nice man. I take it you are here to put an end to his activities.'

'To be honest Zafran, that is something we shall do in the long term but it will not be on this trip.'

'Tell you what, unless you want to travel together you can have a limousine each,' said Jithu.

'Fine by me,' said Allen. 'I have been stuck with him in a plane for hours. Spreading out in the back of a beautiful car is a very attractive idea, after you Jithu.'

'You chose the right car with the right driver Miss Louise. Sadly my brother was correctly diagnosed by Mr Collins. He is slightly backward. Mr Jeremy I feel sorry for you to be travelling in that old banger.'

'Go with him at your peril Miss Louise. He won his licence in a lottery.'

Jithu said something in his own language which brought about a gesture from Zafran.

'I am sure that was probably something downright rude,' said Louise.

'My older brother is not a very nice man, I can only apologise on the behalf of all Singaporeans. Let me assure you that we are an extremely courteous people.'

'Me, the older brother, I think not. It is he who is the older brother.'

'The car was simply pristine clean and sparkled from every nook and cranny.

'Did I detect a bit of sibling rivalry there?' asked Allen.

'No not really, Zafran is correct. I am the oldest. He is my kid brother and I love him dearly. I got him into this business and helped to finance his first car. He's forty now but he will always be my kid brother. He is a very good husband and father. I am Uncle Jithu to two very robust nephews and one absolutely gorgeous niece called Siti. She really is a smart one. Eight years old, however I am sure she has been here before.'

Allen liked her short journey from Changi to the Ascot Park Hotel. She stretched out and chatted away to Jithu. It was just after eleven in the morning local time. Back home it was just after three in the morning. Allen was surprised as to how fresh she was. As the car drew up the drive to the hotel Allen was extremely impressed.

'This is very nice,' she said.

'Indeed this is a very luxuriously appointed hotel. You will enjoy your stay here. This is one of the most beautiful hotels in Singapore at Christmas. They light up all these trees and it is quite exquisite. My little brother is just behind us. Both cars drew up and Aitken said to Allen as she got out. 'I have made sure they have been paid.'

'Thanks Sir and thank you Jithu. That really is the way to travel.'

'Glad you enjoyed it. At least you didn't have to rough it like poor Mr Jeremy. I look forward to being of service to you on Sunday when you return home. Have a very pleasant stay in our beautiful City. If you enjoy good food there is no place finer. The concierge here is nothing short of brilliant. He is worth talking to. Try and take the cable cars to Sentosa Island, the gardens are particularly beautiful. The Dolphin Lagoon with its Pink Dolphins. At night there is a beautiful laser light show. Sorry, I am starting to sound like a tourist guide but we are very proud of our home and we want you to feel at home too. See you Sunday.'

'What a pair, but they are close. My car was absolutely immaculate I assume yours was just the same Sir. I hope you tipped them well.'

'Absolutely spotless, yes I did tip them because they did us a huge favour but the local Government here seemingly doesn't approve of tipping. I am not quite sure what the right etiquette actually is.'

'I wouldn't worry about it Sir, we're foreigners. Just watch the locals.'

'I suppose. They checked in with reception.

Chapter 51

★ ★ ★

~An Old Acquaintance~

The receptionist said, 'We have some messages for you Mr Aitken.'

That was an understatement. There was a huge sealed envelope that the receptionist passed over with J Aitken. Private & Confidential was written on it.

Purbright had been busy.

They had adjoining rooms.'

'We'll unpack, freshen up and I shall meet you downstairs for lunch, say one o'clock Allen.'

'Fine by me Sir. I am keen to see what is in that envelope.'

'Well we can open it together over lunch.'

'I thought you would have opened it now.'

'No Allen, we are a team and we work together as a team. Spontaneity is our hallmark, yours in particular. No we shall open this together. Do you know back home it is after three o'clock in the morning and I am starving.'

'Cannot say I am starving but I am sure that when it is put in front of me I shall probably do it justice.'

Allen was down in the spacious dining room at exactly one o'clock. A waitress bowed slightly and indicated Allen to follow her. Allen saw Aitken sitting with his copy of The Times he had taken from London.

'She intimated to the waitress that she was with Aitken.

As she approached Aitken stood up.

'There was something lovely about his old fashioned manners that Allen actually enjoyed.

'Feeling better. I have had the most wonderful shower. Feel like a new man.'

'Me too, I didn't mean I felt like a new man. I meant I had a wonderful shower as well. This place is, as Jithu said on the way here, a very luxuriously appointed hotel. I could put up with travelling around the world if I was residing in hotels like this one.'

'I think you might need to be extremely rich to do that if this is the standard you are after,' said Aitken. 'This young lady is standing here patiently waiting for us both to shut up so she can take your order for a drink.'

'Oh sorry, what are you drinking. Sir? I always have trouble deciding on an aperitif.'

'I am drinking a blast from my past, Campari, but can I make a recommendation.'

'Go ahead feel free.'

'The lady will have a Charbay Green Tea on ice please.'

The waitress gave a small bow and was gone.

'I am not sure about Green Tea as an aperitif.'

'This you might enjoy. It is alcoholic and on par with say, vermouth.'

A couple of minutes later the waitress came back with Allen's drink.

'God this stuff is absolutely fantastic. I have never even heard of it. Are you a closet alcoholic? You know more about booze than anybody I know. I am dying to see what Purbright has sent.'

'That can wait until coffee as we are here for a serious job so let's enjoy a pleasant lunch. Look at this plate of antipasti, now that is what I call first class.'

'Probably in price as well, Sir. Purbright will have a fit.'

'I didn't choose this place Purbright did, well technically ADI did. Semantics really. Purbright cannot expect us to stay in a place like this and go down Orchard Road to the MacDonald's.'

'I think you will find that he does,' said Allen. 'This stuff goes down too easy.'

'Then you will be glad to know they make a Pomegranate version as well.'

'My pal Amanda loves Pomegranate. I could probably get her hooked on this stuff if the Pomegranate is as good.'

Lunch was superb.

'Now it is time to do what we came for. Let us have a look in this missive from Purbright.'

Aitken ripped open the envelope.

'Hold it Sir, hissed Allen. 'There's a guy approaching us.'

'Hi I see you got my envelope. Sorry to say there is an awful lot more in this envelope'

With that he offered Aitken another full A4 envelope.

'Please sit down,' said Aitken. 'Can we get you anything?'

'Yes please, it's hot I'll just have a beer, Thanks. Make sure you tell that Pseudo Scot that my beer is on the expenses. That old bugger Sergeant Dunbar practically converted Purbright to being as tight as duck's arse underwater. I think the bugger keeps his money in his sock where he cannot reach it. I often wonder if he is crossed with an owl. You know the thing, wise and hunts at night. Take it, it's not a bloody letter bomb. Mind you it contents will probably be explosive and be the end for some crooks. Sorry, where are my manners, it's Jeremy and Louise isn't it? Bill Reynolds at your service. In another life I was a colleague of Purbright. We actually came through Hendon together. Frank was always going to be a brilliant cop. We both got made up to detective about the same time. Frank was ahead of me by about eighteen months but he was ahead of most people anyway. We were put to the East End with real villains in those days. The villains didn't fear the police back then. Top you as soon as look at you. Frank and I were having a ball. We were locking them up as fast as we could. Then tragedy struck. We both suffered major attacks. Frank got taken down first. Shot by a Bank robber. Smashed the guy to bits and cuffed him while Frank was bleeding like a stuck pig. He came damn close to dying. I hated going to hospitals back then. I had never spent as much time in the damned place and eventually he pulled through. The night that the ward nurse told me that he was finally off the danger list I went out and bought the best bottle of champagne I could afford and I drank to Frank's recovery. Five month later it was my turn to be in hospital. I would be in there for a little while, like a couple of years.'

'Good grief what happened to you?' asked Louise.

'Simple Louise, I put away the two sons of one of the local crime barons. Rape and GBH. A right nasty pair, so twelve and ten years each was a good result. The case finished on the Thursday. The following Saturday my wife and I were downtown with my ten-year-old son. He had just been picked, not only to represent his school but the whole local area. The wife and I decided that he should have a new pair of football boots. We bought this pair of Le Coq Sportif, much dearer than we meant to spend but they were absolutely fantastic. Jimmy was just ecstatic with them. We were making our way back to the car. All Jimmy wanted to do was to get home and get into these boots. The wife and I were in great humour just seeing the joy on his face. We were crossing the road when this Transit van came from nowhere at high speed. We never stood a chance. My precious wife and son were killed instantly. Two other members of the public died that day on that crossing. I was hit fair and square. Sadly, unlike my wife and son, I would survive. I wouldn't know anything until a hundred and fifty three days later when I came out of my coma to discover the awful truth. Thirteen major operations and two years later I left hospital in a wheelchair. I was told it was unlikely I would walk again. Purbright moved heaven and earth to nail the guys that ran us down. He even nailed the crime baron. What followed for me was a long time spent in physiotherapy. Two years later I met Jasline. She is a Singaporean and the one that made me walk again. Two years later and we were married. I walked with her out of the ceremony to a very happy life. A son and a daughter followed. Jasline is nine years younger than me. We came out here after my Jessica was born and we have been here ever since. I love the place and the people. I have a job in security and there is nothing much coming over me. Just every now and then I think about my first wife Ruby and my boy. He would have been twenty-eight by now. When they were killed, it was Frank who paid for both the funerals and the headstones for my lass and our son. He wouldn't hear about taking any money until the compensation was paid. It was a long time before I got compensation. Maybe he is not as tight as we all make him out to be. Anyway how is the old bugger? He hasn't long to go until he is driving Barbara crazy, getting under her feet. I don't think Frank will do retired well. I just cannot see it. He obviously didn't trust putting this stuff through on anyone's Internet so he asked me to help.'

His beer arrived. He lifted the glass and toasted Frank Purbright.

'You make sure he knows that he has paid for this beer. This last bunch of stuff came through at ten past three in the morning UK time. Most people would be giving it Zeds, not our Purbright. As I say he is a bloody night owl. Oh, there's my Jasline waving through the glass. I need to go. If there is anything I can do to help my card is there. Give me a bell.'

With that Bill Reynolds was gone. As he walked away the two detectives both observed that he walked with a funny rolling gait. He was also extremely bow legged.

'Dried his long johns over a barrel' said Aitken.

'My God you do have some of the weirdest expressions. I must admit it does look a bit like it though. He wouldn't make a defender at football would he? He would be getting continually nutmegged.'

'Now it's my turn to be surprised by your expressions. I am totally surprised you even knew that passing the ball through someone's legs is a nutmeg. I thought you absolutely detested football.'

'I do, the snag about living with a couch potato that loves all forms of sport you become like a passive smoker. You have no intention smoking you just get press-ganged. Ask me about Bull Riding or Handball, minority sports they may be but I am closet expert.'

'What did you think about Bill Reynolds?' asked Aitken.

'He certainly is a fan of the Super,' said Allen.

'With good cause it would seem,' said Aitken. 'Right let's have a look at what Purbright has sent us.'

Chapter 52

★ ★ ★ ★

~Dispatches from home~

The envelope contained a dossier on every one of the ADI so called 'Knights' However, Purbright was no closer to finding out about Wendell Fanshawe than were Aitken and Allen.'

'Where the hell has he dug this out from?' said Allen.

'I wouldn't know. God only knows where he finds this kind of stuff.'

There was a lengthy report about the whole status of the case and what was obviously Purbright's current thinking. He mentioned he was having major problems cracking their Afghan friend George Vitra. Then Purbright discovered that he had two eighteen-year-old twin daughters back in Kandahar. Purbright then threatened him that the British Army would pick up his daughters for interviewing if Vitra got his meaning. Vitra thought Purbright was bluffing. Purbright explained that a visit from the army to his daughters wasn't as bad as what they had done to Amy Anderson when she was executed. Purbright explained he wasn't getting the Army to execute his daughters. He wanted them to be alive so that they were aware of the shame you had brought about for them. We would also ensure that we would make them aware that what was happening to them was entirely your fault. Vitra capitulated. He would not admit to any part in Amy Anderson's execution but simply his part in the prison poisoning.

Vitra denies knowing Wendell Fanshawe. He is also very coy about the tattoo. He claims he was drunk when he got it done. The design isn't what he wanted and he doesn't think it was what he chose. Purbright is going to organise a video of his two daughters in Afghanistan just to show he isn't bluffing and that should loosen Vitra's tongue.

'I am slightly surprised at Purbright's tactics. Not very nice in reality.'

'Allen, get real, Purbright would never harm a hair on those two girls head's. Just prompting Vitra's memory, nothing more.'

'The problem I have Sir is that if they belong to this little boys club for grown men there might be some code of chivalry they live by. This guy simply might not crack. Have you considered that?'

'I am sure the Super has.'

'Anyway I assume that you have equipment with you to bug this meeting.' said Allen.

'Yes but the problem is how to do it? I am sure that these guys will be taking no chances and will sweep the room. I saw a guy talking with Lee Johnson that we do not have a photo for from Purbright. He wasn't hotel staff and it looked very much like they knew each other. I am convinced that they will have support staff here. By the way I saw the lovely Nadine Kraft, at least I think it was her. I went past where they are holding their meeting and I am positive it was her giving out a whole bunch of instructions to the hotel staff.'

'What did she look like?'

'Short, dark haired, trouser suit, high heels. Very expensive clothes, shoes and jewellery.

Not particularly pretty. Plain is a more accurate word.'

'Wears Dior glasses?'

'Yes, navy ones.'

'Then it was her I passed in the corridor. She was standing speaking to a tall man in a grey suit, blue shirt, white collar and no tie. She was speaking to him about security. To be exact all I caught was 'there must be total lock down by nine thirty.'

By chance Sir did you clock the watch he was wearing? He was standing fiddling his signet ring with his other hand. I am positive that it was the pink gold Duomètre. I would say that this was the guy Walker Young that checked Melissa out.'

'That's the guy I saw speaking to Johnson. That's good because I think the meeting starts at ten. That means they will have swept the room by then. Somehow I need to get my bug in after that and before the meeting starts.'

'Do you think you can?'

'Well Allen if I cannot do it we have wasted a lot of money coming here. What I am hoping is that this is an extremely high-class establishment so they will lay on drinks and water and probably biscuits for the first session. What I need to know is if they are having a working lunch or are they coming out to the dining room. Personally I think that once inside they will stay put. Again I am hoping that all the food for the day will go in at the last minute. Why I think it is continuous is that Collins is booked on a plane to Mumbai for six o'clock Friday night. They are all gone by nine o'clock Saturday morning.'

'It is a high risk strategy but probably you are right,' said Allen. 'How are you going to achieve it Sir? What is Plan B?'

We need the route from the kitchens and we ambush the food en route. I shall ignore your question about Plan B.'

'How do you propose to ambush the food?'

'You Miss Allen are going to create a diversion in one of the corridors that's being used to ferry the food to the meeting room.'

'How am I going to do that?'

'Good grief, I don't know. Take all your clothes off and run naked down the corridor. What the hell, surely you can think of something, OK?'

'Don't worry, of course I can, big trip, badly wrenched ankle, all the hotel's fault, scream the place down threaten to sue the ass off the hotel.'

'Yes, that would do it for me.'

'I am sure that taking off my clothes and running naked down the corridor might also do it for you but that isn't going to happen.'

'I am pretty positive that it would do it for most men but it wasn't quite the diversion that I had in mind.'

'Glad to know it. I was beginning to wonder what I had to do in the line of duty. By the way how did you recognise Lee Johnson if you have just opened the envelope.'

'Slow Allen, slow.'

'I suppose Purbright passed stuff to you on that posh phone you have.'

'Quick Allen, quick. What do you mean posh phone?'

'Well it is, complete poser's job.'

'Charming, I could do without the thing. All this damned phone is.... is nothing more than hassle. This was simply a free upgrade. I didn't even ask for it. The supplier was simply trying to keep me on the hook.'

'Still looks like a poser job as far as I am concerned.'

'Right lets get out of here and go to one of our rooms so that we can study the mug shots for these guys and all the info in here.'

Two hours later they were doing a reconnaissance to get the routes from the kitchens to the meeting room.

'Right I think I am happy,' said Aitken. 'I think I know the best place to ambush the food. That short piece of corridor close to the kitchen has a blind spot, it's almost perfect.'

'I do not think as guests we should even be there,' said Allen.

'Even better,' said Aitken.

Chapter 53

★ ★ ★ ★

~A little Eavesdropping~

Back in the hotel reception area Aitken said, 'Fancy a visit to the pool?'

'I suppose so, are we finished for the day?'

'No, but I have a feeling it is where we will find our gallant Knights. Let's have a quick look and see if we can spot them.'

At the pool there was a group of eight men that they recognised from the photos that Purbright had sent.

'That's good but where are the rest? I'll have a look into the main bar. We may have to split up. Come with me to my room and I shall give you a little machine to take to the pool with you. It does a little eavesdropping. Looks like an I Pod but it is in fact a directional microphone and it has a recording facility. I have a couple of them and I shall take my computer to the bar and my device. I shall sit and appear like some geek who cannot do without his electronic gizmos.'

They passed the main bar and there in a corner another eight Knights sat.

'There they are, the last four are due in later this evening. Notice anything about them?'

'Yes, they are grouped in either Operations or Business Development. The guys in here are the Operations guys.'

Twenty minutes later Allen was lying out on a sun lounger only twenty feet away from the ADI guys. She simply looked like she was lying listening to music on her I-Pod'

In the bar Aitken was also sitting with his notebook computer in front of him and he seemingly was connected to his music. In fact he had a film up on his computer. One of the ADI got up and probably went to the rest rooms. He looked at what was playing on Aitken's screen as he walked past. Aitken then heard him say to his colleagues. 'The guy there needs to get a life. He's sitting there watching a Bruce Willis film on his computer. Probably all the action he ever sees.'

'Right guys,' it was Samuel Eshe that spoke. He had slightly surprised Aitken with his appearance. He had originally expected Samuel to be coloured. He may have had an African name but he was an Afrikaner when he spoke and was white.

'I have to go to the airport with Nadine and meet Mr Collins.'

'He must be going to tear a strip of you,' said Wayne Harding.

'Or maybe, just maybe, he might be going to say thanks. My theatre of operation is running as sweet as it comes. Not like that bush operation you run.'

'It might be bush but at least it makes money. Better than some guys, that right Naresh?'

'I think you are under some misinformation about the level of our activities. I will blow your figures out of the water. Yes I suppose we had better go and get ready for dinner. I believe it is now going to be in main dining room.'

'I thought it was going to be in his suite,' said Wayne Harding.

'Mr Collins has changed his mind and we are dining in the main dining room. I have dined here before and the food is just fantastic.' said Lee Johnson.

'Right, I am going to shower,' said Harding. 'Those BD guys are still sitting poolside. I think a few of them are going to get their arses shredded tomorrow. North America has been a huge disappointment. Tamblin has dropped a right bloody fortune thanks to the DEA. I am glad I am not in his shoes.'

'Don't think you have got much worries, you Skippys' all stick together. You will have to seriously blot your copybook before John Collins is going to take action against you.' said Naresh.

These two were obviously quite friendly as the banter between them demonstrated.

The meeting broke up and Aitken finished his drink. He then walked through to the main dining room. The moment he entered a waitress came across.

'Sorry Sir but we are closed at the moment preparing for dinner.'

'It's OK, I am booked for dinner and I just wanted to have a look around. I like to see where I might sit, that is Maitre d' permitting. He smiled at the waitress and she slightly bowed and smiled a small smile. She's seen it all, the pretentious, the self-important, all the ones that thought they should have the best location in the room, or what they perceived to be the best location.

'Do you mind if I just walk round and straight out?'

'I suppose, yes, please go ahead.'

Aitken could see the big table off to one side of the room. Exactly fifty seconds later he thanked the waitress and took his leave. He put a bug at each end of the table, proof that it had been a successful walk round. He would record everything in his room. Aitken had a pleased expression on his face as he went to see if Allen was still there. He met the ADI guys coming through the door from the pool. Allen was stretched out on the lounger.

He walked over and Allen got up.

'I take it that your lot are going to get ready for dinner. Collins is coming in shortly. They are all dining in the dining room. Seemingly business talk is taboo until tomorrow morning. I have bugged the table. Everything shall be recorded in my room. I am going to go for dinner myself. We are going to the hawker barrows to eat the local food. You are a curry fan so you should have a good evening. We will go and have a Singapore Sling in Raffles first. Sit in the long bar, scoff the peanuts if they still serve them. Have to shell your own. Then we shall head to the Hawker stalls to eat.

An hour later it was dark and they were in a taxi heading to Raffles.

'You hungry Allen,' asked Aitken.

'In fear of soliciting some smart comment, I am starving.'

'No, that was a serious question I am the same. I think it is going to be a quick aperitif and then off to the stalls. They may sound like it is a bit informal but let me assure the food is brilliant. Well it certainly was the last time I was here.'

Allen loved Raffles. Aitken said, 'we can come back Saturday and have proper tea and tiffin.'

'That sounds good to me,' said Allen.

The walked around the Hawker stalls and suddenly Aitken caught sight of a chef very stylishly flipping and turning a flat style pancake.

'Ah a showman, he's flipping Prata.'

'He's a flipping Prat? That's not nice Aitken. You don't even know the guy.'

'You know what I said Allen. This guy's good. Prata's a bit like Naan bread, a distant cousin possibly. Comes I think from Madras or Chennai as it is now. Can I recommend that if you want a curry, Roti Prata with either a meat or a vegetable curry? I see a guy doing Bak Chor Mee, he also has Sambal Stingray. This is just brilliant.'

So it would prove to be. Both had a sumptuous feast of food.

'Don't know about you Allen but I am running out of steam. Back to the hotel, a nightcap and hit the sheets.'

'I think that would do it for me Sir.'

When they got back to the Ascot Park a number of the ADI guys had taken over a corner.

Aitken and Allen came in and sat down at a table at the other side of the room.

'Can you pick up on what they are saying Sir.'

You pop your handbag up on the table and I shall pop this little baby behind it. I will then slowly move things around to see if I can pick up what they are saying. Pop this in your ear, its wireless and hopefully we might hear some little titbit.

The waitress arrived. 'Armagnac please,' said Aitken.

'That sounds good. Same for me please.'

By the time that their drinks arrived they were receiving loud and clear. The talk was conditioned by what had obviously been a convivial evening. The talk was male and fairly crude.

Then Wayne Harding spotted Aitken. 'There's that sad bastard who was watching films on his computer. That can't be his wife. He has a ring on and she has none. No they are definitely not a couple.'

'She was sunbathing at the pool this afternoon. I wouldn't say no to her, she is seriously fit. What is the deal with them?' Ross Morgan was the man asking the question.

'I would lay odds he is a Doctor of some kind. Singapore makes a fortune out of being a medical City. You can find some of the finest consultants here,' said Johnson.

'What's she then? What nationality is she? I love the people watching game,' said Harding.'

'She is his fantasy and I would say she is definitely European. I doubt if she is his Secretary. Actually the threads are so good that she actually might be his business partner,' said Morgan.

'Very good Ross, I could buy into that. What about the old boy and the young thing on the table next to them? He is shagging the arse off her and what an arse,' said Harding.

'What a damned waste,' said Johnson. 'That is a case of a guy who has pots of money. Normal circumstances and that little honey wouldn't look twice at the guy.'

'What about the two guys in the alcove? Pair of queers those two.' said Harding.

'That's highly possible,' said Morgan.

'Yeah they are more our Bard of Avon's type I think. Why doesn't he get his arse on a plane and join our meetings. I prefer to work for a boss that I have met.'

'If he knew you said that he would have your arse in a shredder,' said Morgan. 'Collins has met him and that was a few years back. He hasn't looked outside England in the last eighteen months. His condition is debilitating so it means he cannot travel.'

'What the hell is actually the matter with him?' said Harding.

'He suffered a deep vein thrombosis on a flight back from LA and it damned near killed him. He refuses to fly anywhere, don't know about you guys,' said Ross Morgan, 'but tomorrow really is a big day. I am going to bed. I want to be fresh and thinking clearly.'

The rest of the group agreed and they all started to get up to leave.

'We have to arrive 09.50 for a 10.00 am start. Do not be early Collins hates that.'

'Don't worry Lee, we know the scores. Collins will appear at 09.55. Load of bollocks if you ask me,' said Harding.

Aitken and Allen sat where they were until the ADI people had left.

'Well that was a little bit useful. We know that Fanshawe definitely resides in England. What we also know is that he suffered a DVT that nearly killed him. Somewhere he got hospital treatment for that. He might have had it in flight. The Avon reference, was that a reference to would be Shakespearian actor or possibly a cross reference as to where he lives. Could he possibly live in the Stratford area?'

'That's something worth pursuing as is finding someone receiving treatment for a deep vein thrombosis. I would imagine that with Fanshawe's money it would have been private. That is going to make it more difficult. I am off to bed, was there anything else that you got from what they said.'

'Yes, that you men you are all the same, coarse and crude.

Goodnight Sir.'

'As a chastened member of the male species I shall say Goodnight.'

'Sleep on this Sir, Ross Morgan was strangely very defensive and almost knowledgeable about Fanshawe.'

'Allen, that is indeed a very interesting observation.'

Chapter 54

★ ★ ★ ★

~A Small Diversion~

At breakfast the following morning they were both nervous. Allen for once wasn't even hungry.

'This has got to work Sir,' she said.

'Tell me about it. If we don't pull this off a certain Superintendent Purbright is going to be well ticked off.'

Just over an hour later they were hanging about outside the kitchen when they heard a voice say 'Right Jennifer, you get that stuff up to the Stanford Room.'

'Right,' said Aitken, 'plan into action.'

Twenty seconds later, the kitchen doors swung open and Jennifer appeared pushing a large trolley laden with all manner of food and drinks. She looked slightly surprised to see two guests coming towards her, as no guests should have been in this area. Next thing the woman fell over and started screaming about her ankle. The man came towards her and asked if she had any ice on her trolley. Jennifer told him rather abruptly to not touch a thing on that trolley. She would get ice from the kitchen. Thirty seconds later she was back with a bag of ice wrapped in a cloth. The woman was screaming about a loose carpet. Jennifer said she had to go and guests shouldn't even be in this area. At that moment a guy looked out from the kitchen. 'You still here Jennifer, forget it I shall take up the second trolley myself. James you take the third,' he shouted back into the kitchen. 'You get back here pretty damned quickly Jennifer as the fourth trolley will be complete.'

He looked at Allen; still sitting on the ground and just shook his head.

When the corridor had cleared Allen stood up and the pair of them walked back to Aitken's room.

'I take it you were successful Sir?

Yes, but the problem is if they take away the trolley that will cut down a couple of bugs.

Aitken started off the recording from the beginning. They were running about eight minutes behind real time.

The first thing they heard was Jennifer complaining about Allen's histrionics about her ankle. 'Probably nothing the matter with her,' said Jennifer, 'these rich people are all the same.'

'So that's what she thought of your small diversion,' said Allen.

The guy with the second trolley was moaning they were late.

When they got to the Stanford Room they would find Nadine Kraft in vile mood.

'You are eight minutes late. Where the hell have you been? I thought that this was supposed to be one of Singapore's finest.'

The guy apologised and told Nadine it would take only a few minutes to empty the trolleys.

'Don't bother it's too late and anyway it's a bunch of men. They wouldn't appreciate the lay out. They can simply help themselves. Now go, go.'

'Oh yes,' said Aitken, 'even better; we have six bugs in that room. Only a last minute sweep could stop that. Right lets go to real time. They should be filing in. Five minutes from now and Collins makes his entrance.'

Chapter 55

★ ★ ★ ★

~*The Knights of the New Order*~

'**R**ight,' said Aitken, 'we are now in real time. Let's see how good our little surveillance system is.'

Aitken opened up the speaker and the sound quality was fantastic. They could hear lots of movement in the room but strangely no speech.

'That's concerning,' said Allen. 'I would have thought that we would have heard them speaking. Lots of background noise but no speech.'

Then someone sneezed. That was loud and clear as was someone saying 'Bless You.'

'Obviously they are not very chatty with each other. They are probably nervous.'

Five minutes passed and Aitken was starting to get perturbed.

Then a voice announced.

'Please be seated. The meeting is brought to order. Let us first swear the oath of allegiance.'

There followed an oath sworn by all present.

'We the Knights of the New Order swear that we shall serve our leader, our cause and our beliefs in that we shall bring about a new order within the world whereby capitalism shall be our servant. We serve until we die. The Knights of the New Order.'

'Well there's a shocker for starters. Here was me thinking that their Holy Grail might be money when in fact it was money all along.'

'Big surprise that Sir.'

Before Aitken could say anything else the voice in the room started speaking again.

'Right Gentlemen, this is an extraordinary meeting brought about by several events that were avoidable and should have been avoided. To compound our problems further we shall not be joined by George Vitra today. He was arrested on board the plane at Heathrow taking him here. Rather stupidly he managed to get himself caught on CCTV when we took out the two incompetents whose job it was to eliminate the Anderson girl. One survived the prison attack so we still have a need to eliminate that guy. I have no idea what the hell is going on as we spent a fortune in eliminating the girl. So why was it her executioners were arrested within hours? The plan was superb so what when wrong? Ridgeon should have done better and he has paid the price for his failure. You will notice that a vacancy now exists in Europe. Mr Fanshawe has someone in mind. His name is Byron Mann.'

'The Byron Mann? The biggest hedge fund manager in the world,' asked a voice. 'I would have thought he wouldn't have subscribed to our philosophy.'

'Quite the opposite. He is doing what we are doing which is to build enough material things and sufficient finances to dominate the market through short selling and runs on some of the biggest financial institutions. Mr Fanshawe says an alliance with Byron Mann shall speed up our own ambitions by as much as two years. Gentlemen can I introduce you to Byron Mann.'

Obviously Byron Mann had entered the room and the next few minutes were spent as each member around the table probably shook hands being introduced to Byron Mann.

'As John has mentioned I am Byron Mann and after meeting Mr Fanshawe we are pooling our resources to help each other. I shall bring some forty six billion to the table, Euros that is. Together we can start to dominate the market. Jointly we can take out and take over some of the biggest financial institutions in the world. I am convinced that it is going to be like knocking down tenpins. We need to get to about three to four trillion to control a large number of the Forbes five hundred. That is my estimation of critical mass. Do not forget you do not need to own all the company, just the majority.'

John Collins spoke again.

'Welcome aboard Byron, we need to swear you in. Before we swear you in you must ensure us that you clearly understand the rules of membership. If a Knight of the New Order is captured and where that capture may lead to other knights being endangered we shall eliminate that Knight.'

'Mr Fanshawe has briefed me completely even about our latest developments. The conditions of membership are acceptable to me.'

Byron Mann was sworn in.

After this Collins said, 'we shall address our immediate issues before going through our meeting agenda. We have a problem in England. This is where the Anderson girl accessed the private e-mail records of Mr Fanshawe. We still do not know what she has learned. Her computer is being worked on. Those useless bastards at the Police IT department cannot crack her passwords. We need to get that computer. They have two decent enough people working on it but their minds are elsewhere. They get married in ten days time in Mauritius. I think Anderson was so brilliant that her computer is impenetrable. What I fear is that she left the keys to the lock somewhere. She didn't leave it with her brother or her best friend Melissa. Somewhere the key is out there. Of that I am positive. Anderson was smart enough to know she was in danger even to the extent she knew her life was in danger. She was eliminated but not without huge incompetence by Philip Ridgeon. Mr Fanshawe's plan for her execution should have been foolproof. What it didn't legislate for was the fact that an idiot was used to carry it through. Now that problem is compounded in that we have Vitra locked up. We have had Arthur's top man in to see him and try and get him bail. That was refused. The damned guy that arrested him is the biggest bloody Rottweiler in the police force. The lead detective is a guy called Aitken and he has a very sharp assistant called Allen. They were the two that visited Ridgeon. He thought they were a pair of country hicks. These were the two who were responsible for catching up with our hit squad. They were also the two smart arses responsible for this guy Purbright arresting our man Vitra. I am trying to line the three of them up for elimination. The problem is I am not sure whether to eliminate them or whether to eliminate their families as a lesson. I shall take a show of hands on this.'

'Surely as Knights we only take out the immediate opposition,' said Mann.

'Under normal circumstances, that is the rules of engagement Byron. We haven't faced such a threat before. Personally, I favour taking out the cops. Leave any of these three alive and they will probably hunt you to the ends of the earth.'

'You can sodding well bet on that,' said Aitken with venom in his voice.

'Let's have a show of hands. Three options, the cops, their families or the cops plus their families. No abstentions allowed.'

'These guys are talking about eliminating us,' said Allen.

'Then we had better eliminate them first,' said Aitken.

The Knights cast their votes.

'Gentlemen, that is it, a clear majority to eliminate the three police only. I shall arrange a hit team. We need photographs of the three. I shall arrange that later. I think we shall recall the team that eliminated Ridgeon. They are very efficient and have excellent rates.'

At that moment a voice came over the speaker. The voice was rich and mellifluous but sounded old.

'I think that you may have a problem there John. Please all be seated Gentleman. I think that you shall find that our Albanian friends are also under lock and key courtesy of those three police that you mentioned, Purbright and his team. You do right to eliminate these three officers. The Albanians are held under the Terrorism Act in a high security unit. We need to eliminate them as well on an urgent basis.'

'I wasn't aware of this Sir. When did you learn this?'

'I had a little assistance from someone in homeland security. May I suggest another team, Viktor and his two Chechnya mercenaries? I know they are very expensive but they are good. I am quite prepared to sanction their costs under the circumstances. They are also very imaginative and I am rather fed up with this Purbright fellow and his team. They have become a major irritant.'

'Sir, do you think they would have access to doing an exposure to radiation?'

'Nice idea Howard, all too slow I'm afraid. We need to get these guys off our backs quickly as possible.'

'Well I am very glad that I shall meet my end by a slightly quicker method than radiation. My problem is with just how imaginative Viktor and his Chechnya goons can be.'

'Fortunately Sir, they have no photos of us, just as well.'

'I think Allen we need to keep a very low profile. We certainly do not want them to get the slightest inkling we are here.'

'What happens if they return to London on the same plane as

us?' asked Allen.

Fanshawe continued. 'Do you know what irritates me about this Purbright fellow. He isn't even important. He is not with any of the big boys he isn't even in SOCA here. We happened to eliminate someone on his patch. He is parochial and we are international so we should be able to control one insignificant plod and his two flunkeys.'

'Do you hear that Sir, here, Fanshawe definitely lives in the UK?'

'Sir, said Collins, 'I warned Ridgeon that these two police were very good and Aitken is no fool. He has an amazing track record in bringing major criminals to boot. His new partner, his previous was eliminated, is also very sharp. She bedazzled Ridgeon allowing Aitken to probably bug Ridgeon's house.'

'Ross,' said Fanshawe, 'I must compliment you on your choice of execution method for the Anderson girl. After I had written that I was convinced that it had merit. Sadly an inconsequential person in a film studio didn't even bother to read it, just rejected it out of hand. I still have to square the account with that guy. This damned minor problem that prevents me flying prevents me from going and blowing the moron to kingdom come.'

The pair listening detected the change in Fanshawe. The venom and hate in his voice was there for all to hear. Then he changed back again to Fanshawe the theatrical.

'These police officers, I think there is all the more reason to speed up their departure. Their time to expire upon the stage has come. Theirs will be a good death, exeunt omnes, they go out.'

'There is the old ham coming out,' said Aitken.

'Great actors obviously never die, they just go out Sir.'

'Something like that Byron, but hopefully I have some years yet before that exit.'

'I would hope so Sir, we have so much to accomplish together.'

'Yes we do, jolly exciting isn't it.'

'There's our non politically correct Daisy Sims, that's her poofter talking,' said Allen

'Can we get back on track please,' said Collins.

'He's no fun our gallant knight Collins. No fun at all Byron.'

Again Fanshawe sounded quite effeminate then suddenly the voice changed and it was like a different person was speaking.

'Right can we have an update of progress to date. Round the table if you please. We shall start with Business Development first.

Mr Tamblin, Mr Reed I hope you have better news than at our last meeting, in fact we shall start with you Mr Tamblin. What is happening in the Americas?'

Chapter 56

★ ★ ★ ★

~Do you believe these guys? ~

There followed a lengthy session of all the Business
Development and Operations Directors giving reports. Sadly
for Mr Tamblin he failed to impress Mr Fanshawe and he was
promptly informed about that.

'Mr Tamblin, it appears that again you disappoint. I shall bear
this with a patient shrug for sufferance is the badge of all our tribe
but that patience extends to only a further three months. Further
disappointments would mean that we would have to terminate
your contract. You do understand exactly what I am saying Mr
Tamblin?'

'Do you think he is Jewish Sir? The Merchant of Venice,
Shylock quote. What do you think?'

'I don't know, I think that was just the 'luvvie' in Fanshawe. He
could be Jewish, but that makes no difference other than it gives
another avenue to examine.

The meeting took the format that each Business Development
Director gave a chapter and verse about their operation and how
they had performed against targets. They also had to outline their
future plans and how much they could increase turnover. Some of
the figures being spoken about were astronomical.

The best report came from Barratt Gold for the Russia's.

'Right Barratt, how have you done?' asked Fanshawe.

'Overachieved by 38.8%. Will sustain this penetration through
the next twelve months and increase it by some 25 to 26%. Still not
happy with sales. That's it Sir.'

'That's definitely it Barratt, if every area was performing like that we could have this meeting over in five minutes. Ross Morgan almost matched Gold and it was obvious that Morgan was a slight favourite of Fanshawe's. After telling Morgan 'Well done Ross' Fanshawe asked Morgan if he had taken in any good shows. He had, been in Hong Kong and caught the RSC on tour with King Lear. Sir Edmund as King Lear.'

Fanshawe almost squealed with delight, 'Oh, you lucky, lucky man. Please do not tell me more or I shall cry with envy.'

'He was immense Sir, truly immense. You know him of course, don't you Sir?'

'You bloody creep,' said Allen.

'I am delighted to say that it has been my pleasure to press the flesh with Sir Edmund. He was back here at home doing Othello two years ago and we had a lovely dinner.'

Then there was that sudden jump again to a different persona.

'Right Mr Russell I hear we are projecting a slow down in Australia, care to enlighten us as to why?'

Fanshawe was a very hard taskmaster.

The meeting broke for lunch. Thirty minutes then it was back to work.

The meeting continued in the same mode as the morning session. The guys who were in Business Development could sit back and see their Operations colleagues getting grilled.

At a quarter of an hour to three Collins went back to the UK situation.

'Can we highlight our objectives on the UK front. Byron, I take it you are ready to accept the responsibility in this area? This is a task that we did not anticipate having to set you. However you appreciate that you are now a fully fledged Knight of the New Order.'

'Holy shit, do you believe these guys,' said Allen. 'Knights of the New Order. For crying out loud, grow up the whole bloody lot of you.'

Aitken just smiled.

Collins continued. 'Do you think you can eliminate the guys in high security Byron?'

'Yes, I should be able to do that and get right rid of Vitra plus that little weasel that still survives from the Anderson job. I would be more than hopeful of recovering or destroying her computer, probably the latter.'

'That is excellent news,' said Collins. 'If you concentrate on those issues I shall personally arrange for negating the police threat emanating out of the UK. I have to go there in two weeks so we should try and tie up all these loose ends by then. I take it I can get help from you Ross. Perhaps you can arrange to be in the UK for that period.'

'Nice one,' said Aitken. 'You have shifted responsibility to Fanshawe's blue eyed boy. If this all goes to rats you are not going to be left holding the baby. Have I got news for you, it is going to rats. We shall make sure of that.'

Collins continued, 'I want to have a look at the UK operation just to get an idea if there are any concerns within the staff.'

'Are you paying me a visit then?' asked Fanshawe.

'Sir, I wasn't planning to. I hate to impose.'

'Oh I think you can impose John. I think I would like a personal report on developments, it would be very beneficial.'

'Sir I appreciate the invite and I look forward to our meeting.'

'Like hell you do,' said Aitken. 'You know damn well that you cannot fail on any facet of the tasks ahead. Fanshawe probably noted how you were moving responsibility to his favourite so Fanshawe has just placed your nuts on the anvil. Failure to complete the UK tasks shall mean that Fanshawe will bring the hammer down. Mind you it will not actually be Fanshawe bringing down the hammer it will be us. Look out nuts!'

'Right my Knights; I have to bid you a fond adieu. I am going tonight to a small local performance of Two Gentleman of Verona. I am quietly sponsoring the career of a young lad who is of considerable talent and showing much potential. For those that I am pleased with, continue the good work. For those with whom I am displeased, beware. I do not tolerate slackers. Each Knight is equal, just some are more equal than others.'

He laughed as though he had said something witty. Then his mood almost somersaulted.

'Get to work, the lot of you. I am impatient for better progress.'

Obviously Fanshawe had then rang off.

There was a lot of sudden chatter within the assembled cast. Collins cut it dead.

'Right you heard the man. Time to get the finger out. Tamblin, I am travelling on to see you after the UK. Those guys in Columbia are bending you over and shafting you. Two bloody payments made, two bloody shipments intercepted. Close to a billion up in smoke. You are damned lucky that Mr Fanshawe didn't terminate your membership here and now. Right, you are all out of here tonight. Sorry two of you are first thing tomorrow. I know it's the weekend but you need to get to grips with things. Unless there is any other business I think we can wind up this meeting of the New Order with our oath.'

Oh Please,' said Allen. 'Hard to believe grown men can do this.'

'Not a Mason are you?' said Aitken.

'My dad is one and I cannot think they would behave like this. You a Mason Sir? There's a lot in the Police Force.'

'No Allen I am not and I think their membership in the Police Forces might be dropping. I also think that is probably something from a bygone era. I don't know, because I am not interested. I know something I am interested in and that is Collin's forthcoming visit to the UK in two weeks time. I would go as far as say that I am very interested in Mr Collins's visit to the UK. We shall ensure a welcome wagon. We shall put him up at one of Her Majesty's finest establishment. He might come in but he will not be going out.'

'What had you in mind Sir? Windsor, Balmoral or Sandringham. Sandringham is nice this time of year. Scotland on the other hand is supposed to be quite cold at this time of year.'

'Then Scotland it is Allen. Not Balmoral, you were close though. No, I thought HMP Peterhead. Nice contrast for someone from the tropical North End of Australia or who lives in Myanmar. A bit of a nor'easter coming off the North Sea. He would love exercising in the yard with that blowing up his kilt.'

'Do you know something, if I wasn't already aware of it already I would say that you can be quite vindictive.'

'What do you mean if you weren't already aware? Pray tell me what vindictive action have I taken against you in the past?'

'Never mind the past Sir, what about the present? You drag me half way around the world on a luxury flight and put me up at one of Singapore's finest hotels. You then feed me some of the finest food and drink. All that when you know I could be back home with my loved ones and Saturday would be the start of my weekend. Instead you expect me to work. If that isn't vindictive what is?'

'I can see that I need to get a person who is of a more robust character to partner me. I probably need to find someone with a public school background who is more accustomed to discipline and no little adversity.'

'Don't bother Sir, I shall have to get accustomed to no little adversity.'

'Some little adversity might just mean getting assassinated. I think we need to do something about that.'

Chapter 57

★ ★ ★ ★

~Shaking hands with a Crocodile~

Collins and the Knights had sworn their concluding oath and goodbyes were being said. 'Right all of you out, someone please send in Nadine,' said Collins.

Nadine obviously came in and joined her boss.

'Everything go smoothly Sir? Food OK?'

'Food was excellent, meeting was shit. I am heading to Mumbai tonight. Naresh Gupta has set up a massive deal and if we can swing it, it is huge. I have kept it up my sleeve as I think I shall need it. The shit that Ridgeon and Vitra have dropped us in is immense. I think that this is the biggest threat we have ever faced since we were formed. I have to go and see Fanshawe when I am in England.'

'Do you want me to make the travel arrangements, Sir?'

'Yes Nadine, fly me to Bristol, two weeks this Sunday. I do not need overnight accommodation. Organise a limo from Bristol and then back for the night flight to New York. That useless sod Tamblin has dropped over nine hundred big ones. Old Fanshawe is talking termination. I wouldn't be surprised if that is something I have to organise when I get across the pond. These bloody limeys are my immediate problem. Do you still have a number for Viktor Farsai?'

'Yes I do. I do not particularly like the man. You get this impression that you are shaking hands with a crocodile. On a day when he is hungry he will eat you immediately after shaking hands. I take it we have a contract for him?'

'Actually we have three. Three police officers from a police station in the UK. They hole up in a station called Railton and the three I want Farsai to contract are a Detective Chief Superintendent Frank Purbright, a Detective Chief Inspector Jeremy Aitken and a Detective Constable Louise Allen.'

'That might not be as easy as you think Sir.'

'How's that Nadine. It's not too difficult to eliminate someone when they are not expecting it.'

'Yes but what if they are expecting it?'

'Are you telling me we have a leak?'

'No Sir, well not one I would know about. No, it is just that when those police called on Philip Ridgeon I did a background check on them plus their Boss Purbright. Purbright is as tough as nails, been shot in the line of duty. He has a track record of bringing down major criminals. His DCI Aitken is probably as hard as nails. Four years ago a gang of four yobs to use the limey term, tried to mug him in a dark alley. He disarmed and hospitalised all four. Allen is equally tough. She is a self-defence expert, champion fencer and supreme shot with a pistol. She was also the UK Universities Chess Champion. She is tall, blonde and seemingly beautiful.'

'Do I detect a note of jealousy there Nadine?' said Collins teasingly.

'You are right Sir, it pisses me off. Bet she can bloody well cook as well. That brings me nicely to the interesting fact about Aitken, he is married to the celebrity cook Rosemary Aitken.'

'She cannot be that big a celebrity as I have never heard of her.'

'You don't watch cooking programmes. You don't even cook.'

'Maybe just as well we decided against contracting on the families. Knock off some celebrity cook and all hell might have broken loose. The limeys are funny about their petty celebrities.'

'I think you might be right about that Sir.'

'Are you still coming back Tuesday Sir?'

'Yes. Try and get Viktor to meet us in London on the Friday before I go to Fanshawe. I know he is shy about personal appearances but I want his input to make sure we are successful. We need to conclude this UK business before I meet the Chief.'

'Do not forget, next Thursday is Bryan's birthday. A special one too as he becomes a teenager.

'Shit Nadine, I bloody well had forgotten. Can you get him something?'

'I can, the latest Wii is in the crosshairs, but you will need to send and do the card. Do you want to put in some Australian money.'

'Yes pop in two thousand.'

'You need to watch your time, your cases are packed and at the concierge beside reception. Limo is booked and will be here in twelve minutes time. The account I shall see to.'

'Allen, I will be back in five,' said Aitken. 'You keep listening to them.'

Nadine Kraft was still speaking.

'Are you sure you do not want me to come to Mumbai with you? Everything is fixed up and Naresh is meeting you at the Airport. You have your usual suite. So you can hold private meetings. Unfortunately the US Secretary of State is in residence up until tonight so we cannot have it swept but I would think the job has already been done.'

'I would have thought so. Anyway I have the security team on another small project just now. I am sure that bloody Harding is fiddling us. Young and his team will be in Australia next week. Anyway, absolutely no one knows that I am going to Mumbai and certainly not our keen DEA investigator. I cannot believe their ham-fisted efforts can you? Usually they are a class act. We cannot rate or they would send someone better.'

'Maybe she is not all that bad if Tamblin has lost two shipments to the DEA. Anyway it is not her you worry about. Her boss Brad Michaels is the one to beware of.'

'I am not so sure that she is good, I think it is more Tamblin who is the incompetent one. I think I had better get going. What time is your flight?'

'About an hour and a half after you leave.'

'Right then Nadine, thanks for everything. You and Tony have a good weekend and I shall see you Tuesday.'

'Thanks and good luck in Mumbai.'

'Christ, I nearly forgot we need pictures of those three Police guys.'

'Don't worry Sir I will have those long before Viktor actually requires them. Bye!'

'Bye.'

Aitken came back in. 'Anything of further interest?'

Allen related what had happened and Aitken's ears pricked up when he heard that Collins and Gupta would probably work in

Collins's suite in Mumbai.

'I have bugged his luggage.'

'Yes but you would need to be able to pick it up. I take it we cannot pick it up here?' said Allen.

'No but I know someone who can.'

'That is something that you and Purbright have in common. You always know a man who can. Actually it is quite worrying, as they always seem to be shadowy figures.'

'You are both like, well not to put too fine a point, dodgy, the pair of you.'

'Charming, Purbright would love to be called dodgy. He is going to love that one.'

'Oh great, so you are going to drop me in it.'

'Having been tarred with the same brush as Purbright I think we have the right to reply. Insults aside, I may be able to access Collins and Gupta and what this big deal is.'

'I suppose you know that all this stuff we have obtained is illegal and would not be allowed as evidence in court.'

'That only holds good for us poor ordinary policemen there are a number of other agencies who could present this stuff in court and it would stand up. Anti terrorism, terrorism funding, any number of reasons why they had to covertly listen in to such a meeting, national security and all that. Funny thing is they wouldn't be far out at that. If ADI were to achieve their goals they could screw up the financial markets and with it national security. Really and truly it is time to put them all inside.'

Chapter 58

★ ★ ★

~A Sam Russell on the rocks~

That night they did another round of the Hawkers 'restaurants' and got back to the hotel for a drink quite early. When they had sat down with a drink Allen spoke.

'Well I must admit, it is good that our Round Table has departed, well all bar two and they are not around. At least for tonight we can relax. Especially now we know that we are marked down for elimination.'

'You have no idea Allen how pissed off Purbright is about that situation. The idea that someone has taken out a contract on him has really got up his nose. I asked him to explain the difference as he had taken out a contract on them. Two things, he said, firstly I am only terminating their activities, not their lives and secondly I am not a bloody criminal. Not a very happy bunny is our Superintendent.'

'Aitken's mobile went. He answered it. Much to Allen's surprise the conversation was in Russian.

After the call was over Allen said, 'I never knew you spoke Russian, that was Russian wasn't it?

'Yes, it was a friend of a friend from Oxford days.'

'Russian friends, Oxford, you are not another Kim Philby are you?'

'Communism was all but dead and buried when I was at Oxford, do I strike you as having those leanings? I hardly think so.'

'Oh you never know, I never knew you spoke Russian. No I think you are a rampant capitalist. Far too fond of La Dolce Vita to be anything else.'

'You make me sound a hedonist Allen.'

'Whatever rocks your boat, whatever rocks your boat.'

At that moment a very well dressed young woman, probably in her early thirties sat down at their table next to Allen. Allen looked at her slightly bemused. Allen then spoke to the woman.

'I am sorry but we are having a private conversation can you possibly sit elsewhere. There are a number of empty seats.'

'I am not going anywhere and you two are going to sit and listen to me.'

'Wrong approach whoever you are,' said Aitken. 'I am sitting here having a quiet drink and we are having a private conversation. Come on Allen let's take ourselves somewhere a little more private.'

'Okay sorry but can you please remain where you are. My name is Kristy Armstrong. I am with the DEA out of Washington. We are trying to ascertain exactly who you two are. You are tracking our target and you are not Interpol. Are you Mossad?'

'I assume when you say that we are tracking your target can we assume you mean John Collins amongst aliases that he uses.'

'So you are tracking him. In that case you can back off.'

'There you go again. You really are a bossy person. Neither me nor my companion here work for your organisation nor are you our superior officer. I am very close to telling you what to do and where to go.'

'Sorry, but if you scare off Collins you will have wasted a lot of painstaking work we have put in chasing him down.'

'Fine, say so in the first place. Do not try to punch me between the eyes, as I shall then knock your lights out, woman or not.

Allen was slightly taken aback at Aitken's attitude. This was a side that she hadn't noticed before. Maybe Nadine Kraft's earlier assessment that he was as hard as nails did apply. This was a very cold and steely Aitken.

Aitken continued. 'I do know who you are and IS have watched with amusement over the past few days as you and your team have clumsily tried surveillance on the ADI meeting. Collins has been equally amused especially after they found all your bugs you had placed in their meeting room. They even know the type of the bug and who uses them. They correctly identified your department as doing the job and bugging the room.'

'I suppose you are going to say that you were successful and that you in fact did bug their conversation.'

'It's possible, anything's possible.'

'You had better not be holding out on me,'

'There you go again, that aggressive streak. I could just see you as a Sergeant Major in the Army.'

'Sorry,' said the woman. 'I have had a real shit week and these jackasses have given me the run around all week. Needless to say I have a boss back in Washington DC not smiling too much. Can you help me?'

'No, I cannot.'

'Kristy Armstrong's eyes flashed fire then her shoulders slumped.

'No I cannot, but my Boss probably will. Can I see your ID?'

Kristy Armstrong complied and she was who she claimed to be.

'Right, I am Detective Chief Inspector Jeremy Aitken and this is my colleague and partner Detective Constable Louise Allen. We did indeed bug Collins in his meeting. I do not have the authority to let you listen to it. We are heading back home tomorrow. Are you stationed here or are you going back to DC? If you are a stop off in London then come see us. My Super is a man called Frank Purbright. More than likely he will help you.'

The weight that lifted off Kristy Armstrong's shoulders looked to be immense.

'Do you mean that you are simply a pair of detectives out of the UK. You are not with any of the majors. Are you SOCA then? You are a long way from home.'

'No, afraid not and yes we are some way from home. A very ordinary policeman and a policewoman that said, Allen here is a rather good detective. Thing is Collins took out a contract on a young woman on our patch. They executed the poor girl, right in front of her family. My boss Purbright takes a very dim view of that sort of thing happening in his manor. For you to get him to agree to back off Collins you are going to have to make a good case. Mind you, Frank Purbright thoroughly enjoys horse trading.'

'If that is the case, then I am sure if we cannot do him a favour at the moment we can put down a marker.'

'You are already speaking his language. Can I get you a drink?'

'Yes please. A Sam Russell on the rocks.'

'Well well J&B not JD, Justerini and Brooks, not Jack Daniels. The old country influence somewhere?' said Aitken.

'Yes, you are quite correct, my granddad is from Scotland and it is his favourite tipple. It is now mine. He is quite proud of the fact that he has led me astray. My Mom is his daughter and she doesn't drink. Granddad says that if she wasn't his daughter and the fact that he loves her he would disown her for not drinking especially the true whisky. He keeps telling me that forty two whiskies go into the J&B Rare Blend.'

'You do know,' said Aitken, 'that J&B supplied alcohol to George III. I blame J&B for losing us the Americas. The stuff they supplied was so damned good that he drunk far too much of it and rotted his brain. Instead of sending in a real army to put down you colonial upstarts he dithered in an alcoholic haze and hey presto we had lost America. All went downhill from there on. Brief resurgence under Victoria, she closed the account with J&B. After that it was back in favour with Edward VII, somewhat of a bon viveur and once more we were heading down the slippery slope losing all Victoria's hard gained Empire.'

'Ignore him Kristy, there is probably some single fact in there and the rest is bull.

'Aitken said, 'The bit that J&B supplied George III is correct.'

'Told you, didn't I,' said Allen.

'Kristy Armstrong laughed it was a hearty laugh. 'At least I can tell Granddad a fact that he probably doesn't know about J&B.'

Chapter 59

★　★　★

~*We can work together*~

'How long have you been on Collins's case?' asked Allen. Just over a year, him and his friend William Tamblin. Tamblin has been trying to flood the US with all manner of drugs. Fortunately we have managed to kill the freight but we are unable to nail Tamblin. He maintains that façade of legitimate businessman with ADI. '

'I wouldn't worry about him too much,' said Aitken. 'According to our boss Tamblin was someone that ADI recruited whereby they believed the Curriculum Vitae,' said Aitken.

'What do mean by that?' asked Kristy.

'According to my boss, Tamblin was a West Coast dealer that got lucky. Dead man's shoes and good work by your colleagues eliminating his predecessors left Tamblin in a position of power. He was literally over promoted. He has animal cunning but he isn't up to the job that ADI expected him to do. He is in grave danger of being terminated by ADI.'

'In which case he will probably pop up back in the West Coast,' said Kristy.

'No, when we say terminated we mean terminated as in dead,' said Allen.

'You got to be kidding me. We know Collins to be possibly a psychopath but that is stretching things a bit.'

'Tamblin has been told and he knows the consequences of failure. Your department's efforts have put Tamblin on Death Row if he cannot increase penetration in the North American markets.'

'So Collins has told him that he is to be terminated. That must be one mother of an incentive scheme. Here is me thinking that Michaels back in DC is a pain in the butt.'

'You seem to think that Collins is calling the shots. Collins has a boss,' said Aitken.

'That I find almost impossible, no boss has ever shown up on our radar. No, I think you have to be mistaken,' said Armstrong.

'Look, when you get to London we can give you chapter and verse. Meantime take our word Collins is definitely number two. You can scoop up all the drug peddlers. We are after the Boss. He was the guy who sanctioned the hit on an innocent young woman. That's the guy who at this meeting here has also sanctioned a hit on our Boss Frank Purbright and the two of us. Just like we were bugs to be eliminated. Oh we are definitely after Mr Big. Like I say we can work together, we would welcome the help as these guys are scattered all over the globe. We cannot use the evidence we have obtained but you can.'

'That is true, we most certainly can and we would line up others to ensure that we are legitimate, national security, homeland security, terrorism, the works. We can screw these guys to the wall so hard that they will never ever be able to move again.'

'One word of advice to your boss, do not try to screw with our boss. Purbright is straight and honest. He will work with you. You will quickly alienate him if you think you can try and bully him. That is really dangerous, very dangerous in fact. It is a measure of the regard these ADI guys hold him in that they have commissioned a hit on him.'

Armstrong thought that might just go for you two as well but left it unsaid.

'Message received and understood. Brad Michaels unfortunately is very accustomed to getting his own way. He is a New Yorker of Irish extraction. He takes a goddam' day off, every year, on March the seventeenth, to celebrate St Patrick's Day. Goes and gets very drunk on Bushmills Irish Whiskey. He has a hair trigger.'

'That could be a combustible mix with Purbright. He too is a whisky drinker, single malts from the western isles of Scotland. We will just have to hope for the best Kristy.'

Chapter 60

★ ★ ★ ★

~*Kristy Armstrong*~

'How long have you been with the DEA?' asked Aitken.
'Coming up five years in August. I am a Chicagoan, from the Windy City. I studied Business Law at Stanford. When I graduated I came back home and joined the Police Force. Do not ask me why. Probably I thought it was going to be glamorous. That was a laugh. How wrong did I get that one? I made detective quite quickly. Promotions by others probably saw me, like Tamblin, over promoted. That said I worked my butt off to balance the books and I grabbed the opportunity with both hands. My parents were horrified by my choice of career. They live in Miami now. Dad made a lot of money from the construction business. He retired early. Mum railroaded him into moving to Florida and he absolutely hates it. He misses Chicago and tries to get back as often as he can, which is good as I see him quite a bit. He didn't want me to do Police work, he thought it was too dangerous. If only he knew the half of it. I've been raped by three guys at the same time. They were high on drugs. Two months later I was shot twice by a guy completely stoned out of his mind. We got called to what we thought was going to be a domestic. It was a domestic all right. The guy had shot the wife, the mother in law and his two children. When I approached the door to the place he stepped from the shadows and shot me twice. First bullet went through my shoulder and the second I took in the stomach. I managed to blow his head off before I hit the ground. You can see where this is going. I applied for a transfer to the drug squad and they gave me it. From

there I was eventually recruited by the DEA. I've managed to lock up a few pushers.'

'You said you were raped. That must have been horrible.'

'I don't want to go there Louise, I still cannot wash myself clean to this day. Fortunately I didn't contract anything. We managed to track them down, which was rather unfortunate for them. The first two we found in a house playing poker. We marched in and they immediately pulled guns. My partner Dave immediately shot both. Dave is a fantastic shot and he shot the peckers and the balls off both. Rather messy but it didn't half make me feel good. The third guy heard about what had happened and walked in and gave himself up. The two Dave shot both died of their injuries. Needless to say there was an inquest and Dave was suspended. Fortunately everything turned out fine and Dave was reinstated.'

Allen felt like saying something about a gun culture but decided against it.

'Third guy is doing twelve now. Anyway that is more than enough about a very boring subject. How long have you two been a team?'

'Nearly a year now' said Allen. 'I cannot believe how long I have put up with him.'

'Is that all the time it has been?' said Aitken. Aged me a good ten years Kristy. I was only a stripling of some thirty-two years when she was allocated to me. Now look at me I'm forty....., well over forty.'

Yes Aitken, he thought, you got that right, well over forty

Kristy laughed, 'What are you two like?'

'I suppose I could get worse partners if the truth be told, not much worse but worse nonetheless,' said Aitken.

'Me,' said Allen, 'I request a transfer every single day and every single day my request is ignored. The problem is the Super cannot get anyone else to work with Aitken so I am stuck with him.'

'I think you will find that the reality is that I am stuck with you Allen. Do you have a partner Kristy?'

'Do you mean in the DEA or in life. I basically work on my own now or occasionally I am part of a team. In life I have a partner back in Chicago and her name is Mel. She is a Doctor. As you can imagine being raped was doubly bad for me. Mel was pretty cut up about it. You guys married or what?'

I am not married but I have a partner Jonathon who I live with.

My Boss here is married to the cook Rosemary Aitken.'

'You are kidding me. My Mel is a serious fan of your wife, both from a cooking perspective and from a lust perspective. Those violet eyes and that divine tush; I have to throw cold water over Mel when your wife is on the TV. When is she coming over to make more programmes?'

Allen smiled and thought that there was no way that Aitken was going to tell Rosemary that she was the object of lust for some lesbian in Chicago or that she had a divine tush. She was also wondering how Aitken was coping with Miss Armstrong's rather forthright expression. Still he seemed to be cool about it.

'Good question,' said Aitken. 'Rosemary never quite knows. The Producers decide all these things. The next port of call is looking like being the Emirates. That too is not firmed up.'

Kristy Armstrong looked at her watch and shook her head.

'You guys are going to have to excuse me but I have to phone home. Can you leave details with reception of where to get to your place in the UK? Really been a pleasure meeting you. I shall see what I can get to keep your Super happy.'

With that Armstrong got up and left.

'Well that was different,' said Allen.

'It certainly was,' agreed Aitken.

Chapter 61

★ ★ ★ ★

~Just a Barrow Boy~

'Right before we were interrupted what I was going to talk about was what we need to do to keep us in one piece. Purbright has been shot once and is not keen on a repeat. I am not keen on even a first time and I assume you are similar. Farsai is currently in Cambodia of all places so I would expect he will probably stop off in Myanmar on his way back home to either St Petersburg or Perpignan in France.'

'Are you telling me Purbright tracked him down in that timeframe?'

'Yes, I got a text while we were eating at the Hawkers Market.'

'I wished to hell I knew how he does it.'

'So do I,' said Aitken, 'because he has even picked up on the possible names of Farsai's Chechnyan friends. Our meeting here with Armstrong probably means that they are going to have first chance at Collins.'

'That's surely not a bad thing. We are going to need help as we are dealing with such an international organisation. At the end of the day we are after Fanshawe. That is one screwed up man. Did you see the amount of times he changed personalities today?

George Royston is the nasty personality, Wendell Fanshawe the theatrical and nicer component of his personality. The problem is they blur. There is almost a third persona which is a hybrid of the two.'

'Yes, I agree, both about Fanshawe and the fact we need more help. The question is how much is Purbright going to allow

Collins to go elsewhere. Collins told Ridgeon to organise the hit on Amy. Then there is Ross Morgan who had the sycophantic idea to use Fanshawe's original script to wipe out Amy. There is something interesting about Morgan. More information is surfacing about him. He might be the Asian Business Director and live in Hanoi most of the time with a 'wife' and family but very interestingly he has a second 'wife' and she lives near Oxford. He frequently visits the UK to see her. Travels in under a different passport. The alias he uses is Peter Landsdowne. She lives as Mrs Peter Landsdowne. We have an address and it is a seriously wealthy neighbourhood. One of his neighbours plays football at the very top level. Houses fetch close to five million in his little backwater.'

'My God, so he could have been in the UK masterminding Amy's death.'

'No Allen I do not think so, or he would have fallen into the culpable category. The very opposite was the case. He was up for praise.'

'Does that mean Sir, that if we give Collins to the other agencies we can lift Ross Morgan and Wendell Fanshawe? I know that we are due to be eliminated but I am more worried about Byron Mann's claim that he can wipe out four people. Vitra and his cronies and our little weasel friend Dobra.'

'Yes, I was coming to him as we have history. I admit that is an extremely worrying claim. He was pretty confident that he could achieve his task. I think he probably has a solid plan. He will be keen to prove a point to Fanshawe. Mann is just a barrow boy made good.'

'What do you mean a barrow boy?'

'Exactly what I said. He started off street trading in the East End. Maggie Thatcher's Britain was the making of Arthur Mann. He was the original 'Loadsamoney' and he then changed his name by deed poll to Byron to give him more street credibility.'

'So if he doesn't have the background he will find it difficult to crack the establishment in Britain.'

'Doesn't need to Allen, money does it for you. Mann has tried to change sides of the tracks in his persona and lifestyle but when he wants something done it is back to his shady and somewhat sleazy friends for help. I tried to nail him down about six years ago when he beat a prostitute so badly that she died. Oh I haven't forgotten Mr Mann and I should personally like to nail his ass.'

'Does he know you personally?'

'No, because we didn't have enough evidence to bring him in for questioning. I would derive extreme pleasure from putting Mann away for a very long time.

At that moment Aitken's mobile went.

'You realise you are on my mobile Sir.

The caller obviously said something.

Sir you can hardly expect me to be sitting in my room waiting for a phone call from you especially in a five star hotel and with an expense account. Tell you what, I shall go to my room, you have the number. Phone me in five.'

'That I assume was Purbright.'

'It was, the problem is he is eight hours behind so he still has a lot of the day left. I shall return. Order me another of those, a large one this time as I might need it.'

Chapter 62

★ ★ ★ ★

~*You speak to yourself*~

Thirty minutes later Aitken came back and sat down.
'My God, said Allen. That was a long five minutes. Your drink
will be here, well exactly now to be precise. I told them to hold it
until you returned.'

The waiter who had ghosted in and laid down Aitken's drink
had simply ghosted away having first checked if anything else was
required.

'You have to admit they have service down to an art form. I
sent all the materials we have collected over the past two days and
Purbright is a very happy bunny. He says he is going to have a
spring sale.'

'What do you mean a spring sale?'

'Oh, he is having a sale alright. The stuff we have collected is
dynamite actually and he will offer it up to the big boys in return
for markers and favours. The deals will come with handcuffs. He
wants Fanshawe, Mann and Morgan.'

'You make them sound like a firm of Solicitors.'

'No, these are just plain ordinary crooks, they will never be
found wearing legal wigs.'

'Aitken, that is absolutely a terrible innuendo, especially as you
are a member of the law enforcement society yourself.'

'Well there are times when they give me the pip. They have
helped some amount of guilty scum to walk free over the years.'

Allen was slightly taken aback by the fierceness with which
Aitken delivered his comment.

'What does he think of the fact that Mann is going to be able to take out four targets, or more accurately try?'

'Like me he is tempted to let him be successful but we are not allowed to. We are going to keep our powder dry on that one and try to stay abreast of developments. Surprisingly he has got Homeland Security; I think he might be asking our American friends to tap Mann's phones. Purbright isn't fond of Americanisms unless they actually pertain. He is trying to organise the same for Morgan's house.'

'He has been busy then.'

'Oh he has, but he hasn't cracked Vitra yet.'

'I bet that is not going down well.'

'You could say that, I think you will find that it is our task to interview Mr Vitra on Monday. Could in fact be our first task after debriefing.'

'I think we have a very busy time ahead of us when we get back. I was sort of going over all the things we have to do when we return. I was having a question and answer session with myself,' said Allen

'Is that the only way you get sane conversation when you are out with me? You speak to yourself, speaks volumes about the standard of my company.'

'You know exactly what I meant Sir. I just ask myself something like, do we actually need to spend effort on Amy's computer in view of all the new developments we have. I think we do. I think we can nail down Fanshawe through Amy's computer. I agree with their assessment that somewhere a key exists to open up that computer. He was talking in metaphors and I suddenly thought what if it was a real physical key. I have sent Laura a task to check Amy's physical keys. I want them all identified and I hope that one exists that we need to find a lock for. Laura is busy on that. I am annoyed, as I should have thought of it earlier. The guy that works with Amy will help identify any works keys. I am slightly surprised that ADI haven't beaten us to the keys.'

'That, Allen, is brilliant, simple but brilliant. I can almost guarantee there is a good chance you are right. Like you, now that you mention it, I am surprised ADI have not asked for their keys back. Tell you what Allen, if that's what speaking to yourself does, you can sit there for the rest of the evening and chat away to yourself until your heart's content. I will not interrupt you. Have you spoken to yourself about Fanshawe by any chance?'

'You are partaking of the Michael Sir. I have to admit that I have. We now know a lot about Fanshawe. He is possibly using an alias to live somewhere in the Stratford area. I did wonder if it was something Shakespearean he was using. Trouble is a name from one of the plays is a bit obvious, but I couldn't think of a sensible one. Christopher Marlowe is a possibility but would attract too much interest. I am sure it will have a 'luvvie' connection. The other me argued that he might live there but still not officially exist. He still maintains the invisible man role. He is possibly living in a property which is in someone else's name. Bottom line is all we need to do is to follow Collins from Bristol Airport to his destination then keeps tabs on him and Fanshawe. Problem for me is I want to identify Fanshawe before then.'

'Why Allen, why can you not wait?'

'Because you said you wanted to arrest them all simultaneously. I think that we should organise gathering this whole lot up in one operation, co-ordinated on a worldwide basis. Every one picked up within a few minutes of each other. No chance for them to speak to each other. All trussed like Christmas turkeys.'

'Well that was my theory but I think that is going to be difficult to achieve but it has merits. I think you would push the limits of even Purbright's negotiation skills to get all parties to agree to that. That said it has a lot of gain for us, no cross chatter. We scoop up the legal eagles and the accountants. Fortunately they were all present so they share culpability in the plans to eliminate three officers of the law like wot we is.'

'Who writes your scripts Aitken. Have you been watching those old Morecambe and Wise repeats again?'

'Worse Allen, you even knew the reference. Maybe you are older than you maintain.'

'Comments like that will cost you tea and tiffin at Raffles. I shall hold you to that promise. Do you know I held that drink off so that the ice wouldn't melt and you haven't touched a drop yet.'

'The problem was your riveting conversation. Cheers Miss Allen, here's to dodging the assassin's bullet.'

'I'll drink to that.'

'Do you fancy getting up early tomorrow and doing a bit of sightseeing. We can finish off with tea and tiffin. There is a heck of a lot to see in this place. I am going to go down to the shops and see what gifts I can get Rosemary and the monsters.'

'You are horrible Sir, they are not monsters either of them.'

'Sorry Allen, you are right. They really are a smashing pair of kids. Come on then, shops stay open late here, you can get Jonathon something. I saw the most fantastic cuff links on display at the Airport and the shop is just around the corner from us.'

'Yes, that might work. He loves his shirts and his cuff links. Come on, on your feet.'

'Hey, this was my suggestion and now I am being railroaded.'

'Railroaded my ass, I have it on good authority, your father no less, that you are as tight as a duck's bottie under water. Come on, spend some money on your loved ones.'

I'll probably spend more on Jonathon's cuff links than you will on the whole family.'

'I find that rather judgemental Allen. You have no idea how much I am willing to spend on my family. I am sure that it will be more than adequate.'

'Oink, Oink, flap, flap, and pigs will fly.'

'Allen you are heading for a sound thrashing.'

'I am heading for the shops where I, as one of the poorer members of society, shall probably spend more than I can afford by purchasing goods yet again on my credit card thereby helping both the UK and global economies.'

'You frequently accuse me of bull Allen. You have raised it to an art form.'

'Pure flattery Sir, I was taught by a master, you.'

'That does it Allen, let us shop.'

'Then let the elderly show the youth the way.'

'You really are bordering,' said Aitken smiling.

Chapter 63

★ ★ ★ ★

~Taking Silk~

The following day they were up early and out. A really super morning followed. Finally they arrived at Raffles for Tea and Tiffin. That was to prove as wonderful as it sounded

'You now know why everybody goes on about this place. This is one of these places that leave an indelible stamp on its patrons. There are only a few hotels in the world that have that mystique.'

'I would agree with that Sir. Actually thanks to your efforts it has been a pretty good trip and I have thoroughly enjoyed the experience. Hopefully we can reap the benefits of your work and put these people behind bars. What did you buy Rosemary?

The change of topic actually caught Aitken by surprise and he replied 'Silk' before he meant to say it.

'Silk? Silk what, silk scarves, silk stockings, silk suits, silk tops, silk nightwear or perhaps silk underwear? Pretty wide-ranging material silk. Care to elaborate Sir?'

'Well just silk Allen, what else do you need to know?'

'Oh, chapter and verse Aitken, you are not sliding out from under this one. If you are taking silk home I am truly in need of detail. Was it a silk teddy, silk bra, silk panties or maybe even a silk Basque?'

'Jesus Allen, keep your voice down.'

'Oh sorry Sir, you are going a nicer shade of red. Mind you that sun is strong out there. Tell me something, was the present for you or Rosemary?'

'Aitken finally laughed, 'Probably both of us, happy now?'

'Not really, I wanted a description of colour, style, the whole picture but I note your discomfort so I shall let you off the hook. Well no, not quite. Silk is cheap here so did you spend more or less than a three figure sum?'

'My God, you really are a woman, you are extremely nosey.'

'I shall ignore the sexist comments, just answer the question.'

'Well firstly I disagree silk is cheap here. That has not spread to the emporium that I gave my business to. Yes it was a lot more than a three-figured sum. Perhaps we may go up a tier. Can we now change subjects.'

'Wow Aitken, serious money, I am proud of you. I am just looking after Rosemary's interests. We girls have to stick together and without a little prodding I doubt if you would have returned home with anything worthwhile.'

'Well I reckon Rosemary is going to be delighted with your use of the cattle prod.'

'Cattle prod, my God you love to exaggerate. A tiny, slight prod, a small word here, a small word there and you call it a cattle prod. Would I be right in assuming Rosemary is not a nag?'

'No she's not, what makes you ask that?

'Because Sir, you really do not like to be nagged at, even in the slightest degree. You obviously are not subjected to it.'

At that moment Aitken's phone went.

'Damn, I meant to have this on vibrate. I hate it going off in a restaurant.

'Oh hello Dad, surprise, surprise, I am still in Singapore. This is costing you a fortune.'

Allen kind of guessed that Aitken Senior pointedly explained to his son that roughly he could not give a shit about how much it was costing although Allen knew James Aitken would have far too much class to put it in such graphic terms. Whatever it was Aitken Junior seemed chastened.

'Your call Dad, what was it you wanted to tell me?

Aitken listened patiently. 'You are kidding me.' 'You are sure about that? 'That is fantastic.' 'Well I never.'

These were interspersed by gaps in which Aitken Senior was telling his son what was obviously very interesting news.

'That is just brilliant Dad. Well done, glad to know that the old grey cells are working as well as ever. I am looking forward to seeing you. Oh how did Charlie get on at his interview?'

The response from the other end was obviously to Aitken

Junior's liking.

'Brilliant, thanks for that, please thank Chris as well. See you tomorrow. I have a small present for you. I need it now after that piece of detective work. See you Dad, thanks.'

'Well would you believe that Allen? Dad has located the early episodes of Z Cars with Wendell Fanshawe in a bit role. He did not act under the name Wendell Fanshawe which is his real name. You are going to be well pleased with his name, Hector Speed, a combination of Shakespearean characters, pretty good by you Allen.'

'Speed is from the two Gentlemen of Verona, where does Hector pop up?'

'He is in Troilus and Cressida, Allen.'

'Of course Sir, it would be something like the Hector of the Greek epic Troy. That is totally egotistical and totally understandable for Fanshawe. The name was more likely to be Shakespearean than Arthurian. This Knight thing came later. Come on, I am fascinated to know how your father tracked down what must be some very rare footage.'

'Well quite amazing really. Seemingly he published a book in the early eighties which was written by a woman who considered this era to be the great and golden age of television. He vaguely remembered her mentioning that she had a large library of tapes of these classic programmes. He tracked her down and happily she is still alive albeit in her early nineties but clear in mind. She was delighted to hear from Dad and even more delighted when he visited her in the Cotswolds. Seemingly her book was well written and had made her a very nice earner in later life. She was able to show Dad the early episodes. Dad recognised Fanshawe right away and the credits gave his name as Hector Speed.'

'That has to be some piece of detective work. We are getting tantalisingly close to Wendell Fanshawe, George Royston or Hector Speed or whatever else he calls himself.'

'That is still the problem Allen, that is all we are, tantalisingly close. We are still not there yet. Still this is going to cost me a large Bombay Sapphire and tonic.'

'There you go, Purbright's mentor Dunbar would approve. He would be saying there has to be a limit to your extravagance laddie, ye dinna want to be treating the old man to a meal do you? If it was me I would only be thinking about a single dram.'

'Allen, you need to stop watching those old repeats of Star

Trek. Scotty the engineer, you are getting far too much exposure to that terrible Scots accent.'

'Yes, pretty bad wasn't it.'

They both laughed. Allen looked at her watch.

'Hey, have you seen the time. We need to get back and pick up our stuff so that we can get to the Airport. Back to chilly Britain.'

'I know Allen, but it is home.'

Chapter 64

★　★　★

Putting the 'Hems' on Purbright

T hey both slept quite well and the flight was on time. Jonathon was there to greet Allen and she seemed very pleased about it. Aitken was much more surprised by who was there to greet him. Frank Purbright stood waiting outside the customs. Allen was more than slightly surprised to see him as well.

She came across and asked, 'Is everything OK, Sir?'

'Yes Detective very well indeed thanks to the fine work you two have done. Mrs Aitken was coming to pick up our man here but I suggested due to the nature of the hour I would drive him back home. I can get up to speed on the drive. Have a good weekend, what is left of it. I need you at your very best for Monday morning. I hope that you are going to have more success in interrogating Vitra. As I say, good work Detective, well worth the trip. Oh take this with you, I shall be briefing Aitken on the way home.'

'Thanks Sir, see you Monday morning.'

In Purbright's car it was obvious to Aitken that Purbright was seething.

Something wrong, Sir?'

'You can bloody well say that again. Some bugger is trying to put the hems on me.'

'Sorry Sir, I do not know the expression.'

Oh it's a Dunbar one. In Scotland there are some sheep that no fence can keep in. They always manage to get through. I like to think that I am one of those kinds of a sheep. I can get through whatever fences are popped in front of me even if I am not supposed to. What happens is that the shepherd puts a wooden cross thing around the errant sheep's neck, which prevents the sheep from getting through the fence. Seemingly this restriction device is called a hems. Some bugger is trying to fit me up with one. That Mann guy is back home and he is wasting no time to use his money and influence. I was called into the Assistant Commissioner's office this morning at have past bloody eight in the morning. There was a senior figure from our security services. I was given an extremely no nonsense dressing down by Jenkins. I was seemingly targeting ADI as being responsible for Amy Anderson's death when there was nothing whatsoever to connect ADI with such an event. Anderson was about to be terminated by ADI as she had a serious drug habit and had became a liability within the company. Unless I could come up with proof of my damaging allegations ADI were going to take us to court for defamation. We have been nobbled. Well there is something they have greatly underestimated and that is no bugger nobbles me when I am in the right.'

There was practically smoke coming out his ears. Aitken had seen Purbright go off the deep in the past but this was a cold fury. This was really dangerous. He didn't give Mann much of a chance in the long run.

'I take it you have kept quiet about our little trip to Singapore.'

'For the time being I have. Mann is not going to know that we have an inside track.'

'I thought you would have used our Security Services to bug Mann.'

'I think I used the expression Homeland Security.'

'You farmed it out to the FBI?'

'No Homeland Security is a privateer. They are a company in Northampton ran by an old friend of mine. They are damned good at surveillance.'

Aitken laughed. 'What if it is found?' It is an illegal wire-tap.'

'Oh I think what might be on there is going to be in my spring sale.'

'I take it you are still having a spring sale Sir?'

'All the more need now, more than ever I would say Aitken. I need to get our products in front of parties who are prepared to act on what they purchase. You did a cracking job out there and I am not letting that go to waste. I've had a very good offer from that wee lassie Armstrong who you met in Singapore. She and her boss Michaels are coming in on Tuesday. I want you and Allen to accompany me to the meet. This is going to be a very clandestine meeting away from the office. This is a hire car I hired on the spot. I thought that they might have bugged my car. My friend Des is coming in with his team to sweep our offices, cars, phone lines and mobiles. Mann has moved at such a speed, he has to be having inside help. We might have been tantalisingly close but now we are some way from getting to these people. Believe you me Aitken we are going to nail them. As I said, nobody puts the hems on me. I have given a message to Allen so that she knows to stay off the phone.'

'Do you think you could have been followed here Sir?'

'No, not a chance. What I haven't managed to do is check out your father's gem about Hector Speed. Who the hell does this guy think he is, Sir Laurence? Hector Speed I ask you? I need to know that I am bug free. If I am not, all hell is going to break loose.' If our phones are compromised we go on to Pay as You Go. I do not care what it costs.'

'Sir, I think that is a good idea anyway. They can get our mobile numbers and scan for them. Let's make it damned difficult for them. Let us cut a deal with Michaels. I am told he has a lot of your characteristics.'

'That's funny because I was told he has a short fuse, a hot temper and likes to get his own way.'

'I rest my case,' said Aitken.

Purbright laughed and with it he relaxed.

'Aye, it's good to have you home laddie. There will be a few at home thinking the same shortly.'

The rest of the journey passed in a much lighter mood. They both formulated their plan of action and what they were going to do to enable Purbright to go through fences that he wasn't allowed to.

Chapter 65

★ ★ ★ ★

~We are merely Messengers~

Monday morning was a horrible morning, heavy rain and driving winds but warm and humid. Demisting the car on the way to work was a major problem for everyone. As usual in these conditions, the journey took much longer. The inevitable crashes caused by the guy who flew past you, the guy who had better eyesight, better brakes and better driving skills!!

When Aitken and Allen got to the station Purbright was in his office.

'Come in you two and close the door. Meet my friend Des. Des is going to give you the quick once over. Five minutes later Des announce you two are clear. Can I have the keys to your cars please and your mobile phones. He was given their keys and phones and Des left Aitken and Allen alone with Purbright.

Right, this place is bug free but the phones are tapped. That goes for my home phone. My mobile is still OK. That is just as well as Michaels and I made our plans on it. Des thinks that is just a matter of time for them to be bugging our mobiles. They cannot get easy access to the actual records, i.e. who you have phoned, who has phoned you. That is pretty tight but they can scan and listen in. My car is not only bugged for sound it has a GPS tracker in it.'

'Who the hell is doing this Sir?' asked Allen.

'People Mann has paid with sweeteners to do it, that's who. Not necessarily our security forces but privateers, just as Des is a privateer.'

'You make him sound like a pirate Sir,' said Allen.

'Don't know about him being a pirate but he is a bandit, the prices he charges. We shall keep the bugs in place but feed those who are listening the biggest amount of horse manure that you can imagine. Right, I want you two to go and scare Vitra shitless. He still has some inkling that ADI are going to rescue him. Go and set him straight. Meantime I am going to work on a strategy of deception.'

When they got to the jail Vitra was already in an interview room waiting for them.

'Who are you?' he asked. 'A couple of Purbright's lackeys.'

'In that we work for Purbright you would be correct.'

'Well Purbright tried to fool me into telling him about something I know nothing about. I called his bluff. My daughters are in no danger from that old man. You can interview me for as long as you like but I'm giving you no more than I gave Purbright and that was zilch.'

'Who told you that we were here to interview you?' asked Aitken. 'If someone did they are feeding you bullshit. No, we are merely messengers.'

'What the hell are you on about?' demanded Vitra.

'Are you thick or something? What do think a messenger does? We are not bloody here to dance with you Vitra. We are simply here to pass on messages. Firstly Mister Vitra, you misjudge our Superintendent. He doesn't bluff. Your daughters look quite beautiful. Your youngest is only a little older than my own daughter. I believe they reside close to the beautiful village of Sher Surkh. What we are about to do is have the local troops spread the rumour that your daughters give their favours to the troops.'

'Jesus, you cannot do that, it is like signing their death warrant.'

'I thought you were a Muslim. You blaspheme in your own religion. Anyway that is the first message. According to Purbright he gave you ample opportunity. Anyway that is your funeral or to be more accurate,' said Aitken smiling, 'your daughters' funerals.

'You Bastard.'

'Tut, tut, that's no way to speak to an officer of the law. I could deem that as a personal attack and I would have to break your sodding arm just to teach you a lesson.'

Vitra recognised the viciousness in Aitken and for the very first time Allen knew Vitra was just a little afraid.

'You are mental,' said Vitra.

'Perhaps I am, perhaps I am,' said Aitken.

Allen could see the disquiet within Vitra growing.

'Right Detective Allen, please convey to Mr Vitra our further good news. His daughters will likely get stoned to death and he is likely to get de-stoned to death. They are going to have your balls Vitra. We are going to do nothing to stop them. I find this whole episode so very amusing. Your mistake Vitra was misjudging Purbright. Purbright is a bad poker player because he doesn't know how to bluff. I hate poker. Crosswords man me. Feel free Allen to explain where his nuts are going to depart to.'

'You really are something else Aitken.' said Vitra.

'Mr Vitra I am Detective Constable Allen. You have already put your daughters in extreme danger because you thought Purbright was bluffing. Do not judge the DCI Aitken wrongly either or you are going to be in even bigger trouble. We had you removed from the plane when you were on your way to Singapore to a meeting of the Knights of the New Order, the venue being The Ascot Park Hotel in the Stanford Room with the meeting to commence ten o'clock sharp. By the way, apart from Mr Ridgeon, who you prevented from attending, you were the only other no show, which is maybe just as well for you. Barratt Gold has done a fantastic job on the Business Development side and you seemingly are not servicing the clients. It appears that you have been more interested in servicing ladies in the various Russias that you are supposed to be looking after.'

Vitra was now sitting like a rabbit in the headlights.

'Your action of eliminating Philip Ridgeon has meant there is now a vacancy. Give Wendell Fanshawe his due he acted quickly. So quickly in fact that it came as a surprise to the assembled cast. Only John Collins knew about it and oh, probably Nadine Kraft. In fact, I actually do know she knew, nothing probably about it.'

'You two are both the same, you are both nuts. It is a bloody game to you both.'

This time it was Allen who came across as vicious.

'Vitra, it is no bloody game to us. You cold callous bastards executed a vibrant young woman in front of her family. If your two daughters are cannon fodder as a result of the war that your people started, so be it. If you think we actually give a shit about you and your daughters, dream on. Purbright wasn't bluffing. You screwed that well and truly up and neither my boss here nor I have any time for you or your daughters. I am simply carrying out an instruction I was given this morning. I do not even want to be here with a lowlife scum like you but I have to, it goes with the territory. Now shut up and do not interrupt me again or I shall break your nose. Is that clearly understood?'

Vitra sort of mumbled 'Yes'

Aitken had a quiet smile to himself. He was sure that Vitra was thinking that he'd gone from one psychopath to an even bigger one.

'Right, where was I?' said Allen. 'Oh yes Fanshawe's replacement for Ridgeon is none other than Byron Mann the world famous hedge fund financier. Sworn in as a Knight of the New Order. Got what we thought was a bummer of a first task. Eliminate your two Albanian friends, finish off the job you botched and then for the *coup de grace,* finish you off. He already knows you are all in solitary in high security institutions. That did not seem to bother him. He assured Fanshawe he would complete the task.'

It was obvious from Vitra's body language and expressions that he knew Allen was telling the truth. He had no idea how she had obtained her information but he knew she wasn't bluffing. Purbright and his team were nothing more than a bunch of psychopaths.

Allen continued. 'There is more news. You could say good news, bad news. Made us laugh though.'

'I'm bloody sure it did,' said Vitra.

'I warned you,' said Allen and drew back her hand.

Aitken said, 'Easy Tiger.'

'Sorry Sir,' said Allen.

Vitra meanwhile had covered his nose with his hands and he took them down.

'That would have been a waste of time. I will break your nose even with your hands there. It is all about the sheer speed and exerting sufficient force, easy with a sitting duck as a target. Anyway I digress. Oh yes, what was it that made us laugh, I remember now. You might call this out of the frying pan into the fire. Bottom line is we are going to allow Mr Mann to take out your Albanian friends and the one you screwed up on. You however, have value it appears. We are having a Spring Sale and you are our special offer. There are several interested parties. So far one of the US agencies has put in the best bid. A Mr Brad

Michaels is able to extend his hospitality. As you might know already, Brad Michaels is responsible for Mr Tamblin spending over nine hundred million and getting nothing in return. Mr Tamblin, similar to your own good self, will not fall upon his sword so Fanshawe has given Collins the task of creating yet another vacancy. All I can say is if that's what being a Knight means I am glad I am excluded on a gender basis. If Brad Michaels is to be believed you may yet land up back home in Afghanistan. You might not see much of it and you sure as hell will not be happy to be home.'

'Look I have heard about this type of shit. It is illegal, you are not allowed under the Geneva Convention to do this.'

'I wasn't aware you were a prisoner of war,' said Aitken. 'Actually you are not anything or anyone any more. Detective Allen here has been busy. You simply do not exist anymore. We have wiped the records clean. You are not even in our custody anymore.

DCI Aitken is correct. I have had you expunged from the records. That slightly negates your chances of any further legal representation. You shall be put on a plane tomorrow night and after that we have no further interest in you.'

'Right Detective Allen, unless you have anything else I think we are finished here.'

'No Sir, there is nothing else I need to tell Mr Vitra.

'You two are sodding joking, I have rights.'

'You had rights, those are now cancelled,' said Aitken, 'just as your membership of society has been cancelled.'

'That's illegal,' protested Vitra.

'We are only the messengers. You created the circumstances you now find yourself in. I put your chances of survival twelve months from now as no better than twenty per cent. I rate your daughters' chances even lower.'

'You call us Muslims barbaric.'

'Do not try that racist, religious shit with me,' said Aitken. 'I don't hold with it. Cut me and I bleed the same colour as you and I feel the same pain. Actually it is you who is the barbaric one. In fact, you are a murdering bastard and it wouldn't matter which race, religion or creed you were.' There was genuine venom in Aitken's voice.

'You had your chance and missed it, there is nothing we can do about it,' said Allen.

'I am sure there is,' said Vitra.

'No, Allen is right, we cannot do a thing. Purbright is the only guy who can keep you here and I am sure he is probably not that interested any more.'

'What if I gave him what he wants. Will that save my daughters?'

'Honestly Vitra, I do not know. Are you saying that you are willing to co-operate? I am not taking this to Purbright unless you are definite about this. If you really knew Purbright you would know why I need a very definite yes from you.'

You could almost hear Vitra thinking that Purbright must be something else if this guy is scared to phone him.

'Right, I will give you what you want if you can give me a guarantee that nothing will happen to my daughters.'

'I cannot give you that yet as I have no idea what the status is in Kandahar.

Purbright was seriously ticked off with you. Your only hope lies in the fact that it was the weekend and even that isn't a guarantee knowing Purbright. I shall phone him and we can only hope.'

Aitken phoned Purbright in front of Vitra.

'Sir, Vitra is willing to testify if you stop the actions you were taking in Kandahar. He does not want to be handed over to any other agency.'

There was obviously a response from Purbright.

'I told him there might be a chance with the weekend. Problem is they are ahead of as in time terms. Can you check and ring us back. We will wait until we hear from you. In the meantime we shall take Mr Vitra's statement. He can sign it if you are successful. Thanks, Sir.'

'Right Vitra, Purbright did activate that on Sunday. Hopefully the propaganda has not gone out yet. Purbright is going to check his contacts.'

They spent the next forty-five minutes getting Vitra's written confession and still no call from Purbright. They then sat for another forty minutes and then Aitken's mobile went off.

The three all jumped despite the fact that they were waiting for it to ring. Purbright was on the line.

Aitken listened intently then rang off.

'You Vitra, are a very lucky boy. The guy Purbright needed to speak to was at lunch. Fortunately our British diplomats are quite often slow to react and this guy hadn't done a thing about actioning Purbright's instruction. Right now things are held in abeyance subject to your signing this document. Purbright is not happy about disappointing Brad Michaels. There could be some fall out from that Allen.'

Vitra signed the documents. Aitken phoned Purbright to tell him to put the stop on his supposedly proposed action. They scooped up their confession and headed back to Railton. Vitra had gone very quiet. He knew that whatever happened he was facing a long time in jail.

'Well Allen, that nailed down John Collins as the one who instructed the hit in the prison. There is enough to ensure that he never leaves the country when he comes a-calling.'

'I'll tell you what Sir, it's a fine situation when we are being spied upon by the criminals, it really hacks me off. I was slightly surprised you didn't go for broke and get him to confess to his part in illegal ADI operations.'

'He is well and truly stuffed and he knows it. We shall revisit that topic later. I think he might have bridled at us trying for a series of confessions that could see him get twenty years. As it is he has got rid of a low life and will probably be out in eight years or so by his own reckoning. Do not worry Allen he is not getting away with a single thing.'

Chapter 66

★ ★ ★ ★

~*Tai Kwando*~

Back at the station Purbright shouted them into his office. All the team were there.

'Well done you two, that at least means we hold Collins when he pops in to visit. I have here a number of Pay as You Go phones. We only use our mobiles to mislead. I have briefed everyone about where we are, apart from you two but you shouldn't need any briefing. One thing, do not forget this is not the only case of importance going on in this office at the moment so take special care that you do not hold up any other investigation. We have been made the target of some rather well off criminals. It seems that my car has been bugged complete with a GPS tracker system, as has Detective Allen's. Aitken's banger is bug free. Why does that not surprise me? The criminals probably thought it was abandoned.'

There was a lot of laughter. Aitken wasn't too amused.

'Mind you it could be that he lives behind big gates and twenty foot high railings with a security system to rival Fort Knox where as Allen and I along with vast human population reside in ordinary dwellings where we leave our cars on driveways, streets and places like that.'

Again there was more laughter.

'Perhaps,' said a wag. 'The criminals have recognised the brains behind the team. Allen is the brains and Aitken the muscle. No need to bug the muscle.'

Again there was another round of laughter.

'You are probably right at that Jimmy,' agreed Purbright. 'Mind you I don't fancy your next task Jimmy.'

Jimmy slightly reddened and wished he hadn't been so bold.

'Right said Purbright. You are all briefed. What we need to give is the impression we are still after ADI. We still think they are involved. No mention must be made of any other member than John Collins or Wendell Fanshawe, the elusive, impossible to find Mr Fanshawe. Absolutely no mention must be made about Byron Mann, as far as he knows we are in complete ignorance of his existence as a Knight. No reference must be made to the Knights of the New Order. We can mention that Allen has this hypothesis that the tattoos on Ridgeon and Vitra mean something, possibly heraldic. We want to show and demonstrate ideas but we also want to demonstrate that they are on the wrong wavelength. We will maintain that Vitra is not cracking and not looking like cracking. Take care that we make no reference to his location. He is being moved shortly to another high security unit. We stay with the fact that Amy's computer is totally impenetrable.

Mind you that is not a lie. What is the latest with your work in that area Laura?'

'I have acted on Louise's instruction and the good news is that I am down to only one key of Amy's that I cannot account for. Problem is I haven't a clue what it's for.'

Laura held up a rather odd looking short key. What was odd about it was the strange shape of the head of the key.'

'Amy Anderson was a Tai Kwando participant,' said Jimmy.

'How do you know that?' said an amazed Laura.

Because I belong to a Tai Kwando club and we have that type of key. Mine is a different club if colour is anything to go by. Our keys are black. Pink is a strange choice of colour. I have no idea which club that belongs to, if indeed it is a club key. It must have been someone who visited my club or hers, as I have never seen anyone else with a similar key even when we go away for competitions.'

Are you sure she couldn't have been a member at your club.'

'No I think I might have remembered a babe like her.'

'Tell me something Jimmy how do you know what the key number is?' asked Allen.

'Simple, it is written on them.'

'Not on this one Jimmy.'

'Let me see it. Yes, it is the key to locker 56. Sorry, it is in Korean symbols.'

'So I suggest you get your ass around to your club and see if this opens locker 56 and if it doesn't we need to find the club that has the locker this opens.'

'No problem Laura, you only had to ask,' said Jimmy. 'Even if it isn't our club I am fairly convinced that it cannot be from either the area where Amy lived or where she worked.'

'Let us hope,' said Purbright, 'that this gives us the password to this computer. I think our luck needs to change as our dynamic IT duo Malcolm and Jo Jo are shortly leaving us to be wed. We need to give them a leg up with that computer before they leave for their nuptials. Two weeks from today computers will be the last thing on their minds. We also need to look to its safety. Mann was confident he could destroy it. Let us make sure he doesn't. We need to pick this computer up now and keep it here. If we are right in that Amy has stuff in this locker, then we get our soon to be weds over here instead. I think we should leave a decoy computer in its place. Then if they do succeed in making their target they will think they have got rid of Amy's computer. John, can you take care of that. Our IT guys can shift stuff onto a dummy for destruction.' Right, you know your briefing, stick to the rules. We are playing for high stakes here.'

Chapter 67

★ ★ ★ ★

~He seemed to go on rising forever~

At that moment Purbright's desk phone went.
'Good Afternoon Sir, what can I do for you?'

The caller was likely to be the Assistant Commissioner.

'Well Sir I think you can understand that I am well displeased when someone tries to interfere with our enquiries. I couldn't care what that guy from Security thinks or says. ADI are guilty as hell.'

There was a gap as Purbright listened.

'Fine Sir, I hear what you say. I shall lay off ADI as you suggest but I do it under extreme protest.'

There was obviously more chatter by the other party.

'Someday Sir, when we are finally proved to be right I want you in here to apologise to my hard working team. I agree we have a guy in custody who was one of the murderers but they were only a hit team. We really should pursue the people who were responsible for commissioning the hit. That person was John Collins who gave the order and ADI whose interests he was protecting.'

Even in the room the assembled staff could hear the shouting coming from the other end of the phone.

'Whatever you say Sir, but if we ran for cover every time someone shouted litigation we would never solve a crime. Someone up high has nobbled you guys.'

The party on the other end obviously went ballistic.

'Sir I am not particularly saying that you have been nobbled but if you haven't been nobbled then someone above you most certainly has been.'

The entire assembled cast collectively thought that Purbright had balls, very big ones.

More shouting at the other end.

'Right Sir, we agree to disagree. I shall do what you instruct Sir and lay off. I think we get the message. That said, I should explain to my team that we have simply been nobbled. If you want to go ballistic so be it. I do not lie to my team. I think I shall ring off before I say something I might regret, goodbye Sir.'

The assembled room all collectively dropped their heads. They knew you could light a cigar off Purbright when he put down that phone. He stood up and for those sitting near his desk he seemed to go on rising forever. He pulled himself to his full six feet four and drew in a deep breath and said 'bloody man, he will be the death of me. Right let's get going and prove that clown wrong. He had better be man enough to come in here and apologise.'

The room cleared in record time.

'Not you Aitken and Allen, close that door.'

'Some bugger is squeezing that idiot's bits, problem is they probably cannot find anything to squeeze. I do apologise Allen but he really is a ball less wonder. Obviously pressure is raining down from on high. I am going to phone you shortly on your mobile and relay his instruction. We will then appear to be backing off. Tuesday we have Brad Michaels and Wednesday I want you two to take in a little culture at the home of our Bard. Fanshawe is out there and our systems are all being spied on so it is down to old-fashioned legwork. The stuff we used to do before we had all these computers. I hope your idea on those keys is a winner Allen. We are so damned tantalisingly close to nailing these sods and now we are being pushed back. Mann might be sticking it to us now so we need to stick it to him. I am going to arrange to move our four people that Mann is supposed to eliminate out of his reach. Michaels is willing to host them until we can put the rest away. They shall be ferried away by us and they are going to one of the US Air Force bases for a little Rest and Recreation. We need to assure Vitra we haven't sold him up the river.'

'I think he might be a bit twitchy about being put up by the Americans,' said Aitken.

'I will go and tell him personally and why we are doing it. Right, Farsai is due to go to Myanmar tonight in fact in two hours time he leaves Cambodia. We all know where he is going and who he is going to see, Nadine Kraft. I am now certain we have the names of who his two associates are. They are a Yakov Mihailov and Dimka Fedoseev. I have a wee birdie singing on the wires that tells me they are presently at home in Grozny. I tell you assassination is a good career as it certainly pays well. They both live in two huge mansions amongst the rich and famous in Chechnya. The Russian authorities are keen to talk to both. They have incited a number of uprisings not for any reason or purpose other than disorder. They were used for the assassination in Lahore and the Thai job was also Farsai's work. No political objective, they just did it for the money. Farsai was supposed to be the organiser. This damned snooping on us is slowing us down. I have concerns that once Mann finds out that he is about to let Fanshawe down we might become the soft target option. I want to know at all times where Farsai's men are and exactly where he is. I intend to take them out before they take us out. I am hopeful we can pick up on when they move and where they actually go. Right, let's get this whitewash stuff on the move. By the way we are taking a run in the back of a police van tomorrow. We are travelling, hidden in the van, to Slough. There we are meeting Brad Michaels and Miss Armstrong at a private house. This is a safe house far from prying eyes. Laura and John are up front doing the driving. I am not even taking a chance on being clocked. This really is a covert meeting. Brad Michaels I think is keen to work with us.'

'Well Sir I may have quite a bit to give him. I should, with a bit of luck, have the transcript of the Indian deal. This is the one that Collins is keeping from Fanshawe. I am having it forwarded to somewhere that Mann couldn't possibly know about it. Come with me Allen and we shall go and see if our bait has caught a fish.'

'I hope that it's a big fish Aitken. The more I can give Michaels the better, the more I get for us. Let's see what is in your net.'

'I take it we are using different pool cars all the time?' said Aitken.

'You take it as right. Do not forget that these are much newer vehicles than you normally drive Aitken.'

'Fine sir, I shall drive them with care. I get the message.'

Allen smiled at Purbright and she was positive there was a twinkle in his eye.

Chapter 68

★ ★ ★

~Nanny Watson~

In the car Allen asked, 'Where are we going Sir?'
'We are going to see a wonderful old lady of nearly ninety, Nanny Watson to be precise.'

'I take it we are talking your Nanny Watson Sir? I wasn't even aware that you had a nanny.'

'Well I did and a lovely one she was. My Mum was never too strong and Dad decided that two boisterous children were a little bit too much for her. Nanny Watson came when I was four. She would become one of the family just as Ken the Gardener did.

She lives close to Haslemere. She really has a chocolate box house.'

When they arrived Allen could see that Aitken wasn't joking. This was the full chocolate box house job. Aitken rang the doorbell. Allen expected some little old lady to answer the door. The door was answered by an elderly woman all right and nearly as tall as herself and ramrod straight. She simply reeked of class and the cut glass voice confirmed it.

'Well young Jeremy you finally found a little time in your busy schedule to visit an old lady. Please come in.'

Inside the house was immaculate. Aitken made the introductions.

'Nanny this is my colleague Louise Allen.

'Pleased to meet you Louise, my name is not actually Nanny but Priscilla Watson. I take it I would be right in saying that you look after young Jeremy here?. He can be a handful at times. Quite a wilful child at times but you haven't turned out too bad other than being a bit forgetful about visiting his rather old and infirm Nanny.'

Allen thought that Nanny Watson was about as infirm as the Rock of Gibraltar.

Nanny picked up both Aitken's hands and looked at them.

'Glad to see you are keeping those nails clean and in good shape. Jeremy used to bite his nails, quite the most disgusting habit. I hope that you shall take tea.'

'Yes please Nanny. I take it my stuff has come in?'

'Yes, it is on the escritoire. Louise can you give me a hand.'

'I have a feeling that my ears are going to burn.'

'Do not flatter yourself young Jeremy, you are not that important. We girls have far more important things to discuss. This young woman has all the grace of a debutante and the matching dress sense. Please come and tell me what this summer fashions are likely to be. Sadly all too impossible at my age but it is nice to imagine.'

Allen had immediately taken to this amazing woman. Priscilla was a serious class act.

Aitken picked up the e-mail. This was the condensed version and was thirty-seven pages long. The detail that had been collected was fantastic as was the scale of the deal that Gupta and Sanjeev Bajani had closed with Collins's help. The deal would put just over two and a half billion dollars in the ADI coffers. This would get Collins lots of brownie points with Fanshawe. This would also get Purbright lots of brownie points with Michaels. This was heavy duty in that arena.

The two women returned to the room animatedly chatting and laughing.

'I assume that is what you want. You have been skulking in corridors again hoping to hear something to your liking. Doesn't always work out in life but it is probably a useful tactic in your profession. I had such high hopes that young Jeremy here would have a Chair in Oxford by now. Is it ordinary coffee for you Jeremy, or one of these number of different names they give coffee these days so that they can charge you more?'

'Black coffee is fine Nanny.' said Aitken.

'That's my Ronald there Louise. He was a Captain in the Royal Artillery. Killed in '44 by our US cousins in what has to be the biggest oxymoron of the lot, friendly fire. Sadly it took me decades to stop hating the Americans and everything American. I was on holiday on a cruise in the Mediterranean some eleven years ago when I met an American lady purely by chance at the dining table. She was my age and from Wichita Falls in Kansas. The cruise was scheduled to take in Italy. Her husband had died in Italy during the War. She had never been outside the US since he died. Her husband and five of his colleagues had taken a direct hit from a twenty-five pounder. The trouble was, it was from a British gun. I knew from experience that it would have been, very likely, a Royal Artillery piece. My hate stopped that day as did hers. When I told her my tale we just hugged each other and quietly sobbed. I sobbed an awful lot more last year when she passed away. Dorothy had become a great friend. You did say black? I have no idea how you can drink it like that. Mr Aitken would never dream of taking coffee like that.

'Look, it is just fine like that Nanny.'

'I was speaking with Kate Winstanley. It appears that you have employed an apprentice to Ken for the garden, the young Allardyce boy. Glad to see that some of Mr Aitken's goodness has rubbed off on you. Personally I suspect Rosemary's hand at the tiller.'

'And you would be right. I got well and truly outflanked there. I was no more than Rosemary's messenger.'

How are my 'grandchildren?' Rosemary came by just over a week ago with Amelie and I must say I got quite a shock. That cygnet is well on the way to becoming a very beautiful swan. Fortunately she has inherited her mother's looks. Who's looks did you inherit Louise?'

'Well rather oddly they are my Grandmother's. My grandmother is just a lovely person. We love her dearly. I try to see her as often as I can. She is a widow and lives in Cheltenham.'

'How wonderful to know, that there are children who have grown to adulthood and still have time for the elderly in their family, isn't that so, Jeremy? How nice, to see someone actually enjoying tea and not picking at their food Louise. I like this partner of yours Jeremy.'

'You do not need to worry about Louise picking at her food she'll scoff the lot given half a chance.'

Jeremy Aitken, that is both a coarse and a most ungallant thing to say. You were never raised to be that rude. Is it this job? Is mixing with the criminal classes lowering your standards?'

Louise could almost feel Jeremy cringe and she came to his

rescue.

'I do not think so Mrs Watson. I think he was merely joshing.'

Well he can keep that kind of joshing for his rugby club friends I think an apology is in order.'

'Sorry Nanny.'

'I should think so too. Let us speak no more of the matter. It was nice to hear you call me Mrs Watson, Louise. We had only been married the eight months. Saddest part was we had no family. We knew that we were going to win the war and we decided to wait until after the war, that was a big mistake. Mind you it was lovely to look after other people's children. Sixty-five years I have been calling myself Mrs Watson. Helps keep the memory of Ronald alive. He was such a handsome man and what a dancer.'

The old lady then completely changed tack.

'That seems a thoroughly bad lot you have got yourself in with. They really do need locking up.'

'You read this then?' said Aitken.

'And why not? That came in on my broadband and was printed on my paper using my printer and ink cartridge. I think I have every right to read it. If you didn't want me to read it, send it somewhere else. I have a bone to pick with my ISP, provide Internet service that's a joke. Fifteen Meg, codswallop! If that system is breaking seven Meg I shall eat my hat. Dead slow and stop that's what speeds it has. Before you start blaming my computer, I have a new, all singing and all dancing, faster than a speeding bullet dual core job. Brain the size of a planet to quote Marvin.'

'Allen had to smile, Priscilla Watson was something else. She had obviously embraced the latest technologies to the extent that she was so very comfortable using them. Allen's mind also turned to Daisy Sims another nonagenarian, the two probably couldn't have been more dissimilar in background or cultures but they did share one thing in common. They were both thoroughly enjoying life and living each day like it was their last. At that great age it very well could be your last one.

'Look Nanny we are going to have to cut and run, my grateful thanks for the use of your Internet.'

'Anytime Jeremy, anytime. It was lovely to meet you Louise. Do you like my beautiful cottage? Mr Aitken bought me this as a retirement home. He has a gardener keep my gardens beautiful although I potter a bit myself. I like growing stuff in the greenhouse. Ken taught me a lot when we worked for Mr Aitken.'

She kissed Louise continental style and then hugged and kissed Jeremy.

'Come by soon with that wonderful family of yours. The sun comes up every day. At my age I never know, there might be a day soon when it comes up and I do not. You take care out there, especially with all those bad people about. That goes for you too Louise. You know where I live, drop in when you feel like it.'

Chapter 69

★ ★ ★ ★

~Emma Gaylord~

Louise was quiet in the car.
'You OK?' asked Jeremy.
'Yes, I am. I was just thinking about Mrs Watson. She is such a very alive person. Her comment about the Sun coming up one day and she will not. It was quite sad.'
'I wouldn't worry about Nanny, she will go on for ever.'
'That's the thing Aitken, she will not.'
'I know Allen, I know, I just try not to think about it. She's a real smasher though.'
'I would go along with that. Did your bug in India prove worthwhile?'
'I should say so; the scale of these guys and their operations is mind blowing.'
Allen read the document.
'Well that is pretty explosive. That should sort out Banjani and Gupta for a long time. Purbright's going to enjoy this tomorrow. What a bargaining chip. He is going to gorge on this.'

Back at the station things had moved on with the team. Amy Anderson's computer had been recovered from IT and a substitute loaded up and installed in its place. Interestingly Malcolm and Jo Jo had managed to progress further with the computer in that they had accessed a list of transactions for ADI, which Amy had designated as probably monies from illegal transactions. There was a very large amount of detail. Malcolm said that there was no way that she could have collated this information without either hacking in to company systems or alerting someone that the information was being accessed.

Purbright reckoned that there was enough for the Serious Fraud Squad guys to become involved but he wasn't going to inform them just yet. He wanted things to carry on as normal until he could scoop up the whole lot. The day he picked up the criminals would be the day they closed their operation down. Malcolm reckoned there were enough access codes in this one file alone to be able to let the SFS have a field day in the ADI computers.

Jimmy had also been busy. The key didn't fit the lockers in his club but he had found out where the other club was. What had happened was that a few years back Jimmy's club had been owned by a husband and wife team. They had separated and the wife had set up another club and she specialised in women members. This was the club that Amy Anderson belonged to.

Her family knew she was going to a gym they just didn't quite know where. They thought it was near Amy's work.

Melissa was the same, she thought Amy was just going to a gym and was slightly surprised it was a Tai Kwando club.

'Mind you, knowing Amy it is not something she might mention until she had become extremely good at it, a third Dan or whatever they have when you are very good at Tai Kwando.'

Much to Jimmy's frustration Amy's club closed on a Monday. He would have to wait until Tuesday.

Back in Purbright's office the three of them poured over the documents from India. Purbright was almost purring. 'Michaels is going to kill for this stuff. I reckon we can raise a pretty good joint campaign between us and one that would put away the entire lot for a long time. How was Mrs Watson, I take it still as sharp as ever?'

'Yes Sir, apart from her broadband operating at a snail's pace, she was fine.'

Allen was slightly surprised that Purbright knew Nanny Watson.

'You know those fingerprints that you uplifted for Nadine Kraft in Singapore? Well Aitken I have had some rather interesting news regarding Nadine Kraft. She is another one that sails under a flag of convenience. Her real name is Emma Gaylord.'

'You are kidding me,' said Aitken.

'You are going to have to help me here,' said Allen. 'I have no idea who Emma Gaylord is.'

Purbright continued. 'Fourteen years ago a pair of young German backpackers were in Australia as part of their gap year after they had completed University. They disappeared off the radar somewhere near Darwin. They would be found almost two months later in an outback farm building. They had died in the most horrific circumstances. They had been tortured, sexually assaulted and practically starved to death. Another three months passed and amid growing public pressure the Australian police announced the arrest of a young couple in their early twenties. The pair was a Darren Alderney and an Emma Gaylord. The two were as guilty as hell but bang in the middle of the trial Emma Gaylord escaped from the women's prison she was in. She killed a prison warder in her escape. She then disappeared off the face of the planet. Now she has popped up again, reinvented and in a position of power. Still helping to kill people so that should be right up her alley. The Australians will be simply delighted to get her back in custody. Again we shall sit on that until the right moment. I am still working away on the other fingerprints that you took Aitken. Who knows what it might turn up but I doubt if it will surpass the Kraft one.'

The next hour was spent formulating their presentation and what their strategy was going to be for the meeting with Brad Michaels.

'Right you two it is going to be an early start. We need to be in the safe house for eight o'clock tomorrow. I have been thinking about your trip to the West Country tomorrow. You can leave when we get back here. That will probably just be after lunch or slightly later. I have laid on lunch at the safe house.'

Back in Aitken's office Allen spoke. 'I have a bone to pick with you Sir. I knew nothing about all your little efforts to lift fingerprints of our ADI guys. I am trying to learn the ropes. How can I if you keep excluding me with that kind of action. Can I assume that somehow or other you have also bugged Nadine Kraft, would that be the case?'

'Yes Allen, I am sorry. I completely accept that I am in the wrong. I should have briefed you.'

'Yes, I reckon Purbright probably knew that I didn't know. He is brilliant at picking up on things like that.'

'Allen, I will make sure that there will be no repetitions. Believe me we are a team.'

Chapter 70

★ ★ ★ ★

~Brad Michaels~

The following morning dawned clear and bright but cool. Laura and John were ready and waiting. Purbright, Aitken and Allen took their places in the rear of the van, which had been reversed into a loading bay out of sight. The journey to Slough was a fairly quiet one. When the Van stopped it was inside a big garage to the house. When the garage door was closed everyone got out.

'Right follow me,' said Purbright.

He walked through the house. Aitken and Allen noticed that all the blinds were drawn. They walked into a large drawing room and there sat Brad Michaels and Kristy Armstrong. They both stood up.

Michaels looked at his watch and remarked 'Good, bang on time.'

He stood about the same height as Purbright. As he moved forward there was a slight almost imperceptible limp in his left leg. He offered his hand to Purbright. Allen noticed his hands were massive with huge fingers.

'Good Morning, Brad Michaels at your service.'

'Nice to meet you Brad, Frank Purbright here and this is Jeremy Aitken and Louise Allen.

Allen was slightly taken aback at what was obviously going to be a first names meeting. She was particularly surprised to hear Purbright use Frank. Hell would freeze over before anyone at Railton called Purbright by his first name. She certainly wasn't going to.

Michaels shook hands with Aitken and Allen and introduced Kristy to Purbright. More handshaking.

'Good Journey Brad?' asked Purbright.

'Yes, no complaints,' was the reply

'Right then let's get down to business,' said Purbright.

This seemed to be right up Michaels's street. No bull. No time wasted.

'Right,' said Purbright, 'we need your help. As you saw from my briefing documents this is a massive operation we are bringing down. All the stuff we have gathered would be inadmissible in our courts and in our jurisdiction. We do not try to kid ourselves. We are simply at the place where they murdered that girl. I do not allow that on my patch. Coming to the UK in about ten days are Collins, possibly Viktor Farsai and definitely two assassins. Also, Ross Morgan will be here. The one elusive man that we are so tantalisingly close to is the big boss of this operation Wendell Fanshawe.'

'Until I received some of your reports Frank we had never even heard of the man. He is a bit out in left field anyway, a bit of a weird character it seems.'

'I think you could put it that way,' said Purbright. 'We want, provided you are in agreement, Fanshawe and Mann as they are truly British. Collins and Morgan will also be arrested in this country. Collins is all yours as he really is an International criminal. I take it arresting all these guys simultaneously in different place gives your organisation no problems?'

'None at all, thanks for turning over Collins. That is one dude I shall take great personal satisfaction in nailing.'

'Then you can accompany us Brad, and be the arresting officer.'

'I might just take you up on that kind offer. What a rush that would give me.'

'Feel free, it is Byron Mann I am after for the others it is Wendell Fanshawe.'

'For me it would be Nadine Kraft,' said Kristy Armstrong.

'Well Kristy, you might just have your wish come true. Aitken lifted some fingerprints when he was in Singapore and she is in fact Emma Gaylord.'

'The Backpacker Murderess, that Emma Gaylord, Frank?' said an astonished Brad.

'The very one and the same, Brad. She is still ordering and

organising murders.' said Purbright.

'Right then Kristy, she is all yours.'

'I might have to go to Myanmar to arrest her Sir.'

'You can go to the North Pole if you have to. The Australians are going to love this one. They are going to be absolutely delighted. I have a good friend who is well positioned in the Police down there. I am sorry Frank but I think you have just earned me a huge steak at his expense. I am not stealing your thunder it's just I have known John for years. Gaylord's escape was a bit embarrassing at the time.'

'Brad, as long as we lock this entire damned crew up I have no problem who does what or when. Gaylord has managed to accumulate ten million Australian dollars. That should square away expenses. I just want Mann. I take it personally when someone sets out to execute me. You will be glad with Jeremy's next piece of espionage. This is an edited part of the overall discussions, which we have on tape. Here's a copy for you both.'

Michaels and Armstrong sat quietly and read through the transcript.

'My God Frank, these guys are operating on a massive scale. This is something else. This is close to mind blowing. There are a lot of names mentioned here that we will need to identify. In the timeframe left we are going to have to work our socks off to make sure that we are able to not only gather up the Knights but a lot of their Squires. Obviously we have been shadowing for some time and all we needed was a breakthrough. We have a substantial amount of information about these ADI guys. The Fanshawe guy and the Knights of the New Order was news to us.'

The next few hours were spent thrashing out a complete plan of action and who was doing what and when. At exactly twelve o'clock they heard a vehicle arrive.

'That is lunch arriving,' said Purbright. 'My people who are on guard shall deal with it. A couple of minutes later Laura popped her head in, lunch is in the dining room Sir. John is on watch.'

'Thanks Laura, make sure you both get fed as there is plenty to eat.'

Aitken was more than pleased when he got to the dining room. Where the hell Purbright had sourced the food he had no idea but it was first class. Purbright and Michaels had obviously hit it off. They sat and chatted away to each other like they had known each other for ages. Allen had rarely seen Purbright in such an expansive mood.

Kristy and Louise were also chatting quite a bit and Aitken suddenly found himself almost excluded. He took his new mobile out and looked at the number of text messages that had come from the office. Most interesting of all was the fact that Amy's key had opened locker 56 in the Cheam Street Tai Kwando club. Inside the locker were all manner of things relating to ADI and obviously passwords to her computer plus two sticks. Malcolm had come round from the IT depart with Jo Jo and they were busy accessing Amy's computer. Aitken reckoned that by the time they were back they would have some information on Fanshawe.

Fed and watered the meeting was starting to break up.

The Americans were going to be leaving first. Everyone went to the garages. A blacked out car sat next to the unmarked police van. Michaels and Purbright shook hands.

'You take care Frank. Watch that guy Farsai and his goons that they don't sneak in under the radar. I'll give you as much help as I can. Jeremy and Louise, I have to thank you for some amazing work. You have pulled us forward by at least eighteen months in this case and we shall probably take down the whole network. This will make some difference at street level. Frank, I have something for you. I have done something about your problem of being bugged. This box here contains a dozen rather special mobile phones. This is on par with what our President uses. You can use it in total secrecy by simply pressing that button there. They are so goddamned expensive that I will need them back. Hell you three can keep yours. You now know how to reach me and I know how to contact you without someone eavesdropping on us. Thanks for lunch. Right, Kristy we better get going. We really have a lot to do. See you all.'

Chapter 71

★ ★ ★ ★

~Another Tantalus lock opened~

On the way back to the station it was obvious Purbright was in good form.

'Well I liked Michaels. That is a guy to get things done. No patter, no bull, just dead straight. If he couldn't do it he told you. That was a really worthwhile meet. I think he will enjoy putting the hems on John Collins. He's right in that we need to ensure that Farsai doesn't come in ahead of expectations. What gave with Kristy Armstrong and the Kraft woman, obviously a bit of history there?'

'Singapore Sir, Kraft rumbled Kristy's attempts to bug the meeting. The ADI security people swept them up and Kraft walked into the Bar where Kristy was sitting having a drink and dropped the bugs on the table and told Kristy to stick them up her big dyke of a very nasty word. Kristy might be a lesbian but that doesn't mean she likes being called a dyke. Retribution shall be extracted I can assure you,' said Allen.

'Sir,' said Aitken, 'I have received a text that they have found Amy's locker, the stuff that can open up the computer. That plus the two memory sticks that Malcolm and Jo Jo were after. I think it is still quite complicated. Jimmy said something about algorithms or something like that was what he thought. Suffice to say that Malcolm and Jo Jo are at Railton working on Amy's computer. We are hoping to get something that will help us later today and tomorrow.'

'I hope you are right Aitken. Good shout on those keys Louise.'

'Laura and Jimmy did all the legwork.'

'Well we have under two weeks left to wrap this up. By God Aitken, you gave this the right name in calling it the Tantalus Case. We started off so well and we made quick progress. Then we could see the baddies just couldn't get to them. We need to find Fanshawe and I feel we can finally put this to bed, eat the fruit and drink from the pool.'

Allen was always fascinated by Purbright's depth of knowledge. He might not have a University degree but he was one of the smartest people she had ever met.

When they got back to Railton the place was humming. Purbright assembled everyone from the whole station.

'Right firstly thanks for your time. I think I need to explain a few things to you all. We started out with the murder of a young accountant, one that has now escalated in to a major international conspiracy of drugs, money laundering and other nefarious activities. We put considerable time and effort into identifying and arresting those responsible for her actual execution. The problem is that someone commissioned the hit. I should like to think we would have been able to convict those who instigated the hit. I am convinced that the company ADI was responsible for the murder of Amy Anderson. I have been told in no uncertain terms by Assistant Commissioner Jenkins that I have to back off ADI. We shall comply with his orders. The resources that we had tied up in this case shall be redeployed to other cases. There are at least nine other important cases we are working on in this office. That and a host of minor ones that in their own way, are equally important. So it is business as usual in this station with one small exception. Someone is spying on us so take care, all of you. We are going to create a no go area in this station. The public entrance and space for the public is going to be limited indeed. If I catch any member of the public who isn't under arrest beyond the door from the reception desk all hell is going to be let loose. Is that understood? We are battening down the hatches. Now, all back to work and the Tantalus team to my office for your new assignments.'

In Purbright's office they all dragged in a seat and sat down. Aitken stood at the back. Laura and Louise were busy speaking about something.

'Heads up please,' said Purbright. We can talk in here I have had this office swept. I am going to brief you all about this morning's events and where we are on this case. Firstly you are each getting one of these little beauties courtesy of Brad Michaels. Lose or damage one of these babies and I shall personally skin you. When this case is closed we return these.'

Purbright talked for almost forty-five minutes.

'That is where we are. Now we are going to blow some smoke up Jenkins's rear end. I was partially right when I said you will be re-deployed but this project is not being wound down, quite the opposite. Not this coming weekend but the weekend after I want us all to arrest those in the UK and our friends from Washington to arrest the others around the world. Our big problem is still this Fanshawe guy. We are no nearer finding him.'

'I might be able to shed some light on that Sir,' said Laura. 'Louise asked me to check out something that Fanshawe said in Singapore about taking an interest in a budding thespian who was in Two Gentlemen of Verona. Last Friday there were no less than seventeen companies doing the Two Gentlemen of Verona. They varied from Kirkwall in Orkney to the Penzance Players version. The one that interested me was one presented in Bristol. This was quite a serious production by the Travelling Troubadors and Minstrels Company, which I have never heard off. That said they played to a full house and this Thursday to Saturday sees them in Bath with the same production. Now what is funny is that one member of the Travelling Troubadors is called Henry Speed. Taking that coincidence and pressing on I tried to track down Henry Speed and it seems that for once it isn't a stage name but his actual name. Rather than take a chance on these damned snoopers I worked on my own Internet at home once Des had checked it out. I am really hacked off about these sods bugging us. Anyway Henry Speed was born in Middlesex General twenty-two years ago and his mother is a Sylvia Sherwood. His father is given on the Birth Certificate as Robert Speed with an occupation given as Accountant. I tried tracing the parents. Sadly Sylvia Sherwood died some fourteen years ago from a heroin overdose. As far as I can determine the parents never married. The father seems to also have disappeared from the face of the earth but you are going to love one fact about Robert Speed. He was born forty-six years ago. The Birth Certificate is interesting to say the least. Father is given as Hector Speed a gentleman who gives his occupation as an actor. The mother is given as Caroline Faubert. This is a publicity photograph of Henry and he is certainly a good looking young guy.'

'Fancy a toy boy, do you?' asked Peter Wainwright.

Laura just glared at him.

'These are stills photo of Wendell Fanshawe from his Z Cars days courtesy of Mr Aitken Senior. Another good looking guy and look how alike they look, grandfather and grandson and shut up Peter. If not I will come over and squeeze your family jewels so bloody hard you will pass out.'

Peter looked down and a few of the audience smiled and some men winced.

Laura continued. 'Caroline Faubert is a member of the Faubert family, the hotel and restaurant chain Fauberts or rather they were. She attempted to make a career for herself treading the boards. This must have brought her into contact with Fanshawe.'

'Do you know I was almost positive Fanshawe batted for the other side,' said Allen.

'More likely that he swings both ways, doubles his chances on a Saturday night,' said John.

'I tried to tie that down Sir, but I haven't been able to come up with a boyfriend. Actually he may very well be hetero. The Faubert family did not approve of Hector Speed and Caroline was spirited away to Monaco and taken out of the reach of debauched theatrical types. Wendell got his revenge on the family. Just over three years ago he had Mann basically make them go under even if they were financially sound. Mann did a whole bunch of short selling of their shares and things like that. I am never quite sure how these things happen but sufficient to say the Fauberts landed up practically broke. If not broke certainly on their uppers. All the Fauberts with the exception of Caroline Faubert who lives in Monaco in total luxury has a penthouse overlooking the harbour.'

'Everything in Monaco overlooks the harbour,' said Jimmy.

'Thanks smarty-pants, I meant the bit where the racing cars go alongside the water and through that tight chicane.'

'The Marina,'

'Yes Jimmy, the Marina. Do you know if it was a man up here reporting there would be none of these smart assed comments from us girls.'

'Yes Laura, the next guy that interrupts you, it'll be me that will be interfering with his family jewels, I'll be bloody well cutting them off,' said Purbright.

'Thank you Sir, so let's cut to the chase, this little property is worth a cool eight million in our money and whose name is on the deeds?'

'Hector Speed's I would guess,' said Aitken.

'You would guess correctly Sir,' said Laura. 'Young Henry went to RADA and was in fact a star pupil. I also checked to see if Fanshawe, Grandfather Speed or whoever he may be went through RADA and I couldn't find any reference that would match. Henry is on the cusp of a very promising career in acting. This is his first major tour. He has an address in Cheltenham, a National Insurance number and his Inland Revenue is up to date. What I have been unable to determine is whether he and his father and grandfather have any contact. I'm convinced that Fanshawe and Caroline are in contact. That said trying to obtain phone records in Monaco, well let's face it, we couldn't. I think because of the proximity of these performances to Stratford on Avon or that area I am convinced that Fanshawe will attend all the performances. That is it Sir, for the moment anyway.'

'Well Laura I think you have done a fantastic job there, apart from the odd clown who interrupted, that was truly excellent work. I think that just opened another lock to the Tantalus.' Purbright was obviously delighted.

Chapter 72

★ ★ ★

~A little mischief~

At that moment there was a knock on the door it was Jo Jo. Purbright signalled her in.

'Sorry to interrupt Sir but we have been recalled. There has been a security breach in our department. Amy's computer has been completely destroyed, well not Amy's computer but the dummy one. The power seemingly went off today and we had the power company in to repair it. The power is now back on but Amy's computer has been power surged with catastrophic effect. We shall obviously maintain our position that we were out sorting out stuff for Saturday.'

'I thought it was a week on Saturday that you were getting married Jo Jo,' said Purbright.

'I wish it was Sir because I am not organised yet. My engagement ring has been away as it is a combination with my wedding ring. They are still not back from the jewellers. No panic there, not much. We are finished on Thursday night and fly out early Friday for our wedding Saturday. The good news is Amy's stuff is fantastic. If you thought the previous file gave you enough to go to the Serious Fraud Squad you should see what is on 2 + 2 = 5. That is absolute dynamite. You could arrest all the Board members on that stick alone. That file shows that Amy was also a very talented accountant. The only real problem is Fanshawe; he sends all his e-mails from Internet cafes. He sends them from Bristol, Bath, Tewkesbury, even Cardiff but never from his home. The printer will need someone to keep feeding it until it is finished. There are mountains of stuff to print. Sorry it has taken so long to crack but we have to admit that girl was practically a genius at computers. If only she had joined an honest company.'

Jo Jo looked into the distance and for the briefest moment the tears swelled in her eyes. Then the radiant smile returned.

'That's it guys. I am off to organise a wedding.'

Thanks Jo Jo,' said Purbright. 'Pass on my thanks to Malcolm. Jimmy here will look after the printing. All the very best to you and Malcolm for your wedding.'

'Thank you Sir.'

Jimmy's face was a picture.

'Right, that's one of you deployed. Now, can I see to the rest of you and get some work done here. Wainwright I shall start with you.'

There were a few smiles in the audience. Wainwright is going to get a stinker thought the audience. He did.

Fifty minutes later Aitken and Allen were back in Purbright's office.

'I think you can hold off for a day and catch young Speed's performance in Bath. Go via Cheltenham and look up Henry Speed's address. Go early Allen and you can catch tea at your Grandmother's.'

'I would, except that she is visiting my Mum,' said Allen.

Allen was stunned that Purbright knew her Grandmother stayed in Cheltenham, so typically Purbright.

'My contact in Myanmar has said that Kraft is meeting Farsai tomorrow morning at her place. That from my point of view is fine, as I have had my contact bug her house before she got back from Singapore. Collins has stayed on in India. He has gone to Chennai as part of this big business deal. Hopefully we can get some details of Farsai's contract. Hopefully we then know when he is coming to get us.'

Allen thought here we go again, another of Aitken's contacts, one in Myanamar this time. At times it was almost irritating.

'What about that situation with Amy's computer?' asked Purbright. 'Fortunately it was the dummy one that got destroyed. I would imagine Mann now thinks he has got rid of a key piece of evidence. He will be reporting to Collins his success. I am so looking forward to telling him the truth. I am glad we are managing to keep our tabs on Farsai.'

'I think we need to fight back in a way that will deflect some of

Mann's energies,' said Allen.

'You have our attention Louise. What have you in mind?' asked Purbright.

'Mischief Sir, mischief. I think it is time that the rumour mill was started. I think we could do well to report the possibility of a financial alliance between Mann Financial and ADI. Why should that occur if both are successful? Is it possible that one or both are in trouble and a joint venture might be a parachute. We have it on good authority that ADI took a very big hit recently on their North American operations.'

'Oh I like that Allen, that really is mischief and I know the exact man who will publish it and also suggest selling the shares. That is positively wicked and they will be hard pushed to deny it and they will have to use a lot of energy to scotch the rumour.'

Purbright sat looking at his spot on the wall. Suddenly he shot up from his chair almost making Allen jump.

'I should like to get that out tonight in the late editions. That will give the Nasdaq guys time to start selling. That should start a run. Out the pair of you, I want to stitch the sods up. I love it Allen, just love it.'

Outside in the corridor Aitken said, 'Now that was truly inspired Allen. Take the battle to Mann. Put him on the back foot. If we can get a run on their shares we certainly will rattle the pair of them, him and Fanshawe. I think it is fair to say Purbright enjoyed that as a strategy. All that chess training pays off.'

'Possibly,' said Allen.

'I am going home to get Rosemary to purchase tickets for Thursday's performance of the Two Gentlemen of Verona, that is, if it isn't sold out. Did you know it is Shakespeare's smallest cast in his plays? Odds on Speed is probably Valentine, he has the looks for it.'

'Valentine and Proteus that's the two Gentlemen wasn't it?'

'You must have been sitting up in class that day, Miss Allen.'

'I didn't particularly like Shakespeare, I thought it laborious.'

'Well that's a critique I have not heard before. I hardly think his writing was laborious. Flows pretty well as far as I am concerned.'

'What I meant Sir was that it was hard labour for me to sit through it. For me it was laborious. There are many writers I like better. I do not get excited about Dickens either. Try getting immediately into a Tale of Two Cities.'

'Are there any other of our National Treasures in the literary field that are about to be assassinated?'

'Not at the moment Sir, should I think of any others I shall kindly issue a three-minute warning so that you can take to the Anderson shelter or should that be Aitken shelter. Are we going to Cheltenham in the morning Sir?'

'Yes I think we should, I would be surprised if we learn anything but you never know. I have hardly seen the kids so I will not be in until nine as I want to take them to school.'

Purbright had been busy and the late edition had indeed started a run on ADI and Mann Financial shares. Nearly twenty three per cent had been wiped off the value of the two companies. In the Singapore STI ADI shares had gone further down. The morning television programmes were now ringing warning bells. Mann had been invited onto the breakfast slot. The big problem was that Mann tried to say that there was no problem with Mann Financial nor was he aware that there was a problem with ADI. What he was not prepared to comment on was this joint venture scenario. He had absolutely no idea where that idea came from.

'Then why was it that Mann Finance bought over 60 million ADI shares ten days ago.'

'Mike, that was not Mann Finance. Correct me if I am wrong but I think the guys that bought those share were Resurge Ltd, I wasn't aware that had anything to do with me or Mann Finance.'

'Normally Byron,' said Mike Connell, the financial man for the television programme, 'I would agree with you except for the small fact that Resurge Ltd is a wholly owned subsidiary of PRM Ltd which in turn is another offshore company and that in turn another wholly owned subsidiary. The parent in this case is Yamata Holdings, which in itself is a wholly owned subsidiary of Prima Inc then Diablo Holdings and on we go until guess the parent. You can see this ship coming in. The ship making port, the final parent, is Mann Finance.'

Mann's face almost contorted with fury. 'My Connell, we have been a busy bee. This interview is over.'

'ADI is obviously in trouble,' shouted Mike Connell at the quickly disappearing Byron Mann.

'Well folks you heard it here first. Mann Finance has been baling out the fastest growing company in the world, ADI. Maybe they flew too near the sun and like Icarus the wax on their financial wings has melted. Their Far East stock plummeted last night and I think I can predict a run on ADI today once the FTSE opens for business. I am not sure it will do too much good for Mann Finance either. They could, just could, be perceived to be backing a loser.'

The Tantalus team were all gathered around the television. Purbright was smiling like a Cheshire cat.

'Boy oh Boy! Mann is going to love that. Another bad day and he is going to be so busy putting out fires he isn't going to have any time for us. We are now able to pick up on his phone calls and I cannot wait to listen in to some of them. I tell you what Allen, you really have caused mischief.' Purbright was ecstatic.

'Anyway you two let's have a quiet word before you depart. God I love it when something goes to plan and that really went to plan. Mike Connell is very good and he really did his homework. There is absolutely nothing litigious in what he is saying. Mann cannot even put a legal wheel clamp on Connell. Mann was absolutely seething.'

Allen was slightly amused and amazed at Purbright's sheer pleasure in Mann's discomfort. She thought to herself that there might be history there.

In his office Purbright was back to all business.

'Right, anything from the Far East and Farsai?'

'Basically Sir, Farsai has taken the job, five million, three up front and a further two on completion. Completion date is set for a week Saturday. He has told Kraft he can have the hit men in the UK a week on Thursday. He will be flying in on the Thursday and meeting with Collins on the Friday. I am slightly surprised at their choice of day, a Saturday. We are not likely to be together. I would have thought the Friday a better bet. Maybe they are acquiring a target each with a timed completion. The only reason for delay can be the money. Collins may actually have to pay them the cash. He phoned Fedoseev and Mihailov from Kraft's place. They were happy with the money and would set up their own travel arrangements. There was lots of other chatter but we will pass that to Brad and his team. Fortunately Collins is still meeting people in his hotel suites and we are still picking up on him. He is fuming about this run on ADI. He firmly put the blame in Mann's court. Fanshawe has been on his case and told him to get his ass back home and sort things out. Collins put that call on speaker as he was obviously pacing about in his suite. The two and half billion-dollar deal certainly made Fanshawe a lot sweeter. Collins said that as

Fanshawe was responsible for hiring Mann he would be better equipped to deal with him. I do not think that comment went down at all well. Mind you that was before Mann's spectacular show on this morning's television. Now Collins is even more convinced this is all Mann's fault and Collins is distancing himself from Mann. This is what it is going to be like when the manure starts hitting the fan. There is no honour amongst thieves and they can call themselves Knights of the New Order or whatever but they will soon be fighting each other to save their own skins,' said Aitken.

'Well, you two, you had better get on your travels. Let us hope that Wendell Fanshawe will no longer be a phantom but takes flesh in front of your eyes. Do not forget the expenses Aitken. There are far too many good restaurants where you are going.'

'I shall bear that in mind Sir.'

As they walked out into the corridor Aitken said to Allen, 'I guarantee at this moment Purbright is trying to think what I meant there when I said I shall bear that in mind. He will be thinking that it is bloody unlikely that I shall have the expenses in mind. He will be positive it was that the area has a lot of good restaurants is what I shall bear in mind.'

'You are probably right,' said Allen.

Back in Purbright's office that was exactly what Purbright was thinking.

Chapter 73

★ ★ ★

~*Amateur Dramatics*~

They arrived in Cheltenham just after eleven thirty. The news had told them that the run in ADI shares and Mann shares had continued. Purbright had been slightly surprised that Mann's phones had been quiet with no calls from ADI personnel. He had made several calls but these were all routine calls on the financial front to prop up his share value.

The Sat Nav had taken them to a leafy suburb. The address for Henry Speed was in a low-rise block of luxury apartments, apartment number eleven. There was complete security. They walked around the property and found that this was a rather substantial property. The property had a tall wall going all the way around. Numerous trees looked over the wall suggesting a large internal space. There was an electronic controlled entrance at the rear through gates for vehicle access. A sign said that number five was for sale and also that number eight was for let. The estate agent was given as Galvez Luxury Homes.

'I think we should get round there and see what kind of prices these places command. I have a feeling that young Speed is in a place that no budding actor could ever afford. I think we need to arrive in a limousine. Let's hire one. Are you any good at amateur dramatics Allen?'

'As far as I am concerned Sir, something to be avoided at all costs.'

Fifty minutes later they called in to Galvez the estate agents.

The receptionist was extremely snooty.

'I am sorry you cannot see Mr Galvez about that particular property, certainly not without an appointment.'

'I am sorry,' said Aitken, 'we are simply passing through. This property was a tip off by a friend. We have a prospect for next year's Gold Cup and we should like to have a place locally.'

'Seems extreme considering the meeting lasts only a week, wouldn't a let be more convenient?' enquired the receptionist.

'The week is purely the culmination of several months' preparation and for me I like to have hands on involvement in the training. I am sure there are other properties locally. The thing is that property seemed to have a very secure setting.'

Aitken stood and shook his head.

'Come Louise, I see no further need to waste any more time here. This would never happen in Russia, in my country.' Aitken said this in Russian.

'Darling please speak in English. You know I cannot understand Russian.'

'Then I think it is time to learn.' Aitken seemed extremely irritated.

'Please darling, calm down, this is Britain, sometimes things take time.'

'At that moment a man of about sixty came through from a back office.

'Is there a problem Mrs Barratt?'

'This gentleman here was enquiring about apartment number five. Unfortunately he has no appointment.'

'I do not know if he has an appointment but he certainly has an excellent choice in tailors. Would I be so bold as to say that classic high-twist wool suit is supplied by these fine tailors.'

He opened his jacket to reveal the makers.

Aitken smiled, bowed his head and offered his hand.

'Dimka Eltsin, delighted to meet you Sir.'

'Likewise Mr Eltsin, Simon Galvez at your service.'

'This lady here is my companion Louise Connaught.'

Further handshakes followed.

'I am quite sorry but we are purely passing through. We are heading to Stratford to see the birthplace of Shakespeare. This is a rare event for me, taking two days off. I am not sure Louise is overly happy with my proposing to look at properties. If you cannot manage a brief tour I shall have someone come and make an appointment and do an evaluation but that does not ever give you the … what is the word I am looking for?' He then spoke to himself in Russian. Ambience, that's the word, the feeling of what makes it a home as opposed to simply being a house. I bought an apartment in Cannes once in that manner and without an appointment. When we actually went to stay in it the ambience was totally wrong. Remember that apartment Darling, it was just so unwelcoming. A building has to make you welcome if you know what I mean.'

'You are totally correct Mr Eltsin. I could give you a brief tour so that you get a feel for the place.'

I take it all the fellow residents have been closely vetted. I personally have MI5 clearance. I can supply references.'

'I doubt if they can supply such references as MI5 but they are the rich and famous and we have never heard of anything untoward happening. Most are older.'

'Good I do not want young people making a lot of noise, such as some of these pop stars and worse footballers.'

'As I say the people are in the main highly successful and a little bit older. Actually we do have one youngster, I forgot young Henry Speed. He is a budding Shakespearean talent. If you are into that then his is a talent to watch, literally.'

'He would not be having any wild parties would he? You know how these theatrical types are.'

'You do not need to worry there, his grandmother owns the property and I think any misbehaving by young Henry would see him quickly homeless. Anyway he is quite a serious young man.'

'What size and price are these apartments?'

'Number five is approximately two point eight. The flat comprises six bedrooms, four en-suites with five public rooms. There is a two-bedroom servant's apartment in the roof space. Parking is available for four vehicles on the ground floor. A games room along with a gymnasium is also on the ground floor. Look, there are so many things, let me get you a specification. We are looking at just over five hundred square metres. Is this the type of property you had in mind?.'

'It is, provided all the gardens are maintained by anyone but me. Gardening is not my thing.'

Aitken laughed like he had made a funny joke.

'I don't think you will ever be concerned with gardening.'

Mrs Barratt had passed specifications to both Aitken and Allen.

Aitken looked as if he was seriously studying the document.

'I tell you what this is definitely a property that interests me. Rather than a whirlwind tour why do we not make a proper appointment? Then we can come and give this the complete appraisal. Can you please be honest with me, it is going to be a couple of weeks before I return from Russia, will this property still be available?'

'I would almost certainly say more than likely. If you give me a contact number I shall let you know if any other interests occur.'

'I am sorry but I do not give out my number. Only eight people in the country have my number, Louise here is one, the Prime Minister another. My people shall contact you next week. You commented on my suit and got it correct. Two can play that game. Your shoes, Kent shoes by Grenson if I am not mistaken.'

Galvez smiled, 'Mr Eltsin you should be a detective.'

This time it was Allen who smiled.

'I am sorry for imposing upon your time Mr Galvez and I thank you for the Specifications Mrs Barratt. You shall be hearing from us. Come Darling, let us now visit Stratford and hopefully step back half a millennium.'

Chapter 74

★ ★ ★ ★

~Another family member~

With their Limousine paid off and back in their own car, Allen had a dig at Aitken.

'Boy Sir, you are so full of bull. Do you know what worries me? You were so damned comfortable playing that role that I think that maybe the real role-play is what you do during the working day. Perhaps behind closed doors you are not Dimka Eltsin but some English gentleman, the high-twist wool suit from Saville Row. Jonathon is loaded and has some great clothes but I would doubt if he even knew what a high twist wool suit was. I am extremely worried by you being so damned convincing, far too convincing if you ask me. Christ you even knew the bloody type of shoes he was wearing.

'Mr Eltsin, you should be a detective.' Funny thing that Mr Galvez, seeing it is a role that he plays when he is not being your upper crust English toff.'

'Are you quite finished Detective Allen. You seemed more than adept at sliding into the role play yourself.'

'I would need to be role playing to call you darling,' said Allen laughing.

'By the way I guarantee the Grandmother is Caroline Faubert. There is our Guinevere.'

'Yes, that's almost a certainty for me,' said Aitken.

'Do you know something, Fanshawe owns the stuff on the continent? I could guess that they have reversed the situation here. I am sure that Caroline owns other properties in this country and that is where our Wendell Fanshawe hangs his hat. I need to get Laura to check this out.'

'I see Laura has become your researcher lately.'

'Sorry Sir, I didn't mean it to appear like that. We are both the same as far as status goes. You have me worried now Sir in case she thinks that as well. The reason I ask Laura is that she is simply brilliant at research. Take the Hector Speed, Caroline Faubert thing, that was simply brilliant detective work. God I hope she doesn't think that Sir.'

'I think if she did she might say something,' offered Aitken.

'God I hope so.'

Allen phoned Laura and obviously expressed the concerns that she hoped she didn't think she was being used as a researcher and that Allen would do the same for her.

'Louise, stop worrying, has Aitken been stirring it up.'

'Well yes, he was the one that mentioned it, I hadn't thought about it. The thing is you are just brilliant at that stuff. You always manage to get so much more than just the facts.'

'Put me on the speaker Louise.'

Louise opened the channel for Aitken to hear Laura.

'DCI Aitken you should be ashamed of yourself. You are causing my friend to have serious doubts about our working relationship. Louise and I are a team. She has the ideas and I try to verify them, we work well together, especially without any male interference.'

'Ah, the sisterhood joins ranks again.'

'If that's how you choose to see it, then yes we do. I shall get you your information Louise and do not let that big bad man you work for bully you. Those types need reporting. Bye Sir.'

'Bye Laura,' said Aitken sounding quite resigned.

'Well now, that was me told not to interfere. Women, why were they ever allowed into the police station other than to clean it and to make coffee.'

'You keep that up and I shall tell every female at Railton what you said. See if you then get home in one piece. Tell me something Sir, do you still have all the photos of the ADI guys with us?'

'Sudden change in topic, yes is the answer but why do you ask? The files are in the boot. Do you want me to stop at the next service station?'

'Yes, there is something I want to check out.'

When they stopped Allen went to the boot and a few minutes later she came back in and sat down with a file in her hand.

'Right Sir, this is a picture of Hector Speed alias Wendell Fanshawe. This is a picture of the grandson Henry Speed. They are seriously alike but another family member exists that is also a spitting image. Look at this and see if you agree that this is the third member of the group.'

With that Allen handed Aitken a photograph.

'Bloody hell Allen, that is absolutely brilliant. We have found Robert Speed alias Ross Morgan. This is Caroline Faubert and Wendell Fanshawe's son and the father of Henry Speed. This also explains Wendell Fanshawe's benevolent mood toward Ross Morgan in Singapore. It was patriarchal behaviour. Fanshawe was simply the proud father.'

'There is an amazing family resemblance on the male side. There may be sisters for Henry. I doubt if the Fauberts let Caroline out of their sight so there are probably no other issue there. I would also suspect that Caroline owns at least three houses in the UK possibly more. Sir it is almost four o'clock can we put on the news?'

The news came on and once again the topic was the run on ADI and Mann Finance. Shares in both companies had rallied slightly in late trading as Mann himself had pumped in large amounts of his personal fortune to prop up the shares in the company.

'Well Miss Allen you really put the cat amongst the pigeons. I do not think you will be on Mann's Christmas card list once he finds out the responsible party. I have a distinct feeling that our leader is going to tell him and with great pleasure too. I detect a history there but I am not sure what it is. I have history but I think Purbright really wants to square the account for something.'

'Yes I thought the same. So you do not know either?'

'It will probably come out in the wash once the Super has Mann under lock and key.

Chapter 75

★ ★ ★ ★

~A slight discord in Camelot~

'I Wonder how Laura is getting on with finding out about Caroline Faubert's properties?'

As if on cue the phone went and it was Laura.

'Hi,' she said. 'You were correct Louise. Caroline Faubert is a serious property owner in this country. Nothing unusual about that as the Fauberts were seriously wealthy and it was well documented that Caroline and the rest of the family had been estranged. When the Fauberts lost their fortune it was not a shock that Caroline was not brought down with them. I suspect that originally Fanshawe's money came from Caroline but latterly he used it to make a fortune and started backing money into her. Sorry, I am rabbiting; good job the Super cannot hear me.'

'I can though,' said Aitken.

'I wouldn't say too much if I were you. You are in rather dire need of brownie points.' said Laura.

'I'll hush my mouth then,' said Aitken.

'I think you had better Sir,' said Allen smiling at Aitken.

'Cut to the chase woman,' said Aitken.

'You see, you cannot help yourself. Purbright all over again, that's what it is. Caroline Faubert owns no less than seven properties in the UK. Apart from her grandson's apartments she has a property in Bristol, Bath and Tewkesbury. There is nothing in Stratford. There is another fairly recent acquisition, just over two years ago, close to Oxford. She has a property in Chelsea, London and a large estate in Perthshire, which was originally one of the family properties. That is all that is registered in her name. I have checked the electoral roll for all the properties and Henry Speed shows up as the only person domiciled in any of them. All taxes and bills are paid up to date. All properties are therefore being used from time to time. As I get more information I shall keep you posted. I shall endeavour Sir, to be clear and concise and nothing superfluous in my conversation. Oh Louise, have you seen the latest collection from Stella, it is simply fantastic.' With that she rang off laughing.

'Too damned smart that one,' said Aitken in a mock growl of Purbright. 'I think we have Wendell shuttling around the three properties in the west. Henry we know is a bona fide resident in Cheltenham and I would say that Ross Morgan is in the Oxford property. The Chelsea pad is probably Wendell and Caroline's and the Scottish estate is probably something that goes back to happy memories for Caroline, possibly childhood ones and hence her retaining it especially if it was once the family's place. Does Caroline Faubert have any siblings and if so is it really an estranged family. Doesn't probably influence this situation, I am just curious.'

'Nosey is more like it Sir. I shall have my 'researcher' look in to it should you wish. I would think that your summary of the properties would probably hold up quite well. The downside is that Fanshawe has a large number of boltholes he can go to. This makes it much more difficult to cover all his movements.'

'Hopefully we are able to check all his movements if we ever actually find out where he lives. Right, let's get to this hotel and get fed. Rosemary has organised every thing and the tickets for tonight's performance of the Troubadors should be waiting for us. We are in the Dress Circle because I want to be able to have a good look around.'

Aitken's phone went and this time it was Purbright. Aitken told him of Allen's latest discovery. Purbright found that a very interesting connection. He told Aitken to put it on the speaker.

'Hi, great work Detective on the Morgan connection. That is a very interesting connection indeed. Detective Baynes has had another good day with tracing down all Faubert's properties, makes for very interesting reading. You then ask the question, are they all in it together? Our American cousins are trying to tap Caroline Faubert's phone but you can imagine her living in Monaco makes her a bit of a protected species. Anyway according to them she is not in Monaco at the moment but is here in the UK. She came in two days ago and I would suspect either Chelsea or Scotland. Anyway what I called you for was that in the last half hour we have just listened to a very interesting call that Mann made to Collins. I think we can safely assume there is no love lost between the pair of them. Collins introduction in Singapore was a PR job simply because Fanshawe was listening and Mann is Fanshawe's man. Have a listen to this recording.'

The recording started with Mann telling Collins that the four targets he had to eliminate had literally disappeared off the face of the earth.

Collins response was, 'Do you know what time it is in Rangoon? I have just travelled from Chennai early today and worked my socks off to stabilise the company.'

'You are not alone' said Mann, 'I have had to put over six hundred million of my own money into Mann Finance to prop up my company because people are of the opinion that I have backed a turkey in ADI.'

'I think you have forgotten that your recent television performance was influential in people coming to that conclusion,' responded Collins.

'I am not taking that from you. I am putting huge reserves at your disposal and you need to be thankful for that.'

'Thankful, you must be joking, thankful for what? You have wiped almost seven billion from our balance sheet.'

'I am not taking that from you. I shall speak to Wendell about your arrogance.'

'Please feel free. I am sure Wendell is in the mood to discuss the situation. Do not expect the polite and pleasant Wendell. Your name is shit at this moment in time. Mind you, rightly so. I cannot believe your television performance. What the hell were you thinking about? As for your boast that you would get rid of those four guys to Fanshawe, it seems you cannot find them, well tough because that really is your problem. Maybe you do not have the contacts that you were boasting about. If I were you I would ask a more pertinent question, why would the authorities hide four prisoners that we have put out a contract on? I keep going on about those three police, Purbright and his team. They really do have a fantastic track record. Could they be a step ahead of us?'

'How the hell can they be? They have direct instruction from their superiors not to do any further investigation into this case.'

'As far as I am concerned you can any issue amount of instructions to that kind of detectives. They are going to turn around and stick it so far up your arse you can wipe your nose with the order.'

'Purbright laughed, 'At least he got that right. Collins is nobody's fool.'

'Are you trying to tell me that Purbright and his team hasn't spirited four people away and taken them completely out of the system.'

'Of course he has, I would put money on it. Can you find them in the system?'

'No, they are not registered anywhere,' said Mann.

'I tell you Mann, you are starting to worry me. I can almost guarantee that there is something that smells here and it isn't your bloody awful aftershave. Perfume is for poofs'

'You bloody uncultured Australian. They are damned right when they say the scum of Newgate lingers on.'

'Maybe we are, but we do not pretend to be something we are not. Acqua de Parma, I heard you telling Ross Morgan. Typically, he's another culture vulture who thinks that it is simply one of the finest colognes in the world. What the hell is wrong with just keeping clean? Women like a bit of sweat occasionally. Mind you three failed marriages, three women who left you to shag someone else. The only shagging they gave you was for a heap of money. You might have a lot of money but you obviously have a little dick.'

'I am telling you, you cannot speak to me like that,' Mann blustered.

'I can and I will because it is only a matter of time before I have to clean up the shit that you have dropped us in.'

'Why can't you clean up the three police quicker than a week on Saturday?'

'I have arranged for that. It is costing a cool five million to get rid of your problem. I am not changing those plans. I am overseeing that project myself so I know I can deliver instead of making idle boasts. In the meantime Mann I shall just leave you with your balls in the crusher, that's if you have any.'

'I am not going to forget this. I shall dig myself out of this hole and when I do I shall have your head on a platter.'

'Problem is Mann, you are digging and the real problem is the hole is getting deeper. In the meantime you need to get to the bottom of the situation with those four guys. People do not just disappear. Are your contacts high enough placed?'

'They bloody well should be. They work in the Home Office and they are people I trust implicitly. They should know where every person in the UK is.'

'Then something is seriously amiss. I shall put Nadine to work. I shall go and see her in the morning. Now if you don't mind I should like to get back to sleep. My problem is that your problems are now my bloody problems. And one last thing, do not ever call me a bloody uncultured Australian again or I shall radically alter your appearance when we next meet, Knights of the New Order or not. Good Night.'

'Well,' said Aitken. I detect a slight discord in Camelot. Our Knights are forgetting the code of chivalry.'

Chapter 76

★ ★ ★

~Finally, the forbidden fruit~

'I am perturbed about that phone call. I have a bad feeling about it,' said Aitken.

'Me too,' said Purbright. 'I share your concerns. I sense Collins is seeing dangers coming toward him. The problem for us is his conviction that we are out to get them and that he is included.'

'I would call that a reasonable conviction,' said Allen, 'given the circumstances.'

Purbright laughed. 'I suppose I have to concede that. It is just that I have this uneasy feeling about this conversation.'

They talked some more about what Brad and Kristy were up to. Seemingly they had been to quote Brad 'working their butts off'. They were close to making a raid of all the Knights a week on Friday, the day that Collins was due to arrive in the UK. They were having a problem with two Knights who were going on vacation. They were struggling to find out where they were going. Tamblin amazingly was one of those who were taking a vacation.

'If anything happens or there are new developments I shall keep you posted. They are under stress thanks to us and it is something that they are not enjoying. They are going to regret the day that they murdered someone on our patch. Enjoy the Two Gentlemen of Verona.'

'Thanks Sir, actually I think it might be a very good production. We shall let you know if we finally see the elusive Wendell Fanshawe.'

'If you do let me know, no matter how late it is.'

'We shall Sir, trust me on that.'

That night they took their seats early in the second row of the Dress Circle right in the middle which gave them an excellent view of the Orchestra Stalls and the private boxes off to the sides of the theatre. They watched as the audience filtered in. They saw no one that they thought was Wendell Fanshawe. Finally the houselights went down. Aitken was correct, young Speed was cast in the role of Valentine and he was very good as an actor. The talent was there for all to see. He was head and shoulders above the rest.

As the lights went on for the interval, Aitken heard the sharp intake of breath from Allen.

'You've spotted him too. There were times when I wondered if this guy really did exist. He came in about five minutes into the performance. I am sure the events of the day have occupied his time.'

'He looks quite old' said Allen.

'That is because he is quite old.'

'He's younger than your father yet he looks older than him. He is getting up and leaving.'

'Yes and we need to be on his case. Hopefully he is just going for refreshments.'

Fortunately Fanshawe was indeed going for refreshments, he was in the bar. He was speaking to a couple of people. He was a tall man. The once good looks had not survived the ravages of the passage of time. He was now too thin and gaunt. The theatrical projection to the voice was still there. The voice was as effeminate as Aitken and Allen had heard previously. They heard him say to the shorter of the two men he was talking to that he had made a good choice in young Speed as Valentine as he was quite outstanding. He then broke off the conversation to say that he had seen someone that he wanted to talk to.

Much to Aitken and Allen's amusement as they passed the two men the shorter one said. 'I cannot stand that old poof. Young Speed is good alright, I would go as far as say he is a jewel in our crown and we don't need some old queen making designs on him, the lecherous old bastard.'

'Who is he, that guy? He has been at all our performances of this run,' said his companion.

'Oh, he was a bit actor in the early days of television, did a couple of episodes of some play or something and thinks he is Laurence bloody Olivier. He is called Fenshaw or something like that. He did tell me his name but I have forgotten it.'

'Ah,' said Aitken, 'such is the firefly that is fame, nothing more than a brief flicker.'

Fanshawe was having a conversation with a couple that he obviously knew and it was all about the play that they were watching. This couple were obviously theatre buffs and clearly knew their stuff. The bell went, drinks were quickly devoured and people headed back to their seats.

The production was an extremely enjoyable one and Aitken and Allen both enjoyed it thoroughly. As they stood to give the cast a well deserved standing ovation Aitken said,

'There are some perks to this job and that was one of them.'

'Yes Sir, I would agree that was an excellent production. Speed is very, very good. Well, well, did you see that? Fanshawe and Speed definitely know each other. Did you notice the gestures Sir?'

'Yes, there was the glance, then the small hand gesture by Speed and Fanshawe increasing his applause in response. They know each other alright.'

'Right we need to get out of here to make sure that we cover Fanshawe's exit. I would suspect that he is going to his Bath property. The address that Laura sent is odds on where he will spend tonight. That means he is here for tomorrow night. If we can confirm that he is there I shall have Purbright send him a shadow, probably Jimmy. He can be a smart mouth at times but he is a very good detective.'

By the time Wendell Fanshawe left the theatre Aitken and Allen were in their car. Just as Fanshawe came down the steps a blue convertible Rolls Royce glided to a halt in front of the steps. A full liveried chauffeur got out, nipped round the car rather quickly and opened the door for Fanshawe.

'He might have proven elusive and lives out of the limelight but he knows how to do it with style,' said Allen.

'I couldn't care how he lives, well that's not quite true especially if it is at the cost of human misery and the dope heads addicted to the drugs his organisation have sold them, then I do care. I am just glad we have found him at long last. I have tasted the forbidden fruit. Locking this whole lot up will be the quenching of my thirst.'

They followed the Rolls discreetly so not to alarm the driver. Thirty-five minutes later the Rolls turned into a drive with large gates leading to a very large house. Only a few lights burned in the house.

'That's the address that Laura gave us for Bath,' said Allen. 'That there, appears to be very wealthy real estate.'

'I am going back to check the Roller doesn't leave. In the meantime I am going to post the Super and get Jimmy up here. He will need relief as he cannot cover Fanshawe twenty four seven.'

They stayed for a further forty minutes and when all the lights in the house went out they decided to call it a day.

Chapter 77

★ ★ ★ ★

~*We are working in the dark*~

The following morning Aitken and Allen had just ordered breakfast and the waitress had poured coffees when Purbright called.

'Can you two go somewhere that we can talk, something has come up.'

'No problem the phone in my bedroom has a speaker facility. Give us two minutes.'

In Aitken's bedroom Purbright told them to listen to another recording picked up in Rangoon and coming from Nadine Kraft's house. Collins had called on Nadine. They now picked up the conversation from the front door into the house.

'Morning Nadine, This is a result of the conversation I told you I had with Mann. I want a bit of help from you,' said Collins.

'Sir, I was just about to call you. I think a very serious problem has come up. I was acquiring identification of our targets in the UK and look at who has popped up. Two seconds and I shall send them on my mobile.'

There was a brief delay while Nadine transmitted the images.

'Recognise this two?'

'Christ Nadine, that's the sodding two who were guests at the Ascot Park.'

'You are quite correct Sir. That bitch is definitely the woman from the Ascot Park. She passed me one day wearing a pink and black Gavin Sutil dress, a Safor clutch bag and a pair of matching shoes. You do not forget someone dressed like that. Less is more and she had mastered it beautifully. That bitch is Detective Constable Louise Allen from Railton Police station in the UK. Look at the clothes on the guy. These two must be the best damned paid detectives in the land. Handsome sod, pity you are going to wipe him out. That is Detective Chief Inspector Jeremy Aitken. Their boss is Detective Chief Superintendent Francis, or Frank as he is known, Purbright. Now why would a lowly DCS pop two detectives to Singapore at what would be substantial costs? They came here for a reason. They must have had a specific task that they had to perform. Care to hazard a guess Sir?'

'Nadine why I am here is that Mann's four targets have disappeared. They have disappeared completely off the face of the earth. Why should that happen unless someone had inside track that we were going to wipe them out. How would they know that? They would only know that if they had managed to do what the Americans so patently failed to do. They bugged our meeting.'

'How could they do that? We swept the room. That is how we found the American bugs.'

'How long was that before the meeting started?'

'About twenty five minutes Sir.'

'Right, who or what came into our room after that?'

'Waiters delivered four trolleys of food.'

'The waiters bugged the room then.'

'We didn't allow the waiters in. We took the trolleys from them. They wanted to set the table properly but as they were eight minutes late we forbade them.'

'The Bastards, they bugged the sodding food. They had to do it. That is the only way they could know we were taking out the four inside. Nadine, they will also know that we are taking them out as well. Christ we need to mix things up now. Fanshawe will go berserk if he finds this out.'

'They are only a couple of ordinary cops they cannot use the stuff they might have, it would be inadmissible in court.'

'Purbright has probably worked out a solution to that small problem. He will have cut a deal with either SOCA or MI6, the CIA or some agency. I think we need to keep this to ourselves at this moment in time. Mann would make hay with this. I think that we are all in serious trouble. I wish we had never killed that stupid accountant. We should have paid her off instead. I need to think this through. Maybe we should leave these three cops alone and sacrifice some of our Knights. Tamblin, Morgan and Mann that is maybe the three we should stitch up. Christ, Nadine this is a fine mess. We need to stay calm.

'You are right Sir; we are in deep trouble so it is essential we keep our heads. I think we need do what we have to do and then go walkabout. You are paying too bloody much alimony anyway. Thanks to you I am worth over ten million Australian. I fancy a new life in Europe. I think you need to go walkabout as well.'

'Nadine, I think that idea has merits. I think we shall just run with our original plans so as not to scare the others. I can raise about three hundred million Australian. I think it is a bit of plastic surgery for me and go and live in Brazil.'

'My problem is I would like to be the one pulling the trigger on that blonde bitch Allen.'

Collins laughed, 'what have you against the fair detective?'

'Exactly, fair as in blonde and beautiful, with legs that nobody mortal should be allowed to possess.'

'Nadine, sometimes these goddesses are a disappointment in the bedroom department. Let's face it, she is thirty and not married. That should tell you something. You are a sexy woman yourself so forget her. Those legs will not be walking anywhere shortly.'

'Yes and I wish I was pulling the trigger.'

'I think it might be better if you leave that to the professionals. I am going back home. Are you going to be in all day?'

'Yes Sir, I want to check up on these three targets. Mann is obviously useless, so I think we need to use someone we can both trust. I know a guy in the UK Government that I can blackmail. Hell knows how he got a job in such a prestigious establishment but even they can make security mistakes. If he wants to keep the bloody job he'll do some legwork.'

'Sir, I know you said on the phone that Mann thinks Purbright has been scared off. I agree with you Purbright is probably a bloody Rottweiler. I would doubt if anything or anyone scares the bastard. We killed someone on his patch and it is obviously personal.'

'Kraft, you can bet your sweet ass it is,' said Purbright.

'I want to know what they are up to. Where are they? What are they doing? Where are they going to be a week on Saturday? Aitken is a family man. Do his kids do something that proud Daddy watches on Saturday? Purbright probably bowls, Allen the Gym, they must all do something.'

'Good Nadine, I shall leave you to get on with it.'

'Bowls, me bowl, that's an old man's game for when you have been put out to grass,' growled Purbright.

'In that case you can follow her logic,' said Aitken.

'It's a damned good job you are miles away after a comment like that,' said Purbright. 'I would bloody well show you that I am some way from being an old man.'

'Seriously Sir, I am surprised we even got that recording as I would have thought they would be sweeping their own places by now,' said Allen.

'Funny you should mention that because that was earlier today. Six hours later the transmission was destroyed, said Purbright. 'They obviously discovered your bugs Aitken. Now we have a problem. We are working in the dark. They could bring the hit forward and we need to be on our toes so that we are not the next victims. Jimmy and Ken with support are on the Fanshawe watch. They have seen him earlier walking his dog in the grounds. We are getting a tap done on this property and the ones at Bristol and Tewkesbury but we are having a bit of a problem in Tewkesbury. Brad's team are having problems with a local judge. He thinks the Americans far too gung ho, so he is reluctant to grant their application for a tap, and that's with Brad using the terrorist card as well. I need you two back here for a council of war.'

'Right Sir we are on our way.'

Purbright rang off.

'Right Allen back to finish our interrupted breakfast.'

'Good idea Sir.'

They ate a hearty breakfast and as they walked out the dining room the waitress said, 'Are you checked out Sir?'

'No not yet,' said Aitken, 'why do you ask?'

'Because only your first breakfast was included. You will be charged thirty nine pounds for the second breakfasts.'

'You must be joking,' said Allen. 'We were called away urgently. We didn't even drink the coffees. I think we should refuse to pay that Sir.'

'If you are refusing to pay I shall have to call security, and if you still refuse after that we shall call the Police.'

'We are the Police and that is why we were called away,' said Allen. 'We are here because we are investigating a murder. There is my warrant card and if you persist in charging us for food that we did not receive I shall arrest you for robbery.'

'Sorry I didn't know you were the Police, I think I can turn a blind eye this time.'

'Thank you very much,' said Aitken flashing a dazzling smile at the woman.

'Come on Detective Allen let's get back to the station.'

Out in the foyer Allen said, 'thank you very much? Thank you very much Ma'am you were trying to roll me for thirty nine quid and you say thank you very much.'

'Purbright is going to love you. You have just saved him thirty-nine Great British Pounds. Threatened to arrest the poor woman for robbery, that is what you call an abuse of power. I cannot wait to bring him the good news.'

The journey back was uneventful. The slight rally in ADI and Mann Finance shares had stalled when the US markets had opened and another six per cent had been written off the Mann Shares and just over eight per cent loss in the ADI stock value.

Chapter 78

★ ★ ★ ★

~Lunch at The Little Red Rooster~

Back at the station they were all shocked when Purbright said the whole Tantalus team was going out for lunch at the Little Red Rooster pub.

When they got there Purbright said, 'do not sit down we are dining upstairs in a private room.'

They went upstairs and there waiting was Purbright's man from Homeland Security who had debugged the cars, the phones and the station.

'I take it that it is all clear?' said Purbright.

'I would have been stunned if it was anything else. You can talk as much as you like without any one snooping. I shall scan you all though just to make sure that nobody has had a clothing bug planted.'

All checked they sat down at the table.

'Right, food is there,' said Purbright. 'Tea, coffee and soft drinks are there. No alcohol as we are all working. Help yourselves and we can then have a War Council.'

Fed and watered they all sat up as Purbright started to speak.

'There are elements of this enquiry that I have kept to a few on a need to know basis. We are now at that stage when we all need to know. We have obviously battened down the hatches against the establishment who has told us to lay off ADI and Mann Finance. There is good news in that we are close to wrapping up the Tantalus case. There is bad news in that the so called Knights of the New Order have a five million contract on my head along with

Aitken's and Allen's.'

There was a collective intake of breath.

'You three been upsetting the criminal classes again?' asked John.

'It would appear so John. I do not intend them to cash in on the contract. A week from now as far as we know from intelligence received earlier today, John Collins and the hit team will be in the UK. Also coming in next week is Ross Morgan who just happens to be Wendell Fanshawe's son that he had with Caroline Faubert.'

That brought a gasp from the audience.

We have cut a deal with the DEA out of Washington. A Brad Michaels is heading their team up. Whilst what we have collected is inadmissible in our courts; Brad's team can use it as all manner of acceptable evidence. The plan is that next Friday we pick up all twenty of the Knights of the New Order plus the accountants, the lawyers, Mann and Fanshawe. That said Brad has two of the Knights going on vacation and the problem is Brad doesn't know where.'

'He does now Sir,' said Laura. 'I was speaking with Kristy late last night and the two who are missing are Bill Tamblin and Al Bergeinmeister. As it happens I know some people in the travel business and it appears that Tamblin is doing the Trent Jones Trail and Bergeinmeister is heading to Saint Lucia this weekend.'

'The Trent Jones Trail,' said Kevin. 'What is that?'

'You are not a golfer are you Kevin?' asked Laura.

'No I am most certainly not. I subscribe to the Mark Twain school of thought, a good walk spoiled. Give me orienteering any day.'

'Trent Jones is a famous golf course designer in the USA and you can follow a trail of Trent Jones clubs. That is what Tamblin is doing,' said Laura.

'Great research again Laura,' said Purbright. 'That means, provided we can pick up Fanshawe, Mann and Morgan on the Friday plus Collins and his hit men, we have the rest including Nadine Kraft picked up by Brad's teams. Kraft in particular is being scooped up by Kristy Armstrong. I would like to be a fly on the wall for that meeting. Henry Speed, Fanshawe's grandson, would appear not to be connected with ADI in any shape or form. On Friday Collins is being picked up by Laura's team. Brad Michaels is accompanying Laura. Laura will allow Brad to be the arresting officer. I shall pick up Mann. Kevin you are firearm trained. I want your team to pick up Farsai and his two hit men. These are photographs of the three, Farsai, a Dimka Fedoseev and a Yakov Mihailov. Get to know these faces well just in case they slip in under the radar. There are also photos of Collins and Morgan, Mann you should all recognise anyway and the last one is the one we received from DCI Aitken last night. This is the phantom, the Tantalus, the elusive Wendell Fanshawe. He is incarnate, the human embodiment in flesh. Just looks like an old man, not one that is amongst the biggest drug dealers in the world. Kev, picking up Farsai and his hoods means that you have to be very careful out there. The public is often the problem. These guys seem to prefer to carry handguns, albeit cannon, .44 or .45 calibre Magnum type. I have no idea how good they are as far as being a crack shot goes. Their last two assassinations simply was a case of filling the victims full of lead. If they resist in the slightest you know what you have to do.'

Kev just nodded.

'John you are going to keep tabs on Ross Morgan once he arrives. Aitken and Allen are going to pick him up early. Aitken and Allen will then go and arrest Fanshawe whom Jimmy is presently watching. Fanshawe is liable to have the stuffing knocked out of him if he knows that his son has been picked up as well. After I arrest this lot I am arranging to get straight on television and make the announcements. I intend to stick it straight up those who tried to gag us. I shall organise that the TV companies call on our Assistant Commissioner only a couple of minutes ahead of my broadcast. That bastard is going to get one of the biggest red faces ever.'

The entire assembled cast thought that you do not mess with Superintendent Frank Purbright.

Purbright then briefed them all on the conversations they had collected. There were copies in all the folders. He then covered off the fact that their bugs had been discovered.

They read through all their stuff in silence.

'Wow, said Laura. Nadine Kraft doesn't like you Louise. Mind you what I see in her photograph you cannot blame her.'

Kristy detests Kraft and Brad Michaels is sending Kristy to pick her up,' said Allen. She called Kristy a Dyke and it didn't go down well.'

'I thought Kristy was a lesbian,' said Kev. 'Where's her problem.'

'My God,' said Laura, 'Men! Just because someone is a lesbian doesn't give you the right to call them a Dyke.'

'Why are you protecting them? Are you a lesbian Laura?' asked Kev.

'No I am not. For someone so brainy you can be seriously thick at times Kev. It is about respecting other people, regardless of race, colour or creed. That should not be difficult to grasp.'

'Right then Miss Baynes you tell me why it is that I smoke and nobody gives me respect for my choice in that direction.'

'Res Judicata Kev, as I said for someone so brainy you can be seriously thick at times.

'I bloody well must be because I have never heard of res judi something.'

'Res Judicata,' said Aitken. 'A case in law, already decided.'

'In other words she has already decided I am thick,' said Kev.

'Something like that,' agreed Aitken smiling. Aitken also thought to himself that it was going to take someone very smart to better Laura Baynes in a game of words. He was pretty convinced that she took no prisoners. Purbright obviously agreed with Aitken.

'If I were you Kevin I wouldn't get into a war of words with Detective Baynes. You might just get shredded,' said Purbright.

Kev took it very good humouredly, 'you might be right at that Sir.'

'Right,' said Purbright, 'I want this operation to be seamless. We are working in other people's manors so we will need to be courteous and keep the locals informed of what is happening. If we are lucky enough for Fanshawe to stay put in Bath, I can get a lot of help from Barry Stevenson. Fanshawe lives on his patch and fortunately Morgan lives on Jimmy Barr's patch. I can get a lot a help on both locations.'

Allen had a sly smile. With Purbright there it was again, he always knew a man who can. She wondered if she would ever acquire the kind of knowledge or the contacts that Purbright had. She doubted it. The system had changed and probably wasn't as intimate as it was when young Purbright had been coming up through the ranks.

'I have included a briefing document in the packs so that you all know clearly your roles and your chain of command. If you have any questions do not fail to ask and have it clear in your head that you know exactly what you will be doing one week today.

Richard, I want you to take over from Jimmy in Bath Thursday night. Jimmy is coming with me Friday morning.'

A few eyebrows were raised but nobody passed any comment on Purbright's decision that Jimmy was accompanying him on the Friday.

'Right let us address one issue and that is the hit team. Those guys might be activated early. In light of that I shall have uniform to protect our three properties. I think that we need to get armed as well. I detest guns but I think that we need to be playing in the same game. Do you two know how to use a firearm? Allen?'

'Yes Sir, shot quite a bit at University.'

'You Aitken, you OK with a sidearm?'

'Yes Sir.'

'Good, then I shall indent for firearms.'

'Remind me Louise,' said Richard, 'not to piss you off next week.'

'No,' said Louise smiling, 'you had better walk the line.'

'That's the danger Sir,' said Richard. 'Arm these guys and they are already using Americanisms. God help any poor guy they catch speeding. He'll be dragged out of the car at gunpoint. Spread across the bonnet... sorry hood, with gun to temple. You were doing thirty-one in a thirty mile per hour limit. Y'all know how serious an offence that is.'

They all laughed.

'Problem is,' said Purbright, 'that we have a very serious situation. These guys have done some of the biggest and highest profile assassinations. We all need to be extra vigilant. Hopefully I can pick up on their travel plans. Collins and Morgan are both scheduled to arrive in the early hours of Friday morning. Those bookings are made. Farsai and his team were scheduled to come in Thursday.'

'Are we picking them up at Heathrow Sir?' asked Kev.

'Kev, I am beginning to wonder about you. Laura is bloody right you can be thick at times. No I am going to let them come into the country, let them disappear and see where they turn up. They will turn up as well armed and dangerous and intending to add to the number of orifices that I possess. I have just the exact amount that I require at this moment in time. Any other, as I can recollect, would be both superfluous and painful or just plain bloody fatal. What the hell do you think I am going to do? Morgan can get in, he is harmless and we need him when we arrest

Fanshawe. Farsai and his team, we hit them before they deplane and the same goes for Collins. Collins would have been let in to help us find Fanshawe. Now we have finally found Fanshawe we do not need Collins to act as a pathfinder. Laura and Brad pick him up before he deplanes. He is going over to Brad Michaels for interrogation after we charge him with the murder of Amy Anderson.'

'Are we handing him over after charging him Sir?' asked John. 'Isn't that going to complicate things?'

'I appreciate where you are coming from John but Collins is a big fish and Brad needs to offset what are huge costs. If he has the head of Collins on a silver platter to display he will have harvested a huge amount of credibility. He has taken down one of the biggest drug dealing organisations on the planet. He has arrested all their key personnel and he also has the head of operations. He will definitely get a pat on the back for that. Bear in mind we shall all make money as we gather up the enormous revenues from ADI's and Mann's ill gotten gains. Pity we have nearly ruined them. I doubt the remaining few billions is enough to offset Aitken's expenses from Singapore. These, at this moment in time, lie unopened on my desk. I am absolutely terrified to open the envelope.'

There was a lot of laughter in the room. In what was a very serious situation, the very light heartedness of Purbright's comments went some way to lifting their spirits

'Right any questions, if not, let us get back to work and get our ducks in line for next week.'

Chapter 79

★ ★ ★ ★

~*Are you still a straight copper*~

As they came into the station yard a uniformed officer walked past them and said Jenkins is here. The Officer never stopped walking, just spoke as they passed.

When they got through the door Jenkins was standing there with a face like thunder.

'Where in hell's name have you lot all been? Purbright, you and I in your office now.'

'Sir I give out the invitations to my office not you. This is my patch. Dave, what interview room is free?'

Dave the desk Sergeant said 'number three is free Sir.'

'Thanks Dave, right Sir, follow me. We can talk in there.'

A fuming Jenkins followed Purbright.

Out in the entrance the rest of the team were all talking.

'Boy I would love to be a fly on the wall in there,' said Kev.

'My money's on the Super,' said Richard.

'That's a no brainer. I feel sorry for Jenkins,' said John.

'Don't forget lads that Jenkins has the power to suspend the Super if he wants to,' said Aitken. 'I would doubt though that he has the guts to do that.'

In the interview room, Purbright had sat down and Jenkins was walking around the room.

'Are you going to sit down and discuss the problems that you have? Nobody comes into my manor and speaks to me like you did, especially in front of my troops. Try that again and I shall have you up for bullying and harassment quicker than you can ever imagine.'

'Well, where the hell were you? I come in here and half the bloody staff is missing including the man in charge.'

'I think that you might find that the time was twelve to one o'clock. I think that is lunchtime in a lot of offices. Next time you care to arrive unannounced choose a period outwith lunch.'

'So where you then?' demanded Jenkins.

'Out for lunch, why can you not understand that simple fact?'

'Yes, but were you all out together, you and your staff?

'Yes we were, do you have a problem with that? We do it occasionally for team morale and team building.'

'Is morale low in this station?'

'It tends to go downhill when they know they have been nobbled by their own people.'

'You are just not going to let that go are you Purbright?'

'Well there have been a few developments on that front and you will be glad to know that ADI have hired a hit team to get rid of myself, DCI Aitken and DC Allen. Five million is the pay off to take us out.'

'You are joking, nothing more than paranoia. A device to allow me to let you back on the case, I don't think so.'

Purbright's voice was one of cold fury.

'Look Jenkins, I do not give a shit about a contract out on me. I bloody well do care about a contract out on two of my officers. If you do not take this seriously I shall go above you. If any of my officers get harmed through your incompetence I shall ensure that your career is permanently damaged. In fact I shall make sure it is over. Is that clear Jenkins? I know you have been nobbled by the Home Office. In one week's time I shall name and shame who is in the payroll of Mann and ADI. You had better be pristine clean or you will go down.'

Jenkins was clearly rattled by Purbright's cold fury so he did exactly the wrong thing, he blustered.

'You didn't do what I told you to. You clearly disobeyed a direct order. I am of a mind to suspend you.'

'God Jenkins, are you really that thick man? Of course I ignored you. They were as guilty as hell. Do you think I am a one-man band? We are going to put the whole damned ADI team away for a wide range of crimes and you are busy trying to protect them. If I were in your shoes I would be distancing myself from that stance as quick as I could manage it. You have less than a week to do it. Suspend me if you want but other people are going to take ADI out and Mann for that matter. Things are outwith my control. I have put things in place to counteract being nobbled. Look me in the eye and tell me are you still a straight copper.'

'Christ Purbright, you have no need to ask that.'

'Answer the question, Sir.' Purbright's tone was quiet and intense.

Jenkins looked at Purbright and he knew that what he said to Purbright in the next sentence was going to have serious consequences.

'Yes Frank, I am still an honest cop and I always will be. I am a political animal but I am still straight.'

Purbright looked at Jenkins and there was a ten second silence. Ten seconds that for Jenkins, his life stood still.

Purbright finally spoke. 'Good Sir, I believe you. Well, you had better come to my office and get briefed on exactly where we are with the Tantalus Case. That is the name DCI Aitken gave it.'

Two hours later Jenkins was sitting just shaking his head in disbelief.

'Frank, this is bloody earth moving. Some amount of shit is going to hit the fan.'

'I would say so Sir. I was going to drop you in the shit next Friday by announcing the arrests on National TV. Now you are back onside I should like if you do that. More the natural order of things Sir.'

'Frank, I would be honoured to announce your successes to the world if necessary. Do you think I could have a word with your team?'

'I do not see why not. I shall go and get them together.'

Five minutes later with all the staff gathered AC Jenkins addressed them.

'Firstly, I shall start with an apology to both Chief Superintendent Purbright and the staff here at Railton, in particular to those working on the Tantalus Case. I was given some bad advice. Advice that was more politically expedient for me than anything else. Frank here bluntly asked me if I was still an honest cop. I answered him that I wholeheartedly was an honest cop and always would be. Your Super has briefed me completely on what is happening and I for one shall be making every effort to ensure that this case is bought to a successful conclusion and that we protect those who are in danger. I apologise to all of you. Over the next few days I shall redress the damage I have done. Thanks for your time.'

Unexpectedly for Jenkins he received a huge round of applause which slightly took him by surprise. The team then went back to work.

'Thanks for that Frank, it was the least I could do.'

'I think you can see for yourself how much that was appreciated.'

'Right Frank, if I am going to perform anything useful I better get back to my office and get working. I shall have the armed response units cover arranged for yourself, Aitken and Allen. I do not think we can take enough precautions. The fact that we have lost all coverage worries me in that they could pull things forward. Keep me posted if you get any more info. Thanks Frank, speak to you soon.'

Chapter 80

★ ★ ★ ★

~A slap in the face~

When Jenkins was gone Purbright called Aitken and Allen into his office.

'Well Sir,' said Aitken, 'that was a bit of a change of tack.'

'Not before bloody time, boxing with one hand tied up your back is not fun. All the phones will be back to normal in a couple of hours. We can do our own research without fear that someone is snooping. Jenkins is going to arrange that we have armed units shadow us until we have Farsai and his cronies locked up. To be honest I am glad he is back onside. It gives us a lot more options. I take my hat off to him for standing up and being man enough to admit how he had got it wrong.'

'Went down well with the team Sir, I'll give him that. What do you want us to do?'

'Something oddball, I want you to go and meet with Mann. His place is near the Gherkin. He is normally in the office every day, weekends included. I want you to go and tell him that you know he is a Knight of the New Order. Tell him that we have enough evidence to arrest him and when we are going to arrest him. We are also going to arrest Fanshawe if we ever find him. You can bug his office as I feel he will react quickly to that kind of news. Mann is a barrow boy made good. He lives the good life in luxurious style and the fear of going back to having nothing is not an option for the Manns of this life. At worst he can throw you out. Tell him that he tried to gag us and that we know he was assigned to get rid of our four witnesses. Tell him that we moved them to safety. Tell him that the arresting officer who will come to pick him up will be James Austin, the officer who arrested him eight years ago for doing ninety six in a thirty mile per hour zone close to a school. A charge that he wriggled out of by using a lawyer, one who is just about as big a crook as he is. This would be the same James Austin that he totally discredited in court as a liar, when all the officer was doing was his job. Mann should have received a prison sentence for that as he had two previous driving bans for speeding. A third strike would have seen him going to jail. Go and really rattle his cage. Oh and one last thing, please introduce him to Detective Louise Allen whose brilliant idea it was to cause a run on his shares. He might like that.'

On the way to Docklands Allen asked, 'why do you think we are warning Mann?'

'I am not quite sure,' said Aitken. 'I think it is part of a divide and conquer strategy. We will need these guys to seriously backstab each other. I think we are out to sow the seeds of that strategy. I think he wants Mann to panic and lash out.'

At Mann's office they found their way barred by the customary PA Rottweiler.

'I am Stephanie DeVries. You have no appointment so you cannot see Mr Mann.'

'Don't need one, this negates the need for an appointment.' Aitken showed his warrant card.

'You are not getting to see Mr Mann and that is final.

'Allen arrest and cuff this woman for obstructing the law.'

'Try that and I shall sue you.'

'You might if you could find a lawyer stupid enough to take your case. I think you might have a job finding such a lawyer. Anyway I gave you a chance. Allen cuff her and send for a Police van to lock her up.'

Allen moved to do what she was told and the woman promptly resisted arrest by smacking Allen in the face. Next second the woman was face down on the carpet with her hands cuffed behind her back. Allen then hauled her roughly to her feet. You could see the red mark on Allen's cheek. She then read DeVries her rights and told her that she was charged with obstructing the law, resisting arrest and assaulting a police officer.

'Get her out of here,' said Aitken. 'It is late Friday so there will be no chance of bail. A weekend in the cells will do her good.'

The commotion was enough to bring Mann out of his office.

'What the hell is going on out there?' he bellowed before he made his appearance.

When he did appear he demanded, 'what are you two doing with my PA?'

'Arresting her for obstructing the law, resisting arrest and assaulting a police officer, that is what we are doing,' said Aitken.

'Well you can stop that immediately and release her.'

'Sorry Sir, cannot do that. Assaulting a Police Officer is a very serious offence and will probably bring a custodial sentence.'

'She was only doing her job. You look familiar, so do you,' Mann said looking at Allen.

'Doing her job or not she is going to the cells. You will probably remember us better from last week at the Ascot Park Hotel in Singapore.'

'Christ you are those two sodding detectives Aitken and Allen. The pair of you can piss off. I have nothing to say to you.'

'Well we have plenty to say to you. We can do it in your office or we can do it downtown. You can share a van to the station with Ma Baker here.'

'I am saying nothing to you without a lawyer present.'

'If that is the case you are going downtown. Our talk was going to be a friendly word of advice in your office. However, if that is how you are going to play it we are all going downtown. When are they collecting DeVries here?

At that moment a pair of uniformed police came out of the lift. A policeman and a policewoman.'

'Is this the prisoner Ma'am?' the policeman asked Allen.

'Yes, take her to the cells. There is her charge sheet.'

Allen walked with the two police to the lift. As they waited for the lift Allen spoke to the Policewoman. 'Cool down this one down, she has a hot temper. Make sure she gets the whole treatment as a criminal, body search, the whole damned works. You have struck your last Police Officer DeVries. I am bloody well going to make sure of that.'

'Don't worry Ma'am we shall make sure that she thinks twice before she does that again. The old cold hosepipe usually cools the hotheads down.'

Stephanie DeVries wasn't so bold now.

Chapter 81

★ ★ ★ ★

~Care to raise it to twenty? ~

A llen came back in and Aitken asked her, 'you OK Detective?'
'Don't worry I am definitely in better shape than she will
be soon. She is getting the full welcome wagon.'

'If you mean what I think you mean, that is an abuse,' said
Mann.

'So is a right cross in the face when I am just doing my job,'
said Allen.

'I shall have my lawyer in there and get her out on bail.'

'No you won't if you know what is good for you,' said Aitken.
'You leave her to cool her heels until Monday morning. She will
get a custodial sentence for assaulting a Police Officer.'

'Are you threatening me you shit?' said Mann.

'Carry on like that and get yourself arrested as well. We are
looking for the slightest excuse to take you downtown. All we
wanted was to give you a friendly word of warning and we land up
in all sorts of bother. Do you want to hear what we have to say or
not? What we are about to tell you will greatly help your future.'

'You are talking in riddles. I haven't got a sodding clue what
you are talking about.'

'You have, but we are quite prepared to talk to you about it.'

'I suppose you had better come in and say what you have to
say.'

They sat down in Mann's palatial office, which had a stunning
view towards the Thames.

'Right, as you correctly recognised we were in Singapore last weekend. We were out there to bug the meeting of the Knights of the New Order. We listened to you be sworn in as a Knight. We also listened to you tell Fanshawe, now there is an elusive gentleman, that you would eliminate four people who were in custody in high security units. That was a bold boast as Collins also told you. Collins doesn't like you very much, does he? Now the problem for you is that we are about to pick you up for dealing in drugs and for the murder of Amy Anderson.'

'Whoa up there, I had nothing to do with the Anderson girl. I am not a murderer.'

'No? How were you proposing to eliminate four people? Blow on them and they would all fall over. I think murder might have been your solution. Do not forget that in ninety-five you wriggled out of a manslaughter charge that had been reduced as a plea bargain. You sold your so-called mate down the river. He has one year left on what was a minimum of fifteen years and guess what prison we shall be sticking you in?'

'You will not be sticking me in prison anywhere; I can assure you of that.'

'You say that and you think that because you tried to obstruct us through your friends in the Home Office, you can prevent it happening. You watch these friends evaporate like snowflakes on a summer's day once they know you have been charged with various things such as murder, money laundering, drug dealing and that's just for starters.'

'You are full of bullshit Detective. You cannot make any of that stick.'

'And you wish Mann. We have even picked out your arresting officer. Remember James Austin, a good honest hard working policeman that your twisted lawyer Collier did a character assassination on. He is going to enjoy reading you your rights.'

'As I say Detective if you thought you could, you would arrest me now. For your information Collier isn't my lawyer he was only appointed for that case.'

'You do not listen, just as your PA didn't listen. I can arrest you now but my boss Purbright has decreed that James Austin will be your arresting officer. He is not here at the moment, so until James is back on duty you might as well enjoy your last few days of freedom.'

'I still do not know why you are here?'

'God for someone who has such a business acumen you are

pretty slow in getting to terms with what transpires once we pick up Collins and various other people in ADI. None of those guys are British. Collins will give you up and you damned well know it. Your only hope of reducing your sentence is to sort out a strategy of what you are going to do once you are arrested. Forewarned is forearmed as they say.'

'You keep going on about when I am arrested. You are just not going to be arresting me or making anything stick.'

'You on the other hand are not taking a friendly warning. My Boss does not do bluffing. You shall be arrested within the next seven to ten days. James Austin is back on Friday so you become fair game after that. Anyway I have completed what I was told to do. Had it been up to me, I wouldn't have bothered to tell you. I would just have swooped and charged you without warning.'

'I have been told you are a hard-nosed bastard Aitken. Do you know something; I have to admire your sheer effrontery? You walk into my office; you bloody well arrest my PA. You threaten me and tell me that shortly that James Austin is coming to arrest me. You really have balls, I'll give you that.'

'I assume the bitch that arrested Stephanie is from the same mould?'

'Mann, the last guy that called me a bitch still speaks with a falsetto voice. Tread carefully,' said Allen.

'First thing you have said in this meeting and it is a threat.'

'First thing you said to me was to call me a bitch. I don't take that from anyone.'

'No, I bet you don't.'

'Just remember when it comes down to it the Anderson girl is at the heart of this enquiry. That is what my boss wants people nailed for. He does not care about your various and nefarious activities. We are charging all of the officers of the company, the so-called Knights, as culpable. You have been scooped up in that net now although technically you were probably an innocent party on the Anderson score. That said if Collins doesn't sell you down the river I shall eat my hat. What do you think Allen?' said Aitken.

'I am not sure Sir, they are supposed to be Knights. I would like to think there is some honour.'

'Get wise Allen, there is no honour amongst thieves and that is basically what we are dealing with here. Knights, that's a laugh. I'll tell you what Allen, I will bet a tenner Collins sells Mann here down the River.'

'I'll take that bet, there has to be a code of chivalry. Tell you what Mann you can hold the stakes.'

'Care to raise it to twenty Allen?'

'I'm not so sure sir.'

'I bet you are not. Too late now, here is my tenner Mann. We'll get that back off you after we make the arrests.'

'Are you two for sodding real? Are you seriously asking me to hold this as a bet against Collins shopping me?'

'Yes, surely you cannot have a problem with that, after all you are going to know about it. If you were putting on a bet yourself I would guarantee you would back Collins shopping you. Tell us which way you would jump if you were Collins. Here is his dilemma, you can save your own arse or you can save the arse of some guy you cannot stand. Now let me think. Mind you Allen, letting Mann here hold our money is maybe not such a good idea. He might try and steal it as it is all the money he is going to be left with. That twenty will be a fortune for you in ten days time.'

'You two are looney tunes, definitely looney tunes. I cannot believe you are betting about an outcome like that.'

'Look Mann, you are all going down for very long time. Depending on how you all react and how you horse trade with the authorities will determine the length of the sentence. I just know Collins is going to stick it to you. He cannot stand you so when the chips are down what is he going to do. Where did you get that idea about honour Allen is completely beyond me? This is going to be the easiest tenner I have won in a long time.'

'You two are seriously nuts.'

'We might be but I can assure you Mann I will be spot on about Collins and what he will do to you. I do not make too many mistakes about the criminal classes. Anyway Mr Mann unless you have any questions we are out of here. Try and use your influence in high places and we will haul you in so fast that your feet will not touch the ground. Try and get DeVries out on bail and the same thing applies. So do you have any questions?'

'Christ, you are being sodding serious. Of course I bloody do not have any questions.'

'Then we shall say goodnight and wish you a good weekend.'

'You really are taking the piss Aitken.'

'Possibly Mann, possibly, I am not taking the piss when I tell you to enjoy what little freedom you have left. One last thing this hard-nosed bitch as you describe her has more than taken her retribution for what I can only describe as your arrogant rudeness to her. Miss Allen here is no bitch and you had better keep that in mind. She is however extremely smart and she was the one who came up with the idea to financially ruin both your shares and that of ADI. You did it to the Fauberts and had we left Allen to her own devices you might be worthless now. That will happen anyway when we arrest you, as we shall be taking all your assets and categorising them as ill gotten gains and subsequently the property of the state. Do not try and move any money about as that is being monitored. Your credit cards are frozen as of midnight tonight. Have a good meal tonight, as it will be one of the last you will enjoy. On that merry note Mann, goodbye, until we meet again.'

'You cannot freeze my credit cards. That is completely illegal.'

'Wrong, when you joined into partnership with ADI you become involved in drugs dealing. Your assets are now regarded as suspect and the property of the state. We are simply protecting our assets. Goodbye Mann.'

'You just had to look for the dodgy deal Mann. You couldn't rise above been a barrow boy,' said Allen.

Mann's response as they both left was completely unprintable.

Chapter 82

★ ★ ★ ★

~Slightly right of Genghis Khan~

Outside the two detectives sat in the car and sure enough Mann was straight on the phone. The first call was to his lawyers.

'He is going to try and get DeVries out on bail. Surely he is not that stupid,' said Allen.

'I would be very surprised if he tries that. I think this is going to be more about saving his hide.'

So it turned out to be. Mann was definitely interested in getting his ducks in line if Aitken's people did what Aitken had said would happen.

'Hello Greg, Byron Mann here. I have just had a visit from the Police, that arrogant bastard of a cop DCI Aitken and his equally arrogant bitch of a sidekick DC Allen.'

'I'll tell you what, I am getting real fed up with people calling me a bitch,' said Allen. 'Really, really fed up. Next person that says that is getting their nose broken.'

'What did they want?' asked Mann's lawyer.

The detectives were slightly surprised to hear the other party. Mann had put the call on speaker. He was obviously pacing about in the room.

'That's the thing, they didn't want anything. They simply came to tell me that they were arresting me shortly along with most of the people from ADI. I take it they do not have a case or they would have arrested me by now?'

'Wrong, I know Aitken and he is a Frank Purbright acolyte, neither man plays poker. You are in serious trouble Byron and no joking. If he says you are going to be arrested you can bet he means it. I told you at the time not to do the ADI deal. This is going to bring you down.'

'Christ, you are supposed to be on my side.'

'Aitken will not be bluffing. I can almost guarantee that. He has something cast iron on you. Is there anything you have been keeping from me? If I do not have the whole picture how can I possibly help you?'

'He is threatening to put me in with Tony Allis. Allis has a year left of his mandatory sentence. Can he do that?'

'Allis is the guy who was sentenced for the sadistic killing of those two prostitutes who were supposedly in your employ. Fifteen years minimum wasn't it. That was not yesterday, that was even before you became Byron Mann. Why are you concerned about being locked up with Allis?'

'He might have a grudge, that's why. I walked and he got fifteen.'

'That only applies Byron if you were guilty of stitching him up.'

'Gregory Fischer-Ward QC is no one's fool,' said Aitken. 'I feel an uncomfortable time coming up for Mann.'

'Well did you set him up?'

'What do you bloody think?'

'What do I think Byron? Well yes, I think you are quite capable of letting him take the fall. That would be without compunction, that's what I think. You have been tried and found not guilty and it is only an issue if you set your friend up for a long stretch. I cannot help to prevent you from being incarcerated in any prison of their choice. What is concerning me is your near admission that you are likely to be heading to prison. Why would you be concerned about sharing a prison with Allis if you didn't think that you were going to prison? If I was I sitting in judgement I would be directing the Jury to find you guilty because I would be quite certain that you did it. Care to enlighten me on what it is that you have done that makes DCI Aitken so positive that you are, in their parlance, going down. If you have done such a deed we need to look at a damage limitation exercise. My problem Byron is that you can have committed any number of crimes and I shall do my utmost to reduce your sentence. If, as I suspect, you have fallen in with ADI and entered into their world of drugs you are looking for another brief.'

'Jesus Greg, you had better bloody well be joking.'

'You know well my stance on drugs Byron. I am slightly right of Genghis Khan when it comes to dealing with those lowlifes. Tell me you have had nothing to do with drugs.' There was a long silence before Fischer-Ward spoke.

'That silence spoke volumes Mann. Find a new brief. This conversation is at an end.' Gregory Fischer-Ward QC hung up on Mann.

Mann let out a long and lengthy string of expletives about how bloody dishonest lawyers were. In the car both detectives smiled at each other.

'Way to go Fischer-Ward, way to go man. I love it, a lawyer, a Queen's Counsellor no less, with a sense of decency. I feel like going round and shaking his hand,' said Aitken. 'Oh he is on the phone again, long distance by the number of digits. Who is he calling this time?'

Fanshawe probably,' said Allen.

Fanshawe it was, a very surprised Fanshawe in fact.

'Wendell, Byron here, sadly I fear we are in trouble. I have had those two detectives around who were in Singapore and bugged our meeting, Aitken and Allen. They are going to arrest me shortly. I need your help.'

Come on Mann,' urged Aitken, 'keep it on speaker.' He did.

The Fanshawe that responded was not the effeminate one. The voice was strong and steely.

'You Byron are not my favourite player at the moment. I think that you need to fall on your sword. You have cost me a fortune. Your performance on our National television was a shambles, a complete shambles. You let a poor player make a fool out of you. I would have been totally ashamed of that performance. What did you just say? Care to expand on your comment, the two detectives that bugged our meeting in Singapore. Are you telling me that a pair of detectives from Britain bugged the meeting of the Knights of the New Order? This is the first I have heard of any bugging. Are you talking about those two detectives we are proposing to eliminate? It seems to me that they are doing a very good job of eliminating you instead.'

'Well you have nothing to worry about, seemingly you are impossible to find.'

'As things stand I wish that you were impossible to find.'

'That is rather unfair Wendell. I called you for help and

considering the amount of money that I am putting up I would have expected help to be forthcoming.'

'Simple Mann, phone my man Collins. He is in charge of operations. I will be phoning him anyway as I have not heard about this bugging of the meeting. Are you sure about this?'

'There is absolutely no question; they have tapes of the meeting.'

'We never said that but you are correct,' said Allen.

'Right, as I say phone Collins.'

'Collins doesn't like me.'

'Be assured Mann, he is not alone in that reflex.'

Without as much as a goodbye Fanshawe rang off.

'The walls of Camelot are starting to crumble,' said Aitken.

Mann's next phone call was to home.

'Hi Darling I am on my way. I have had one of the worst days ever. Let's have a good meal and a good bottle of wine and an early night.

The response took the two listening completely by surprise.

'It's OK Honey, you just get your sexy little tail home here and let Michael kiss it all better.

'My God, there is one ship I didn't see coming in,' said Aitken, 'did you?'

'Never in a month of Sundays.' said Allen. 'Just goes to show, nothing as strange as people. No wonder three marriages and three divorces are behind him. I assume that all of those marriages were probably just a front.'

Not from Yorkshire are you Allen,' said Aitken

'Nowt stranger than folk,' said Allen in a very good imitation of a Yorkshire accent. 'I listen to Andrew Bayliss's cricket commentary and very good he is too.'

'Not bad Allen and you even go on to demonstrate the very veracity of what we were speaking about. Let's get home for the weekend. Our babysitters will be in position. Are you doing anything this weekend? Do not go out unless you have to.'

'Do not worry about that Sir, I am decorating the back bedroom. Jonathon is away for the weekend. His business trip has not gone well and he is held over. He is like a bear with a sore head.'

'You decorating?' said a surprised Aitken.

'Yes decorating, what's so odd about that?'

'Well I thought Jonathon was rather well off financially and you would have had some decorator do it for you. I just didn't take you as a decorating pair.'

'We are not; Jonathon is all thumbs as far as DIY is concerned. I am the one that likes decorating. A job well done is so satisfying.'

'Well as they say, whatever floats your boat.'

'What about yourself Sir, you doing anything?'

'As it is, this weekend has worked out perfect for me as well. Rosemary has taken the children to accompany her on a cooking trip that she is making to Chester. They left about an hour ago. I can keep a low profile and Rosemary doesn't need to know a thing about it. I hope Purbright is going to be all right.'

'I would be more worried for Farsai than Purbright if the two were to lock horns,' said Allen.

'Seemingly our guard dogs have our weapons. We need to sign for them. How good a shot were you at University?'

'Not bad, .22 calibre Pistol, big difference when you fire a .38, bigger difference when you go up to .44, now that is cannon.'

'I shot a fair bit up until I started rowing. A .44 is indeed a cannon Allen.'

Chapter 83

★ ★ ★ ★

~*They are out there, I can feel it*~

The weekend passed without incident. Monday came and final plans were being tweaked. Jimmy reported that Fanshawe only ever appeared to walk the dog early in the morning. Mann was trying to secure the services of a new law firm. Strangely he was finding that quite a difficult exercise. Mann was convinced that Fischer-Ward had tipped him the black spot in legal circles.

Aitken and Allen studied all the stuff that Amy Anderson had unearthed about ADI. Amy had discovered some seven months previously that things were not quite right at ADI. She had kept a personal diary for her normal life. This had been recovered from her locker. The first entry regarding ADI had appeared the previous November. A cryptic 'Something is wrong in this company.' This was followed a week later by another entry. 'I think I am working for a bunch of crooks.' This was followed four days later by another entry, 'I am definitely working for a bunch of crooks.'

Amy had started digging the dirt on ADI. Sadly she was also digging her own grave.

So good was she at computers she had amassed huge amounts of information about ADI activities. She had updated her efforts weekly. A disc was there for every one of her weekly activities. Twenty-nine discs of evidence existed as back ups. They also existed on her computer. They were totally incriminating for ADI.

An entry in her diary twenty-two days before her assassination was the first red flag that she was in danger. 'I think I may have been rumbled and I could be in danger. I will have to wait and see.'

Computer records showed what she had done. She had hacked in to Fanshawe's computer. A single e-mail she had obtained was completely revealing. The e-mail read:

'Good news Darling Caroline, our investment in ADI has returned record profits. An exceptional crop in Afghanistan has contributed greatly. I will discuss things in detail at Allansburn. I count the hours until we meet and I can once more hold your sweet hand and look upon that beautiful countenance. All My Love, Hector.'

Accessing any more of Fanshawe's stuff had been quickly stopped by a device that had blocked any further action by Amy. She had quickly realised that whatever system Fanshawe had it was more than a defensive system. This was an offensive system as well and it started to attack her systems with intent to wipe out what she had taken. Amy had obviously managed to repel the attack but she knew that it was likely that it had identified her system. She had reported in her diary that Fanshawe's system was on a parity with the CIA or MI6. Apart from the fact she had dug deeper and found out that Allansburn House was in Perthshire, Scotland and owned by Caroline Faubert there was no other pieces of information stored after that date. She had obviously shut down all activities on the ADI front in the last three weeks of her life. She had realised her life could be in danger. Sadly her assessment that she had been rumbled would prove all too fatal for Amy.

'I take it Sir that you draw the conclusion that our Guinevere is not an innocent in all of this. His reference to an exceptional crop in Afghanistan doesn't mean they have invested in growing grain. She knows exactly what the hell they are growing,' said Allen.

'I am positive that given that reference she is also as guilty as hell. You are right Louise, she is in on the act. Guinevere sinned in Arthurian legend and so has this one. People never fail to amaze you. Caroline Faubert probably has more money than one person would ever need in life yet she involves herself in trying to get more. There seems no sense to such an action.'

Monday passed and Tuesday was uneventful. There was a lot of chatter between Purbright and Brad Michaels. Aitken was getting impatient. Purbright had more or less restricted their movements.

Wednesday followed exactly the same pattern as Tuesday.

Thursday morning dawned bright. Caroline Faubert was still in her flat in Chelsea. Fanshawe was still holed up in Bath. Then suddenly a big cloud appeared on the horizon. Farsai and his guys had not arrived on the flights they should have.

Aitken and Allen were sitting in Aitken's office when the news came in.

'This is driving me nuts Allen, I have a bad feeling. Farsai and his guys, they are out there, I can feel it,' said Aitken.

'The airline bookings have not been cancelled. The same goes for Morgan and Collins. Their reservations are still in place.'

'Allen they are here already. I just know it. They have somehow come in early. I think we should make a small trip to Oxford. Morgan might know that we bugged Singapore but nobody ever mentioned where he lived. So he will feel comparatively safe.'

Aitken pleaded his case with Purbright and strangely enough Purbright acceded to his request provided that the armed baby sitters went along. The two cars set out for Oxford with the armed response unit riding shotgun. Aitken and Allen were in an unmarked police car.

Chapter 84

★ ★ ★ ★

~Acquired as a Target~

Driving to Oxford Allen said we are being tailed. The black Toyota Avensis. They are not our guys. In fact where are our guys?

As if to answer Allen's question the babysitter's called. 'Our car has broken down twenty-three miles out of Oxford, where are you two?'

'Now nearly three miles ahead of you and we think we have just been acquired as a target. The driver is on his own in a black Toyota Avensis. I am coming up to a filling station and I shall get off and see what this guy does.'

Aitken drove into the filling station and parked at the pump.

'That's us off the road and he has driven past without stopping. Maybe we got it wrong but I don't think so. Is the breakdown serious?'

'Yes, it is terminal Sir. We were watching the Avensis, he was definitely on your tail and he was speaking in his Bluetooth. We will have the locals pick him up. Be very careful as I agree with you, I think you have been acquired as a target.'

'I am going to fill this vehicle up with diesel and come back for you. I am not too comfortable at the moment.'

Aitken filled up the car. He poked his head into the car. 'Keep a weather eye out for company Allen. We may not be alone. Gun to hand.'

'Well I am not going to be sitting sleeping am I Sir?'

Aitken stood rather impatiently in the queue. It was then he saw the Mercedes with blacked out windows pulling up just off the filling station.

'Oh shit!' he said. He yelled at the teller 'Call 999 and ask for back up for Detective Aitken of Railton. Do it now.'

He ran to the car just as two men in black got out of the rear of the Mercedes. They were carrying heavy-duty cannon. They started walking toward the forecourt and Aitken and Allen's car. The car was facing the two gunmen. When they heard Aitken kick the car into life they stopped and immediately adopted a shooting position. They were standing about four feet apart.

'Get down,' screamed Aitken as he gunned the car toward the two gunmen who opened fire. Several bullets passed through the windscreen, so many that the screen simply disappeared. This was just as well as Aitken had lost his vision. Miraculously none of the bullets hit their intended targets. When the screen disappeared he was twenty feet from the gunmen. They decided to take evasive action. That is where they made a serious mistake. They both went in the same direction. Aitken simply followed them and ran them over. One gunman went under the wheels, the other came up off the bonnet and stuck in the now open front windscreen. Once again he could barely see where he was going. He slammed the car into reverse as Farsai got out of the passenger seat of the Mercedes. He braked hard, rammed the car into first and booted it toward the Mercedes.

'Shoot the Bastard Allen, don't miss.'

His instruction was followed by the crash of the revolver in Allen's hand. Her aim was true. Farsai was standing behind the open door of the Mercedes. He was bringing his gun to bear as Allen's bullet hit him under the left eye socket. Aitken ramming his car into the door made sure Farsai would never assassinate any other person. As it turned out neither would Fedoseev or Mikhailov. Aitken slammed the car into reverse and came along side the Mercedes.

'Allen, shoot that Bastard as well.'

'No, No, I am not armed,' screamed Collins.

'Collins I do not give a shit whether you are armed or not. Amy Anderson wasn't armed and you shot her like an animal. Now it is time to return the favour.'

Collins screamed for mercy. 'No, No, you cannot do that it would be murder.'

'Allen do what I tell you. That is in an order.'

'No, please, no, I will give you anything, anything you ask. I am worth millions.'

'Anything Collins, anything at all?' said Aitken

'Name your price, a hundred million Aitken. You wouldn't have to work again.'

Collins was visibly shaking.

'I am not after money all I want from you are the heads of Wendell Fanshawe and Byron Mann. We have paper here. You do a signed confession now and you live. You are still young enough to be out of prison even after ten years. Do not do it and I shall do to you what you did to Amy Anderson, one bullet through the forehead and one through the heart. Allen here is a crack shot. What is left of Farsai's head will testify to that. I assume that you could pull that off Allen.'

'No problem Sir, it would be my pleasure. Can you believe this guy? He orders an execution without any compassion. Then when it comes to his turn he is yellow through and through. A shot through the head will throw him back. The seat will momentarily keep him upright, long enough for a second round through the heart. Yes, I can do it Sir, just give the word. I'm sure the pain will be very brief if that is some consolation Collins.'

Allen's delivery was cold as ice. Even Aitken wasn't too sure if he had said yes would she have shot Collins. He would ask her some time later and all she would say was, 'We will never know.'

Collins was crying by now. 'Look I shall sign anything you want. Just have her lower that bloody gun.'

'Right, get out of the car and we will sort out the paperwork.'

Just then their radio went.

'You two OK?' It was their babysitters.

'Yes we are, just. Farsai and his team are probably all dead. Well Farsai is very dead. I have a guy in the windscreen with his neck broken. He is very dead. The other guy I ran over twice so he is probably very dead. Collins who was acting as driver is under arrest. Other than the fact that Allen is such a crack shot that thanks to her shooting it made Collins wet himself. That apart he is still in one bit. Our car is slightly bent; well to be honest it is a lot bent. The Super isn't going to be too happy about that.'

'Good work Sir, we are in a car and we are two minutes away. The really great news is that you are both in one piece. I think Purbright might forgive you bending his precious vehicle. Mind you what we hear about him, maybe not.'

Aitken and Allen could hear the laughter in the police car.

Chapter 85

★ ★ ★ ★

~Annie Oakley~

A itken's mobile went, it was Purbright.
Thank God you answered. Are you both OK?'

Yes Sir, we are fine. I cannot speak for Louise, as she has had to blow someone away. She really is a crack shot. Saved our damned lives I can tell you. We have Collins here and he is in some state. Amazingly a total coward, he is just standing outside our car. Sadly he has wet himself and is looking pretty miserable. He was willing to give up Wendell Fanshawe and Mann in exchange for Allen not executing him exactly in the same fashion as Amy Anderson was executed.'

'I am glad to see that you have used your time usefully since they attempted to assassinate you. Getting a confession after that kind of stramash is definitely maximising your time. Great work the two of you, just great work.

'What is a stramash?' asked Allen. I take it is another of Dunbar's Scottish words.'

'Aye, it is that Louise. It means when there has been a wee bit of a commotion. Are you OK lass?' The delivery was close to pure Dunbar even if it hadn't been intended.

'Sir I have been better. That said I should sleep a lot better tonight knowing that we are no longer assassination targets. Here are the support units. Looks like they probably got sabotaged Sir. Anyway we are now on programme. I'll be OK, but thanks for asking Sir.'

'Tonight, I'll be sleeping better as well. Brad Michaels is going to be a happy bunny. He has just flown in. That is going to be a great welcome gift, Collins's head on a platter. I am amazed at Collins. I thought he would have been tough as nails. Just like Mann being gay, something I would have never thought of. I am absolutely over the moon that we can tie down Fanshawe and Mann. I suppose I had better let you get tidied up there. Any bugger taking pictures yet?'

'Probably Sir,' said Aitken, 'we have yet to get out of the car. By the way it is in very bad shape. I used it to run over the two gunmen and I had to take out Farsai and the Merc door together. He was already dead thanks to Annie Oakley here. Farsai is spread over the forecourt quite a bit. I assume that this is going to mean one helluva lot of paperwork.'

Aitken I am aware of your love of paperwork, it's on par with mine. The only way you could have gotten out of the paperwork on this was for you to be shot. Good luck with it. Bye.'

They could both hear Purbright laughing as the line went dead.

'He seems happy,' said Allen.

'More relief than anything else, I would guess, the mere fact that we are both alive. He would have picked up our predicament on the police bands. I used my name and Railton when I had the girl in there call the police. Anyway how are you Louise? I am sorry you had to make that shot and I am sorry what we had to do ended three people's lives but it was definitely them or us. Let's get things tidied up here. I think we can forget Ross Morgan. Tomorrow early as planned will do.'

'You two OK?' enquired one of their escorts. 'Looks very much like you had a bit of pitched battle here. Look at the state of this place, three guys dead with one in bits. There are absolute loads of spent cartridge cases strewn everywhere. Two cars wrecked and a guy who has wet himself. We are going to take forever to write this one up. Last time I come out with you pair. Why the hell can you not just fill up at a filling station like everybody else?'

'I did,' said Aitken.

'I know and you didn't pay for it. That's why she called the Police.'

Again the humour came from a sense of relief.

'Oh shit, I didn't pay. I had better go and square up.'

'You are not going anywhere near that counter, we shall sort things out and back charge Purbright. My Super will love getting money out of that old scrooge. We shall stick on a fifteen per cent uplift administration charge and it will wind him up.'

'Thanks, firstly we need to get this guy here to write down his confession before he changes his mind.'

Aitken need not have worried. The level of carnage had all been too much for Collins. He also knew that he had come close to being shot himself. Aitken was right; he would still be youngish when he came out. What would he get? He reckoned he would be sentenced to ten years probably, maybe twelve tops. He would serve eight with good behaviour. He would have three hundred possibly nearer four hundred million when he came out. Giving them Fanshawe and Mann, the latter whom he couldn't stand, was worth it.

Chapter 86

★ ★ ★ ★

~Bit of a close call~

They took Collins to a local Police station where Aitken had him write out a confession implicating Fanshawe and Mann. Three hours later and he was still writing. Just five minutes short of four hours he put down the pen having signed the confession. He was charged with organising the murder of Amy Anderson.

Half an hour later Brad Michaels walked into the station with Frank Purbright. He shook hands with Aitken and Allen. He had a smile a mile wide.

'Bit of a close call for you two today. Best thing that could happen to these types. You live by the sword and you die by the sword, saved us all a goddammed fortune. Downside I hear is you wrote off a perfectly good police car. What were you thinking about? You cannot beat up on police equipment like that, well not one of Frank's vehicles, not according to some of your colleagues at Railton.'

'Tell me who said that and I shall sort them out for spreading malicious rumours about me,' said Purbright.

'You know me Frank, I am hopeless with names,' said a smiling Brad Michaels. 'I hear our man has written a novel.'

'I think you will like it. This is not a work of fiction. Another twenty minutes or so and the typed up copy is ready. They were typing as he wrote it.'

The girls were even better than their word; ten minutes later Collins signed four copies of his confession for Aitken and Allen. Once Collins had completed this task Purbright and Brad

Michaels joined him.

'Do you know who I am?' asked Purbright.

Collins, who was now much cheerier, said 'You are Detective Chief Superintendent Purbright.'

'Yes, I am the one that you paid out five million to eliminate along with Detectives Aitken and Allen here. I am totally pissed off with you but sadly I am not going to be able to demonstrate just how pissed off I really am. Can I introduce you to Brad Michaels of the DEA Washington facility? This man is one serious powerful operator and he is definitely not going to be your friend. He is taking you back stateside where you will face additional charges.'

'You cannot do that. That is illegal. I will say my statement was given under duress.'

Purbright and Michaels both fell about laughing.

'You wrote a sodding book man,' said Purbright. No Judge or Jury in the land is going to believe that. That is the best laugh I have had in ages. What do you think Brad. Just when you think you have heard it all.'

'Sorry Frank, can't speak,' spluttered Michaels with tears running down his face.

'Thanks Collins,' said Purbright, 'that is simply one of the best in a long time. As for you having a wee trip to the US of A, I think you will find that we can and we will ship you out. You were going there anyway to get rid of Tamblin. Tell you what Brad, why do you not tell Tamblin what Collins was coming to do to him and bunk them together. Tamblin is a serious jock and Collins is seriously yellow. Now wouldn't that be fun?'

'No, I couldn't do that Frank. Who would I have left to give me a good laugh? Mind you Collins you will have to go some to top that one, 'under duress,' just brilliant.'

'You will be coming back here for your murder trial. What kind of sentence can he expect over there Brad?'

'Hard to say Frank, a liberal Judge thirty years, a hard liner Judge, possibly life meaning life, somewhere in that range, hard to say. According to Amy Anderson there is just so much to charge them with. Fortunately she will extract her revenge from beyond the grave.'

'Talking of Amy, we'll have fifteen years waiting for him here,' said Purbright.

Collins rounded on Aitken. 'You promised me a lighter sentence if I cooperated.'

'I never promised you anything of the kind. What I said was that if you gave me the heads of Fanshawe and Mann that I would stop Allen from blowing your head away. I clearly kept my promise.'

Collins went very quiet. His whole body language was one of defeat.

'Right you two, having wrecked a perfectly good police car I suppose you want a lift back to the station. I suppose there are going to be a few questions that the media will want answering about what happened at the filling station. I have spoken with the Assistant Commissioner and he says he will stonewall it completely until we do our thing tomorrow. The media have turned up at the filling station but we have huge screens up and we have the area well cordoned off. Fortunately none of the many witnesses had the presence of mind to film what had happened either during or after the event. They know you were involved Jeremy but that is all. We have been asked if we had suffered fatalities. The AC has told them that there were fatalities but we would not be confirming anything until the next of kin had been informed. That will throw them although one witness had reported that the guy had said he was a policeman, well it looked liked he and a woman survived. They were in the car that ran down two other guys who had been shooting at them. They shot another guy who had got out of a black Mercedes with a gun in his hand. They totally wiped him out by running into the car door he was sheltering behind. They then backed up and the woman pointed a gun into the damaged Mercedes. A fourth guy got out of the Mercedes with his hands up. Other cars then arrived and armed guys had got out of them. Then normal police cars arrived and then more big vans came and put up screens. Nobody could see a thing after that.'

'Very good witness statement if he was that accurate,' said Aitken.

'He was a she in this case,' said Purbright.

'That explains it,' said Allen. You can rely on a woman to get it right,' she said with a smile.

'You can rely on a woman to be dead nosey,' said Aitken.

'Do you know,' said Brad Michaels, 'you two sound like an old married couple.'

'If I was married to him I would be giving him poison.' said

Allen.

'And if I was married to her, I would be taking it. Boom, Boom, the old ones are the best,' said Aitken.

They all had a good laugh. Even Purbright smiled.

Underneath each had recognised the release of tension from the events of the day.

When they got back to Railton there was a huge amount of media gathered outside. The entrance had been blocked off.

'Get down in the back and cover your heads, said Purbright, you cover up as well Brad.'

Purbright drove straight in and round to the roller door where they took prisoners out and in. Here they were out of sight from the public.'

Purbright got out and walked through the station to the assembled media.

'Go home all of you. There is nothing here. The Assistant Commissioner has made a statement and until tomorrow there is nothing we can report.'

'Who was in the car?'

Purbright looked at the reporter and shook his head. Sorry to disappoint you but nothing more than a couple of car wreckers we picked up. They had done thousand of pounds worth of damage and they had to be taken in. I merely picked them as I was closest. The job has more mundane aspects than glamorous ones.'

In the station everyone watching the television live report had a good laugh at Aitken and Allen's expense. Brad Michaels obviously had a great sense of humour under the gruff exterior. The description of the pair as a couple of car wreckers amused him no end.

Outside Purbright continued with his report.

'You can interview them if you want but like so many of today's young people they may tell you where to go in purple prose. I am also telling you where to go and that is home. You can stand here for hours and all you will be doing is wasting your time. You know me when I have something to say we will give you plenty of warning.'

'Something big went down today involving your people. Are you denying that Frank?'

'No Eddie I am not and yes it did involve my people.'

'We are positive it was Aitken and Allen. Are they OK?'

'Eddie, Assistant Commissioner Jenkins said it to you all earlier. There were fatalities. So far we have not been able to inform the next of kin so we are not releasing a statement until we have carried that out. I am sorry but we have to respect that. We would anticipate an announcement about today's events around midday tomorrow.

If you contact Assistant Commissioner Jenkins's office at around eleven tomorrow morning they should be able to inform you.'

The assembled media accepted Purbright's statement. If nothing else he was straight.

Just as they were starting to leave a voice said, 'Something is not right here Purbright. I think you are blowing smoke up our....'

Before the voice could complete the sentence Purbright said, 'Ah the disbelieving voice of the Mercury. Mr Sullivan, no matter what you are ever told you never believe it. I am sure that you get up in the morning and look in the mirror and you don't believe yourself either. Mind you I wouldn't blame you.'

The departing crowd had a good laugh at Sullivan's expense. The seasoned Hacks knew there was no love lost between Purbright and Sullivan.

'Sullivan you can stand there until eleven o'clock tomorrow and as I said nothing will be announced before then. I do not really care whether you believe me or not but I can assure you that is what will happen. I equally do not care if you do stay here until then.'

Sullivan turned and marched off without a word.

Aitken and Allen were later taken home in a police van out of sight of any prying eyes.

Chapter 87

★ ★ ★ ★

~*Just remember he isn't Bone China*~

The following morning they were duly collected and taken to Railton.

The sun was up even though it had just turned five am. The day was dry and looked like it was going to be pleasant.

Purbright announced, 'It is a good day to catch criminals. Let's get the show on the road. Are you OK Brad? Anything you need?

Yes and No Frank, I am all set up and there is nothing I require. I have every target under surveillance and all my guys are in position. Shall we go fishing and see what we catch. I take we are still calling on Morgan at zero eight hundred.'

'That is a confirmation Brad, let's put this thing to bed,' said Purbright.

Aitken and Allen finally got to the door of Ross Morgan's house and rang the bell. There was a full minute's delay then the intercom kicked into life. A woman's voice said

'This had better be bloody important Richard. I am right in the middle of getting a good seeing to.'

'I am sorry to disappoint you but I am not Richard,' said Aitken.

'Who the hell are you? How did you manage to get past Richard at security? Even my Mum cannot get to our door unannounced.'

'Well when you announce that you are in the midst of a good seeing to you can be thankful it wasn't your Mum. Anyway, as it is, no offence taken here.'

'Look I do not know who the hell you are but we are not seeing anyone so piss off before I call the police.'

'If you do, you would get the most unbelievable speedy response. We are here already, even before you phone. You cannot beat that for speed. My name is Detective Chief Inspector Aitken and I am here to arrest your husband. Tell him not to try and escape as the entire house and area is surrounded. Equally do not try to phone anyone as your phones are temporarily disconnected. That includes your mobile services as well.'

'You cannot just switch off our phones.'

'I think you will find that we can and have. Anyway as you live in a time of Caring Constabularies who are much more aware of social issues, you will be glad to know that we have been briefed with the very latest recommended time for making love. Seemingly the optimum time is eight to thirteen minutes. We suggest you return to what you euphemistically referred to as a good seeing to. This will be the last time that you enjoy that pleasure, well certainly with Mr Morgan, for some time. The time is seven forty seven and if you do not answer this bell in thirteen minutes time at eight am exactly we shall break the down door. Thank you.'

Mrs Morgan's response was totally unprintable. The intercom went dead.

'Aitken you really are full of it,' said a smiling Allen.

The guys standing around ready to break down the door if need be were also smiling. They would not be needed in battering ram terms. Two minutes later the door flew open to a Mr Morgan in dressing gown and slippers enquiring in further unprintable terms as to who they thought they were and what were they doing there. Susan his wife stood similarly attired, except she had bare feet, in the hall behind her husband.

'I am Detective Chief Inspector Aitken and this is Detective Constable Allen. James Ross Caldwell Morgan or Peter Oliver Landsdowne or should we try Robert Speed, all aliases used by you, we are arresting you for drug trafficking, money laundering and murder. Read him his rights Detective Allen. Behind Morgan there was a thump as Susan hit the floor. Allen just carried on reading Morgan his rights.

'OK lads, cuff him take him away,' said Aitken.

'In your bloody dreams mate, I am not going anywhere and I am certainly not going anywhere in handcuffs. Call Lester, Honey, he will have this sorted out in two minutes. I can assure you, this motley bunch of flatfeet are wasting their time.'

Mrs Morgan lifted her head and groaned. We cannot call anyone as they have disconnected all our phones. Why are they calling you all these different names?'

'What the hell are you talking about. You jerks cannot do that, it is illegal.'

'What I want to know is what they are talking about Morgan?

'You are under arrest and you are most certainly coming with us,' said Aitken.

This time Aitken's voice was all menace.

'You might think us a bunch of flatfeet but we are arresting you. Let me assure you there will be no bail, no Lester Goldsmith or any other legal eagle will be able to get you that. I can safely predict that you are not going to be in circulation for the next thirty years. Try that for size Morgan. Get this lowlife out of here. Just remember he isn't bone china. Strip and search him at the prison, you never know where these drug dealers have drugs.'

'No problem Guv, we flatfeet shall take good care of him.'

Morgan visibly paled, he knew the inevitability of what was about to happen to him.

Ten seconds later Morgan was cuffed rather unceremoniously and equally unceremoniously bundled into a police car.

His wife was still lying on the hall floor sobbing. Allen went in and helped her to her feet.

'Try and get yourself together. Your husband is going to need all your support over the next few days and months,' said Allen.

'Tell me something; is all that your boss said Peter was charged with, is it true? Are you sure you haven't got the wrong man?'

'Mrs Landsdowne, I am sorry but we have not got the wrong man. There are no mistakes. Your husband is totally guilty of what he has been charged with.'

'God, that is just too horrible to contemplate. I love Peter but if he is guilty of what you say I am just not sure.'

Susan Landsdowne wasn't bluffing. Louise Allen was convinced that she hadn't a clue about her husband's activities.

'I need to phone my Mum. Of course I can't, the phones are out.'

'I think you will find that your phone works fine,' said Allen. 'You phone your Mum, does she live far away?'

'No, she can be here in just under an hour. She lives close to

Oxford.'

'Would you like someone from victim counselling to come and see you? I can arrange it.'

'Victim counselling, what do you mean?'

'Unless I am very much mistaken you are a victim of your husband's actions and there are some excellent people out there who can help you with this. As I say you are a victim.'

'I suppose I am.' Susan Landsdowne looked totally bewildered. 'What I am struggling with is what his actual name is?'

'His real name is Robert Speed. We have been tracking him as Ross Morgan and you know him as Peter Landsdowne. In the meantime you might be better going to your Mum's. We shall be searching your house. I am sure that you understand that.'

'That is horrible, but yes, I suppose, I can understand it.'

'If you do not feel up to driving to your Mum's we can have someone drive you there.'

'Thanks but I will be OK. The drive will get my head around things. I had better get tidied up. Just my bloody luck, I only had it confirmed last Thursday that I am pregnant. Poor wee thing is going to have a murderer as a father.'

'I have to go but that WPC over there is Lucy Ashton. I shall have her look after you.'

'Thanks Detective, I am sorry for being rude earlier.'

'Look, you just look after yourself. Just remember that Mr Landsdowne is still going to be your baby's father.'

Aitken looked in on Morgan in the Police car.

'Right you arrogant so and so I am going to sort you out big time. My next port of call is to pick up your old man. Some of our other flatfeet are in Chelsea and guess who they are picking up? A clue is that it is a woman who should have stayed in Monaco.'

'Christ no! She is an old woman. You cannot arrest her.'

'Care to bet Morgan. Your whole damned family is corrupt. Maybe we should pick up Henry as well.'

'Now you are bloody joking. He really is innocent.'

'If you want him to stay on the outside you had better start writing a very accurate account about ADI activities and who was responsible for Amy Anderson's death.'

'This is all about that girl isn't it? You and that bitch follow us to the end of the earth over the death of a nobody.'

'You really are the most arrogant Bastard. She wasn't a nobody to her family and loved ones. If you ever call Amy a nobody again I shall personally take you in to an unfurnished room and teach you a lesson in life.'

'Excuse me Sir.' It was Louise Allen.

She spoke to Morgan. 'Did you just call me a bitch?'

She didn't wait for a reply. All they could hear was a bone crunching smack and blood flew from Morgan's nose, a nose that now lay at a crooked angle.

'Sorry Sir, he resisted arrest.'

'Of course he did Detective. Of course he did. I am glad you were able to subdue him. Well-done Detective Allen.

'You've broken my nose,' groaned Morgan.

'I'll break a bloody sight more than your nose if you ever call me a bitch again.'

'Morgan you know what you have to do to keep Henry out of jail,' said Aitken.

In the car on the way to Wendell Fanshawe's Allen asked Aitken, 'I take it you didn't like Ross Morgan or whatever he is called very much.'

'You got it in one. You know whether you are a major crook or you're not. That arrogant stance that I am above arrest by some of them gets up my nose. That 'I am untouchable' attitude. The one that did it for me was the one that Amy Anderson was a nobody. That guy is going to the toughest bloody jail we can find. '

'I think he got your message and I can assure you he was definitely winded when he realised what was happening,' said Allen.

'So he should because he is going away for a long time. I think he was a lot more than winded when he got your message. In the last nine months so far two guys call you a bitch and they have both landed up with a broken nose. Remind me never to upset you.'

'Sorry about that Sir, that was unprofessional but God it felt good. I must admit I felt a bit sorry for his wife, poor woman obviously had no clue about his nefarious activities,'

'These guys were like a secret society. Everything relied on their total secrecy.'

The next fifteen minutes was spent in comparative silence apart from Allen calling some young idiot in an Astra a complete wanker.

'By the way Sir, where did you get that little statistic about the optimum time for having sex, eight to thirteen minutes.'

'Oh, that wasn't bull, contrary to your critique about my being full of it. Some study group came up with that.'

'Then sir I had better check with Rosemary if you are coming up to even the minimum. Eight minutes wasn't it.'

'Allen, it is just as well that you are driving or I could be joining Morgan in the dock.'

'What happened to the Caring Constabulary with its social conscience? You do not seem to belong to that Constabulary. You seem to be of a violent nature wishing to actually inflict bodily harm on me.'

'Having just smashed a nose to pulp how can you accuse me of a violent nature. Allen, I worry about you.'

'Do not sir; I am getting my full thirteen minutes.'

'Allen, just shut up.'

Chapter 88

★ ★ ★ ★

~ The Tantalus unlocked~

They arrived at Wendell Fanshawe's house and reported in to Purbright.

'Right Sir we are position. He walked the dog earlier, so we should have a positive result. We are ready on your command. We are four minutes from the hour.'

'Go on the hour mark. I am outside the Mann Centre. Mann has arrived in his office. Laura is in position in Chelsea. Brad has also his guys in position across the world. Speak to you shortly when we complete.'

Aitken ran the bell to the intercom. A voice said 'Yes?' in a questioning manner.

'We should like to talk with Wendell Fanshawe.'

'I am afraid that no one of that name resides here. This property is the home of a lady.'

'OK, shall we try Hector Speed or do you want any further aliases. We know he is there. This is the Police, my name is Detective Chief Inspector Aitken and this woman you can see on your monitor is Detective Constable Allen. You have five seconds to open these gates or we break our way in.'

The five seconds passed and the gates started to open.

Aitken spoke in to the microphone. 'Correct decision.'

They drove up the drive to the double doors to the house.

The right hand door, as they looked at it, opened. There stood the man who had been the chauffeur the night they had been at the theatre.

When they got out of the car he spoke. 'Mr Fanshawe will see you now.'

'I think you have that the wrong way round,' said Aitken. 'We will see Fanshawe now.'

They followed the man into a large drawing room and there they could see the back of a wing chair. The top of a man's head poked over it and they could see his hands on the arms of the chair.

The two detectives walked around either side of the chair and sat down in two other chairs opposite.

'I do not recall asking you to sit down. You are in my house. Your actions are so symptomatic of today's society, no manners, no breeding.' This was not the voice of the effeminate Fanshawe.

'I know,' said Aitken, 'a pretty bad state of affairs when some one cannot stand up to greet his guests in his house not that it will be your house for much longer. The proceeds of crime, we shall acquire it on behalf of the state. As to breeding what would you expect from the son of a Music Hall singer.'

Allen thought nice one Aitken. For a moment she also thought that Fanshawe was about to have an apoplectic fit. She watched with interest as he struggled to get control.

He finally snapped. 'What do you want?'

'We simply want to arrest you, that is all,' said Aitken. 'Yes, we are here to arrest you.'

Fanshawe laughed, 'Are you some cheap music hall comedian. Do you know who I am?'

'Oh I know exactly who you are. The real question is do you actually know who you are?'

There was a small tic at the corner of Fanshawe's left eye the only outward sign on Fanshawe's face that Aitken's barb had struck home.'

'You are those two detectives who followed us all the way to Singapore because your stupid Chief Superintendent believed that my company was responsible for the death of a drug crazed employee of ours.'

'No, we do not believe ADI guilty of Amy Anderson's murder. We know that you are. Another thing Amy Anderson was not drug crazed. She never ever touched the filth that ADI poured into the market.'

'Are you on something Detective?'

'No I am not and you know it. Charge him with murder Allen

and read him his rights. By the way Fanshawe, whatever you do, under no circumstances call our lady detective a bitch. Your son Ross made that mistake. His handsome face is far from handsome now. I have warned you. Allen here suffers badly with PMT and this is not a good day for you take chances. For a moment there you represented a Goldfish when I told you about your son. If that is a problem then I have much worse news. At exactly this moment at 44 Arlington Mews, Chelsea a colleague of mine Detective Constable Laura Baynes arrested a Caroline Faubert. That leaves only young Henry at large.'

'You cannot arrest him he has done nothing wrong.' There was a sense of panic in the voice.

'Your son Ross said that and it is probably the case but we feel that we can make a case against him.'

'He is innocent.'

'He is only innocent if you sign a confession to what you actually did and that was to order the execution of Amy Anderson. That is the only deal on the table that will keep young Henry treading the Boards. We watched him perform as Valentine. I'll tell you what, he was head and shoulders above the rest of the cast and they were no slouches.'

'Yes, I must admit, the boy's got talent.'

'I would go further Fanshawe, he's got major talent. That said I am more than willing to flush that talent down the drain if you do not cooperate.'

'This is blackmail.'

'Blackmail is such a seedy word, a grubby word, no I think this is nothing more than horse-trading. You sanctioned Amy's death so you are not being stitched up for something you didn't do. Who knows, whatever you may write in that confession could keep Miss Faubert out of prison.'

'You really are a vicious bastard Aitken.'

'If you think I am vicious then meet Detective Allen. Our detective is as sharp as a lance. It was she who devised the run on your shares. ADI is practically bust thanks to her.'

Fanshawe glared balefully at Allen. He opened his mouth to say something.

Aitken jumped straight in. 'Fanshawe remember what I told you, what not to call Detective Allen.'

Fanshawe closed his mouth.

'Detective Allen, have uniformed remove the prisoner.

This house is closed off subject to investigation.'

'What about my man Reynolds?' asked Fanshawe.

'He's looking for accommodation as of now. If you have any money in the house I suggest that you pay the man what is due.'

'Thank you Aitken. Reynolds, come with me man.'

They adjourned to a library and Fanshawe opened a safe. He had just activated the combination when Aitken put his hand on the door.

'If you do not mind I shall open the door. There could be a gun in there.'

There wasn't. Fanshawe stepped forward and took out a bulging envelope.

'Reynolds you have been a faithful retainer these past eleven years. My grateful thanks, some terrible things may be said about me over the next few weeks and months. Do not think ill of me.'

'Thank you Sir, this is far too kind. You have been an excellent master to serve. There is no way I shall think ill of you.'

'You may not see me again. I am already in God's waiting Room and I fear that prison will speed up the appointment with my maker.'

Fanshawe had gone back into the effeminate voice he affected as Fanshawe.

He then spoke in a totally different voice. 'In God's waiting room Fanshawe, that's a bloody laugh me old cock sparrow. You are a damned atheist.' The voice was hard and definitely East End.

Fanshawe then spoke in his effeminate voice once again. 'You really are a Pagan, George Royston. You always have to bring it down to basics. You would have never made an actor.'

'I am not too sure you that you made one Fanshawe.'

'Your barbs cannot penetrate my armour George. Show an old man a little kindness.'

Aitken shook Fanshawe by the shoulder. 'I am sorry Wendell but we need to go.'

'Oh, it's you Aitken. We are going now?'

'Yes we are, now that you have seen to your man Reynolds we must move on.'

Fanshawe had returned. 'Don't worry Reynolds I shall ensure that nothing untoward happens to you. Right let's get this over with.'

Chapter 89

★ ★ ★ ★

~I would look away Gentlemen~

In the car Allen said 'I take it you didn't feel sorry for Fanshawe back there?'

'Sorry, did I feel sorry for a guy that sanctioned the execution of an innocent young woman? You got to be joking. He is getting what is coming to him.'

'He will not see freedom ever again Sir, nor does he deserve to. I wonder how the others are getting on?'

'Hopefully, they have finished our side of things and hopefully Brad's teams are picking up their targets. I would like to be a fly on the wall when Kristy picks up Kraft or Gaylord as she really is. There is no love lost there. I think there will be a lovely feeling for Jimmy Austin arresting Mann. I think Purbright is brilliant at that kind of thing. He always has the situation at his fingertips. It is like Laura nailing Faubert as thanks for all her research. Purbright is interviewing the three we have arrested today. He loves the cut and thrust of the interview room.'

When they returned to Railton there was a mood of euphoria in the station. Brad Michaels was holding court. His teams had enjoyed a one hundred per cent success rate. There wasn't a single Knight at large. They had done it with style and all the arrests had been done on camera.

Brad Michaels said that the arrest of Bill Tamblin was particularly hilarious. He was playing golf and definitely playing around. The team knew he was with a woman in the room who wasn't his wife. When they broke in it was two o'clock in the morning. Tamblin and the lady were in the suite having only come in an hour earlier. The team had obtained a master key and walked in unannounced. What happens next may require the ladies to look away and definitely for the men to look away. The team would find the couple en-flagrante. As you can see the woman tries to cover her modesty.

'Sorry Mrs Tamblin we are arresting your husband.' The so-called Mrs Tamblin now stops trying to cover her modesty.

'What did you mean Mrs Tamblin. There isn't a Mrs Tamblin. Well, if there is, I sure as hell aint her.'

'You are not Mrs Susan Tamblin of 1547b Eldorada Way, Fort Worth?'

'As ah said, Ah sure as hell aint. OK Tamblin out with it. Are you married you two timing bastard?'

Tamblin was standing there stark naked looking at his feet and not answering.

He muttered 'Sorry Donna.'

'I would look away now gentlemen,' said Michaels.

Well Donna, also standing naked went off it, completely off it. She attacked Tamblin with such ferocity that it took four agents almost five minutes to get her off Tamblin. The problem was that the fair Donna had grabbed Tamblin by the genitals and nearly twisted them off. He was screaming the place down.

Michaels said, 'I bet all the lights in that Motel were coming on as they do when Fred throws the 'cat' out in the Flintstones.'

They finally succeeded to break Donna's grip but Tamblin's genitals were in a bad way. They were bleeding badly from where she had dug her nails in.

'He interviewed later in a high pitched voice,' said Brad.

'Have you got Kristy's arrest of Kraft?' asked Allen.

'Yes, said Brad, it was one of the early ones in. Kristy definitely took the wind out of Kraft's sails.'

'Good because I would have been inclined to do the same,' said Allen.

'Here it is, I think Kristy did you proud.'

Brad started the tape. Kristy rang the bell on the door of Nadine Kraft's house.

A voice said over the sound system at the door, 'Who is it?

'Kristy Armstrong of the DEA.'

'What the hell do you want?'

'To arrest you, so you had better come down and open this

door.'

'You can piss off back to whatever rock you crawled out from under. You have no jurisdiction here.'

'I think you will find that I have. Look out your window and you shall see dozens of local police assisting me. I shall count to three and if you do not come out I shall be coming in. Failure to open this door shall be construed as resisting arrest. You are in such a hole as to only make matters worse by your behaviour. One, Two.'

She never got to three, the door was opened by Nadine Kraft.

'Nadine Kraft or Emma Gaylord to give you your correct name I am arresting you for murder.'

The mention of Emma Gaylord was like a punch in the stomach for Nadine Kraft.

She tried to bluster that she had never heard of Emma Gaylord.

'Do not waste my time Gaylord; we know who you are and what you have done. Take her away.'

'Hang on I am not dressed. I have nothing on below this.'

'You are involved in drugs so you are going to be strip searched anyway and internally examined.'

'I suppose you will be watching you sodding dyke.'

'Good grief no, you are just too ugly. I most certainly do not want to see you in the nude, not if I can possibly avoid it. Mind you most of the men in the station will probably watch. One piece of advice to you, call me a dyke again and I will break your bones, is that clearly understood. You six guys take her back inside, strip her and get her dressed. Do not let her go into a closet, cupboard or a drawer. Give her what she wants from her instructions. She must stand in the middle of the room at all times. After that take her down town, strip her again, search her internally, cold shower and prison garb. Keep a very close watch on her. The Australians will be here very shortly to pick her up.

Do not bother to tell them that you have strip-searched and examined her. They will do it anyway. I should tell you Gaylord that you will be accustomed to the word dyke inside because one of them is going to make you her bitch, even someone as ugly as you. You topped a woman warder I think it is fair to say that the next twenty years for you are going to be seriously shit.'

'I have a son at school what is to become of him?

'We know that and we traced his natural father who has agreed to take him.'

'His natural father? No bloody way.'

'Well it is that way or no way. Otherwise he is looked after by the authorities.'

'You really are a first class bitch.'

'According to you the class bitch is Louise Allen. Louise is serious class and think yourself lucky that she wasn't the arresting officer after what you said. You definitely would have had broken bones.'

Chapter 90

★ ★ ★ ★

~New Transport~

Purbright poked his head in 'Come on team the AC wants you all out there for the press conference. You too Brad. You OK about doing a television interview?'

When they got outside into the station yard it had been fenced off and behind the fences were masses of media including national television cameras.

'Right,' said Jenkins, 'Firstly, thanks for your presence here today at the culmination of what has been a major international case which has been brought to a very successful conclusion by some exceptional co-operation between ourselves and the DEA out of Washington. Yesterday we had a major incident in which three people were fatally wounded. The three were part of an international hit team who were contracted to take out Detective Chief Superintendent Purbright, DCI Aitken and DC Allen. These three were heading up a team working on what we called the Tantalus Case. This case started with the execution of a wonderful young and vibrant woman called Amy Anderson. I am glad to inform Amy's parents James and Emily Anderson and her brother Jason that today with the huge and invaluable help of this man beside me, Brad Michaels of the DEA, Washington and his many teams that we have arrested every person who had any involvement with Amy's death. Their assistance and willingness to work together with my team here at Railton was the main contributory factor in the success of this joint venture. All of these twenty-five, sorry Brad it is twenty-seven isn't it? You have been busy, haven't you? What I was trying to say before I got my maths wrong is that they are all involved with ADI and represent all the senior officers of that company. The other person arrested but not employed by ADI is Byron Mann.'

This brought a huge gasp from the assembled Media.

'Ladies and gentleman of the media can I introduce you to Mr Brad Michaels. Brad please, the floor is yours.'

'Thank you Assistant Commissioner Jenkins, I think I need to redress the balance in this partnership. We have for the past four years been aware of the various activities of ADI. We understand why DCI Aitken named this as The Tantalus Case. We have come tantalisingly close to cracking the case on several occasions. Every time when we thought we had them we have been left just out of reach. The breakthrough came thanks primarily to work conducted by DCI Aitken and DC Allen and their support team here at Railton under the guidance of Chief Superintendent Frank Purbright. ADI were money laundering but much more importantly their phenomenal growth was built on the back of being one of the largest drug dealers in the world.

For us in the DEA it is unbelievably huge and should give us some breathing space. The amount of drugs that will be off the streets is simply immeasurable. I think I can speak for all of my teams throughout the world and express our grateful and heartfelt thanks to Frank Purbright and his team and to AC Jenkins for the immense cooperation he has given. That is it for me, I am going to celebrate with my staff and rightly so.'

Jenkins who was almost purring took over again.

'That's it; we achieved for us the most important task. We arrested those responsible for Amy's death. A word of warning to all those criminals out there, if you are inclined to criminal ways you don't do it on Frank Purbright's patch as you will be caught. However, that said my message as an Assistant Commissioner, to the criminal classes is to actually commit your crimes on Frank Purbright's patch because I know you will be caught.'

He looked at Purbright and Purbright gave a brief nod and a half smile.

The media had lots of questions and Jenkins and Brad Michaels took them all.

Purbright was now back at work interviewing.

Allen said to Aitken, 'Great political speech by Jenkins.'

'Now, now, Miss Allen, let us not be cynical.'

After that the whole team decamped to the pub plus the logistics team from the DEA.

A couple of hours passed and Frank Purbright still had not joined the party.

Jimmy Austin came in; he had been helping Purbright with Mann's interview. Jimmy had loved reading Mann his rights.

'Sir, the Super hasn't quite finished yet but he has given me two letters for you. I do not know what that one is but the second one is your new transport seeing that you are in need of new transport. This envelope is seemingly important. Purbright said to make sure that you settle this one right away.'

Aitken opened the letter. What it contained was an invoice for ten thousand eight hundred and twenty three pounds for a written off Police Ford Mondeo. The people present cracked up.

'Right let's see your new transport,' said someone.

Aitken opened the letter and inside was a picture of a tandem.

This brought out all the wags.

'Louise you need to be up front steering on that new transport. Aitken cannot pass a Mercedes without running in to it.'

'Worse,' said another, 'he runs down pedestrians.'

'I think Aitken would definitely get the better of the deal. I cannot imagine Louise wanting to sit behind that rear end.'

'Especially if the beautiful Rosemary had made a bean cassoulet the night before.'

'All right you lot I get the picture. Wait until I see the Super,' said Aitken.

'When you do, you can buy him a large Jura Malt.'

Frank Purbright had walked in and announced his arrival.

'Do I detect that you are not overly impressed with your new transport?'

Coming Soon...

Join Aitken and Allen in their next case: **The Impediment Case**

In The Impediment Case the Registrar asks the guests at a wedding if they know of any impediment why this couple should not be married. This was answered by the crash of a high velocity rifle from the back of the hall. The bullet would be the ultimate impediment as it hit its target with fatal consequences, the target being the groom.

Aitken and Allen soon discover that all is not as it seems with this groom. His past has reached out and finally caught up with him. Other murders would follow and for Aitken and Allen it is a complex case to unravel. What starts out as a possible revenge killing picks up momentum and past crimes surface that could unlock what is happening in the present. The problem for Aitken and Allen is that the suspects may have friends in very high places. Equally the guilty may have fled the country. An old enemy from Purbright's past surfaces and Purbright can bear a grudge better than most. Can Aitken and Allen solve this complex case and can Purbright square the account with his nemesis.

For information on the author and his works visit:

www.stuartmcbain.com